To Heal or Not to Heal

By Kathleen Willett

Chapter 1

Kansas loomed large. Which made sense, since it *was* large. Most states west of the Mississippi River tended to be large. Unlike their counterparts east. Mitch remembered doing jigsaw puzzles when she was a little girl and giggling at the fact that some eastern states, Rhode Island for instance, were too small to be a piece all unto themselves. In fact, if you thought about the entire United States as a cake, it could take all of Rhode Island, Connecticut, Massachusetts, New Hampshire and Vermont to satisfy one's sweet tooth. But Kansas. Kansas would be a fair helping. And for folks like Mitch, who enjoyed eating, California was even better. Come to think of it, Alaska would be edible, too.

"Whatever are you thinking?" Rebecca poked Mitch's arm. Her bad one. Actually, that was either arm lately. Ouch.

Ah, yes! The ex-Governor, ex-Senator Fairbanks. Fairbanks like as in Alaska.
"I was thinking how delectable you are."

Reb's eyes narrowed. Not in anger. In fact, it had been a whole long time since Reb's eyes had narrowed in anything save ecstasy. In a really broad definition of the term.

This looked like her "I still don't quite get it" expression. Rather than explain further, Mitch just asked, like a kid, "Are we there yet?"

Things had happened since their last visit to Kansas. Monumental things.

Lisa was healing. That in itself was monumental and worthy of attention. But an addendum was attached to that particular item. She was healing physically. She could hardly help it, with all the doctors and nurses prodding her along. They could do wonders in the wound-healing department. Everything else was up to Mary. If you looked up the word "faithful" in the dictionary,

1

Mary's picture was sure to be there as illustration. You couldn't find a better example of a faithful, loving partner. Some people didn't measure up the way Mary had. Marriages and relationships were sometimes destroyed over what Lisa and Mary had been through. What do you do when your lover comes out of a fire with third-degree burns on their head, face and arm? If you were a decent person like Mary, you started right in with the reassurances. Which, although Lisa needed to hear, were probably getting on her nerves by now. Lisa had been beautiful once. Stunning in fact. The operative word being "once." For her, the loss was, well, monumental.

If someone could invent a box where people could put their anger, and have it make a difference somehow, they would be rich. And Mitch would have bought a few hundred dozen. If the wackos in Kansas had had such a box, the fire would've never happened. And she and Rebecca wouldn't need to be going back to Kansas to sort through the aftermath. Aftermath was such a fitting word. If a family described their dysfunction in bomb terms, it would be safe to say that Rebecca's family was going through a Hiroshima about now.

It wasn't bad enough that Lisa had nearly lost her life in a house fire at the Kansas family homestead. No, the real news bomb had come a few days later when it was discovered that Rebecca's niece, the spooky Miranda, had set the fire. The bad blood in the family would've nauseated a vampire.

Mitch wasn't satisfied with the explanation, however. When was the last time Mitch had been satisfied anyway. Well, not counting *that*.

"You've got that look on your face again," Reb noted for the record.
"How do you drive and study my countenance at the same time?"
"Driving is easy. The road is straight."
Mitch nodded. Sounded about right for Kansas.

2

Chapter 2

New York was a whole different story. Trish and Robbie finally had time to find out all by themselves. When they had discovered that Conners, the last remaining relative of Albert Rosenthal, was dying, they stayed and sent Robbie's parents' home with their bodyguard. Not without a fight, in the figurative sense. Silver Smith, the family bodyguard extraordinaire, wasn't at all happy leaving Trish and Robbie without protection. To her way of thinking, Rose and Max had already been threatened by the nut case that was sending Rose weird notes. Silver had responded by confronting aforementioned nut case and breaking her arm. The fact that it all happened at the art auction of the last known Rosenthal painting had been a macabre two-for-one-deal for the press. Come for an auction, stick around for an attempted stabbing.

Ah, yes, New York. Trish had to remember to not give the place a bad name. The assailant had come from another state entirely to do the dirty deed. If revenge was a dish served best cold, this entrée was close to the freezing point. The woman had carried a grudge for over fifty years against Rose for the death of her cruel, rapist Nazi brother. And the upshot was that Rose hadn't even killed the bad seed brother. Nope, the Nazis had saved her the trouble. He had had the audacity to impregnate Rose and was executed for the sin of racial mixing. Never mind the fact that he had crudely aborted the fetus to cover his tracks. You know what sticklers those Nazis were about the rules.

And so, for quite a number of years, Rose and Max had been childless. Until one day, a miracle came into their lives, the beautiful Roberta. It had been such a temptation to spoil the girl rotten, but they resisted. They raised her to be a wonderfully thoughtful, gentle girl. Isn't that what any husband wanted? And then, along came Trish. And the idea of a husband evaporated like so much smoke. Rose and Max took a bit of time to adjust to this "modern" situation. To their eternal credit, this took about ten seconds. Well, maybe five? And it didn't hurt that their new daughter-in-law had soon become a multimillionaire. Didn't this only happen in the movies? And on game shows?

Part of the burden with having so much money was the responsibility that came with it. Trish had decided to take care of all of Conners Rosenthal's medical bills. At first this seemed like it could turn into a huge bill. Conners was totally disabled in just about every sense of the word. It was Robbie's educated guess that there had been some sort of trauma at birth. Conners was what most people called a vegetable. But for some reason, Trish and Conners had connected on a level. He would attempt to say words to her and they had sat together for hours. When they first met, it was known that he needed much in the way of care, and funds were dwindling. Trish had figured that he would need millions and millions to live out his life in comfort. Millions and millions she was willing to give. Millions and millions that Robbie had absolutely agreed to.

Millions and millions weren't going to be needed now. It wasn't going to be long. Conners had liver cancer with complications. He was a shell of his former self, if that was even possible. And Robbie didn't quite know how to handle Trish's profound grief. If ever there was a time when part of Trish was dying too, this was that time. Robbie had seen her share of grief, having worked a number of years in geriatrics. But she had seen grown children grieve much less over dying parents than Trish now grieved for Conners. It was as if she was losing Albert all over again, and Albert wasn't even a family member. If it were possible for Robbie to love Trish even more, she would have.

"You want to go get some dinner?" Robbie asked.
Trish jumped about a mile at the sound of Robbie's voice.
Robbie rarely insisted on much, but where Trish was concerned, she was assertive about food. Given her head in the matter, Trish could very easily waste away, much like what Connors was doing now.
"It's time for dinner."
"You go on. I'm not hungry."

4

Robbie squeezed Trish's arm, enough to make an impression, both literally and figuratively.

"Keep me company anyway."

Trish looked up into Robbie's eyes. No use arguing, especially where food was concerned. Robbie managed to lure Trish clear off the grounds of the facility to a place where they didn't even have to eat off trays. How wonderfully different. There were so many sins on the menu that once Trish smelled the aromas, she indulged deeply beginning with a delectable appetizer of deep-fried mushroom caps followed by a steak and finishing off with a double order of mocha brownie pie.

"How did you know I was this hungry?"

"I could see it in your ribs."

"So, you've been checking out my ribs, huh." Trish made it sound mysterious.

"Only the ones that were sticking out," Robbie answered clinically. It dawned on Trish that everything had been overwhelmingly clinical lately. Between Lisa's burn injuries and Connors' cancer, life had been defined more in medical terms than anything else.

"Let's head back to the apartment," Trish said quietly.

"You don't want to swing by the hospital?" Robbie wanted to be sure she heard right.

"Connors is in good hands."

When they arrived at their temporary home, Trish made sure that Robbie was in good hands as well, so to speak.

"You haven't lost your touch," Robbie remarked as she held on to Trish afterwards.

"I'm sorry I've been ignoring you."

"You don't need to apologize," Robbie insisted. "I don't feel ignored."

"You haven't been my top priority lately."

"That's okay. I don't always need nor want to be your top priority."

"You don't?" Trish was puzzled.

"It's never been my goal to absorb all of your time and energy. I've watched other people ruin their entire relationships trying to be the end all and be all to each other."

5

"I guess I have as well, although there must be other relationships where that works just fine."

"Name one," Robbie challenged.

Trish though about it so long that she fell asleep.

Chapter 3

Mary was sitting patiently beside Lisa's bedside. It was an important day and she didn't want to miss any of it. It was the day that Mary was going to be instructed on how to care for Lisa's wounds. If that didn't sound like a necessarily pleasant event, then one really didn't comprehend how inextricably wound care was tied to eventual freedom from the burn unit. All Mary needed now was a steady hand and nerves of steel. And maybe an empty stomach.

"You're just one big grimace this morning, aren't you?" Lisa remarked.

"I didn't know you were awake!" Mary tried to cover her frown tracks with a bright smile.

"I've learned to wake up quietly."

"You have?"

"It's the only way I catch your unguarded facial expressions."

"I see. So, what did you observe today?"

"The same thing I notice whenever you think I'm not looking."

"Which is what?"

"What else? Unmitigated disgust."

Mary tried, and failed, to make eye contact with Lisa. She wouldn't cooperate and Mary didn't feel like facing the issue. All the literature Mary had read about the depression that burn patients go through did little to help her cope with Lisa's moods. They both had access to counseling, but it didn't seem to be making a dent in the wall that Lisa was building up around herself. Today, of all days, wasn't a good time to start a fight, but the closer they got to discharge day, the fouler Lisa's temperament became.

"It wasn't disgust you saw on my face," Mary made her stand clear.

"What was it, then?" Lisa dared her to answer.

"Hunger."

Lisa didn't reply. If Mary had hungers, she didn't want to hear about them. Any of them.

"You want something from the cafeteria?" Mary offered matter-of-factly.

"No."

Mary nodded and left the room. Further conversation would be pointless now. She went to the hospital cafeteria and absently filled a tray with breakfast items. Everything had been tasting alike for about a week now, so it really didn't matter what she ate. Whatever might not be too painful on the way back up seemed to be the main criteria. Halfway through some egg substitute omelet, she became aware of someone wanting to share her table. It was Hilary.

"Would you care for some company?"

Mary didn't want to be impolite, but she had to think about her answer. What do you say to a former lover who used to knock you around? Well, to be fair, Hilary had sought help soon after their separation. She looked good in her greens.

"Have a seat."

"Thanks. I eat alone a lot. It's nice to have someone to talk to."

"Yes, it is."

Hilary waited a moment and then went right to the heart of the matter.

"I haven't seen you looking this miserable since you and I were together."

"We weren't always miserable," Mary answered diplomatically.

"Still, you look like hell. What's going on?"

"It's just been a long day."

"It's only seven-thirty in the morning."

"Well, then it's been a long week, okay!" Mary became testy, which Hilary interpreted as a good sign.

"Sounds to me like you need someone to get all bent out of shape with."

"I already have a therapist."

"I imagine so, but you're already mad at me. Might as well make good use of that fact."

"I'm not angry with you."

"You're not?"

"I got over being angry with you a long time ago."

"So, now, it's Lisa's turn."

"I'm not angry with her either."

8

"What, then?"

"Burn recovery is a long process. I'm just tired."

"Then, that's okay. I just thought that Lisa was going through the normal depressions that go with being a burn patient. You know, withdrawal, anger, an exaggerated sense of being repulsive to look at. Makes most folks want to pick a fight."

Mary hated it when Hilary knew it all.

"You read all about it in your textbooks I suppose?"

"Oh, sure. That's like first-year stuff."

When Mary and Hilary split up, Mitch arranged for Hilary to go away to medical school. Far, far away at the time. No one would've ever guessed that coincidences would once again bring them so close together.

"I hate to cut this short, but I need to get back to Lisa's room."

Hilary only nodded, keeping to herself the comment about hearing the bell for Round 2.

Hospital staff were patiently waiting for Mary. They knew well her dread and admired her fortitude. As they went through the processes, it sort of came in handy that Lisa had been temperamental earlier. It made Mary less nervous.

"Have you had nurse's training before?" the day-shift head nurse asked as they finished up.

"No."

"You handle yourself like a pro."

"Thanks," Mary said. Her knees weren't quite what they had been earlier, but she was still standing. The real pros gathered up their supplies and left. Lisa, who had been stubbornly weaning herself off pain medication, was now gritting her teeth in obvious discomfort.

"Can I get you something?"

"No."

"Not even an aspirin?"

"Especially not an aspirin!"

"How about a pair of boxing gloves?"

"A pair of what?"

"As long as we're going to be fighting every day, they might come in handy."

"Wouldn't be a fair fight. I only have one good arm right now."

"Oh, I'd figure out a way to make things even."

Mary sat gently on the bed and took hold of Lisa's good arm.
"What are you doing?"
"I'm waiting out the pain with you. I caused it so it's only fair
that I help you through it. Now squeeze my hand."
Lisa did so, a tiny bit.
"Oh, come on! You can do better than that!"
Lisa squeezed a little harder.
"Not good enough. Try to break my hand!"
Goaded on by frustration, Lisa squeezed as long and hard as she
could. The pain became very real for Mary, who winced in
sudden agony.
"Damn, for a girl, you sure are strong."
"Watch who you're calling 'girl.'" Lisa tried to remain gruff.
"Oh, I do. Every chance I get," Mary touched Lisa's hair, and
then her face.
"I need someone to be angry with," Lisa explained out of the
blue. "Someone safe."
"I'm here. I'm safe. You can be as angry with me as you need
to be."
"I'm trying. Honest."
"I know. Now, try to get some sleep. I'll be right here," Mary
said as she kissed Lisa's forehead.

Chapter 4

Mitch stirred awake. She really hated sleeping in hotel rooms. It was a relatively new-found hatred. Maybe if she and Reb were on the French Riviera…Now, that would be okay. But, no. Here they were in flatline Kansas. Courtroom proceedings were pending.

"Did you know that there are two basic types of crimes?" Reb asked in lieu of "good morning."

Mitch directed her one open eye toward Rebecca. Even sitting in a wheelchair and holding a law book, she was undoubtedly the most gorgeous woman on the planet. Not that that was all that attracted Mitch to her. Heck no. Rebecca was also a brilliant politician and a real brainiac.

"Huh?"

"Did you hear me? What are you thinking about? Are you getting out of bed anytime soon?"

Mitch processed the questions before answering. "Yes, your brains, and why don't you come over here and make me?"

Reb, in turn, thought about the answers, the middle one in particular. "You were thinking about my brain?" She used the correct form of the word, since last time she checked, there was only one brain per person.

"Yes, Ma'am."

Reb wheeled closer. Maybe she was considering Mitch's third answer? Mitch could only hope.

"My *brain*?" Reb was emphatic in her curiosity.

"You're a brilliant woman. Tell me about the two types of crimes. What are they, civil and criminal?" Mitch took a stab.

"No. The first type of crime is when someone does something that is usually okay to do except for a legal prohibition. The second type of crime is when someone does something that is more or less universally recognized as being wrong."

"I'm not sure I follow?" Mitch was still fending off sleep and felt out of her element.

"Well, take liquor, for instance," Professor Fairbanks was just getting warmed up.

"What about it?" Mitch might know a little bit about this, having once been the owner of a bar.

"It's okay to sell alcohol to people over a certain age, but not to minors."

"Okay," Mitch yawned. Again. This was going to be a long morning. They were all turning into long mornings lately.

"But, if you consider the act of murder, well, that's always wrong. There's never a case where it's okay to murder someone."

"Except for self-defense."

"Perhaps, murder and killing weren't the best examples."

Rebecca took to studying Mitch long and hard. It was, more or less, her Schoolteacher Look, and we all know what that's like.

"Are you purposefully trying to be argumentative, or is it merely accidental?" she asked.

Mitch knew when she was losing the argument to a former Debate Club president.

"I'm merely being the Devil's Advocate. Get off my case. I'm not the one who chose to debate the finer points of the law at seven thirty in the morning!"

Mitch rolled out of bed, knowing full well that the third concept of being joined by Reb was now a thing of the past. She went to the bathroom and took a shower. When she emerged, things were quiet. Too quiet.

"You want to know what I think?" Mitch figured out a logical ice breaker.

"I'm sure you'll tell me."

"I think it's about time you talked to your sister."

Ah, yes. Reb's sister, BeBe. In a community of pillars, she was the pillarest of them all, if that was even a word. Mitch's very first encounter with "Aunt BeBe" was when the formidable woman knocked Mitch clear flat down. It was a lucky sucker punch, coming out of the blue in a hospital waiting room. Mitch had just flown in from Washington DC to rush to the bedside of Reb after her accident when Aunt BeBe cold cocked her with a mighty sweep of her hand. It left Mitch red-faced, bruised and stunned. Once everything was sorted out, Mitch dropped the charges. But, true to her pillar-of-the-community form, Aunt BeBe couldn't, in turn, drop her animosity toward Mitch. As far as she was concerned, Mitch was the Anti-Christ who made

Charles Manson look like an altar boy. Which made it all the more strange that it was Mitch suggesting to Reb that she talk to BeBe.

"I'm sure the lawyers wouldn't approve."

"To hell with the lawyers," Mitch said pointedly. "The sooner we get this all worked out, the better."

"You don't understand. I'm prohibited from talking to BeBe or Henry or Miranda pending the court case."

Ah, yes, Miranda. Mitch had once referred to her as the Patricia Krenwinkel of Kansas. She was the spooky daughter of BeBe and Henry and now found herself on the other side of the phrase, "The People Versus." She had been seen leaving the scene of the fire that had engulfed the homestead farmhouse where Mary and Lisa were living. Mary was in church at the time, but Lisa and houseguest Reb had been in residence. Lisa had saved Reb's life, no doubt about it. In the process, she had been seriously injured. If she had died, Miranda would've faced a murder charge. As it stood, there were still a multitude of charges including arson. The motive was unclear. Reb had one theory, Mitch another. Which, perhaps, accounted for the general surliness that enveloped them lately. Rebecca had decided that BeBe had instilled into Miranda a jealousy over the terms of the estate thereby inspiring Miranda to burn down their former home. Reb was ticked. Mitch figured instead that Miranda had fallen under the influence of the local fundamentalist church leaders. This group raised homophobia to a whole new level, from thought to action, not to put too fine a point on it.

The church congregation had taken to picketing the house not long after Mary and Lisa moved in. As events escalated, news crews descended. Before Lisa and Mary had even gotten a good start on redecorating, their place and their neighbor, Mr. Bixby's, place were both pretty well burned beyond recognition. And all Bixby had done was to be a good and decent guy to two new-comers, who, just in case anybody cared, had treated him better than BeBe and Henry and Miranda ever had.

So, Mitch had taken to bestowing to Miranda the "Charles Manson mob mentality" benefit of the doubt. Hence the Krenwinkel moniker.

"Maybe that's best," Mitch shrugged.
"What's that supposed to mean?" Reb was still primed for a fight.
"With the mood you've been in lately, I'm sure no fences would be mended."
"Well, maybe if you ate breakfast once in a while, you'd be easier to live with, too!"
"Best idea I've heard all day. Let's go to the diner."

The morning was so beautiful that they left the van at the hotel and meandered on foot over to the local eatery. You could smell the bacon grease a mile away. Since arriving in town for all the pretrial motions, Reb had been a stickler about two things: diet and proper public appearances. As far as diet was concerned, they had been on a virtual organic regimen. Mitch could hardly complain, she was feeling fit and healthy. As for Reb, she hadn't developed even the slightest hint of a pressure sore. But every once in a while, Mitch developed a special craving for salty, greasy food. And like sexual cravings, Reb let her indulge. So before the clock struck nine, they were sitting across from each other over plates of pancakes, bacon and eggs. Mitch fairly moaned with pleasure as she tasted each temptation in turn.
"Enjoying yourself?" Reb asked like she knew the answer already, which she of course did.
Mitch looked up rather sheepishly. "Was I talking to my food again?"
"Just enough to convey that I don't bring you here often enough."
"Oh, you bring me often enough," Mitch assured her with a wink.
"I'm sorry if I was cranky earlier," Reb stated in a whisper.
"You weren't cranky," Mitch answered honestly. "I'm just not very good at legal debate before breakfast."
"I'm just really afraid of what I might say to my sister once I get started."

14

"You can practice on me. After all, I'm quite used to it."

"I'm really sorry about that."

"I'm not," Mitch reached across the table to take Reb's hand, which was against rule number two, no public displays of affection. She pulled back. It was going to be a long, long trial. "So, what would you say to BeBe?"

"Why do you take Miranda's side in this?"

"I'm sure any mother would take their child's side."

"I'm not asking her, I'm asking you. Why do you defend Miranda?"

"I'm not saying that what Miranda did was okay. I just feel that there was a conspiracy and that she shouldn't take the fall all by herself."

"And that's why you keep calling her by that Krenwinkel name."

"That right. Imagine how frightful it would've been back in 1970 if Charles Manson had walked away a free man?"

"And that's what you see happening here?"

"In a way."

"So, you think the trial is a waste of time."

"No. It's just incomplete justice."

"Well, it's all we can hope for now."

"When are we going to rebuild the farmhouse?" Mitch asked.

"I didn't know we were?"

"We're not?" Mitch stopped eating.

"You would want to?"

"It was insured, wasn't it?"

"Right."

"So, we might just as well. Unless you had other plans?"

"Who's going to live there if we do rebuild?"

"Let's worry about that later."

"Now that you don't have the restaurant to keep you busy, maybe this would be a good project."

"Anything to keep me busy," Mitch nodded.

Reb became thoughtful. "I just don't understand how religious people could do things like this."

"Don't forget, Patricia Krenwinkel was a Sunday school teacher."

Reb shuddered and then announced, "I'll call the insurance company today so you can start getting bids."

15

"Utopia is a small town. We might be getting 'bid.'"

"If anyone can get good 'bid', it's you."

"And if you don't hurry up and eat your breakfast," Mitch intoned, "you're going to have to worry about me trying to do a whole lot more than hold your hand in public!"

"I'm eating as fast as I can," Reb stated as she quite deliberately slowed down. It was *just* like her.

Even with all the sexual innuendo, when they got back to the hotel room, they spent more time on the phone than in each other's arms. This was now pretty much typical of their established relationship. They knew they would catch up with each other later. Depending on what kind of elaborate plans they could dream up for a new house, the insurance settlement might need a bit of a boost from Mitch's pocketbook. More information would be forthcoming from the contractor just as soon as Mitch and Reb formulated a basic floor plan.

"Of course, everything must be handicap accessible," Reb stated.

"Goes without saying. Do you want a hot tub?"

"Where?"

"That was my next question."

"You sound like you want to live here."

"It might make a nice vacation home."

"A vacation home? In Kansas?"

"Doesn't work for you?"

"People don't build vacation homes in Kansas. People build vacation homes in Aspen. Or Hawaii. Or the French Riviera." The third location jolted Mitch. Hadn't she been thinking about that earlier? Had she talked in her sleep? Or had Reb read her mind?

"Okay, so no hot tub. Fine."

"Well, you don't need to be petulant about it."

"I'm not being petulant. I'm just wondering who we're building this house for?"

"Whoever buys the family homestead, that's who," Reb was firm.

"You're selling the homestead?" Mitch couldn't believe what she was hearing.

"I think it's the logical thing to do."

16

Mitch listened to this pronouncement with the ears of a lover. This meant that she tried to hear more than was being said but didn't challenge. One of the secrets of a good relationship was to take things in stride.

"In that case, I think it ought to be big enough for a sizable family and a hot tub would be a grand selling point."

"Fine. Pencil in a damn hot tub."

"And a swimming pool."

"A swimming pool?"

"Great for kids. Nothing quite like a dip in the pool on a hot Kansas afternoon."

"Why don't you think about a merry go round while you're at it," Reb teased.

"Actually, I was thinking more along the lines of a Ferris wheel."

"I think a merry go round is a better choice," Reb defended her idea.

"Why?"

"Well, if a Ferris wheel gets stuck, then people might be trapped way up high. That can be very dangerous. But with a merry go round, you just step off the contraption."

Mitch wondered sometimes why she even bothered to debate this brilliant woman.

"So, a merry go round it is. A hot tub, a swimming pool, a merry go round. Anything else?"

"Oh, gee, maybe a couple more things like a bedroom and bathroom for instance!"

"The mundane stuff." Mitch nodded with a smile.

"Just don't get too wrapped up in your work. Remember, we're selling the place."

"Right."

Rebecca knew without even being psychic that she was in for an uphill battle. Why it was that Mitch was more inclined to want to keep the property was anyone's guess. Kansas, so far, hadn't been very welcoming to them. The impending trial wasn't going to help at all. The tone of the legal actions was teetering day by day depending on whose spin you listened to. In some ways, it was like the proverbial "gay student being beaten up at school" kind of instance. Most of the time, the perpetrator's sole defense was the simple assertion that the gay student brought it all on themselves by virtue of the fact that they were asking for it. There were communities big and small across the nation that had this unwritten law that said it was okay to bash gay people. Setting their homes on fire was just an added attraction for some folks. If Mitch and Rebecca rebuilt, what were the chances that everything wouldn't be burned down all over again? It was as if Mitch was reading Reb's mind.

"We just have to have faith," Mitch patted Reb's hand.

"You know what the Bible says about faith, don't you?"

"No, what?"

"It says that of the three: faith, hope and charity, that the greatest of these is charity."

"I'll pay extra special attention to works of charity."

"It never hurts."

"Got any more Biblical insights?"

"Not offhand. Why?"

"They seem to come in handy once in a while."

"Should I buy you a copy?"

"I wouldn't have time to read it."

"You could do the next best thing."

"What would that be?"

"You could go to some sort of church service."

"I suppose so," Mitch sounded unconvinced.

"I can tell you're not wild about the idea."

"I just haven't been to a real church service for a long time."

"Were you dragged to church every week as a child?"

"More or less."

"And you were taught, however insidiously, to hate yourself."

"That's right, but not just because I was gay."

"Why then?"

"I was taught to hate myself because I was a sinner."

"You weren't supposed to. Jesus loved sinners."

"That wasn't the problem. The problem was that I was taught to try to not be a sinner."

"And that was a problem?"

"Sure."

Why?"

"Because I was also taught that it was a terrible sin to try to be as perfect as God."

"I think I see your point."

"You're a quick study. It took me years to figure out the contradiction. I tried to be just good enough to not be too bad of a sinner but be just bad enough to not get on God's jealous side."

"Well, if it's any consolation, your attempts to be both good and bad make you a great lover."

"Have I been bad?" Mitch asked, but didn't look too worried.

"In all the best ways," Reb twinkled. The stars in the heavens might just as well pack up and move on. They could never compete when Reb twinkled.

"We might need to rent a house while we're building," Mitch suddenly switched back to the original topic.

"We could move a trailer onto the property."

"You think you could maneuver around in a trailer?"

"Haven't you seen some of the newer models? Many of them are pretty spacious."

"Including the bathroom?"

"Especially the bathroom. Lots of senior citizens buy these things for retirement. In many respects, they are perfect for folks like me."

Mitch thought about this for a second or two. How long would it take before the press and public started to speculate on how or why the honorable ex-Senator Fairbanks had transformed to trailer trash? Maybe this wasn't such a good idea after all.

"You don't like trailer living, I take it?"

"Oh, it'll be perfect!" Mitch tried to put on a joyous face. For the most part, she succeeded. Reb gave her serious consideration for so long that even the usually unflappable Mitch was, well, flapped.

"Is it something I said?"

"No. It isn't. I don't know what it is."

"Not even a clue?"

"It's like if we were in a spooky movie, the spooky movie music would be playing."

"You mean that kind of music where everyone but the lead character knows that the ax murderer is just around the corner? That kind of spooky music?" Mitch took a glance over each shoulder, *just* to be on the safe side.

"Not that spooky. More along the lines of one character just now comprehending something crucial to the plot."

"And what are you comprehending?"

"I'm comprehending that for whatever reason, we'd better get a really, big nice roomy double wide trailer."

"Why?"

"I think we're going to need it."

Mitch, who for the most part didn't argue much with Reb, decided that this was no time to start and instead cracked open the phone book. Of course, trailers weren't under the letter T, at least not the kind they were looking for. They didn't need to transport horses and such. What they were looking for was a manufactured mobile home. The biggest dealer in manufactured mobile homes was in Wichita.

"If they're mobile, why don't we just have one delivered?"

"You want to buy one sight unseen?"

"You don't think that's possible?"

"I think we need to have you maneuver through it in your wheelchair before we plunk down any hard cash."

"You are so sensible."

Mitch was actually taken aback. Not often was "sensible" one of the adjectives that described her behavior.

"So, should we jump in the van or call ahead for an appointment," old sensible Mitch asked.

"Let's do both. Let's get in the van and call and warn them."

"I'm packing a suitcase first."

"Why?"

"Because it's the sensible thing to do."

In truth, Mitch always tried to remember to pack a suitcase. One never knew when one was going to get stranded or decide to stay overnight. Meanwhile, Reb called the mobile home dealer, who was more than happy to set up an appointment for later in the afternoon.

"Business must be slow," Reb surmised.

"Or maybe they just know that we mean business."

"Two women with more money than sense?"

"Not necessarily."

They took turns at the wheel through the long drive and still arrived at the appointed time. Two salesmen were waiting for them. Mitch wondered if there was going to be a fifty-fifty split of the commission. They showed Mitch and Reb several models. Within about an hour, they had their choice narrowed to two. This was going to be a tough choice. Or was it?

"We'll take both," Mitch shrugged.

If Reb was surprised, she hid it well. So did the salesmen.

"These two," the senior of the pair pointed to the two homes in question.

"That's right. How soon can you have them delivered to Utopia?"

"Within a few days."

Mitch nodded. That would give them time to stock up on all the supplies they would need to run a household. Mitch signed the paperwork on the first line and Reb on the second. Their hands were tired by the time they were done and the only signature left was the one on the bottom of the check. Mitch made it out like it was for groceries.

"You understand that I need to call the bank on this kind of transaction."

"Perfectly understandable," Mitch nodded.

That call took all of about thirty seconds and the deal was set.

"You sure you don't want to buy one more, just for the road?"

"We'll know where to come if we do," Reb answered sweetly but firmly. She was ready to be anywhere but there. They shook hands all around and then Mitch and Reb loaded back up in their van. Reb spoke first. "I'll await your explanation until we get settled for the night."

"You want to stay overnight in wild, wooly Wichita?"

"Sure, what the hell."

Mitch found a decent hotel and they were in a three-room suite before you could say, "You want extra pillows?"

Which they did. They always tried to get extra pillows. It made things infinitely more comfortable for Reb. Mitch spent extra time helping get Reb all arranged.

"Are you stalling?"

"No, why would I be?"

"Then tell me why we just bought two homes. Are we splitting up?"

"Heavens no! In fact, having two homes will prevent us from splitting up, don't you think?"

"And that's because…?"

"And that's because you and I know that we need a little elbow room once in a while."

"We do?"

"We always have before."

"We never have before."

"Almost always!"

"I don't understand what your mean."

"We have rarely had to live full time, 24/7, in a place as small as one of those mobile homes. I bought two so we can have some extra storage to avoid a lot of clutter."

Reb sensed an "and" tacked on the end of the thought.

"And what else?"

"You and I need breathing space."

"You plan on doing a lot of breathing?"

Mitch inhaled and exhaled a couple of times. "On a daily basis." They watched TV, ordered up dinner from room service before it stopped for the night and generally did a lot of breathing. There was enough air for them here and now.

"Besides," Mitch broke the silence, "we might have overnight guests from time to time."

"Who are you thinking of inviting – Melissa Etheridge?"

"Haven't you heard? She's had enough of Kansas. No, I was thinking more along the lines of Mary and Lisa and Trish and Robbie."

"Wouldn't this be slumming for Trish and Robbie?"

"Hard to tell. They haven't had a chance to spend their new-found fortune yet."

Chapter 5

The vigil continued. Every day, Trish would get out of bed early, shower, make half-a-pot of coffee, drink one cup, get dressed in jeans and a soft shirt, kiss the usually still sleeping Robbie goodbye on the forehead and take off for the care facility. Once there, she would check on Connors to see if he made eye contact, which he hadn't lately, and then settled down to read the local newspaper. That would take about ten minutes. Trish read fast. Then, she would delve into the stack of books she had stashed there. Every weekend since their arrival, Trish and Robbie visited the bookstore during their time together. They would sleep in on Saturday and then go out to breakfast. The local eatery had a nice assortment of ethnic treats. That was a fancy way of saying that Robbie was in lox and bagel heaven. After breakfast, they would go to the bookstore and shop for various titles. Trish by habit would pick out one or two from both the fiction and non-fiction best seller lists and then selected an eclectic mix from mystery, self-improvement, poetry, and gardening. So far she had learned that no murder mystery was complete without a red herring, walking was good exercise, Rome rhymed with comb, and mint would take over your garden if given half a chance.

After the bookstore, they went shopping for groceries and supplies. Robbie was a God-send in the area of making a house a home no matter where they were. She was being a good sport about apartment living which included traipsing back and forth to the washer and dryer most of Sunday in order to get the laundry done in time for Monday. Trish had told her two or three times that she should just send it all to the dry cleaners, but Robbie resisted. She had done Trish's laundry almost from the start. It was less of a chore and more an act of intimacy. Besides, we all know how hard the cleaners can be on clothes.

Once they had this shopping finished, they went back to the apartment and spent time together cooking, cleaning and watching TV. What they weren't doing much of lately was making love and planning for the future. Robbie understood the part about not planning for the future. Until they came to a finality concerning Connors, it didn't seem appropriate. And honestly, she wasn't too surprised about the lack of sexual activity. Trish had a lot on her mind.

"Robbieeeee."

The voice made her look up. Trish caught her eye.

"You were deep in thought."

"No I wasn't. I was just thinking."

Trish nodded like it all made sense.

"Tell me what you were thinking about."

"It was just random thoughts."

"If you look so serious over random thoughts, I wonder what serious thinking must do."

"You don't think I'm capable of serious thoughts?"

"I didn't say that," Trish defended herself calmly.

"Of course you didn't."

Trish knew one thing for sure. Robbie was uncharacteristically on edge and there were two ways to alleviate that tension. One was arguing. The other was a lot more fun.

"Would you rather argue or make love?" Trish asked point blank.

"Excuse me?"

"You heard me. We can argue or make love or perhaps a bit of both. What are you up for?"

Robbie gave the impression that she was giving this serious thought.

"How about we make love and then, if we still feel like arguing, we can do so."

"Sounds like a good plan to me."

As readily as Robbie had agreed to the plan, she wasn't about to be rushed. She had been patient. Now it was Trish's turn to know what it was like to wait. And ponder. And go very slowly.

Trish shook for five minutes off and on after her orgasm. When she regained her wits, she turned her full attention to Robbie. What a true and loving partner she had been to put up with all of Trish's withdrawal. To offer her nothing more that humble lovemaking felt so inadequate. And yet, Robbie responded so

24

sweetly. If there was any tension left in her body after Trish was finished, it was buried too deep to locate. Maybe it would surface on the next go around.

"It's my turn to ask. What are you thinking about?" Robbie inquired as they rested in each other's arms.

"I'm thinking about what I'm going to do to bring you to another climax in about thirty minutes."

"Oh, I don't think that will be necessary," Robbie said, but her body had other ideas. Even now, as Trish touched her here and there, she was stirring.

"It certainly won't require much thinking. Your body tells me already what it likes."

"I'm sorry if I've been on edge lately."

"Don't ever be sorry about that," Trish ran her fingers up and down Robbie's abdomen. She hadn't mentioned it, but Robbie was beginning to show weight loss through this area. Trish didn't know whether to tell her she was proud or to worry.

"Your hand is driving me crazy!"

"I planned it that way."

"Can we talk about a subject we've been avoiding lately?"

"We've been avoiding something?"

"We haven't talked much about the future."

"That's a pretty big topic," Trish said, "Don't suppose you'd narrow it down some for me."

"Okay, how about 'children.'"

Trish's hand stopped its foray.

"'Children' as in having some," she wanted to clarity further.

"Right."

"Well, we've talked about this before."

"Quite a while ago."

"Is that the ticking of your biological clock that I hear?"

"I'm just not getting any younger."

"Does that mean that you want to be the birth mother?"

"Is that okay with you?"

"Of course."

"Are you sure?"

"Why wouldn't it be?"

"Well, I just didn't know if you were really serious about having children."

"You think it was just a line I used to finagle you into bed?" Trish playfully resumed her hand work.

"It's just that we've been through a lot lately. When I think about it, as heartless as this may sound, we aren't going to be saddled with too many more expenses where Connors is concerned."

Robbie watched Trish for her reaction.

"You're right," Trish nodded pragmatically.

"So, here we are with all this money..." Robbie stopped there. Something else was weighing on her mind. Trish raised up on one elbow so she could see.

"What are you worried about?"

"I'm worried about all the dangers that come with money."

"Like kidnappers?"

"Right."

"So, we'll just hire another bodyguard."

"I don't want to make Silver jealous."

Silver Smith, bodyguard extraordinaire, was hired by Trish to protect Robbie's parents from a wacko. Now that said wacko was out of the picture, Silver had a lot of time on her hands.

"I have an idea!" Trish brightened.

That alone should have been fair warning for Robbie, but she just mildly asked, "You do?"

"When things, you know, finish up around here, let's all move in together."

Trish waited for a reaction from Robbie. And waited. And was just about to elaborate when Robbie spoke up, "I don't think there's enough room for all of us plus a new baby at my folk's house."

"Actually, I was thinking that we should get a new place."

"A new house?"

"Right. Doesn't that make sense?"

"Except for one thing. My folks would probably never move."

"If we got a big enough house with a maid, they might change their minds?"

"They might. But let's remember one thing."

"What?"

"If we ever hire a maid, let's not get one named Mary."

26

Chapter 6

"OUCH!! Goddam it!!! Would you watch what you're doing!" Lisa yelled loud and clear. Startled, Mary dropped the gauze. She had been trying on her own to clean and treat Lisa's burn wounds and was now shaking too much to continue. The nurse took over and Mary left the room entirely. She walked without even thinking about a destination and ended up in the hospital cafeteria. Again. She wasn't at all hungry but went ahead and loaded up a tray like that's what she had planned all along. As she sat at a table for one, a feat she managed by selecting a small table and then moving all the chairs away but the one she was now sitting in, she thought about the prior week. From the day a patient is admitted into a burn center, the primary goal is to help the person prepare for as full and functional a life as possible. It's as if there's a discharge date circled in red hanging over everyone's head. Right now, it felt like Mary was hurtling toward this day and not one bit prepared to ease Lisa back into civilian life. And Lisa's yelling wasn't helping. But that wasn't the real problem. The real problem was that Lisa was withdrawing in every way a person could. She resisted all demonstrations of affection. Mary hadn't had a kiss in she couldn't remember how long.

"Haven't seen you in a while," a voice drifted into Mary's gloom.

"Oh, hi, Hilary," Mary sounded neither thrilled nor troubled by her presence.

"Mind if I join you?" she had already pulled up one of those chairs that Mary had set aside and sat down.

"Umm," was all that Mary said.

"Thanks. So, how's Lisa?"

"Fine."

"Yeah, right. Tell me another," Hilary was in her very own mood as well. Perhaps there was an outbreak of the grumpy virus winding its way through the medical center.

"Okay, she's being difficult. There, are you happy now!"

"Now that you're telling me the truth, yes."

Mary exhaled pointedly, like a teenager, and then resumed eating.

"How difficult is she being?"

"She's in a lot of pain."

"And she's taking it out on you."

"How would you know that?" Mary was skeptical.

"Because you're still shaking."

Mary hadn't noticed it before, but she was unsteady. It had to be the fatigue.

"I'm just tired," Mary explained.

"How can I help?"

"You can't."

"There must be some little thing I can do. I could spend my day off visiting Lisa so you could catch up on your sleep."

"No, thanks. I have too much to learn about her care that I really can't miss a day."

"Okay. Well, I could run some errands for you."

"There's nothing to run."

"I could cook you dinner some night?"

Mary had to think about this one. Before Mitch had left for Kansas, she had arranged for pizza delivery every night to the burn center. And as nice as that was, Mary frankly didn't care if she ever had another slice. Hilary was reading her mind.

"Aren't you tired of pizza?"

"A little."

"So, let me throw together one of my Hilary Martin student-on-a-budget marvels. I do a pretty mean stir fry."

"That's really nice of you to offer, but I think I'd better stick close to the hospital tonight."

"You stick close to the hospital every night. I'm sure you could use a break."

"Not tonight. Thanks anyway."

Mary stood up and bussed her tray before heading back to the room. If Hilary was watching, Mary didn't turn around. There wasn't time for second thoughts about the temptations of stir fry. When Mary got back to the room, Lisa was resting comfortably. It might have been sleep or pretend. Mary didn't care at that point. Anything to avoid another argument.

"Back so soon?" Lisa asked out of the blue. So it had been pretend after all.

"I guess."

"What, did Hilary chase you out of the cafeteria again?"

"What makes you say that?"

"Well, for one thing, you have that 'Hilary chased me out of the cafeteria again' look on your face."

Mary squinted, just to alter her looks. Early on in treatment, there had been talk of having a mirror handy for Lisa. Somewhere in all the shuffle of recovery, Mary had neglected to bring one in. She could use one about now.

"Yes, I admit it. Hilary chased me out of the cafeteria."

"Between that and me chasing you out of this room, you're been a woman on the go."

Having nothing more to say, Mary went over to the window to check the view. Now, no matter what expression was on her face, Lisa couldn't see it. That would serve her right.

"I'm going to yell more in the days to follow," Lisa made it clear.

"You don't yell at the nurses."

"That's because I don't love the nurses."

Perhaps it was best that Mary had turned away. Tears started to form and drip. She was afraid to wipe them away. Here she was. Stuck. She couldn't move and she couldn't trust her voice to speak. If this was one of the benefits of love, it was a questionable one at best.

"I don't even love any of the doctors, would-be or otherwise."

Mary gave this comment a moment to sink in. It dried up her tears pronto.

"Well, that's nice to know," she turned around. One of the things that Mary wasn't going to do was carry around residual guilt about once being in love with Hilary.

"So, when I botch up treating your wounds and you yell, I'll know that it's okay."

"Well, just don't botch things up too many more times."

"I'll get better, I promise."

"You need to stop shaking. That would be a good start."

"Stop shaking. Got it. Anything else?"

"Don't let Hilary chase you away."

"I don't. She's just a good excuse to get out of the cafeteria."

"And we all need that once in a while."

"We sure do."

They spent the day watching TV in between Lisa's tubbing. They had about gone through the entire stock of videos that the hospital had in the library and were considering renting from an outside source. Anything to make the hours pass quicker. When the dinner hour approached, Mary asked, "Am I the only one who's tired of pizza?"

"I thought you'd never ask. What have you got in mind?"

"What are you hungry for?"

"I'd love some Chinese food."

"Anything more specific?" Mary asked, doing her best to ignore the coincidence of Hilary's offer of stir fry.

"I want some hot and sour soup, spring rolls, sesame shrimp, pork fried rice and those wontons with the cream cheese filling." About halfway through the recital, Mary started scrounging for a pencil and paper. She wrote items down and then read it back like a secretary taking a message.

"And tea. And sugar. And almond cookies," Lisa said and then added, "And whatever else you want."

"Got it."

Mary went over to Lisa and bent close to kiss her forehead. "I'm glad you're getting your appetite back."

"I'm trying to get my strength back," Lisa explained in a detached way. It was her knee-jerk reaction every time Mary initiated affection. Mary was now used to it. One day, when they least expected it, their passion would re-ignite. She drove, not to the nearest Chinese restaurant, but one that she had heard good things about from the staff. After checking out the menu, Mary ordered everything on Lisa's list plus some cashew chicken and beef with broccoli. Knowing Lisa, she would want a taste of these as well. Everything was packed up in about twenty-five minutes and by the time she arrived back and unpacked the goodies, Lisa was eager.

"I want the soup first," Lisa was benevolent in her directness. She managed well in spite of only having one functional arm. The soup was history in a matter of minutes and Lisa was midway through Mary's order of cashew chicken when Hilary popped in.

"Something smells good," she remarked.

"Pull up a pair of chopsticks and have some dinner."

"Oh, I don't want to interrupt," she tried to bow out gracefully.
"Nonsense. Come here and try a bite of this beef broccoli and tell us what you think."
"Well, maybe just a taste."
Mary played hostess to past and present lovers as she pushed food in both their directions. She managed to nibble on some of the pork fried rice that Lisa had passed over as they chatted about the benefits of Chinese cuisine. It was one of the few safe subjects they could discuss. Hilary wasn't interested in safe subjects after a few moments.
"So, how's the wound care going?" she asked anyone who cared to answer. Lisa didn't mind rising to the challenge.
"Mary is doing fine."
"I'm all thumbs," Mary was willing to be a bit harder on herself.
"Oh, you'll be just like the pros before too long."
If the remark was meant to suggest that Hilary knew all too well about the learning curve of Mary's tactile abilities, it remained unarticulated.
"I just jump every time she does," Mary filled the awkward silence with her confession.
"Goes without saying," was Hilary's cryptic reply.
"So, how many more years of medical school do you have?" Lisa wanted someone else to be the topic of conversation. A real change of pace for her.
"If I don't get home to study, even more than planned!" Hilary stood to leave.
"I'll walk you to the elevator," Mary the Gallant offered.
"No need for that. It was nice to have dinner with you."
"Drop in just any old time," Lisa remarked like it was Tara and she was Scarlet.
Hilary was gone for about a total of fifteen seconds before Lisa declared, "She sure is still crazy about you."
"I suppose."
"I just have one other question."
Mary steeled herself for whatever curiosity remained.
"Are there any more wontons?"

Chapter 7

If the town of Utopia had thought they had seen it all when Mary and Lisa had done their shopping, they were in for a big shock with Mitch and Rebecca behind the wheel of a shopping cart. After establishing their own line of credit at the bank (Mr. Philbin nearly slobbered all over himself) they commenced to doing some serious buying for two manufactured mobile homes. Not that that immediately compared in scope to the efforts of Mary and Lisa to make a farmhouse a farmhome, but then again, they weren't finished yet. In fact, they were still in the ketchup aisle of the grocery store when the debate opened up.

"Why are you getting two bottles of ketchup?" Rebecca wanted to know.

Mitch smiled. Had it not been for the curious nature of Rebecca, she and Mitch might never have gotten together. Sometimes it seemed that they had been together for years. Other days, it was as if they had just met. Mitch, who had never been one much for politics, had first seen Rebecca on TV the night she won the election of the governorship of Colorado. Having been mesmerized by the vision of loveliness, Mitch couldn't remember much of the rest of the night. Oh yeah, other than the fact that she had also won millions in the lottery. So there she was a short few weeks later: rich, captivated by an unapproachable woman, and enjoying a quiet moment in a bar when her life was transformed by the unquenchable curiosity of Rebecca.

Reb poked Mitch.

"Huh?" Mitch came back to the present. And she was just getting to the good part.

"I *said* that we haven't even used up *one* bottle of ketchup in our years together. Why are you getting two?"

"Because we have two refrigerators now."

"I don't see why that matters. We still only need one bottle."

"Well, what if you're resting in one trailer and I'm in the other one and I want to have ketchup on a hot dog or something?"

"Go on," Reb was in a prodding mood.

"You want me stomping all over your place just for a little ketchup?"

"It isn't *my place*?"

"It is if you're resting there."

"And you can't just quietly walk around while I'm resting? You always have before."

Reb was right on that count. For the most part, Mitch had done her level best to tiptoe around Rebecca's life. They had given each other's space a healthy dose of respect. Sometimes miles of respect.

"What if we have overnight guests?" Mitch wouldn't let go. "Don't you think it would be nice if they had a fully-stocked refrigerator?"

"If and when we ever have overnight guests and if and when they ever want ketchup, they can have ours!"

Mitch got the distinct feeling that they were arguing about something above and beyond ketchup, but wasn't ready to delve into the root of the problem in front of witnesses in the condiment aisle.

Which brought Mitch to a totally different train of thought, something she categorized as the "onlooker syndrome." Mitch had never intentionally sought the limelight. Most of her encounters with it had either been accidental or unavoidable. She differed from such people as musicians or actors, who, upon slaving for literally years to become famous, complained about the phenomenon in autobiographies. Which made them, in turn, even more famous. And perhaps even more complaining. But the day Mitch fell hopelessly in love with Rebecca, she had joined the cadre of people who were followed by those she dubbed "The Onlookers." People were watching them while they shopped today. People watched them eat when they dined out. People watched them when they walked. People watched them when they stood still. People just plain watched. Right now, one middle-aged housewife was watching the entire ketchup debate like it was a first-run film. Heaven forbid anyone's life would be so boring as to watch two lesbians deciding how much ketchup they needed to buy and then breathlessly report back to their bridge club. Mitch decided to give the woman something even better to talk about.

"Excuse me, Ma'am," Mitch looked directly at the woman, who now appeared to be praying for the ground to swallow her up, shopping cart and all.

"Yes?"

"I was hoping you'd give me some advice on mustard?"

"Well, if I can?" she seemed a little less panicked.

"I have a recipe that calls for dry mustard, but I'm always afraid of overdoing it. Is there a way to substitute prepared mustard for dry mustard?"

The woman took a couple of seconds to think it over. "How much dry mustard does the recipe call for?"

Now, Mitch had to do some fancy thinking. Of course she had been making this all up so far. "It says, 'to taste.'" Mitch made it sound like she was picturing the recipe in her head.

"What kind of recipe calls for dry mustard 'to taste?'"

"It was my grandmother's recipe."

"Oh, well, I guess that explains it…but what are you cooking?"

"Oh that," Mitch acted like she was just now catching on. "It's deviled eggs."

"Well, personally, and I'm not a blue-ribbon cook or anything like that, but I always use prepared mustard in my deviled eggs. It gives them a smoother consistency. Start with a tablespoon for a dozen eggs and then, as your grandmother says, taste it. If you like it, then that's how much you use."

Mitch was paying such rapt attention to this explanation that you would've thought it was the secrets to the whole damn universe coming out of this woman.

"Can you recommend a good brand of mustard?" Mitch made it sound like a prayer.

"I always buy this," the woman pointed to a national brand in a yellow container.

"That's good enough for me," Mitch picked a jar off the shelf. "How about you, Reb?"

"Fine," Rebecca tried to sound enthused.

Then, as Mitch usually did, she went one step beyond. "By the way, my name is Mitch, and this is Rebecca," she made introductions.

Of course the woman already knew who they were, but she nodded along and then announced, "I have to be getting along."

With that, the unnamed woman went about her shopping. About three aisles away most likely.

"Is this brand really okay with you?" Mitch double checked with Reb.

"I wouldn't want to second guess the expert. Now, if we continue to debate every purchase, we're going to be here past closing time."

"Okay, okay," Mitch went on to the next item on the list. "Mayonnaise?"

"Oh, dear Lord," was Reb's only response.

They finished up the grocery shopping in time to get back to the homestead before dark. Although it took some doing, the mobile homes had been delivered two days ahead of schedule and hooked up with all the modern amenities in relatively short order. Plumbing and electricity were present and accounted for and even proper ramps led the way to both of the homes.

Mitch unloaded the supplies as Reb availed herself of the bathroom facilities. She was so happy with the fact that she could easily maneuver around the bathroom and actually take a shower all by herself that she had already indulged twice since occupancy. One more wouldn't hurt. Meanwhile, Mitch straightened things up and then sat down on the couch. She nearly dozed off when Reb reappeared.

"Want some company?"

Mitch looked over. Reb was wearing her emerald green nightgown, the one that was so flattering.

"Of course," Mitch nodded.

Reb took little time arranging herself next to Mitch. She had such good upper body strength that she needed no help. Mitch refrained from touching her, knowing that now was no time to foster dependencies.

"I didn't know whether you'd be here or in the kitchen whipping up a couple dozen deviled eggs?"

"I could go and do that now that I have the recipe."

"You didn't buy paprika."

"Why would I?"

"You sprinkle paprika on deviled eggs."

"No, you don't. You put pepper on them."

"No. You put pepper in them and paprika on them."

"Well, if you know so damn much about it, why don't you go out and make them."

"I would, but they're chock full of cholesterol."

"Okay, so what do you want for dinner?"

"Oh, I figured I'd just nibble on your ears for a while."

"That's not going to be very nutritional."

"Who's worried about nutrition?" Reb whispered as she nuzzled slowly.

"I guess I am?"

Reb pulled back. It wasn't like Mitch to be this way.

"You seem preoccupied. Are you feeling okay?"

"I think I'm just tired."

"You seem pensive."

"I am."

"What are you thinking about?"

"I'm wondering how we're going to do it…"

Ordinarily, Reb would have made a wry comment, but it didn't seem like the time.

"Do what?"

"How are we going to talk to every person in Utopia?"

"Is that your goal?"

"You saw what happened in the grocery store. One minute that woman was looking at us like we were the 'two lesbians shopping' exhibit in a gay zoo and the next minute, we were sharing recipes."

"She was a nice lady, once you got her started."

"That must be the answer. If we could just have a nice conversation with every person, it might break down the barriers of prejudice."

"That might work for a lot of people," Reb nodded, "but it won't make one whit of difference where people like Lucinda Cornwall are concerned."

"A person could talk until doomsday and probably never get through to her."

"You said, 'probably.'"

"I know."

"You always hold out hope, don't you?"

36

"I've had too many great things happen to me when I held out hope. Just for the record, you're tops on the list."
"The top?"
"You do prefer that, right?" Mitch was getting over being tired. Talking to Reb usually energized her.
"Actually, I'm beginning to prefer being on the bottom."
"Well, I guess everyone has their preferences," Mitch winked.
"In fact, I prefer your bottom as well."
Now, they were giggling like a couple of love-sick teenagers on a second date. Maybe living in a trailer out in the middle of Kansas was going to be a good idea after all. Mitch disentangled herself from Reb long enough to prepare and serve a modest dinner. It was all the separation Reb could take for one evening and soon they were in bed together, just wrapped up in each other's arms. Nothing more. Nothing less. They were asleep in ten minutes.

The sound of the TV set woke Mitch. She couldn't believe that Reb was up and about so early in the morning. Then it dawned on her that Reb was still beside her in bed. It must have been voices from her dream. And then, she heard them again. Quietly, she slipped out of bed and looked out the window.
"What is it?" Reb woke up.
It took Mitch a second or two to break the news. "They're back."
"Who?"
"The protestors."
"You're kidding, right?"
"Nope."
Mitch took her time getting dressed as Reb weighed the possibilities in her mind.
"What are you going to do?"
"Well, first, I'm going to make some coffee and then see if anybody wants some."
"That didn't work last time."
"And it may not work this time, but that doesn't mean it's not worth a try."
"Wait until I'm dressed before you do anything drastic."

"Don't I always?"

Reb couldn't believe it. Mitch was seemingly excited at the prospect of more trouble.

"You wouldn't be so excited if it was you who got stuck in the previous fire."

"I'm not excited," Mitch clarified. "I just think this is a golden opportunity to continue what we started yesterday."

"Which was?"

"Our outreach program."

Before Reb could offer further comment, Mitch was gone to make coffee. As a precaution, she also called the sheriff, who sounded like he had sat down hard on a hemorrhoid upon hearing the news.

"I'll be right over," he drawled through the pain.

"Oh, take your time. Coffee's only half brewed."

"Right," he hung up.

This was going to be a thrill-a-minute morning. Reb found her way out of the bathroom in about ten minutes. She still looked beautiful, despite the circumstances.

"I hope the sheriff has sun glasses. He'll be here soon and you're dazzling."

"Oh, put a sock in it!" Reb was irritable.

"You're grumpy, I take it?"

"I'm frightened."

Mitch looked at her and said calmly, "You don't need to be."

"And why the hell not?"

"Because I'm here now, and nothing bad is going to happen to you."

Rebecca looked at Mitch like she hadn't seen her in a month of Sundays, which is a little over half a year in calendar time.

There was something markedly different about her. Something Reb couldn't quite put her finger on.

"You want milk with your coffee? We forgot to buy creamer."

"Milk's fine."

Mitch poured like they were at Buckingham Palace.

"Should I have breakfast ready for the sheriff?"

"You'd better hurry. He's pulling up as we speak."

"That didn't take long!"

"He knows the way," Reb remarked dryly.

"I guess so. I could still make some scrambled eggs and toast? How's that sound?"

"Fine. I'll get the door."

Sheriff Clouber was nothing if not the consummate gentleman. His hat was in his hands before he crossed the threshold and was all too happy to have something to eat. The trio talked as Mitch cooked.

"We wanted to make sure you were aware of the circumstances," Rebecca started right in on business as soon as coffee was poured.

"I appreciate that, Ma'am. Always good to keep one step ahead of things round here."

"What's your plan?" Reb bore in.

"Well, that depends on you, I guess. Those folks have the right to peaceable protest under the constitution-"

"You don't need to quote the constitution to me, Sheriff. I was a Senator."

"Oh, right, Ma'am."

Mitch could've sworn she heard that hemorrhoid acting up again.

"Here's some breakfast, Sheriff," Mitch put a heaping plate of eggs and toast in front of him. Next best thing to the diner. Reb got a reduced portion and Mitch stuck with dry toast. Although Reb noticed Mitch's meager entrée, she made no comment. She was still busy making her point to their guest.

"I want to make sure that they, and I mean every single last one of them, stay off my property and give us unfettered access to the public road."

"I understand that, Ma'am, and we'll certainly do our best."

"I don't need to remind you what happened last time."

"Ma'am, we figured that last time was purely a family affair."

Mitch watched Reb. After all, that *had* been Reb's theory as well. It was only Mitch the renegade who saw a conspiracy. And the conspiracy had a name, she was the homo-hating, fag-baiting Lucinda Cornwall. Mitch forgot to check if she was out amongst 'em. In fact, she had forgotten all about taking coffee out as well. Maybe she should do that with the sheriff on the premises, lest she be accused of slipping someone hemlock.

"I'm going to go and see if anybody wants coffee."

"Don't go out there alone," Reb warned.

"Honey, I'm not going to be frightened into hiding out in my own home. Now, I'm gonna go out there and see who's thirsty or hungry and then I'll be back."

She was out the door before the sheriff and Reb could think of a way to talk her out of it. As Mitch walked toward the group, she began to tally their number. There was a baker's dozen. Too bad she hadn't picked up a box of donuts at the store. There wasn't enough eggs left to go around if anyone wanted serious fare. At least there was one bright spot. Lucinda Cornwall wasn't in the crowd.

"Good morning!" Mitch hailed the group like they were her fan club. No one answered back. They had no doubt been briefed on how to handle Mitch Tanner. Ignore, chant, march.

"Anybody want any coffee or maybe something to eat?"

Ignore, chant, march.

Mitch even went so far as to wander in and out of their pint-sized picket line, looking closely at each participant like she wanted to be sure and recognize them the next day, all the while saying "hello" and smiling. The ignoring and chanting and marching continued until something very strange happened. As Mitch stood more or less in the center of the group, she raised her arms in a stretching motion. It was early, after all. For a brief instant, all the protestors fell silent. Not that they had planned it that way. Their strategy was to drown out everything Mitch said. Then, as quickly as the moment came, it passed and no one was sure that what had happened had really happened. Most of all Mitch, who had felt nothing at all but a good solid stretch. When she looked around, the group had given her a wider berth and even lost the march step. One man almost fell over the feet of another, but recoiled at Mitch's attempt to steady him.

"Okay, everybody. I'm buying donuts for tomorrow. Everyone who wants a donut, raise your picket sign!"

Instantly, all the picket signs went down. Well, at least they were listening.

"Don't worry. I'll still get enough just in case. See you later!" Mitch waved as she headed back to the trailer. Reb and the sheriff were waiting on the front landing. Neither spoke at first and then Reb asked, "Are you okay?" in that tone of voice people use when they see someone walk away from a really bad car accident.

"I'm fine, but I have to go into town and get some donuts for tomorrow. And some creamer. You stopping by for breakfast tomorrow, Sheriff?"

He looked as if he'd been struck by lightening. "Uh, um, well, I guess it depends on what happens?"

"I guess so," Mitch was puzzled by his response, but still planned on a donut buffet. She looked at Reb, who still had such an interesting facial expression.

"Well, let's go and finish breakfast and then head into town." Mitch was suddenly hungry for more than toast and ate the leftovers from everyone else's plates. For whatever reason, they had lost their appetites about the time she had acquired one. It didn't take too long to clean up the dishes and get ready for still one more trip into town. Sheriff Clouber gave them a semi-official escort, which means he left at the same time that they did. There were no sirens or lights or any other distractions. Reb would remember this later on. For once, Mitch got to drive. One of the biggest steps forward Reb had made soon after her accident was the ability to drive. It meant such a world of freedom to her that typically she did about ninety-five percent of the driving. Today was Mitch's turn at her five percent. All she had to do was to avoid running down any protestors. It was no big deal, they didn't bother to block access with the sheriff as witness. When they got close to town, the sheriff peeled off the two-vehicle convoy to attend to other duties. With no prior warning, Mitch pulled into the parking lot of the diner.

"What are we doing here?" Reb asked.

"I'm hungry."

"You just had breakfast!"

"I'm still hungry. Come on."

Jessie practically knocked them down as they came through the door.

"Did you hear the news?" she was practically breathless. If this was going to be an announcement about what was already obvious to Reb about the renewed protests, she didn't want to hear about it.

Mitch did. "What news?"

"There was an earthquake!"

"Where?" Mitch followed up like she was going to reporter school in her spare time.

"Here! Right here!"

"Here at the diner?"

"Of course not! But real close!"

"Really?" Mitch was now just polite. She was more hungry than curious.

"It was closer to your place, according to the news."

"How's the chicken fried steak?"

Jessie gave one of her patented head shakes that conveyed a warning. "Go with the corned beef hash and eggs."

"Sounds good."

"I'll just have toast," Reb figured she could get by with that.

"Sure thing, Senator."

Jessie was off to place the order and refill a swarm of coffee cups.

"So, that's what that was," Reb had brightened considerably since they had placed their order.

"What?"

"Obviously you were at the epicenter of a mild earthquake. Did you feel the earth move?"

Mitch shook her head, "But then again, every time I'm around you, the earth moves!"

Reb only rolled her eyes. No use trying to best a sweet talker like Mitch. Besides, being in the epicenter of an earthquake might be just like being in the eye of a hurricane. If anyone could stay calm in the middle of that, it would be Mitch. As Mitch ate heartily, Reb just picked.

"You gonna be hungry for lunch?" Mitch asked between bites.

"Not if I keep eating two breakfasts every day."

"Two half-breakfasts only count as one."

"Then what do two full breakfasts add up to?"

"Heartburn?"

"Let's remember to go down the medicine aisle in the store."

"Okay. We need stuff like sunscreen anyway."

"And creamer," Reb reminded.

"Did we make a list?"

"We didn't write anything down."

"Should we?"

"No. Let's just go down every aisle. I'm in no rush to get home."

Mitch turned the last statement over in her mind throughout the shopping trip. Indeed, Reb was in no particular hurry and all but loitered in the produce section of the store. She bagged up item after item, everything from oranges to cilantro. Good thing they had two refrigerators. All the items Reb chose were perishable. Which would be good for her overall health.

"The fresher, the better," Reb explained.

"A lot like me," Mitch answered.

Now that they had a van full of groceries, they had no choice but to head home. Company was still there and this time, Mitch had donuts. She left a dozen in a box out on the fence post and then worked side by side with Reb cleaning vegetables.

"What are we having tonight?" she asked Reb.

"I don't know. What are you cooking?"

"I don't know. What do you want?"

"One things for sure. I don't want donuts and neither it seems do your guests."

Mitch looked out the window. "The box is gone?"

"One of them knocked it off the fence post with a stick."

"Oh really? Well, I'll pick it up after they leave."

"You'd better do it now before they report us to the sheriff for littering. Besides, it'll get all buggy if you leave it out there."

"Okay."

Mitch was happy to do this chore. Keeping things clean made Reb content. She took a small plastic bag with her as she walked over to the mess. It looked more like someone had done some batting practice than a simple poke with a stick. Donuts were scattered in a ten-foot radius and already some industrious ants were settling down to a party of their own. As the ants had gathered, so had some storm clouds and before Mitch had everything all picked up, a bolt of lightning came searing out of the sky, scattering the group of protestors to their respective cars.

43

Mitch was unfazed. She had seen her share of lightening before and took her time cleaning up the rest of the mess before going back inside the trailer. Rebecca was beside herself.

"Are you hurt?"

"No. Why?"

"That lightening strike was awfully close!"

"Oh, I've seen worse," Mitch shrugged.

"You have not!"

"Sure I have. One time, when I was at the house in Colorado, a big bolt of lightening hit right outside the porch."

"And you never told me this before!"

"You never asked."

"And what am I supposed to do? Ask you every day, 'Oh by the way, did you almost get killed by a bolt of lightening today?'"

"I didn't think it worth mentioning."

The discussion was cut short by the distant sound of sirens. Instinctively, Reb sniffed the air for smoke. Meanwhile, Mitch took a gander outside. The group of protestors had gotten back out of their cars and formed a tight circle. Whatever was going on was the root of the sirens. Mitch went outside and watched from her edge of the property line, right next to where the donuts had been scattered. Reb was soon out there as well.

"What happened?"

"I don't know yet."

About that time, Sheriff Clouber ambled over to them and had a grim look on his face.

"You wouldn't happen to know anything about some possibly poisoned donuts, would you?"

"Poisoned, no. But I do have a bag of donuts infested with ants," Mitch went to get it out of the trash can.

"Don't touch those, Ma'am!" the sheriff stopped her cold.

"Okay," Mitch backed off.

"I'll have to take them into evidence."

"Sure. Come on over and collect them. What's going on, anyway?"

"Lady over there is pretty sick."

Mitch got a glance. The woman was gray and shaky alright.

"Check her for a heart attack before you spend a lot of time and energy tracking down some poison that doesn't exist."

"I just let the doctors do the doctoring."

Mitch was beginning to know how Jessica Fletcher felt. Mitch and Reb watched as they loaded the woman into an ambulance.

"She'll be dead before morning," Mitch shook her head.

"How can you tell?" Reb asked.

The question caught Mitch off guard. How did she know? "I don't know. I just know. Let's go finish cooking dinner. We still have our funeral clothes, don't we?"

"Yes, we packed up everything when we moved out here."

"How did it all fit?" Mitch asked suddenly, like she hadn't a single memory of the process.

"We travel light through life."

"We'd better make sure our going-to-funeral duds are decent looking."

"Let's just cook dinner, okay."

"Sure."

Chapter 8

Conners died as Trish napped in the chair next to his bed. For a moment, she chided herself for not being awake when it happened, but soon felt content that at least he hadn't died alone. Too many other people in this place would suffer that fate. Connors had died much sooner than the doctor's prognosis. Maybe he knew somewhere in his heart that it was time to free Trish of her self-imposed obligations. She called Robbie. "Hello?" Robbie answered. She sounded so alive.

"It's me," was all Trish had to say for Robbie to know.

"I'll be right there," she said and then hung up.

Robbie had been through this dozens of times with the sons, daughters and other relatives of the hundreds of geriatric patients she had known over the years. It never got much easier, but helping Trish through these next few steps would be more wrenching than all the others. Due to Connors' sudden demise, they hadn't made any arrangements. Maybe they thought that there would be some sort of mystical warning, some revelation that would tell them to call the mortuary? They thought wrong. After Trish had hung up from calling Robbie, she notified the staff. Ms. Huber was there within minutes, as were Robbie and the doctor. The body was left undisturbed until the doctor made a final determination and time of death. It didn't take long. No one saw the need for an autopsy and Ms. Huber offered to call the mortuary most used by the facility. Trish checked it over with Robbie, who nodded agreement. It wasn't like they had any real preferences and if Ms. Huber received a kickback, so be it. Connors would be bagged up, ferried away and ready for viewing by the next day. Trish gathered up her books, took one last look around a room she had spent enough time in and then allowed herself to be pulled out by Robbie. They went straight back to the apartment and followed up on the paperwork necessary to break their lease. They were now anxious to be gone. They would view Connors, see to the burial and then leave for home. Rose and Max were both happy and sad at the news. In balance, they were more happy. Connors was no more than a stranger to them, but even Rose shed a few tears.

"We'll be home in three days," Robbie announced.

Chapter 9

Mitch had read the account of Edna Sellers untimely death in the morning paper the day after the lightning bolt. She had died in the ebb of the night from heart disease brought on by the sudden shock and surprise of the lightening. Mitch's donuts had been exonerated and, thankfully, discarded. Now, it was time for what Aunt BeBe would have called the "meeting." It was the gathering of the mourners at the family home the night before the funeral. Mitch was in her best black outfit and still couldn't hold a candle to Rebecca. What Rebecca Fairbanks and black did for each other should be illegal.

"Are you sure this is such a good idea?" Reb asked.

"The poor woman was practically killed on our property. I think we need to pay our respects."

"The woman had been holding up a sign that said, 'You make God want to vomit!'"

"Well, let's not talk ill of the dead."

"Too bad everyone can't follow your example."

"You ready?"

They drove to the address listed in the obituary. It wasn't hard to find. All the streets were straight in downtown Utopia. There were so many cars parked all over that they ended up walking two blocks, which allowed them to blend in, more or less, until they got to the front door where they were immediately recognized. So much for blending in.

They were immediately asked to leave. Get out. Go away. And they hadn't even stepped foot in the door. Mitch and Reb were more than happy to respect the wishes of the family and were willing to let bygones be bygones even though warnings were hollered at them half a block away to stay the hell away from the funeral as well. Mitch just waved it away and walked proud alongside Reb.

"That didn't accomplish a thing."

"Oh, *sure* it did."

"It did?"

"It made us look like the bigger person, or persons in this case."

"You really think so?"

"Remind me to send a sympathy card. I'm sure they have expenses."

"You ready to head home?"

"Sure."

It was about five more minutes before Reb asked, "You aren't planning to go to the funeral anyway, are you?"

"I respect all the wishes of the family."

Chapter 10

The funeral for Connors was attended by so few people that the words of the preacher echoed through the sanctuary. There were no surviving relatives. None of the residents of the care facility where he had lived were able to attend. Trish and Robbie sat in the front pew and were joined by a smattering of local church goers. This was the same cadre of people who attended as many funerals as possible and served punch and cookies afterwards. After Conners was laid to rest next to his mother, Trish and Robbie were on a flight home to Colorado and back in their own bed before the late news.

"It's nice to be home," Robbie noted.

"Uh huh," Trish answered quietly.

Everything Trish had said lately was spoken quietly.

"If you needed to talk about something, you would, wouldn't you?"

"Uh huh."

"Anything on your mind right now?"

"Yes, as a matter of fact, there is."

"What are you thinking?"

"How do you want to get pregnant?"

"Oh that! Well, how do you think we should get pregnant?"

"I asked first."

"I don't want to do it the usual way."

"The usual way?"

"You know, intercourse."

"Okay," Trish nodded. She hadn't even thought about that as a possibility.

"I mean, unless it turns out that that's the only way…"

Trish would die green of jealousy over that situation, but didn't let on.

"I think the major issue is whether or not we want to know the donor."

"I don't," Robbie made it clear right away.

"That was fast. You've been giving this some thought?"

"I don't want the father to be second guessing us as we raise our family."

"But what about the kids wanting to know?"

49

"Do you want to know the donor?"

Trish, who was truly far behind in the thought processes, was playing catch-up.

"No," she finally said.

"So, we agree on that?"

"Yes."

"Well, I guess the next step would be to locate the best gynecologist in Denver."

"And a new house," Trish reminded

Robbie exhaled slowly. "We're going to be very busy."

"If you think that's busy, wait until we have three or four children running around the house."

"We'd better get some sleep while we can."

For whatever reason, it proved to be a lot easier to find a good baby doctor than a new house. This could have had something to do with the fact that Trish had once been a real estate agent. She knew enough about the business to be terribly selective about whatever mansion they were being shown. So far, nothing had stood out.

By contrast, Robbie had settled fairly quickly on a gynecologist, but insisted that Trish go along for the pediatrician interviews. Just so it was clear, the interviewing process went both ways. They had to answer as many questions as they asked. In the end, the doctor and Robbie were both satisfied and that's all that was important to Trish. As soon as Robbie was ready, they would begin the artificial insemination process. After the paperwork was complete, including billing address, Trish took Robbie to dinner. Not just any dinner, but a candle-lit fancy schmancy dinner for two.

"This might be our last chance for a long time to have a romantic evening," Robbie said thoughtfully.

Trish shook her head. "No. Every evening with you is romantic. That's never going to change."

"Just wait until I'm nine months pregnant and waddling through the house! Then, you'll change your mind."

"I'm sure I will. Then, I will think that it's even more romantic."

"Why ever would you think that?"

"Because building a future together with you is the most romantic thing we could ever do."

Chapter 11

Mary was getting better at burn wound care. Then again, she couldn't have gotten much worse. At least, that was her opinion. The medical staff begged to differ with her and was overall pleased at her level of competence. Lisa was still extremely hard to please, but Mary chalked that up to nerves. They were on a countdown to the time when the skin grafting would be performed on Lisa's face. Research had shown over the years that the best success for facial skin grafts was after eschar, meaning that the burn wounds on the face, if allowed to gradually or naturally loosen from the healthy tissue, would produce less scarring. Slowly but surely, that was happening. It was, at best, a time of conflict for Lisa. She wanted to be done and out of the hospital, but she also wanted as little scarring as possible. It made her snappish and irritable about twenty-three hours out of every day. Mary was running out of reserve and good cheer herself. Matters weren't helped when the doctors began to talk about the plastic face mask that Lisa would need to wear for months after her release. Once the final grafting was over, a custom-fit mask would be made that would put the same kind of pressure on the facial grafts as the Jobst garment on her arm. It was enough to make any grown woman cry. Which was exactly what she was doing when Mary showed up at lunch time.
"Hi Sweetie. What's wrong?" were words that Mary found herself saying more days than not as a greeting.
"Nothing."
"It wouldn't be like you to be crying over nothing."
"Well, I haven't exactly been myself lately, in case you haven't noticed."
This was one of those times when Mary couldn't come up with a good reply. If she told Lisa she was being like her old self, it would make her sound like a perennial crybaby. If she told her that indeed she wasn't like her old self, it would further feed Lisa's growing insecurity. She decided to go on a fact-finding mission.
"Are you still pretty upset about the plastic mask?"
"I'm going to look like a freak."
"No, you won't."

"Twenty-four hours a day!"

The worst news about the mask was that it was necessary to wear it at all times, maybe with the possible exception of taking it off during meal times. And we weren't talking about long, leisurely romantic dinners, either. Lisa and Mary knew that the longer the mask was on, the less likely it would be that the scars would be lumpy.

"Once you get through that, the worst will be over."

"Once I get through that," Lisa was snappish again, "I'll still resemble a patchwork quilt."

That much was true. The skin they were planning to use for the grafts was a different color than the skin on her face.

"Then, we'll just get you tattooed," Mary had all the answers.

"Great. Then I'll take my place among the truly weird. Won't that be special!"

"Is there anything I can do to cheer you up?"

"Leave me alone."

Since Mary had asked for suggestions, it wouldn't do to argue.

"I'll be back later."

Mary wandered down the too-familiar hallway to the all-too-familiar waiting area. It was deserted and bleak, not unlike Mary's mood. She sat down and closed her eyes. When she opened them again, an hour had passed and Hilary was sitting next to her.

"You sure have a lot of free time on your hands, for a medical student," Mary said.

"Hello to you too."

"Sorry."

"It's okay. I should know better than to disturb someone who's asleep. How are things going?"

"About the same. And you aren't disturbing me."

"Good. Aren't you two about ready to get out of here?"

"We have the face graft work left."

"And that will go just fine. I have a good feeling about it."

"Well, you're a party of one, aren't you."

"That gets tiring."

"What?"

"Being a party of one all the time."

They were both quiet for thirty or so seconds. A record for them.

"You want to grab a bite?" Mary finally asked.

"A bite of dinner?" Hilary wanted to make sure she heard right.

"How about a late lunch?"

"Okay, sure."

They stood up and walked down the hall together.

"Aren't you going to check in with Lisa?"

"She wants to be left alone."

"Oh, I see," Hilary nodded wisely. "She's at *that* stage."

"She's been at *that* stage for a long time."

"That's normal."

Hilary talked Mary into leaving the hospital grounds for lunch. In fact, they drove miles to a Greek restaurant for gyros. They were substantial and satisfying. Medical students knew where all the cheap good food could be had. As Mary worked her way through the meal, she talked about the various concerns still facing Lisa. So much so that she realized that she had monopolized the entire conversation.

"So, what's new with you?" Mary asked in a way that so much as admitted that she'd gone way overboard on the Lisa and Mary Chronicles.

"I'm just studying and behaving myself. Nothing new to report."

"Nothing new at all?" Mary pressed.

"I don't have a girlfriend, it that's what you're asking," Hilary reported nonchalantly.

"I didn't mean to be nosy."

"Oh, sure you did," Hilary smiled. "And I don't mind."

"Studying keeps you that busy?"

"Not that busy. I'd have time in my life for someone. If I were so inclined."

"Which you're not?"

"Which I'm not."

The silence that ensued was so awkward that Hilary decided to take a chance and elaborate. "I have nowhere to go but down. I've already had the best."

If Hilary thought the previous silence awkward, it paled to this one. Mary couldn't be farther away than if she were on a dingy in the middle of the Bermuda Triangle. Hilary went on anyway. "You know, there probably aren't too many people who can point to one event in their lives and say that this was the one time they had it made and screwed it all up. And that's what I think every single day of my life when I remember what I did to you."

"You're going to have to let go of that someday. I have."

"Maybe someday I will. We'd better be getting back. I have studying to do."

Mary nodded and then asked a long-overdue question, "What kind of doctor are you going to be, anyway?"

"When I grow up?" Hilary smiled.

"Right."

"A pediatrician."

"That's very challenging."

"It's also very rewarding."

"Why did you decide to be that?"

"Because little kids deserve the best of life."

Mary understood. Hilary had been abused as a child. If that had been stopped somehow, maybe she would have never grown into an abusive adult. And maybe Mary and Hilary would still be together. It would've always been like the first month or two. And you would've needed dynamite to get Mary out of the picture.

"Well, I think we should be going," Mary said like it was her idea originally.

"I'm sure we should."

The drive back seemed to go quickly for Mary. Soon, she was faced with the prospect of going back to face the recalcitrance of Lisa. It started right off with a question.

"Where have you been?" Lisa demanded.

"I had lunch."

"Where did you go, Europe?"

"Close. I had Greek food."

"Greek food? I never knew you liked Greek food," Lisa quizzed.

"I don't know if I've ever had Greek food before, come to think of it."

"So, why start today?"

Mary could've easily volunteered the information that it was Hilary's choice, but since she had already used the pronoun "I" instead of "we," she figured that the less Lisa knew about Hilary's involvement, the better.

"I took a drive and ended up there. It's no big deal. I'll take you there when you're discharged from here."

"I'm not going out anywhere for lunch or dinner when I get out of here."

"Why not?"

"Because I don't want to try and eat a meal with people staring at me."

"People won't stare."

"Oh please! People will stare. People always stare."

Mary knew this discussion was fruitless. It was true. People stare. And point. And whisper. It would be a long, long stretch of eating at home. Which was okay. Worse things could happen than eating healthy meals at home with the woman of your dreams. For about six months. Maybe longer.

"If you can't look any more cheerful than that, why do you even bother to visit me?"

"I didn't know that I had to belong to the Order of Perpetual Cheer."

"Are you going religious on me?"

"I pray every day that we won't fight. How's that for being on a spiritual plane."

"Terrific. Just terrific."

"You want me to go get you something special for dinner?"

"Hell no! You disappeared for lunch. I might not see you until tomorrow if you go for dinner."

Mary knew that this was a normal mood for some burn patients. It didn't make it any easier to listen to. She changed the subject. Sort of.

"Are you nervous about the surgery?"

"I don't want to talk about it."

"Once that's done, they're going to cut you loose from this place."

"I said I don't want to talk about it!"

"Is there anything that you do want to talk about?"

"No."

So, they sat in silence as the afternoon dragged on. Things would be different after the surgery. They would have to be. Mary couldn't take much more of this.

55

Chapter 12

Trish couldn't believe how quickly things progressed after
Robbie had made up her mind to have progeny. In fact, she had
made up her mind about several things all at once. She wanted
to have artificial insemination in a clinic by an anonymous
donor. Of course, there was the checklist to consider. Hair
color, eye color, height…
"Do they have any Jewish sperm at this bank?" Trish asked as
Robbie pondered.
"I'm sure they do," Robbie answered.
"Well, you'd better put that at the top of the list."
"Is that important to you?" Robbie asked.
"I'm sure it's damn important to your parents."
"I'm more interested in your opinion. This is, after all, our
baby."
"I already have my wishes coming true. The baby will look like
you. Can't get much better than that."
Robbie nodded, not in a vain way, but rather as if she was
thinking of something else entirely.
"What's on your mind?" Trish had to know.
"I'm going to list the characteristics I want to match in you."
"How?"
"Well, I'm going to fill in your hair and eye color and things like
that. Then, maybe the baby will look like both of us."
Trish pulled Robbie by the hand over to the mirror over the fake
fireplace in her condo and they stood side by side.
"Can you imagine what a combination of you and I would look
like?"
Robbie studied both their faces in the mirror for a few seconds
and seemed lost for words.
"No. What?"
"It's going to be one good looking kid," Trish moved behind
Robbie and rested her chin on Robbie's shoulder.
"And lucky to have you for a mom," Robbie added.
"We're definitely going to need a bigger house."
"We are?"
"I plan on spoiling our children rotten and I can't do that in this
tiny place."

"I'm not sure about the wisdom of spoiling children."

"Did I mention that I also plan on spoiling their mother?"

"Well, why didn't you say so in the first place!" Robbie said with a wink and a smile. Trish snuggled closer. "I figured that was a given."

"I'm already spoiled. I have you."

"Nevertheless, we must begin house hunting this next weekend."

"What if you can't find a house you like?"

"Then I'll just build one from the ground up."

Chapter 13

The protestors were wary, which was delicious irony for anyone paying attention to the history of the situation. Mitch was cognizant of their unease as she met with the architect, John Randall. He, on the other hand, was quite at ease with Mitch. John thought it was a terrific idea to rebuild the homestead from scratch and agreed readily that no expense was too great. Especially when most of it was covered by insurance.

"You're way ahead of old Bixby," John assured Mitch in the cramped quarters of trailer number two. It truly had been a stroke of genius to get two mobile homes for the duration of their stay in Utopia. Mitch mentally patted herself on the back. As Reb rested or read or caught up on exercise in trailer number one, Mitch could meet with people in her own little headquarters. If it seemed odd that Rebecca had divorced herself from the house project, or at the very least asked for a trial separation, it was nothing compared to the goings on between Mitch and the protest group. After the earthquake and lightning episodes, things had quieted down. However, the group, whose sole purpose in the beginning was to intimidate, had now grown leery of Mitch. If Mitch went outside to do any chores, they kept a trained eye on her. If she got too close, they sort of backed away. It was indeed a strange dance they were involved in, a slow waltz across the Kansas prairie. Mitch hadn't caught on at first and then once she did, found it amusing that she could make them back off just by moving closer and practically scatter when she moved her arms up in the air.

Now, hunched over plans for the new house, she thought about John's comment.

"You say Mr. Bixby isn't going ahead with his plans?"

"I didn't say that," John explained quietly.

John Randall was a nice guy. If Mitch had a straight sister, she would have no qualms introducing them. A woman could do way worse than John.

"He's just not going as fast?" Mitch asked.

"I can't seem to get his approval on much of anything."

"Maybe he doesn't want to rebuild?"

"You think?"
"I think he's enjoying city life right now."

Since Bixby's place had been burned down as well, he had taken
to living in a nice hotel room right in the midst of downtown
Utopia. Although Utopia, Kansas would never be mistaken for a
happening place, it was still far busier than an isolated farmhouse
out in the middle of nowhere. In some respects, it was probably
the best thing that had ever happened to him. And the ten or so
very deserving widows in the suburbs of Utopia who had taken
to brazenly call on him. Last time Mitch had visited him, he
looked a little worn around the gills. She made a mental note to
have him come for dinner when his schedule allowed.

Meanwhile, John nodded and then went on explaining the latest
blueprints to Mitch. Despite all the early talk about hot tubs and
merry-go-rounds, Mitch was more or less opting to build a
replica of the previous homestead. Which was interesting since
she hadn't spent much time in the place. John didn't seem to
mind. Mitch talked and he made notes.
"Big kitchens are all the rage now," he smiled.
"And it will be nice to have all new wiring to run all those
modern appliances."
"Is that going to be the defense in the trial?"
"Bad wiring?"
"It might hold up in court."
For a second, Mitch was tempted to ask what side he was on and
then thought better of it. Miranda, the little torch bug that she
was, had already confessed to the crime and the authorities were
checking her alibis for all other suspicious fires as well. John
was probably making small talk. No need to get all huffy over
that.
"I really haven't paid too much attention to the impending trial.
That's Rebecca's bailiwick."

As if on cue, there was a knock at the door. It was none other
than the lovely ex-Senator.
"Hello, Mr. Randall," Reb rolled right into the meeting.
"Afternoon, Senator, Ma'am."

"Oh, let's not stand on formality," Reb said in her best Kansas accent. "Call me Rebecca."

"Yes, Ma'am," he nodded agreement.

That's one of the things Mitch had grown to appreciate, the almost aching need for everyone around here to be polite. Except, of course, the group outside.

"Are our visitors still out there?" Mitch asked Reb as she bent close to give her a kiss on the cheek. It turned in to a rather nibbly gesture, and Reb called upon all her reserve to keep from giggling.

"Yes, I'm afraid so," she gave Mitch a gentle push back up.

"How do they stand the heat?" John wondered.

He was right. Even the early days of summer were blistering. They had already prayed in church for a break in the heat. Here, inside Mitch's little air conditioned cubbyhole, it was nice and cool. She felt guilty.

"So, the two of you have been going over plans?" Reb was apparently ready to be included in the process. About time, too, Mitch thought as she fetched some more liquid refreshments for her guests. Beer for John and a glass of wine for Reb.

"Isn't it a little early?" Reb checked around for a clock.

"It's almost three," Mitch answered like she had Big Ben in her back pocket.

"Oh, okay."

John settled in to repeat most of what he had already told Mitch. That allowed Mitch's mind to wander, not that it needed any excuses lately. It seemed to wander off at even the least temptation. She looked out the window and noticed what could very well be relief in the form of rain on the way. Even a breeze was beginning to pick up. Even so, the protestors could probably stand some iced tea or lemonade. Mitch made a pitcher of each, cheating as she went by using a store-bought mix. No use investing a lot of elbow grease in something that would just as likely be poured on the ground.

"What are you doing?" the snoop Reb had been watching.

"I'm fixing some refreshments for my other guests."

"I don't know why you bother. They'll just pour it on the ground," she remarked.

"Maybe today will be different?"

As Mitch put the finishing touches on both pitchers, nothing fancier than cutting some lemon slices and tossing them in, the sky began to show even more promise of rain. Mitch gathered up her humble offering along with some plastic cups and headed out the trailer door. It was quite a stroll to the area of the front gate and Mitch went real slow to avoid spilling the contents of the two pitchers. Perhaps it was just Mitch's imagination, but the closer she got to the crowd, the farther away they seemed. It must have been their usual backing off approach that they had adopted. Mitch was almost to the fence before she realized almost everyone had scattered and those left were not staring at Mitch but beyond her. Maybe Rebecca had wheeled out as well? Now, she was a sight to be admired. When Mitch turned to see, she saw two things of interest. Indeed, one was Rebecca and she was pointing to something. Mitch followed her general indication and saw a natural phenomenon of a tornado forming in the distant sky. Not being a native of Kansas, Mitch stood for a time and watched the funnel wind its way across the land. It was a thin spiral, not the huge mile wide version that could eat pavement off the highway. In what seemed like an instant, John was at her elbow.

"Come back inside," he yelled at her.

"Why?"

"You'll be safer inside."

"About the last place you're supposed to be during a tornado is in a trailer," Mitch yelled back.

"There's nowhere else to go!"

"Don't worry about it," Mitch surveyed the area. The protestors had scattered in their cars, leaving Mitch with her two pitchers, plastic cups and John.

"Follow me," Mitch walked carefully to the porch where Reb was waiting.

"Do you have a tornado shelter?" Mitch asked Reb like they had a week to debate the issue.

"It used to be in the barn."

The last time Mitch had been in the barn, she had stumbled upon Uncle Henry and the church organist playing a little ditty of their own. In her haste to leave, she hadn't thought to scout around for a tornado shelter opening.

"Do you want to make a run for it?"

"It's in the path of the twister!"

Mitch looked over like this was a spectator sport. Sure enough, the tornado was bearing down on the structure. If it hit the barn, wood splinters would be the special of the day. For better or worse, they went back into the mobile home to avoid the projectiles. As they watched from the window, a truly foolish thing to do, they observed the tornado rip the barn apart in seconds. So much for Uncle Henry's legacy. According to Aunt Bunny's will, the homestead in its entirety had been bequeathed to Rebecca and Mitch save the barn. The barn had been bestowed to Henry, Aunt BeBe's long suffering husband. He had never really taken claim to it since, and now he wouldn't, for sure. Then, having satisfied itself with that snack, the twister seemed to hover for a moment in one spot. In defiance of all reason, Mitch opened the door and went back out on the porch to watch the tornado's next move. It didn't take long to swirl a path around the trailers and head toward the front gate. Good thing the protestors had fled. The area where they normally camped out was the next spot agitated by the swirling finger. Dust was thick through the air and it was unbelievable that Mitch could see anything at all. After it made its impression on this area, the tornado began to lazily make its way down the road that led to town.

"Suppose we should call and warn them?" Mitch asked as she popped her head back in the door. John picked up the phone to do so. Mostly because Reb was still speechless. When she found her voice, it was loud.

"What were you thinking!"

"What?"

"Have you lost your mind?"

"It was my first tornado. I just wanted to get a good look at it."

"You almost got a good look at your maker instead!"

"But I didn't, now did I?"

Mitch went over and gently took Reb's face in her hands. It seemed to placate her just a bit.

"I'm fine. I was never in danger. I'm not sure we can say the same for others in the path of the twister."

Mitch checked in with John, who was busy filling in the sheriff on the events. It wasn't long afterwards that sirens could be heard.

"Is that normal?" Mitch asked.

"It's the early warning system."

"I don't think so," John answered.

"What do you think it is?"

"Sounds like an ambulance."

Unbeknownst to the trio, the tornado had gained both power and speed after the barnstorming and caught up with the retreating protestors. It wasn't a pretty sight. One car was overturned with injuries sustained by all passengers. By the time Mitch, Reb, and John arrived on the scene, an all-call was put out to other emergency crews. Those who had escaped unscathed appeared ready to cast stones at Mitch, but were perhaps held back by the descending press and lookyloos. Before dinner, the scene was uplinked to all major news outlets. Mitch and Rebecca had gone to the hospital to offer comfort and when they were rebuffed, went home. There were three messages on the phone, two from Mary bookended one from Trish. Reb dialed Mary first. It took two or three minutes of assurances before she believed that everything was okay. Except the barn, of course.

"You want to talk to the Tornado Tamer yourself?" Reb asked Mary.

Apparently the answer was "Yes" for Reb handed the phone over.

"You're okay, really?" Mary asked again.

"Oh, sure. Couldn't be better. And yourself?"

The question seemed to catch Mary off guard. Her hesitation was not lost on Mitch.

"You okay?" Mitch followed up with another inquiry.

"Fine, fine," Mary answered too little, too late. Something wasn't right. It was time to talk to mom again. Mitch said so and then gave a look to Reb that indicated her concern. Mother and daughter talked for several more minutes before hanging up. Mitch had occupied herself by starting dinner.

"Need help?"

"Are things dusty in here or is it just me?"

"Things are dusty. What's on your mind?"

"What?"

"You're frying cauliflower."

"It's a new recipe."

"Are you thinking about the accident?"

"I'm thinking about Mary."

"What about Mary?"

"Something's not right. Why don't you go and pay her a visit this week."

Reb actually sat there and studied Mitch for a moment or two. As if she hadn't already studied her enough for one day.

"You're kidding, right?"

"No, I'm not kidding. Why would I be kidding about that?"

"We just pretty much got here and now you think I should go back there and...do what?"

"Find out what's wrong. I'd go, too, but I figure this is one of those mother-daughter things."

"You're not even sure something is wrong."

"Okay, fine. Don't listen to me. I'm just the mother-in-law."

"You don't seem like the typical mother-in-law to me."

"Yeah, I've heard that before."

"You better let me cook and you call Trish."

"Thanks for reminding me."

Mitch was more than happy to let Reb try her hand at frying cauliflower. She dialed Trish. Robbie picked up, all bubbly and happy. Someone should tell her that she was a gift to Trish.

"Does that bum Trish know how lucky she is to have you in her life?"

"I tell her every day."

"Oh, you do not."

"Well, not in so many words, but I drop a lot of hints."

"Is the old gal there?"

"She sure is. We've been watching the news. I'll let her tell you."

"Thanks."

Trish was on the line in two seconds.

"We heard things got pretty windy there today."

"Just a lot of hot air, although people did get hurt."

64

"Is everyone going to be okay?"

"There are two people in serious condition. One is in fair condition. One was treated and released."

"And your barn bit the dust?"

"We weren't using it anyway. But it's going to be hard work getting it all cleaned up."

"But you're all safe and sound?"

"Couldn't be better. What's new with you?"

"Well, we were going to wait and tell you a little later, but we're going to have a baby."

"You are? You're going to have a baby?"

"Well, Robbie is going to do the actual pregnancy, but, yeah, that's the plan."

"So, you haven't killed any rabbits yet?"

"No, not yet. But we're real close!"

"We are happy for you, aren't we, Reb?"

Reb nodded from the kitchen. "Tell them we'll throw them a baby shower."

"You hear that? A baby shower."

"That's so sweet. Thank you."

"It's our pleasure."

They didn't talk too much longer. There was fried cauliflower to eat. Which was really tasty despite the fact that Rebecca had added water and steamed it.

"This is great," Mitch forced a smile.

"It's healthy. Or maybe you don't need that?"

"What do you mean?"

"Haven't you noticed lately that you're impervious to all harm?"

"What are you talking about?"

"Neither tornado nor lightning nor earthquake can stay you from your daily routine."

"It's just a bunch of odd circumstances. I stubbed my toe just last week. Besides, Mother Nature and I go way back. She hasn't killed me yet. No reason to start now."

"And yet, others are falling by the wayside."

"Which reminds me, did you notice that we got that check back that we sent to the memorial fund of that lady who died."

"We did?"

"In shreds, actually. Somebody ran it through a shredder and sent us the strips."

"That's quite a statement."

"You wouldn't believe what was written on the back when I pieced it together. Some folks need a dose of soap in their mouths."

"We could send them some?"

"Maybe we could send cash, instead?"

"Maybe we should just let it go. Not everyone will respond the way you want them to."

Mitch thought about this statement long and hard. Rebecca could no longer respond the way Mitch wanted her to be able to. Her accident prevented that. Still, they managed to work around it.

"I know what you're thinking," Reb cocked her eyebrow.

"No, you don't," Mitch challenged.

"Oh yes, I do. We've been together long enough for me to know that look on your face."

"Remind me to go look in the mirror."

"Too late. The look is gone."

"But not the intent."

"Eat your cauliflower!"

Chapter 14

The day before Lisa's big surgery, Mary had planned to do several special things to lighten the mood. So far, they weren't working. A balloon bouquet had been relegated to a corner where Lisa rarely glanced. Flowers had been put in a bland hospital vase and placed in the sunlight to wilt. A lunch that Mary had special-ordered went virtually untouched and they were fasting after that. There was no eating, not much talking and absolutely no affection. Not even a kiss goodnight. Which wasn't different than any other night, and Mary was beginning to think that she would need to start practicing kissing her hand just to remember how.

Hilary was in the hall.
"So, tomorrow is the big day?" she asked. She knew already. She was keeping track.
"That's right."
"Is Lisa all pumped up as well?"
"I'd say she was more nervous than anything."
"I would be, too. It's not every day you get your face all put back together through the miracle of modern medicine."
"Well, it won't all be done. But it will be a start."
"Yes, it will. Once most of the wound area is covered up, the chance of infection really begins-"
"Could we please just talk about something else?" Mary interjected quickly.
"Sure. Come on. Ten bucks says you haven't eaten dinner yet."
"Ten bucks wouldn't buy dinner."
"Leave that to me."
To say that Mary allowed herself to be lured out to dinner by Hilary wouldn't be an accurate description. She went willingly. It would be their second meal together in a week. If Mary hadn't been so preoccupied with all things hospital, it would've felt clandestine.
"*You* were hungry," Hilary commented about mid steak.
Mary had devoured a green salad, French onion soup, most of a porterhouse steak and a baked potato.
"I guess I was."

"Check out the dessert menu."

"I'd better not," Mary said, but only half-heartedly.

"I'm having some. You might just as well."

"Well, maybe just some ice cream."

"How about some ice cream and chocolate cake and a slice of cheesecake with blueberry topping."

"Okay, but, what are you having?" Mary started to smile and then laugh.

Hilary smiled back. "The pleasure of watching you eat."

Mary looked past Hilary to avoid eye contact. She missed hearing someone say nice things. "It can't be that much fun," she replied awkwardly.

"Watching everything you do is pleasurable."

"Even when I worry about Lisa?"

"Maybe pleasure isn't the right word under those circumstances. But it's still heartwarming to see your love and concern for her."

"I wish she could see it."

"She does. It all goes to some very positive and safe place in her memory."

"You're sure about that?"

"I still have all those memories of you. Even through all the haze of alcohol."

"Maybe we ought to skip dessert. I think I need to turn in early. Be ready for tomorrow."

"Sure."

Hilary paid the check over only minor protestations. They walked out to the parking lot together and stayed in each other's orbit for a lingering moment before Hilary pulled Mary into an embrace. She also didn't fight the kiss. It was there and gone. Hilary was the first to speak. "I'm sorry."

"No, it's my fault."

And that was the truth. Mary had indulged. It was a lot better than practicing on her own hand, but the guilt...

"You want to spend the night at my place? Strictly platonic, of course. Just so you don't have to be alone."

"I've been alone so far. But, thanks for the offer."

Ten times Mary thought to turn around and drive over to Hilary's apartment. And ten times she resisted. And ten times she congratulated herself for keeping her head. She got to her own place and unlocked the door.

"Is that you, honey?"

Even though the voice was familiar, Mary still jumped.

"Mother?"

"Hi," Reb wheeled around the bend. "I just got in a while ago."

"You didn't tell me you were coming. I would have met you at the airport."

"I guessed that you were busy at the hospital with Lisa. You must have stayed late."

"I had dinner."

"Well, I'm glad you're keeping up your health. Why Mitch was ever worried is beyond me."

"Mitch was worried?"

"She thought you sounded tired on the phone."

"She was right about that. Doesn't mean you have to fly out here every time I get tired."

"I don't believe I have?"

Mary was all out of snappy repartee. Reb took up the slack.

"Is there something you want to talk about?"

"Did you have dinner?"

"I'm fine."

"We have to get an early start tomorrow."

"Then we'd better turn in early."

"Do you need anything?"

"I think I need for Lisa's surgery to be over so you can take a breather."

"Hold that thought."

Saying that mother and daughter went to separate corners might have been a bit of an overstatement, but they avoided further confrontations. Mary needed to go to sleep and erase all thoughts of being with Hilary. It was just one silly little hug and kiss, for goodness sake! It took a double dose of a mild sleeping aide before Mary dozed off. The next thing she knew, the aroma of brewing coffee was wafting through the apartment. It was nice to have it ready when she got up. It had been a lonely couple of weeks.

"I'm cooking breakfast. You want eggs?"

"Do we have time?"

"You're not performing the surgery, for goodness sake. How about just a quick piece of toast?"

"I kissed Hilary last night."

"I figured it was something like that. You want butter or jelly?"

"You're not angry?"

"It's not my place to be angry."

"Then, how do you feel?"

"I think a better question is, how do you feel about it?"

"You think I did a horrible thing."

"Do you think you did a horrible thing?"

Mary stopped talking for a moment. She had to stop and think.

"I think I slipped. It's been really tough lately with Lisa."

"Is she still withholding affection?"

Mary nodded.

"You know, I put Mitch through hell," Reb admitted.

"I bet she never went out and kissed anybody else."

"She didn't have a chance. Aunt BeBe kept an eye on her."

"That would do it," Mary muttered. "Is that why you came?"

"I feel like I deserted you."

"You and Mitch needed to get on with things."

"Not at the expense of leaving you alone to go through this. I'll stay out here as long as you need me."

"What does Mitch think about that idea?"

"She was the one who insisted I come out here. Besides, she seems to be coping quite well with all the things that can happen in Kansas."

"She has good coping skills…?"

"She had to. She lives with me."

Chapter 15

Mitch felt absolutely farmy. She had put off cleaning up the
remnants of the barn destruction until she had sent Reb back east.
Then, dressed in a new pair of baggy overalls and leather gloves,
she worked like a hired hand, gathering the remaining wood into
a huge pile. They would either need to burn it or have it hauled
away. Mitch wasn't crazy about the burning idea. It was
probably against the law anyway. She had pondered as she
worked as to whether or not to call Uncle Henry to see if he
wanted it, but figured that would be like rubbing salt in the
wound. How much nostalgia could possibly be attached to
planks of wood. It really didn't matter at this point what the
plans for disposal were. All Mitch thought about was getting all
the scraps into one big pile. As she worked, she usually had a
small audience. About five to seven protestors were present at
any given time. Since the tornado had ripped up the front gate,
there was only an "understood" barrier now. Mitch would
occasionally go toward the front gate area and the people would
back off and nervously look at the sky. This had happened, oh, a
good two or three times before Lucinda Cornwall blew on the
scene. Talk about a gust of ill wind. Mitch had a half a bologna
sandwich in one hand and about five Cheetos in the other when
she approached her side of the property line.
"Good afternoon, Ms. Cornwall," Mitch was being polite
enough.
"Don't you know it's impolite to eat in front of someone!" was
Lucinda's greeting in turn.
Mitch held out her sandwich. "Want some?"
"Absolutely not! I wouldn't be caught dead eating that!"
"I guess you don't want my Cheetos, either?"
"I have come to tell you that your pathetic display of parlor tricks
will not discourage us from our Godly mission!"
Mitch ate another bite of sandwich as she pondered this. She
was, after all, quite hungry from her morning's honest labor.
"Parlor tricks?" Mitch followed up with a question.
"Your attempts to frighten these decent folk will not work!"
The light was beginning to dawn, albeit reluctantly.
"Are you talking about the tornado?"

"If that's what it was, which I *truly* doubt!"

Geez, everything Lucinda said came out with exclamation marks attached to it. Who could stand to be around her very long?

"Everybody else thought it was a tornado."

"Everyone else was under the spell of Satanic forces!"

Mitch finished off the Cheetos and ate the next to the last bite of sandwich. She was down to mustard and crust.

"And, let me guess. You think I'm Satan?"

"You said it, not I!"

Mitch thought about this for a second or two. The other followers, who had under glare from Lucinda gathered closer to the property line, now stood in defiant posture.

"Let me see if I understand this," Mitch got as close to the group as she could without leaving her property. It was a nose to nose affair.

"You think that a woman like me with a crust of bread in one hand and a bunch of Cheetos orange stain in the other has the power to make a dozen people believe that they saw a tornado that wasn't really there? A tornado that flipped over a car with four people in it?"

"Everyone knows that Evelyn Johnson isn't the best driver in the county," Lucinda explained in her own unique way. Everyone else nodded like they had taken driver's ed. together.

"And so now, it's Evelyn's fault?"

"Of course not! Evelyn couldn't help herself when she was deathly afraid of Satan!"

Mitch had a flashback to the day she and Rebecca had joked about a merry-go-round. She now felt like she was on one. Circular logic never was her strong suit.

"How is Evelyn?" Mitch asked. She had been one of the most seriously injured of the group.

"That's just none of your business!" Lucinda exclaimed.

"Why not?"

"Because if we tell you how she is, you'll work more evil on her."

"I don't have time for that. I'm too busy cleaning up my own property. Have you stopped to consider why it would be that I would destroy a building on my own property?"

"A clever subterfuge. It makes you look innocent."

"I give up. No amount of reasoning will make a dent with you." Mitch turned her back on the group and headed over to her pile of wood. Everyone worked until dusk, Mitch with her cleaning project and the group with their protesting project. When the sun went down, Mitch went into town, still in her overalls. If they wouldn't tell her how Evelyn was, she'd by God find out for herself.

Visiting hours were long past, but there was no guard on duty to prevent Mitch access to the hallways of the hospital. It was, after all, a small rural site, not Fort Knox. Finding Evelyn Johnson didn't take too long. Patient's names were on a slide bar at each door. Mitch went into the room and watched the woman for a moment. She was asleep. Or maybe in a coma? Mitch was no doctor. She touched the woman's forehead and said a feeble prayer for her. Then, she left the hospital as she had come and returned home. She showered layers of grime from her body and then flopped into an empty bed. This was what she had tried so hard to put off. She prayed, again feebly, for instant sleep to avoid the ache of missing Rebecca. Her reward came in four minutes.

The pesky sun was there before Mitch was quite ready for it. Whatever ache was there for Rebecca last night had been replaced by a more real physical ache from the backbreaking work the day before. She slowly raised herself out of bed and then wandered out to the tiny kitchen. After looking in the refrigerator, she decided to do what most bachelor girls do. She decided to drive into town for breakfast. The diner was pretty crowded, but Jessie found a corner table for her.
"You hear the news?" was Jessie's first question.
"Probably not. I didn't watch TV this morning."
"You wouldn't hear about this on TV."
"It's something local?"
"You know that woman who was hurt by the tornado so badly."
"The Johnson woman?"
"Right. Well, that's the news!"
Mitch wasn't sure she wanted to hear this news. She'd already heard enough about how she was all the cause of the poor

woman's suffering. One more death would be a blow to the community and more ammunition for Lucinda Cornwall.

"She's well!" Jessie poured a cup of coffee for Mitch.

"She's well?" Mitch sounded baffled.

"Well, not well entirely. But she's out of her coma and the doctor's expect a complete recovery. You want your usual?"

Mitch looked at Jessie. "What's my usual?"

"Two eggs, hash browns, toast and bacon."

"That's my usual?"

"Usually that's what you've been having."

"I guess that's why they call it a 'usual.'"

"Are you feeling okay?"

"Yeah, I guess."

"You look a little tired."

"I've been filling my days with long honest hard work. Just like you."

"You want something different today?"

"How about a Denver omelet?"

"Sounds good for a change."

Jessie couldn't stay longer. There were coffee cups to fill and tabs to tally. Mitch waited patiently for her breakfast and then ate slowly when it arrived. No use rushing back to more toiling in the sun. By the time Mitch had finished, the breakfast crowd was gone. Jessie swung by with the coffeepot and hovered.

"You sure you're okay?" she asked.

"I have an idea. Why don't you come out to the house for dinner tonight."

"Oh, gee, well…I always watch Beyond the Beyond on Tuesday. It's my favorite show. All those weird things that happen to people. Kinda creepy."

"You could watch it at my place."

"Do you have cable?"

"It's on cable?"

"They don't run that sort of stuff on the networks."

"I guess not. Well, maybe some other time?"

"Maybe."

Mitch paid her tab and then headed home to another day of grueling labor. Along with all the cleanup of the barn, she was also working on clearing out all the weeds growing close to the

74

house. A small patch of grass had been nurtured for years when Aunt Bunny was still alive, but it was slowly creeping toward extinction. Mitch had promised to try and revive it while Reb was away. So, after she had cleaned up the tornado damage, she weeded, mowed and watered their little patch of garden. She then decided she should make a list of things they would soon need. Things like fertilizer. And fertilizer... That was all that Mitch could think of offhand. About four o'clock, she rummaged around the kitchen to see what she could toss together for dinner. Wanting to keep things simple, she steamed some vegetables (Reb would be *so* proud) cooked rice and sliced some store-bought French bread. It was long on starch but low on meat. She was just about ready to plate a serving when she heard a tentative knock on the door. It was Jessie.

"Hello!" Mitch was all smiles.

"Hi."

"Come in. Dinner's ready."

"Actually, I just stopped by to apologize."

Mitch was startled. "You don't have anything to apologize for?"

"I do. You just don't know what it is, yet."

"I'm not listening until you get your feet under the table. Come on."

Jessie followed orders and then Mitch put the plate she had fixed for herself in front of Jessie.

"You sure eat different at home," Jessie said it as a compliment.

"Rebecca wants to keep me healthy. The bread is a splurge. You won't tell on me, will you?"

"No, I won't. But I do want to tell you what I came to tell you."

"As long as it's not in the form of an apology."

"Well, it's true that my favorite TV show is on tonight. I didn't lie about that."

"Okay." Mitch nodded as she munched broccoli. Somewhere, Reb had to be smiling.

"I was just, you know, afraid of what people would think."

"What do you think people would think?"

"Well, since Reb is out of town, I thought that they would think the worst. You know?"

"Oh sure," Mitch nodded. "Some people might think we were dating."

"Or sleeping together!"

"They would think that?"

"Some folks think that that's all you gays think about, especially that witch, Lucinda Cornwall."

"Lucinda does have her moments," Mitch chuckled.

"Aren't you afraid of her?"

"Afraid, no. Concerned, yes."

"You're worried about what she's going to do next. I would be, too," Jessie elaborated.

"Actually, I don't worry about what she might so next."

"Well, what, then?"

"I worry that I can't have a decent conversation with the woman. I mean, I'm willing to allow for differing points of view, but I have a tough time with this constant barrage of fire and brimstone monologue."

"Most people do, too!" Jessie confirmed.

"Well, that's good to know, Jessie. I'm glad you came all the way out here to tell me that."

"Me, too."

They finished up with dinner and then Mitch showed Jessie the blueprints for the new house.

"Is it going to be an exact replica?"

"As exact as we can make it."

"That's so sweet. Keeping things the way they were."

And you can come out and visit anytime you want."

"You mean, you and the Senator are staying?"

"I haven't quite talked her into that yet, but I think once we get the place built, I won't be able to get her away."

"Is it…true? About her?"

"Is what true?" Mitch needed a bit more clarity. So *many* things were true about Reb.

"About the accident. She'll never get better?"

"If I understand correctly, in some ways, she'll get worse. For one thing, she's losing bone density because of the paralysis."

"And she has no feeling at all?"

"Not from the waist down."

"She could hurt herself and not know it."

"We try to be very careful."

"Oh, I'm sure you are…I mean…It's not what you think I mean."

"Well, what I meant was that we're very careful in everything that we do," Mitch smiled shyly, "including our sex life. So, it's okay if that's what you meant."

"I didn't mean to pry."

"You're a good friend and good friends never pry. They just express loving concern."

"I really don't have that many friends in town."

Mitch was caught off guard by the statement and sought a well-meaning response.

"You probably have a lot more friends than you think you do."

"I only have friends when somebody needs more coffee," she answered.

It was something to consider. Too many people battled loneliness on a daily basis. Even when surrounded by people, it could still get lonely without a true friend to confide in. They drank cold pop until sunset and then Jessie headed home.

"Breakfast starts early at the diner," were her parting words. Mitch didn't know if it was a statement of fact or an invitation, but smiled and waved as she drove away.

Chapter 16

It was hours and hours of surgery followed by a couple more hours in recovery. Mary was so glad that her mother had been there for her. Rebecca hadn't even thrown brickbats at Hilary when she stopped by to check on the patient. Something else to be grateful for. Lisa was heavily bandaged so the full effect of the surgical success, as reported glowingly by the doctor, wasn't viewable. That time would be soon, and mirrors would be waiting. Mary finally got to sit alone with Lisa in the afternoon. She was groggy, cranky and demanding. For once, it was a relief. Lisa could only have ice chips for a while until the anesthetic wore off. Pain medication dulled her appetite and overall responsiveness. Which worked out for a while because it hurt to chew anyway.

"Why don't you just go home," Lisa said at dinnertime.

"You don't need me to do anything?"

"There isn't anything you can do," Lisa was blunt.

Mary agreed. All those hospital dramas where all things were instant didn't accurately reflect this version of real life. The tedium was deadly. Mary leaned down and searched diligently for a place to kiss Lisa that wouldn't hurt and wasn't bandaged. There was one small spot. Mary kissed lightly. Then, Rebecca took Mary out to dinner. They were both in a shell fish mood. Over lobster, Rebecca brought up a subject which even she wasn't too sure about.

"Have you made plans for the future?"

"No. I've been so stuck in the present that I didn't want to even think about it."

Reb could understand that. It was a tad overwhelming to her as well, this business of the future.

"Mitch is rebuilding the homestead."

"A new house?"

"She's trying to build a replica of the old farmhouse."

"That's interesting. I guess it was a good floor plan at that. A nice big kitchen…"

"And plenty of sleeping space."

"Are you trying to talk me into moving back there with Lisa?"

"I actually don't know what I'm trying to talk about. I'm not going to live in Georgetown. We've already moved out of that house. I sold my place in Denver. Mitch still has her ranch house."

"And the place in Santa Fe. Don't forget about that."

"And now the farm in Utopia complete with two lovely trailers and blueprints that change weekly."

"How is your money supply?"

"It's okay so far. The income from the farm is still going into the estate's bank account. No one can touch that for a few more months."

"But when you can, it's going to be substantial, right?"

"Your Aunt Bunny was one smart cookie. When I die and you inherit the bulk of the estate, you will never want for anything. Ever."

"I think you should provide for Mitch."

"Old Moneybags Tanner? When Jane opens the restaurant, Mitch will be raking in so much dough that she'll need to buy a bank just to hold all of it."

"I guess so," Mary was pensive.

"Why don't you look okay with that?"

"I was just thinking that with all the money floating around, it still sometimes can't fix everything."

"Lisa is going to be okay, you mark my word. Her face is going to heal just fine. And she will kiss you back one of these days."

"I know. But she'll be in the mask for months."

"All the better to stick together as a family. You don't want to stay in Boston, do you?"

"No."

"Will she need outpatient therapy or anything like that?"

"They might have that joy and rapture up their sleeve."

"If they do, we can have her flown back and forth."

"Have you stopped to consider that maybe going back to Kansas will dredge up a lot of painful memories for her?"

"It's something to think about. Those memories will always be there in the background, no matter where she lives. She'll just have to face up to them, so to speak."

"Easy for you to say."

"I guess so. I had very little damage."

The subject of the future was put on the shelf, for the moment.
"Hilary seems to be ever present. Doesn't she ever go to class?"
"She's a brilliant woman. Probably only studies about half the
amount of time as the other students do."
"I suppose."
"She's going to be a pediatrician."
"How nice for her."
"And I'm not going to kiss her again. So, you don't need to
worry."
"I never was."
Mary was quiet for a minute and then she announced, "If Lisa
wants to come back to Kansas, we'll come back to Kansas."
"And if she doesn't?"
"Maybe we can go back to Denver. Back to Mitch's old house."
"Whatever you think is best, but you wouldn't be close to
anyone."
"Trish is there."
"That's the news that I forgot to tell you. Trish and Robbie are
going to start a family."
"You mean, have kids?"
"One at least, to begin with."
"Unless they have twins."
"Or triplets."
"Let's hope for one. One's enough to start with."
"That's the truth," Reb smiled at her first and only born.

Chapter 17

"This is happening pretty fast. Are you sure you're ready?"
Trish asked on the drive over to the fertility clinic. Robbie was,
well, not to put too fine a point on it, fertile. And the perfect
donor sperm were waiting.
"We may have to do this for months. Might just as well get an
early start."
"Okay. But if you get pregnant right off the bat, we'll really
need to find a house. And a maid. And a nanny."
"No nanny! I don't want some stranger raising our baby."
"I like the sound of that, 'our baby.'"
"Me, too. And I'm not too crazy about the idea of a maid
either."
"I'm not going to have you do housework while you're pregnant.
Even if I have to do it all myself."
"That's not how it's going to be. I'm not going to sit around and
get all big and lazy during my pregnancy."
"I'm going to make sure you rest and eat the perfect foods and
take vitamins."
"Well, okay."
Further discussion was put on hold as they pulled into the clinic
parking lot. The procedure didn't take very long, much like the
real thing in many cases. They were out by noon and starving.
Over grilled fish at the closest restaurant to the clinic, Trish
couldn't hold back her curiosity.
"Are you pregnant?"
"We won't be able to tell for a couple of weeks at least!"
"I know, but do you feel different?"
"I'll tell you in a couple of weeks."
"Eat your fish. It's good for you."
"I'm eating, I'm eating!'
"For two…" Trish got in the last word.
After lunch, just to be on the safe side, they went home and
rested in bed. It was a great excuse to cuddle. When Robbie
dozed off, Trish got up and fixed a light dinner of canned
chicken soup and tossed green salad. Robbie ate very little when
she woke up and then went to bed early. Trish followed a couple
of hours later and slept like the proverbial log until she heard

sounds from the bathroom. Robbie either had one helluva case of the flu or the AI had taken hold. When Robbie emerged, Trish was right there to guide her back to bed.

"I don't feel so good," was Robbie's self-diagnosis.

"I guess not. Come on back to bed and let me get you something. Maybe some weak tea?"

"I don't think I could hold anything down right now."

"Okay, well let's get you settled and then I'm calling the doctor."

"Why?"

"Because that's what people do when they're sick."

"I'm just a little nauseated."

"And anything else?" Trish asked as she dialed the phone.

"No."

As the doctor's service asked questions, Trish answered as best she could and conferred with Robbie about things like rashes and such and then hung up the phone.

"What did they say?"

"They said to rest and call back if you develop any more symptoms."

Right now, it was just nausea. No fever. No sore throat. No bumps or lumps or rashes. Just a good case of, Trish crossed her fingers, morning sickness. Robbie was reading her mind.

"It's not morning sickness. It doesn't happen that fast."

"It did with a friend of mine. She threw up the day after. And the day after that."

"Please! I don't want to know any more about it right now."

"Of course not. I'm sorry. The doctor's office also recommends crackers. You want me to get you some?"

"Will it make you feel better?"

"It would make me feel useful and that's very important to us expectant significant others."

"ESO?"

Trish thought about it. She could be very happy spending nine months being an ESO.

"Let me go check the saltine cracker inventory. I'll be right back."

Trish returned in three minutes with a bowl of crackers.

"They might be a little stale," Trish confessed.

"Do we have any tomato soup?"

"I can check."

"Okay."

Trish didn't even know why she bothered. Even if she had a can of tomato soup, it would be about ten years old. And that wouldn't do. She went back in to report on the absence of tomato soup.

"I'll go to the store. You want anything besides soup?"

"More crackers?"

"Good."

"And some ginger ale."

"Okay. Anything else?"

"No."

A trip to the store to buy three items didn't take too long. Trish returned soon with a case of tomato soup, regular saltines and oyster crackers, and thirty liters of various soft drinks. She checked in with Robbie, who was happily napping. It gave her time to heat up some soup for a light snack. Robbie was awake by ten.

"Hi, Sweetie. You ready for that tomato soup?"

"Oh, gee, no, not right now. Thanks."

"Can I get you anything else?" Trish was feeling just a teeny bit panicked.

"How about...a tuna fish sandwich?"

"I know we have that. I'll go mix something up."

"Easy on the mayo."

Trish nodded. It was like a mantra. Easy on the mayo. She went back to the kitchen, turned the heat off under the soup and set about to make tuna fish sandwiches. A can of tuna, some sweet pickle relish, and a bit more mayonnaise than she would admit to. Not only was Robbie thrilled with the entrée, but was truly pleased at the availability of strawberry soda pop.

"You're spoiling me."

"That's the idea."

They ate their meal in bed and then cuddled up. Trish was okay for all of about four minutes before she started to cry. It was a historic moment.

"I have never seen you cry," Robbie was astounded. "Are you okay?"

Trish nodded, "Uh huh."

"Okay," Robbie held her tightly. "What are you thinking about?"

"We're going to be mommies," Trish said through her tears. "Eventually."

"Not eventually. It's going to be nine months from today."

Trish reached over and placed her hand on Robbie's tummy.

"Are you making a prediction?"

"No, I'm just telling the truth."

Robbie smiled and stole a kiss from Trish, which Trish promptly tried to recover.

"I'm glad you're feeling better," Trish said.

"Me, too."

"How long does morning sickness last?"

"Until the kids go off to college?"

Robbie got the giggles and then took her turn with the crying. Of all the defining moments of life, this was a momentous one indeed. Two lesbians, one pregnancy, a case of tomato soup and enough soda pop to float the Ark. All they needed now was a bigger house. Trish had avoided using the "m" word, namely "mansion," around Robbie, but it was definitely what she had in mind. As Robbie dozed, Trish got up and went to her study to go through an old address book to see if any friends from real estate were still in business. After dialing two numbers and getting voice mail, she finally connected with a real live person on the third try. Sara Walburg sounded as bright and perky today as she had years ago.

"Hi, Sara. It's Trish Sullivan."

"Hello! I've seen you on the news this year. How are you doing?"

"Things are great. I've settled down with a nice woman and we're going to need a bigger house."

"And you want my help."

"Exactly."

"But you know all about this. You could do the deal."

"I know. But I'm going to be pretty busy around here. We're trying to start a family."

"So, you're going to need a big house."

"We're going to need a mansion."

"How soon do you want to start?"

"The sooner the better."

"I have time next Tuesday."

"Sounds great. What time?"

"How about ten?"

"Okay. We can talk and have lunch."

"My treat."

"No, my treat."

"I'll arm wrestle you for the check."

"I'll look forward to that!"

"See you then."

Trish smiled as she hung up. That Sara always was good for a chuckle.

"Did I hear right?" Robbie's voice broke the jovial mood.

"You're awake!"

"Did you tell someone that we're going to buy a mansion?"

"Well, yes."

"What were you thinking?"

"I'm thinking about your parents and the baby."

"We don't need a mansion."

"It's 'realtor talk.' Don't worry about it. Besides, if we're going to have five or six kids, we're going to need a big place, right?" Robbie came closer to Trish. "You think we're going to have five or six kids, huh?"

"Only if that's what you want."

"So, you were on the phone with who? A real estate agent?"

"Right. An old friend of mine. Sara. Sara Walburg."

"And you're meeting with her on Tuesday?"

"No, we're meeting with her on Tuesday at ten."

Robbie nodded thoughtfully.

"Is that okay for you?" Trish asked.

"I just hope I'm not still throwing up at ten."

"Me, too."

Chapter 18

Rebecca had stayed two days past Lisa's surgery. It was long enough to both reassure and be reassured that things were going to be okay. Not great. Not perfect. But okay. For now. Mitch had driven out to the airport to pick her up and without further ado, they arrived at the diner for lunch. Jessie more or less waved them to a table and was nothing short of aloof when she took their order. There was none of the usual banter. Just cut and clipped information. Mitch didn't think much about it, being preoccupied by her reunion with Reb. They had chatted about Mary and Lisa most of the drive and now the subject turned to local news.

"What's been going on around here?"

"I got the lawn mowed."

"I meant, what's up with Jessie?"

Mitch looked up, surprised by the inquiry.

"What do you mean?"

"She's pretty cold to us. Did something happen?"

"She came out to the house for dinner a couple of days ago. I think things are fine," Mitch shrugged.

"Okay, what else is new?"

"I got the remains of the barn all picked up. That took a while."

"You look like you've been out in the sun a lot. Did you get a lot of splinters?"

"I wore my gloves. And my hat."

Reb smiled at the image. "You like it here, don't you?"

"I don't not like it," was Mitch's succinct reply. Further explanation was interrupted by the banging of plates. Jessie delivered breakfast and walked away without comment. Reb looked at Mitch. "What did you do to upset Jessie?"

"I didn't do anything. I have no idea what the problem is."

"Well, you'd better start apologizing. We need all the friends we can get, particularly if you're beginning to like it here."

They ate lunch quietly, enjoying each other's company. No check arrived to pay. Jessie stayed busy with other customers, so

Mitch just left money plus tip on the table per usual and left with a wave.

"Did anything else unusual happen while I was gone?" Reb was almost afraid to ask.

"Let me think. No. Wait. One other interesting thing did happen. You remember that woman who was injured so seriously in the car accident?"

"The one caused by the tornado?"

"Right. Well, she's had some sort of miraculous recovery."

"Really!"

"Yeah! One day she was in pretty bad shape and the next day, she was better."

"Well, that's certainly good news. Now, if you can get things cleared up with Jessie, everything will be back to normal."

Mitch didn't say it, but nothing was ever really normal in their life. However, the afternoon did pass without incident. Reb was impressed with the gardening work accomplished by Mitch.

"You want to maybe see my green thumb?" Mitch had her hands in her pockets.

"Gee, maybe later."

"Have you told me everything there is to tell about your trip back east?" Mitch asked out of the blue.

"No."

"Is it serious?"

"No, at least, I don't think so."

"You'd tell me if it was?"

Rebecca considered Mary's aching loneliness. "Were you ever tempted to kiss anyone else while I was recuperating from my accident?"

"Well, I'll admit that for a brief moment, your sister BeBe was almost tempting…"

"And you wonder why I never talk about serious things with you!"

"I'm sorry. I don't mean to make a joke about it. So, Mary's kissing someone else? Oh, gee, let me think…"

"It's Hilary," Reb said what Mitch already knew.

"Is Lisa still holding Mary at arm's length?"

"It would appear so."

"Did you talk some sense into Lisa?"

"I didn't try."

"You want me to?"

"I think you'd better get things straightened out with Jessie first." Mitch didn't say so, but she thought the term "straightened out" was a curious choice of words. She checked her watch and dialed Jessie's home number. Jessie answered on the second ring. She sounded uneasy.

"Hello?"

"Hi, Jessie. It's Mitch. I was-"

"I don't think we should talk."

"I was wondering if-"

"I really can't talk right now."

"Would you like to come over?"

"No! No, really. I'm sorry."

Before Mitch could say anything else, Jessie hung up.

"I she still angry with you?"

"I don't think she ever was," Mitch's voice trailed off. She went over and looked out the window. Their visitors were still there. All seven of them. It was a quiet day. They had sustained over a dozen visitors most days after Lucinda Cornwall had made an appearance. If the group got much smaller, Lucinda would be back. It was almost enough to make Mitch go out and round up some more people herself.

"Did you say anything to embarrass her?"

"I talked about our sex life," Mitch recalled the conversation.

"Well, no wonder she's acting the way she is! You actually talked to her about our sex life?"

"Well, not in Technicolor detail for goodness sake! We were talking about your accident and subsequent injuries. I told her that it was okay to ask about things. Even personal things."

"So, you want to be a one-woman information center about being a lesbian?"

"Gee, I thought I'd leave that chore to Rita Mae Brown."

"Who?"

"Never mind. I think I know what's going on. Let's go."

"Go? Go where?"

"To Jessie's place."

"Are you sure that's a good idea?"

"No. But you suggested I fix things and this is all I can come up with."

They nosed the van past the group of seven. Mitch had gotten so she waved to them. They didn't wave back. They were too busy scowling and scanning the sky for tornadoes and such. It was a short drive to Jessie's duplex. She rented out half of it from an elderly couple supplementing their Social Security check. Jessie was home and opened the door, albeit reluctantly.

"Hi," Jessie said.

"Hi," Mitch said.

"I wish you hadn't come here."

"I can't have a good friend be angry with me."

"It's not that."

Mitch looked at Reb with that facial expression that conveyed, "I told you so." To Jessie, she said, "What is it, then?"

"Why don't you both come in. You're here anyway."

As invitations go, it was lukewarm at best, but that was good enough for Mitch and Reb. They entered the small living room. It was neat and tidy, everything you'd expect from a neat and tidy waitress. Of course, Reb didn't need a chair, but Jessie pointed to the sofa for Mitch.

"Can I get you something to drink?"

"Don't you think you already wait on us enough at the diner?"

"Wouldn't want to get out of practice."

"I'd take a glass of water."

"How about a beer instead?"

"Sure."

"And you, Senator?"

"I'll have that water that Mitch won't be drinking."

"Want some scotch with that?"

"No, thanks. Somebody has to drive."

"Right."

If Jessie was upset, it wasn't showing now. She got the water and beer and some iced tea for herself.

"Well, I might just as well tell you," Jessie said it like she knew it wouldn't do any good to avoid the subject.

"Okay," Mitch nodded.

"People are talking."

Mitch just nodded encouragement.

"About us," Jessie clarified.

"About us, who?"

"About you and me who."

"What about you and me?"

"Since I came out to your house for dinner."

"What? They think we're dating?"

"Fooling around is more like it. They started the rumor that I stayed all night. Now, everybody's saying that I'm a ...you know."

"Oh, Jeez! Now it all makes sense."

"So, I was just trying to be all business-like at the diner today. I'm sorry if I hurt your feelings."

"You didn't hurt my feelings. We were just worried about you."

"That's right," Reb chimed in right on cue, God bless her!

"I just figured that if I played it cool toward you, everyone would stop the gossip."

"People around here have got nothing better to do than to speculate about who sleeps with whom?"

"Hell, it's a full-time occupation with some folks."

"Well, maybe we should take out a full-page ad in the newspaper and set everyone straight!"

"I have a better idea," Reb ventured back into the conversation. "Let's just go on like nothing ever happened. If you let them think that their gossip bothers you, then they've won."

"I guess so. I just overreacted. I'm really sorry."

"Don't think another thing about it," Mitch winked.

"I have an idea," Reb said. "Let's all go out to dinner. As long as people are talking, we can add menage a trois to their vocabulary."

"That sounds nice, but we don't have a French restaurant in town," Jessie was a bit muddled.

"How about the hotel dining room, instead?"

"Oh, that's a really nice place," Jessie sounded hesitant.

"And really public, too!" Mitch added with a mischievous smile.

"Perfect!" Reb was ready for a night on the town.

It took Jessie a few minutes to get ready. After all, it was a *nice* place. By the time she was ready, she looked much more put together than either Mitch or Reb. If they were in a three-person line up and folks had to pick the two most likely to be lesbian, Mitch and Reb would get the votes hands down.

Jessie was right about one thing. There wasn't a French restaurant in town. The only French food available on the menu at the hotel was "fries." However, there were a lot of other goodies, including halibut steak, fried chicken, and prime rib, ordered happily and respectively by Reb, Mitch and Jessie. Mitch hadn't seen that much prime rib disappear in her entire lifetime. Jessie had a healthy appetite and didn't notice if anyone was staring. Mitch realized that she herself was used to being stared at. As long as the restaurant manager didn't throw them out, Mitch was perfectly comfortable out amongst 'em. Particularly in the company of two beautiful women. As Mitch mused about this, Reb was carrying on quite the conversation with Jessie.

"And in a few short weeks, Lisa will be discharged from the burn center."

"That's a long time to be in a hospital."

"It is. And they don't know what their plans will be from there."

"Will they need to stay there for follow up visits?"

"Not really. I think they can fly back and forth if need be."

"And you want them to come back to Utopia."

"I want to be close to them."

"Well, you'll really be close if the four of you share a trailer!"

"Two trailers," Mitch reminded.

"Ten feet apart," Reb added.

"What you may not know, Jessie, is that Lisa is my old girlfriend."

"Oh, I see," Jessie looked at Rebecca and brightened up. "That's certainly good news!"

"Why?" Reb asked.

"Because if the four of you start sharing two trailers, people will forget all about talking about me!"

Chapter 19

Robbie threw up every morning right on cue. Trish didn't need
one of those gizmos with the blue lines to tell her that they were
eight months away from being parents. It was the morning of the
day they were meeting the realtor, which must have made
Robbie even more queasy. They were running late for their ten
o'clock appointment, but millionaires were allowed to.

"Did you call?" Robbie checked.

"Yes."

"Are you upset with me?"

"Heavens no. Why would you think that?"

"You seem nervous."

"It's been a long time since I've seen Sara."

"Are the two of you old *friends*?"

Trish caught the emphasis in stride.

"She stole a couple of sales out from under my nose a few years
back. You have my full permission to be as picky with our new
house selection as you want to be. Might as well make her do a
little work for her commission, for a change."

"Tell me more about her."

"Well, she's about thirty-five and about two-hundred and ninety
pounds and has mousy brown hair and a wart on her left cheek."

"You're making this up!" Robbie exclaimed.

"Nope, not one bit."

Trish snagged the last parking spot in the lot and then hurried
around to help Robbie out of the car like she was ready to deliver
already.

"I'm perfectly capable of getting out of a car all by myself."

"I know. I'm just practicing."

"Thank you."

They held hands as they entered the building and walked down
the hallway to the elevator. Sara was on the twenty-sixth floor.
Real estate paid well for those who stole commissions. Whether
it was truly necessary or just for old time's sake, but they were
made to wait for about fifteen minutes. About the time Trish

was good and ready to find another realtor, old friendships be damned, a comely woman came out to usher them in. They were all seated and everything before Trish realized that something was familiar about the woman. She sat opposite them at her desk.

"Sara?"

"Trish?" she mocked the tone of voice.

"Time's been good to you," was all Trish could think to say that didn't sound like a response from an idiot-in-training.

"And you must be Robbie?" Sara concentrated her charm on her.

"Yes, I am. Trish has told me a little about you."

"And, no doubt, ninety percent incorrect."

"You've changed a bit, Sara," Trish came to her own defense.

"About one-hundred and eighty pounds of change."

"Not to mention the hair color."

"I do make a stunning blond, don't I?"

"Uh huh," Trish couldn't help but nod.

"And you wouldn't believe how hard it was to get rid of that birthmark. Plus a few other things here and there…"

Trish hadn't seen "here and there" but nodded like she knew all about it.

"But, I know you came to me to buy a house, not spend all afternoon strolling down memory lane."

"Right."

"So, Robbie, what would you like in a house?" Sara's eyes twinkled in her direction again.

"Well, I think it's Trish who knows about that sort of thing."

This statement didn't deter Sara. She kept her eyes on Robbie.

"I already *know* what Trish likes. I want to know what you like."

"I'm really not very fussy. Maybe if I saw some pictures or something?"

"I have done some preliminary work on your behalf. There are several homes that I think might pique your interest. I've taken the liberty to reserve the company limo."

"Do you feel like a ride around town?" Trish asked Robbie.

"I've gotten this far."

"Good," Sara sounded genuinely pleased. She left the office to make the final arrangements. It sounded more like a funeral.

"Are you sure this is the same Sara Walburg that you knew?"

"I'm sure."

"She sure has changed."

"She sure has."

Robbie felt Trish's forehead.

"What are you doing?"

"Checking for a fever. You don't look so good. Maybe you're getting a case of sympathy morning sickness."

"I'm fine. Look, if there's even one thing that you don't like about any of the houses we see today, you speak right up. Don't be shy or hesitant at all. Okay?"

"Okay."

"I mean the slightest thing. Color, size, shape, design, location…anything. Anything at all."

"Alright, already. I get your point."

"Okay."

Sara was back to usher them via private elevator to the underground garage. Somewhere between two-hundred ninety and one-hundred ten pounds, Sara had acquired a new walk. A really sexy nice new walk. And the just-above-the-knee skirt was designed for temptation with a strategic slit up the side. Trish only bumped into one wall ever so slightly as she observed the fashion statement. It was closer to a proclamation. Robbie didn't seem to notice Trish's veering off course and held her hand tenderly as they were driven to the first house. It was a large Tudor style mansion. You could tell immediately that Robbie was in awe of such a huge place. Trish was unimpressed. The concept of being the "Lady of the Manor" didn't suit her fancy.

"You don't like it," Robbie caught on at once.

"It's not my style, but let's get out and look anyway."

"We don't have to if you don't want to," Robbie was happy to go to house number two.

"Maybe I'll like the inside," Trish shrugged.

"Whatever you want," Robbie smiled radiantly.

"Pregnancy agrees with you," Trish smiled back.

"Now, don't start that. We're not even sure, yet."

"If you're not pregnant, I'd sure hate to see your bouts with morning sickness when you are!"

"Just don't get your hopes up."

94

"Okay." Trish said out loud. To herself, she said, "Too late."
Suddenly they realized that Sara was paying rapt attention to
them, waiting for a decision about whether or not they were even
going to get out of the car.
"Wouldn't hurt to take a look, would it?" Robbie asked Trish.
"I guess not."

Sara held the door open for them after unlocking the front
entrance. It was one of those huge oak doors that you only see in
movies. The house was empty except for niceties like drapes and
light fixtures. While the master bedroom was on the ground
floor, a stairway led up to the other bedrooms of the mansion.
Robbie immediately decided that this wasn't going to do at all.
There was no way that she was going to be separated by so many
steps from a newborn baby. This was definitely a "nanny"
house. It was surely beautiful with all that honey-colored wood
flooring and a kitchen you could land a helicopter in, but it was
built for people who wanted to put all their responsibilities on
someone else's shoulders. A nanny here, a maid there, a butler
at the front door.
"Anybody want to see the swimming pool?" Sara asked. "It's
gorgeous."
"Is there anywhere to sit down?" Robbie asked suddenly.
"Are you feeling okay?" Trish rushed to her side.
"I'm fine, Sweetie. I'm just a little tired."
"Let's have lunch," Trish said to her and then turned to Sara.
"Have you made reservations anywhere?"
"Just my usual one at the country club."
They walked back out to the limo and got in while Sara locked
up behind them.
"I don't think I'm dressed up enough to go to a country club for
lunch," Robbie fretted.
Trish looked her over. Lately, Robbie had been dressing very
nicely. She rotated all the clothes she bought in New York plus a
few other things that Trish had surprised her with now and then.
None of them were slit up the side, but that never stopped Trish
from having to take a deep breath when she looked at Robbie.
"Maybe we should just skip the country club and go home,"
Trish smiled.

"We wouldn't want to skip out on Sara. She has planned the day, after all."

"I guess so."

"She dresses nice."

"You think?" Trish acted blasé.

"How's the shoulder, by the way?"

"Shoulder?"

"Yeah, the one that you bumped into walking down the hallway earlier."

Trish looked sheepish. "I'll live."

"You don't need a doctor?"

"I'd settle for a nurse."

Further married-type banter was interrupted by Sara, who finally reappeared. She must've been refilling a moat or something "So, lunch it is?" she checked with them.

"Sure," Trish nodded, keeping her eyes on the road. It didn't take the mental capacity of a Nobel Prize winner to figure out that this house wasn't too far from the country club. They were a bit early, but Sara was in the mood to buy a couple rounds of drinks, particularly for herself. As the third scotch arrived for Sara, Robbie's water was replenished and Trish was steeped in tea. By eleven, their table was ready. The menu was perfectly obscene with fifteen-dollar appetizers and thirty dollars and up for just the luncheon specials. It reminded Trish of her old life and she found herself rubbing the shoulder that was the topic of earlier conversation.

"Are you feeling okay?" Robbie asked in earnest now, never missing anything, it seemed.

"Sure, I'm fine. You'd better order one or two extra lunches. You *are* eating for two, you know!" Trish beamed.

Robbie blushed a perfect shade of pink rose. Too bad they weren't home. Which happened soon after lunch, as it turned out. After Robbie told Trish for the third time that eating for two did not mean one of every dessert, they begged off on any further house hunting for the day. If Sara of the Slit Skirt thought that this was going to be a quick commission, she was in for a rude shock. Trish drove home from the office building as Robbie rested her eyes. Maybe this was too much too soon. When they got home, Robbie made an interesting request.

"I want you to take off your clothes and come to bed with me."
It sounded like a fine idea. Once they were together, Robbie
asked a probing question.

"Back at the country club, you drifted away. Where did you
go?"

Trish thought to simply answer, "the old days," but that wouldn't
be good enough. "I was thinking about my life back when I was
in real estate."

"How long ago was that?"

"Not long enough. At least, not for some clear images. Like it
was yesterday..."

"Good images?" Robbie still didn't quite know the lay of the
land.

"I remember a lot of three-scotch lunches with clients. And a lot
of driving around town. And dressing up in sharp clothes."

"Sara looked nice," Robbie said again.

"I can't believe the change in her," Trish treaded carefully. "She
must have been stapled, liposuctioned and shrink wrapped."

"It all turned out nice."

"Oh, it all looks nice and fun and all that, but when I think of
what I have now versus what I had back then, I'd take today any
day of the week."

"Well, you do have more money now."

"That doesn't have anything to do with it. I have you in my life.
I wouldn't trade you for anything."

"I hope you still feel that way in about eight months when I'm as
huge as a house."

"I will always feel that way."

Trish leaned in close to see if her chances of getting a kiss were
in the realm of possibility. Things looked promising until the
phone rang. It was Rose, frantic with news. Max was admitted
to the emergency room with chest pains. Robbie was up and
dressed by the time Trish had organized everything they would
need for an extended hospital vigil. Things like books, gum,
vitamins, pillows, and their address book. And a fistful of cash
for everything else.

To her credit, Robbie remained calm during the drive as Trish
kept things to the speed limit. No use arriving feet first and

causing Rose even more grief. One place they knew their way around was the hospital and they found Rose sitting in the ICU waiting area. She was knotting a handkerchief into a little ball and was so relieved to see Robbie, she held onto her for what seemed like forever. The bits and pieces of information tumbled out of her. Details were scant. Max probably had a heart attack and the doctors were trying to assess possible damage. He wasn't out of the woods. She hadn't seen him yet, the team of medical professionals were still working on him. Hence the hankie. About the time the update was over, a doctor appeared. He gave Rose and one other person permission to see Max for five minutes. Trish pushed Robbie and her mother toward the double doors and then used the phone in the waiting room. Why she felt compelled to call Mitch was a mystery only because she still knew so little about Max's condition. Mitch did a lot of listening and then made the logical decision to fly to the hospital as soon as she could book a flight. Trish didn't call unless it was important, and Mitch honored her instincts about this.

"I'll be there as soon as I can get there," Mitch said as a farewell.
"Going somewhere?" Reb could tell something serious was up.
"Trish needs some support. Max is having heart problems."
"Let's pack."
"You're going?"
"I'm certainly not staying here all by myself with the Kansas 25!"
Mitch nodded.
"Why don't you call and see when we can get a flight."
"Okay."
Mitch had much better luck packing than did Reb with the airlines. There was nothing until the following afternoon.
"Let's drive."
"You feel up to it?"
"Oh, sure. You know me."
Mitch knew alright. Rebecca Fairbanks Andretti was always itching to get behind the wheel. If Mitch didn't complain about the driving speed, they would be there in time for a late dinner. Reb spared no spark plugs and they rolled into town about seven. The hospital was quiet. Trish, Robbie and Rose had settled into one corner of the ICU waiting room. Trish had packed wisely,

particularly the idea of the pillows. Rose was resting her eyes and Trish was making Robbie as comfortable as possible in her arms. Mitch and Reb almost hated to disturb them.

"Hi," Mitch touched Trish's shoulder.

"Oh, hi! You're here already?"

"Reb drove."

Trish nodded like that was all the explanation necessary. Robbie stirred awake and seemed surprised at first that they were all in the waiting room. She gathered her wits quickly and hugged the visitors each in turn.

"How are you doing?" Mitch held onto her.

"I'm pretty shook up."

Mitch gave her another hug.

"Of course you are. What can you tell us about Max?"

"We're still not sure about a lot of things. They're sure he had a heart attack, but we're waiting to find out how much heart damage there is," Robbie was steady during the explanation. She was going to be a source of strength for everyone. Mitch kissed her forehead.

"Can we see him?"

"You two can go in the next allotted visiting time."

"When's that?"

"About thirty minutes."

"Have any of you eaten dinner?" Reb asked.

"Not really," Trish admitted. "No one has been very hungry."

"You should eat anyway," Mitch advised, and then asked an interesting question, "Where's your bodyguard?"

"Oh, you mean Silver," Rose was now awake and talkative. "We gave her a vacation. Even bodyguards need a vacation now and then."

"You don't have someone filling in for her?" Reb took over the questioning like she was still on some Senate committee.

"No. We really haven't had any other problems since our last mishap."

Which, by the way, was a murder attempt on Rose, Mitch reminded herself silently. If a mere murder attempt was a "mishap," what would a catastrophe consist of?

"You three go have some dinner. Reb and I will stay here and keep an eye on things."

"Are you sure?" Trish asked.

"We're sure," Reb confirmed.

About ten minutes went by before Mitch noticed that the various personnel on call recognized Rebecca for the ex-political celebrity that she was. A certain deference was paid to her. One which Mitch took advantage of. She went into the ICU virtually unnoticed and located Max within ten seconds. He appeared to be resting comfortably and frankly, Mitch didn't know if that was good or bad. She went over to the bed and stroked his hair and then his arm. When he didn't stir, Mitch meditated for a moment and then left the area as quietly as she had come. Reb was still holding court with the attending nurses and didn't notice until Mitch had been sitting for some time that she appeared to be drawn and tired.

"You look worn out," Reb told her in a rather clinical fashion. "Are you going to be okay to sit and wait until Trish gets back?"

"Oh, sure."

"You look really tired."

"It's been a long day," Mitch was just this side of irritable.

"But, you're okay?" Reb was not to be dissuaded.

"Why do you keep asking me that?"

"Because I've never seen you look this tired. I'm worried that you're coming down with something."

"Well, if I am, I'm in the perfect place, now, aren't I?"

Reb stopped prodding. It wasn't getting them anywhere.

"Where are we spending the night?" Reb changed the subject.

"How about my old place?"

"I'm sure it's got an inch of dust on everything."

"I guess so, but we should at least check it before we head home tomorrow."

"We're going home tomorrow?"

"Well, why wouldn't we?" Mitch asked back.

"I figured we'd stay a few days, at least until we know for certain about Max."

Mitch didn't say anything. She just nodded and closed her eyes.

Chapter 20

Mary arrived bright and early for the unveiling. Actually, it was more like an unbandaging, but it was still a big day. Big in the sense that Lisa would need a lot of support because everyone had already warned them of what certain Hollywood stars already knew and that was that Lisa was going to look far worse for the wear until her body could totally recover from the surgery. This was nothing more than a glimpse of the final outcome. It had become a mantra for Mary. "It's just a glimpse."

The doctor arrived on cue and without either a preamble or wasted motion, began the process of cutting and unwrapping. He then began chatting like it was a tea party rather than one of the most significant moments in Lisa's life. Perhaps it was his way of lessening the tension. Mary got the first good look and repeated her mantra to occupy her mind.
"Now, I know it looks like you've gone nine rounds with the champ," the doctor said in his calm way, "but the bruising and swelling will go down sooner than you think."
"How soon?" Lisa hadn't seen the damage yet and wasn't in the mood for vagueness.
"Soon," he fought the urge to circle a day on the calendar. What Lisa did know was that even when the swelling and bruises subsided, her face would still be two different shades of color. The skin on the face had a slightly different pigment than the skin on the donor site. Still, it was a splendid improvement from the wound it replaced. Mary started to cry at the relief she felt.
"What's wrong?" Lisa asked immediately.
"You're beautiful," Mary replied.
Lisa wasn't buying it. "I want that mirror now!"
"That's a good idea," the doctor agreed, "Then I can show you some of the details of the surgery."
A mirror was produced and Lisa, after just glancing at herself, listened to the doctor in her best detached manner. She nodded a lot and "uh huhhed" once or twice through his spiel. He was obviously pleased with his work and Lisa allowed him his moment. It wasn't until after he left that Lisa's true feelings

came to the surface. A good analogy would have been a volcano.

"I look like hell! No, I look like worse than hell! Tell me what's worse than hell because that's what I look like!"

"You look fine," Mary tried to stem the flow.

"Oh, that's just great! A minute or two ago, I was beautiful and now I'm just fine?"

"You're beautiful," Mary corrected. Too little. Too late.

"Go to hell!" Lisa turned as far away from Mary as she could.

"You heard the doctor. The swelling-"

"Go away!"

"The swelling will go down."

"I said, go away!"

"You really don't mean that."

"Get the hell out of my room!" Lisa was in eruption mode now and Mary feared for the healing process.

"I'll let you get some rest," Mary kissed Lisa's hand and then headed for the door.

"And stay out!" was Lisa's final admonition.

Mary felt like she was treading through lava as she went down the hallway. Thank goodness everyone was too preoccupied with work to notice the tears streaming down her face. She wiped at them like they were a betrayal. When she most needed her strength, it had deserted her. She was losing the war and there were no reinforcements in sight. She went back to the empty apartment and fell into the kind of sleep brought on by depression.

After the phone rang on two separate occasions, Mary unplugged it. Whoever it was could at least have the decency to let her get a good day's sleep. She had just gotten good and back asleep when someone started pounding on her door. Mary blocked out the noise in her sadness-laden mind. No wonder she didn't hear the subsequent credit-card jimmy of the lock. Hilary was a silhouette in her bedroom door before Mary was fully awake.

"You didn't answer the phone."

"No, I didn't," Mary concurred.

"We were worried."

"We?"

"I was worried."

"You don't need to be."

"It isn't like you to not answer your phone. What's going on?"
Mary sat up a little straighter in the bed, which Hilary took as
cue to approach and sit beside her. It was an intimacy they had
shared before.

"They took Lisa's bandages off this morning."
Hilary nodded. She knew that much at least and the rest she had
heard via the rumor mill but wanted first-hand confirmation.

"And then all holy hell broke loose."

"Of course it did. I'm not at all surprised."

"I wasn't either," Mary admitted. "I'm just running out of
reserve."

Hilary made no comment. Anything would sound inane.
Instead, she took Mary's hand in hers. She would've been
content with that, but something in Mary reached out for more
comforting. She pulled Hilary close into a kiss far more
touching than their previous encounter. Hilary responded for a
moment and then pulled back.

"We shouldn't be doing this," she said softly. "It's not right."

"I haven't been able to do anything right lately. Why should this
be any different?"
Mary leaned forward again but Hilary was ready for her this time
and diverted her to a hug. Her hold was strong and steady,
something she felt Mary needed more right now.

"I'm not in the habit of stealing other people's girlfriends."

"And I'm not in the habit of being so vulnerable."

"Lisa will come around. I promise."

"How can you be so sure?"

"Because she has you to come around to."
With that bit of wisdom, Hilary kissed Mary on the forehead like
a grandmother would've and said, "Go back to sleep."
Mary obeyed right after she heard the click of the door lock.

Lisa was napping as well when Hilary entered the room. It must
have been her day to catch sleeping ladies unawares. She stood
and observed the patchwork quilt that was once Lisa's face.

"What are you gawking at?" Lisa was more awake than she let
on.

"Your face," Hilary was unapologetic.

"Close the door when you leave."

"I don't plan on leaving, at least for a while."

"The sooner, the better."

"I'll leave after we have a little talk about Mary."

"What about Mary?" Lisa was wary.

Hilary moved closer so she could make her point emphatically.

"You want to keep Mary in your life?"

"What in the hell are you talking about?"

"It's a simple question. Do you or don't you want to keep Mary in your life?"

"You don't have any say in the matter."

"You think not?" Hilary sounded smug. This irked an already prickly Lisa.

"Look, I don't have time for word games. Why don't you just say what you came to say and then get out."

"It's pretty simple. If you keep pushing Mary away, it won't be too tough for me to be right there ready to take her away from you. Is that what you really want?"

Hilary waited as Lisa turned over all possibilities in her mind. "I suppose you've already seduced her," Lisa went on a fishing expedition.

"Heavens, no! Mary's still much too much devoted to you to be open to that possibility. But you keep making her cry like you do and it won't be long. So, I'm just wondering, is this like a test you're giving Mary or do you really want her out of your life for good?"

"I don't have to answer any of your stupid questions!"

"No, you don't. At least not directly. But you'd better figure it out for yourself and pronto."

Hilary didn't stick around to witness the thinking process. She had things to do. Like, exit the room before she was tempted to shake some sense into Lisa. She had done what she felt was her duty in this triangular drama. That was as noble as she was willing to be.

Mary slept through the night without eating. She would've been hungry had she not been so blue. It didn't take her long to figure out that her protracted decision over something as simple as whether or not to make coffee was only an artificial gimmick to forestall visiting Lisa. She had never been ordered out of a room quite like that before and she didn't know if she could swallow her anger. By the time she was at the door to Lisa's room, she had a gut full of bile. Lisa was awake, alert and so close to cheery that Mary was tempted to check the number on the door to see if she was in the right place.

"Good morning," Lisa greeted.

"Hello," Mary answered cautiously

"I've arranged for some therapy for us," Lisa expounded.

"Some therapy?" Mary asked, just to keep the conversation going. It was their best one in days and she didn't want it to grind to a halt.

"You know, counseling. We can't go on with me yelling at you and you crying."

"You saw me crying?" Mary was now confused. She hadn't recalled crying in front of Lisa, but things were a blur.

"Let's just say that I heard about it."

"You did?"

"I don't mean to yell or make you cry. I'm just really shook up about…things."

"Things we need to talk over in front of a total stranger?"

"I don't want to push you into this. I'm going to do it regardless. I need someone else besides you to yell at."

"Oh, I'm willing to get some professional help. All this is new to me as well. You're tired of yelling at me?" Mary tacked on the last sentence and then smiled.

"I'm just tired of everything. The surgeries, the staff, this damn room. The only thing I'm *not* tired of is you. So, why I'm yelling at you is beyond me."

"You yell at me because I'm convenient."

"Well, that's got to stop. I'll yell at a counselor or I'll hire someone to just stand here and listen while I yell at them."

"You can do that?" Mary was now curious.

"Well, if you can't, you ought to be able to. Maybe I could start a company when I get better. We could call it, "Yell At Me dot com."

"Yell at me dot com?"

"Sure, think how this would work. People could rant at you on the phone for a fee, like one of those sex chat lines or in person for a little more money."

"I'm not sure about that?" Mary could see complications in any scheme.

"Come sit by me."

It was the first such invitation in weeks. Mary wasn't about to let it slip by. She sat in a spot cleared and smoothed by Lisa.

"Look, I'm sorry I told you to leave yesterday."

"You don't need to apologize," Mary assured.

"Yes, I do. If I'm going to return to the land of real people, I'm going to need to start acting like one."

"Okay."

"And I'm sorry for all the other hundred and one things I've said or done to make you cry."

"It hasn't been a hundred things, but apology accepted."

"And now, I want you to hold me close and give me a kiss."

"What if the doctor comes in?"

"He'll have to get his own girlfriend."

Mary laughed nervously. "Are you sure they allow this kind of behavior?"

"Let's find out."

When Lisa wanted to find something out, she usually went all out. This was turning into no exception. She hadn't forgotten how to unbutton a shirt, hers as well as someone else's.

Someone else, AKA Mary, moaned softly at the mere touch of Lisa's fingertips on her skin. And they were only on button two.

"It's been too long, hasn't it?" Lisa stated the obvious that Mary wouldn't.

"Any time away from you is too long," Mary smiled and then kissed Lisa ever so gently to avoid hurting her.

"You can kiss me harder than that."

"Oh, I plan to. Believe me."

And she was just setting about fulfilling that promise when the pesky doctor walked in on them.

"Oh!" he said with just a hint of bad-boyism. "I should have knocked. Louder. Sorry. So you want me to come back later?"

"No, that's okay," Lisa had nearly gotten herself all decent again, as had Mary.

"It seems that you're in good spirits this morning. That's always good to see."

"I've gotten over the shock of seeing my new face."

"And it won't be that way for very long. Once the swelling goes down, however, you'll be fitted for your mask."

The dreaded plastic mask for her face. The scar-tissue inhibitor from hell.

"I can hardly wait."

"Really?" the doctor was a tad surprised by her lack of sarcasm.

"Every step is a step out of here."

"And I see you've signed up for some couples' therapy sessions."

"Yes, we did."

"That's good. No better group to talk things over with than people who've gone through it."

"So, it's group therapy?" Mary wanted to know.

"Right. Well, unless you have questions, I'll leave you to carry on."

When he was gone, Mary double checked with Lisa, "I wasn't aware that it was going to be therapy en masse."

"It should be interesting, unless you want something a little more private?"

"Privacy is hard to come by around here."

"Don't we know it."

"You don't need to be brave about the mask," Mary said quietly. "I know it's going to be tough."

"Yes, it will be. So my advice is to kiss me while you've got the chance," Lisa tugged on Mary's collar.

"Guess I'd better do what I'm told!"

"Guess you'd better!"

Kissing was about all they got done. Between the noises of the hospital and compelling modesty, further catching up was put on hold. But that was enough for Mary. This, in fact, was way beyond enough. Not yelling at each other would've been sufficient.

Mary slept in the overstuffed chair until lunch appeared. There were two trays. Lisa had arranged that nicety earlier in the day. It was a common lunch, but all it lacked in romance was candlelight. Which was okay since Mary was glowing enough for the both of them. All day. Right through the dinner hour at which time Hilary showed up.

"How are you two doing?" she asked like she had neither scolded Lisa nor kissed Mary.

"We're doing fine," Lisa answered for the both of them.

"That's nice," Hilary was convinced more by the expression on Mary's face than the tone of Lisa's voice. Portraits of Madonna and Child looked less contented. They chatted for only another moment or two before Hilary exited, smiling. If she had a Dorian-Gray-like picture in her attic, it would've shown noticeable improvement.

Chapter 21

Mitch had awakened to hospital sounds and was temporarily startled before she regained her senses. She was alone.
"Oh, good! You're awake!" Reb's voice carried her direction from the hallway.
"Just now."
"I was making room reservations."
"Are Trish and the group still at dinner?"
"Actually, no. They went home."
Something about that didn't compute, and Mitch immediately feared for the worst.
"What happened to Max?"
"Nothing happened. Wait, I take that back. Something did happen. He's improved. Greatly. So much so that everyone is going home, or in our case, to a hotel to get some rest."
"I'm hungry," Mitch announced.
"I'll get you something."
"I'm not eating hospital food."
"I meant, from room service. When we get checked in."
"Can I see Max before we head out?"
"If it's okay with the staff, it's fine by me," Reb acquiesced.
Max looked better. In fact, he looked like he never had a heart attack in the first place. Doctors confirmed that there was no perceptible heart damage and no real need for a lengthy stay in the hospital. He was going to be discharged the following morning if he had an uneventful night. Which was exactly what happened, and in turn, made it possible for Rebecca and Mitch to return to Kansas as well. They stopped at the diner as soon as they hit town and Jessie was back to her usual friendly self. Wagging tongues were just something to be tolerated in Utopia.
"I didn't even know you two were gone!" she remarked after hearing that they were on the way back from Denver.
"We sort of left in a hurry."
"And now you're back in a hurry and none too soon."
"What? What's going on?" Reb asked.

"Well, Lucinda Cornwall has been stirring up her usual trouble."

"Really?" Reb was doubly wary by now.

"She's handing out pamphlets at church, trying to drum up support for the picket line."

"Is it working?" Mitch asked.

"Beats me. I haven't gone out to check."

Mitch shrugged. She could worry about picket lines or lunch. "How's the stew?"

"Why don't you order the club sandwich, instead," Jessie had that knowing look in her eye.

"Sounds good."

"Same here," Reb piped up.

"Sure thing."

When Jessie wandered off, Reb put her chin in her hand. Normally, it was a fetching pose, but now, she looked just tired.

"I guess we should've flown," Mitch observed.

"Driving is fine."

"You look exhausted."

"I'm just concerned about what's waiting for us at home."

"You think Lucinda has whipped the troops into a frenzy?"

"I think it's her new goal in life. And I don't know what to do about it."

"I suggest we get a hold of one of the pamphlets and check it out."

"And how do you propose we do that?"

"How about...go to church?"

Reb stopped leaning on her hand. "Are you serious?"

"Why wouldn't I be?"

"You don't think that that might be considered a tad on the antagonistic side?"

"Hey, we're the ones with the daily parade in front of our house. I'd think that expressing our religious freedom would be the least troublesome activity in the capital of the Bible Belt."

"I'll remind you that you said that after the fact."

It sounded like an "I told you so" in the making, but Mitch didn't care.

"Let's ask Jessie what time Lucinda goes to church."

"Let's ask Jessie what?" Jessie asked. She had two plates full of sandwiches and chips.

110

"We want to get our hands on one of Lucinda's pamphlets."
"Well, why didn't you just say so," Jessie plunked the plates down and pulled out a folded sheet of paper.
"You kept one?"
"Thought you'd like to know what the opposing side has to say about you, maybe?"
Jessie's expression spoke volumes. This wasn't going to be pretty. Before Mitch could even think to reach for is, Reb had it unfolded and spread out on the table. From just a preliminary glance, it was evident that whoever created the document was some sort of font-a-holic. The heading was in some sort of Biblical block letters and was a snap to read, even upside down. BEWARE OF GAYS INFESTING YOUR COMMUNITY!!!!! it proclaimed.
"Infesting, huh?" Reb said.
"Makes you sound like a couple of locusts," Jessie grimaced.
In an artistic font, perhaps Matisse, the document went on, "EVERY DAY, IN THOUSANDS OF COMMUNITIES ACROSS THIS GREAT LAND OF OURS, THERE ARE GAYS TRYING TO UNDERMINE YOUR SCHOOLS AND COMMUNITIES!!!!! THINGS DON'T HAVE TO BE THAT WAY!!!!!!!! YOU CAN DO SOMETHING TO RESTORE DECENCY TO OUR AMERICA!!!!!!!!!!!!!!!!!
This was a bit harder for Mitch to read upside down, and Reb did her the favor of not reciting it aloud. She turned the flyer over to Mitch, having read enough of this kind of blather for one day. Mitch continued to study it. In still another font, something that looked suspiciously like Haettenschweiler, it gave specific instructions on the nature of the protest that was ongoing at Reb's property, including such handy things as car-pooling information and offers of help with signage.
"Maybe I could donate a box of crayons?" Mitch mused.
"Why do you do that!"
Reb snapped. She hadn't done that in a long time.
"Do what?"
"You always make a big joke out of everything."
"I'm not joking. I'd be more than happy to donate crayons to their cause. The more they know that what they're doing doesn't bother us, the sooner they'll give up."

"You think so?" Reb sounded totally unconvinced.

"Sure," Mitch started eating, hoping that Reb would follow suit. She did and things were quiet until Jessie swung by for a check. "Everything okay?"

"When does Lucinda go to church?" Mitch asked her original question.

"Why do you care now?" Reb cut in before Jessie had a chance to respond.

"I still want to see if she's passing out flyers this Sunday."

"She goes to seven o'clock service," Jessie answered, "but she passed the stuff out all day Sunday. How come you were in Denver, anyway?"

"We went to see a sick friend," Mitch answered.

"But he's much better now," Reb added, happy for a change of subject. "Nearly a complete recovery, in fact."

"Like a miracle?" Jessie was getting wide eyed.

"I don't know if I'd characterize it that way?" Reb hedged.

"Like that lady here in the hospital? You know, the one hurt in the car accident? She had a complete recovery!"

"Yeah, but she looked a whole lot worse than Max did," Mitch said offhand as she sipped her tea.

"How would you know that?" Reb followed up immediately.

"Well, I'm no doctor, but I could just see a difference."

"You saw her?" Jessie continued the line of questioning. Mitch felt a little bit tag-teamed at this point.

"Yeah."

"When?" Reb asked.

"I went to see her when you were visiting Mary."

"Why?"

"Why not, for Christ sake," Mitch was getting snappish now.

"No reason to get upset. I was just curious. You went to see a woman in the hospital who hates your guts and pickets your house? It just seems odd."

"We're supposed to visit the sick. It's in the Good Book."

"You're going Biblical on me?" Reb was almost smiling.

"Eat your lunch and let's go home."

Home hadn't changed much. It was still standing. That was a relief. The picket line was a few people longer, maybe due to the flyer? Still, it wasn't a mob. If Lucinda Cornwall had visions of

112

throngs of protestors, she had better get her eyes checked. Or some help recruiting. Bed felt great, at least, that's what Reb reported to Mitch as she watched her unpack.

"You do look comfortable," Mitch looked at the reclining figure of Reb.

"Come over here and try it for yourself."

"Oh, gee, I would, but I'm doing chores."

"Don't you think the chores can wait?" Reb asked in that tone of voice that suggested that, yes, indeed, the chores could wait. Mitch took the cue to heart and went over to the bed. She sat down next to Reb.

"Tell me what's on your mind," Reb inquired in such a charming way that Mitch couldn't resist.

"I think I'm going to help Lucinda Cornwall pass out flyers at church this next Sunday."

Reb thought this over carefully. "Tell me why."

"Because I think it might just put an end to all this nonsense."

"How?"

"If people see that their protests are something we're not afraid of, maybe they'll go away."

"Do you really think that will work?" Reb sounded like she was thawing out if not exactly warming up to the idea.

"It couldn't hurt. Besides, it's been a while since we've been to church."

"It's been never since we've been to church."

"We went to Aunt Bunny's funeral."

"Funerals don't count."

"Sure, they do. They count twice in my book."

"Twice?"

"It's that new math."

"Uh huh," Reb nodded with a smile. Something told Mitch that she wasn't thinking at all about math.

"Can I finish up the chores, now?"

"Nope!" Reb pulled her closer and kissed her. All further thought of chores and math dissolved in Mitch's mind. As well they should.

Chapter 22

Max was tired of being hovered over. And while Rose had not exactly been a helicopter, she had been keeping a close eye on her patient. The doctors had discharged Max with a list of instructions and Rose was following them to the letter. Trish and Robbie put their mansion hunting on hold to help out, but after two days, Max was up and around and not willing to have three fussing women on the premises. So, Trish made another appointment with the realtor to see a house or two. Robbie was still waking up queasy. No change there. But they were up and dressed and out the door before nine for the drive downtown. Four houses were on the schedule, which sounded like an awful lot to Robbie.

"Did you wear your comfortable shoes?" Trish asked as she drove.

"Yes."

"You look really nice."

"Thank you."

"No, I mean it, really," Trish emphasized.

"Thank you, really," Robbie was sincere.

Robbie had taken advantage of her wardrobe from New York. Indeed, she did look sharp.

"I'm crazy in love with you," Trish made her point clear.

"You are?" Robbie feigned surprise. "I would've never known, except, of course, for the way you teased me half to pieces in bed last night."

Trish had to remind herself that she was driving, and swallowed hard.

"You are so bad to bring that up while I'm trying to drive."

"Well, you started it," Robbie the fact hound reminded. "You and your talk about being crazy in love."

As she said this, she was beginning to lazily trace her fingers up and down Trish's gas-pedal thigh. They'd be driving off the road any minute if they weren't careful. Trish caught Robbie's

114

fingers mid way between her knee and heaven and held her steady.

"You're disturbing the driver."

"Okay, I'll stop. For now."

"Besides, it isn't my fault that you have such remarkable control," Trish explained.

They both knew what that meant.

"Actually, it isn't really that," Robbie said.

"It isn't?" Trish was getting just a tad confused, but didn't want to let on.

"I think it's being pregnant that's to blame."

"Oh, I hope so," Trish winked.

"You do?"

"You bet. I look forward to months and months of terribly prolonged orgasms on your part."

"You would!"

It was this kind of jovial exchange that relieved Robbie's mind of all thoughts surrounding the realtor's stunning attractiveness. This time, they went directly from their car to the limo. She was waiting for them and they were off and rolling to the first location like time was money. Which is what all time really was to Sara Walburg. Their first stop was another multi-level affair, which made Robbie feel like her opinions weren't really being listened to. She was too polite to fuss, but it only took one look exchanged between Trish and Robbie to communicate her dismay.

"Sara, do you have anything on the itinerary today that has a lot of bedrooms on the first floor?" Trish asked.

Sara didn't even need to check her notes. "I was saving that for last."

"Can we see it now?"

"Let me make a call."

Things got set up immediately. Big money had that effect. It was quite the drive out to the old Livermore Estate. Benjamin Livermore had been a part of Colorado lore for decades. His contributions to the community were the stuff of which legends were made. Word was that Ben Livermore was a ruthless business man. Although he married a much younger woman, the widow Livermore had recently passed on at the tender age of ninety-three. Whoever had inherited the estate was more interested in possible cash proceeds than being "Lord of Livermore Manor."

When Robbie saw the place, she was still confused. It, too, was multi-storied and huge. Being a fair-minded person, she was still willing to do a walk through. Those comfortable shoes were going to be vital. The door, if you could honestly call that much wood by such a short name, opened soundlessly. This had to be a feat of engineering in and of itself. The entryway to the house was protected by a covered drive-through and the first impression of the inside of the house was delayed by an almost tunnel-like hallway. While Trish envisioned a butler standing attention, Robbie pictured a hall tree for coats and snow boots.

It wasn't until one passed through the foyer that the hugeness of the house became apparent. They were faced with three possible pathways. Four, actually, if retreat was in order.

"We can go upstairs," she pointed to two huge sweeping staircases that wound up to the right and left, "or we can start with the living side of the house," she indicated a rightward mosey, "or the bedroom area." It would be to the left according to Sara's indications.
"What's your pleasure?" Trish asked Robbie.
Dare she say, "The bedroom?"
Trish didn't need to hear it. "Let's start with the sleeping quarters," Trish acted like she picked the choice out of thin air.
"Okay!" Sara enthused. She was just thrilled that they were walking through *something. Anything.*
First came the master bedroom with a master whirlpool bath and a master walk-in closet. All added up, it was bigger than Robbie's old apartment in Arizona.
"This is fabulous," Robbie breathed.
"Oh, and here's the other walk-in closet," Sara pointed out like everyone has two walk-in closets.
"There's two!"
"Well, there's two of you…" Sara noted.

"And soon to be three," Trish beamed.

"Right, so let's go look at the other bedrooms."

It was a short walk down the hall to the next bedroom, which had all the amenities of the first except for the absence of the whirlpool. That made sense, for safety reasons. Except for difference in layout, the next two bedrooms were carbon copies. For an old house, it was quite regimented.

"So, you can have three children before you start to run out of room," Sara explained her version of the obvious.

Robbie figured that they could have five or six kids before they ran out of room, but didn't want to appear argumentative.

"And we can hear everything going on from our bedroom," Trish was already moving in mentally.

"Which was important to you," Sara displayed her listening skills.

"What about the rest of the house?"

"Prepare to be blown away," was Sara's only warning.

Maybe it was just the total absence of furniture or the rather dark hue of the wall coverings, but Robbie wasn't exactly "blown away" by the rest of the downstairs. Not that it wasn't impressive. Its sheer size was overwhelming. They started with a walk through what Sara referred to as "The Great Room." Other folks might've called it a living room, but with its cathedral ceiling, fieldstone fireplace and built-in bookshelves, it probably deserved its grand name. A wet bar, sans booze, was in the north-west corner.

"What do you think?" Trish asked Robbie.

"It could use a new coat of paint," was all that Robbie could think to say.

Next was the formal dining room, stage right. It made it easier to funnel all those heads of state from the liquor to the table. Of course, right now, there was no table, but the room rivaled the Hearst Castle dining room, if only in square footage. Sara was explaining to Trish that, "You'll need to bring the table in piece by piece and have it assembled here. At least, that's what Old Man Livermore did."

Next to the dining room was the kitchen. Naturally. Food could be brought piping hot from room to room in a matter of seconds.

"Are you sure there was a Mrs. Livermore?" Robbie asked as they checked out the truly dismal appliances.

"Of course," Sara nodded, "but I'm sure she never set foot in here."

"A woman never setting foot in a kitchen?" Robbie couldn't believe what she was hearing.

"Mrs. Livermore never had to do anything she didn't care to."

"Even make love to Old Man Livermore?" Trish entered the conversation in her own unabashed way.

"Well, they did have children," Sara mused, not trying to set the record straight one way or the other intentionally.

"So, you're saying that they had a cook," Robbie tried to get back on track. She'd rather talk about dishwashers than the sex life of the Livermores.

"Oh, I'm sure that they had quite the contingent of servants in their heyday. Cooks, butlers, carriage drivers…"

For an instant, Robbie closed her eyes and envisioned a world gone by. Horse-drawn carriages pulling up to the entrance with footmen and polished buggy whips and ladies in layers of taffeta and lace…

"You want me to find you a chair?" Trish broke through the lifelike reverie.

"No, I'm fine. I'm just thinking about where in the world to begin modernizing this kitchen.

Trish and Sara smiled for different reasons. Robbie was pleased about the possibilities of moving in, which thrilled Trish clear down to her pinky toes. As for Sara, can you spell *commission*? Although not as big of a commission as you would expect. She tossed the base price of the house into the conversation, which didn't sound like a whole helluva lot of money to someone who had 88 million drawing interest daily.

"Come upstairs and see the really cool Captain's Walk," Sara was guiding the way with confidence.

"The what?"

"The Captain's Walk. It's a curved walkway around the observation tower."

"Sounds positively nautical," Trish was beaming.

The trio ascended the curved staircase and took the guided tour of the left half of the upstairs. It was distinguished by studiousness. There was a study which was actually more of a library. Built-in floor to ceiling bookcases were the one feature that couldn't be pilfered by the previous occupant unless by crowbar. However, the shelves were as barren as overworked soil. And as dusty. Adjacent to this was the "real" study. This was the place where you actually read the books in natural light while settled comfortably in a barkolounger. An outdoor porch was the Captain's Walk. Since it faced only field, no ships could be noted. It probably didn't matter since Old Man Livermore's ship had come in way before this house was built. The remainder of the upstairs was chopped up into puny bedrooms. "Servant's quarters," Sara explained like she had one or two at home as well.

"We'll never get your mom and dad into one of these," Trish sighed. The first drawback of the tour arrived with a thud.

"They couldn't get up and down the stairs anyway."

"I think we should put them in the master bedroom downstairs," Trish was thinking as she talked.

"You do?" Robbie was caught off guard.

"Sure. We could take one of the smaller rooms and have that cute baby you're busy making in the corner bedroom. Lots of windows for lots of light. That's important to babies, isn't it?"

"Twenty-two hours of sleep per day is important to babies."

"Can I be a baby again?" Trish cajoled as they walked down the staircase.

"You have been going through your second childhood since we met..." Robbie teased.

There was an awkward moment of silence when they all arrived back in the foyer. Robbie looked at Trish and conveyed her feelings without speaking.

"Draw up the paperwork," Trish instructed Sara.

Maybe only Robbie heard it, but it seemed like the house breathed a sigh of relief. Or it could have been just a little drafty.

Chapter 23

The trial of the century in Utopia was off to a slow start.
Compared to this, episodes of old black and white Perry Mason
shows were titillating. A word that probably wasn't even
allowed on TV in those days. In fact, after Mitch had attended
two days, she realized how many shenanigans Matlock got away
with per episode. This proceeding, by contrast, was a real
snoozer, except to Rebecca, who was enthralled in the same way
that a seasoned bridge player was when playing a no trump hand
to perfection. No wonder Mitch felt like the requisite dummy.
She tried really hard to listen to Reb's recap as they ate dinner,
but this was giving her a headache.
"You're rubbing your temples," Reb remarked.
"I'm tired."
"You're getting a headache?"
"Just a bit."
"Eat some more. Maybe that will help."
"Maybe," Mitch didn't feel like arguing the merits of food as a
cure-all.
"Can you even believe my sister," Reb carried on after passing
the potatoes and gravy to Mitch.
"Depends. What about BeBe?"
"Geez, her daughter *did* try and burn me and my daughter to
death. You'd think she'd show a little remorse!"
"And Lisa," was all Mitch added.
"Of course. And Lisa."
"Won't they be called as witnesses?"
"The consensus was that I'd be the best witness. It's generally
known that victims of burn trauma block out details of the
incident."
"Then, why wouldn't the defense call her as a witness? If only
to discredit your testimony."
"Would you call someone to the stand who has been burned so
badly that they have their face encased in a plastic bubble?"
"I guess not," Mitch started rubbing her temples again.

"Why don't you go and rest."

"Who will do the dishes?"

"You don't think I can do dishes?"

Mitch had a memory flash of Reb destroying most of their breakable dishes in a throwing fit not too long ago.

"I've seen what you do to dishes."

"Go rest. I'll clean things up and join you in a while."

Mitch, for once, obeyed her one and only. It took about fifteen minutes for her headache to subside. Which came in handy since the phone started ringing about twenty minutes after dinner. The first caller was Mary, who had been increasingly regular in her updates about Lisa. Impending was Lisa's discharge day. Mary was a cross between excited and nervous. Reb talked to her for quite a while as Mitch eavesdropped. It helped, she rationalized to herself, to ease her headache pain.

The next call was Trish, who burbled out the news that she, Robbie, and their expected child had decided to buy the Old Livermore Estate. Mitch oohed and ahhed on cue, congratulating them on their decision. She promised on behalf of Reb and herself that they would indeed visit again soon. It was only after she hung up that she announced her true analysis to Reb.

"Trish just bought a haunted house."

"The Livermore place isn't haunted!" Reb had heard enough of the phone conversation to make lively argument.

"Sure it is. Has been for years," Mitch argued back.

"Where did you hear that?"

"I don't remember."

"You're making this up, aren't you?"

"Why would I do that?"

"Just to scare me."

"Haunted houses scare you?"

"Don't they scare you?"

"No, not really. I'm much more intimidated by mere mortals like Lucinda Cornwall."

And as well she should be. Sunday was just around the corner and word had leaked out that Mitch and Rebecca were going to hand out flyers encouraging people to join in the protest of their presence at the homestead. Of course, Mitch had a plan. When didn't she have a plan? Step one was to make the flyers. Step two had been shopping for a lot of extra food. It didn't take a degree on rocket science to figure out the plan from there. An Open House was in the works and if Mitch could get her headache to go away, she had a ton of cooking to do. If the plan worked the way Mitch intended, the majority of the folks would show up Sunday afternoon just in time to be tempted by some pretty fierce home cooking.

"How's your headache?" Reb noticed Mitch's furrowed brow, a dead giveaway.

"Better."

"Are you going to be up to cooking tomorrow?"

"I'll be up and out of bed and in an apron before you can say Deep Fried Pumpkin Pie."

"Did I ever tell you that the sight of a woman in an apron is very stimulating to me?"

"I guess we'd better never hire one of those cute French maids with an apron not much bigger that a hankie?"

"I prefer gingham."

"Oh, good," Mitch sighed in mock relief.

"Why don't we go to bed early?"

"Best offer I've had all day."

"Better be the only offer!"

"The best and only offer I've had all day!"

As with all married couples, there were nights when sleep was more important than sex. Tonight was one such night. If they were this tired tonight, they could very well be totally drained by Sunday night if they didn't get their rest.

As promised, Saturday was wall-to-wall cooking. Mitch's menu had bloomed from a modest bacon and egg meal to a full blown brunch buffet. She had studied recipes ranging from coffeecake to quiche and worked all her selections along in stages with the able assistance of Reb.

"You certainly know your way around a kitchen," Mitch remarked during a much-needed coffee break.

"You don't need to sound so surprised," Reb sipped the terribly strong brew that Mitch called coffee. She held back a grimace.

"I just meant that all those years as governor and senator weren't conducive to spending much time checking out new recipes and such."

"I didn't spend that much time being governor and senator."

"Guess not," Mitch nodded. "What was it, about three years?"

"That's close enough."

"You mean we've been together nearly three years!?"

"Hard to believe, isn't it."

"You've never talked much about what you did to become governor, besides win the election, of course."

When stated that way, it sounded like a question.

"Most of it is a matter of public record."

"I really wasn't paying much attention," Mitch admitted.

"You weren't much of a political groupie, were you?"

"Still aren't, but I'm listening now."

"We don't have time to leaf through my resume. You have too many other things on the burner. Quite literally."

Mitch didn't draw a line in the figurative sand, but in the back of her mind, she knew that one day, they would revisit this subject.

Cooking, in the forms of frying, roasting and baking resumed full steam, so to speak. By dinner time, they had both done enough taste testing to qualify for a meal.

"You hungry?" Mitch asked. Silly question.

"No!"

"Me neither. I have an idea."

"You usually do," Reb was arching only one eyebrow.

"Let's talk about floor plans."

"*Floor plans*?"

"Right. In the new house."

Ah yes, the new house. With only fleeting regard to Reb's lack of interest in the impending construction project, Mitch had forged ahead with the most basic design concepts. Like, bathrooms, bedrooms and other standard stuff. Since Reb hadn't committed one way or the other to their future living arrangements once the trial was over, Mitch would be pretty much at a standstill.

"What about floor plans?" Reb asked, looking like she was sorry she was asking even as she spoke.

"I was thinking about adding a second story to the house."

"A second story?" Reb was perilously close to raising her other eyebrow.

"And that's because," Mitch trundled on bravely, "no modern day home is complete without an exercise room."

Reb could see right away where this was heading.

"You want to settle down here, don't you?"

"I just want to know how to plan. I don't mean to nag, but you haven't been able to spend much time in the gym lately. I'm worried about osteo."

"You're right. I haven't been staying in as good a shape as I should. But that's not the issue. The issue is whether or not you want to live in Utopia the rest of your life."

"Where else would you want to live? Name the place and I'll build you another house with my bare hands."

"As tempting as that would be to witness," Reb took hold of Mitch's hands, which were already showing wear and tear from her farming chores, "I will live here in Utopia if that's what you want to do."

"This is your ancestral home. I will stand by you wherever you are."

"I hope tomorrow goes well. It would make it easier to settle in if things calm down a little."

"I worry less about things calming down and more about your health. How about an Olympic size swimming pool to go along with the second story addition?"

"Are you thinking about building a hotel?"

"Well, I hope to have lots of company all the time."

"Like Lisa and Mary?"

"If they need a place to stay, we would have room."

Reb was all out of excuses to remain disinterested in the construction plans, and promised to study them in detail after the Sunday open house. The plan was really quite simple. Mitch and Rebecca were going to hand out their flyers inviting everyone to their trailer complex for a buffet at the same time Lucinda was handing out her poisonous flyers. When, at the crack-of-dawn six-thirty service was over, and Lucinda found out about the plan, she blew her cork. There was nothing quite as satisfying as being the burr under the saddle of the sanctimonious. Everyone took a flyer from Mitch and she began to fret that she hadn't cooked nearly enough food. She and Reb beat a hasty retreat home right before the ten-o'clock service got underway in order to be home and ready by eleven. As promised, Jessie was the first guest and helped to put the final touches on the table decorations. By noon, Mitch relaxed. There had been no onslaught, but a few curious folks showed up. They were a brave lot who withstood the withering glare of Lucinda, who had taken up the vanguard post at the front gate. Because there were but a handful of guests, there was indeed enough food for all, including seconds for Bixby and his date, and thirds for a guy named Earl. He, Earl, wondered if this was a one-time deal or if there would be more of these.

"You think we should do this every week?" Mitch took an informal survey.

"I'd come."

Mitch nodded. That was good enough for her. As she cleaned up the kitchen, she checked the attendance outside through the kitchen window. Only two or three new faces were out there. Contrasting that with the dozen people at the party, it seemed to be a victory. Twelve to three. Sounded like a baseball score.

Things wrapped up about three. Mitch had the chance to talk to everyone and suggested that they all bring a friend next week. Bixby was worried that it wouldn't be the best idea to bring two dates, so Mitch exempted him from the request, that sly fox. As she ushered the last guest past the prying eyes of Lucinda and company, Reb and Jessie were washing the serving trays by hand. They made a good team, enjoying their work to the point where Mitch didn't want to interfere. It didn't work out that way.

"Grab a dish towel," Reb instructed.

The old adage proved true. Many hands made light work and everything was polished, stored or otherwise disposed of properly in short order.

"How's Mrs. Cornwall?" Jessie asked.

"Just glaring. Not much else."

"Mrs. Cornwall has a way of raising glaring to an art form."

"Are you free to help out next Sunday?" Mitch wanted to stop talking about Mrs. Cornwall and took the direct approach.

"Now, Mitch," Reb was in lecture mode. "We can't ask Jessie to give up one of her days off every week."

"Oh, heck, it ain't no problem. I get a free meal out of it and a chance to keep current on this soap opera!"

"Who could ask for anything more!" Mitch smiled.

On the following Tuesday, Mitch of the Bright Idea Clan, decided that if handing out flyers at church worked so well, she could garner an even bigger turnout by spreading the word early and often in downtown Utopia. She had the notices printed up, handed out, and an advertisement bought and paid for in the local paper.

By Friday, two things were drawn: battle lines over who could draw the biggest crowd on Sunday, and some new blueprints for a second story addition to Mitch and Reb's new house. Construction would begin soon. In the meantime, Reb was taking inventory of the larder. Mitch had gone overboard, definitely. Jessie had been their advisor, but in true Mitch fashion, they had bought about twice as much as Jessie recommended.

"Okay, I give up. How many quiches are you going to bake?"

"At one time?"

"Altogether."

"I haven't decided yet."

"Give me a ballpark figure."

"How about a dozen."

"Just a dozen? Only a dozen?"

"I could make more."

"No! Twelve is fine!"

"I would think so. Especially since we also have hot dogs and hamburgers. You think we have enough sweet pickle relish?" Reb checked the pantry. "Yup."

"You thing the weather's going to hold?"

"This time, yes. Not for much longer, though."

Autumn had held its own for a respectable amount of time, but it would soon bow to the inevitable scourge of winter. For whatever reason, this didn't seem to deter the contractors from carrying on with the building plans. Materials were being trucked in despite the picket line and formed an ever-growing impressive pile of potential house.

Jessie couldn't stay away. She showed up to help after her Saturday shift at the diner.

"You're gonna need a lot of food," she predicted, "if what I heard at work is any indication!"

"Oh, good!" Mitch was honestly overjoyed. "Should I pick up a couple dozen donuts first thing tomorrow?"

"At least. You might even want to phone ahead. I'll pick them up, if you want?"

"I'd appreciate that. Why don't we get a couple of every kind."

"Don't forget the ones with the maple-flavored frosting," Reb finally entered the conversation. From a usually healthy eater, it was tantamount to a confession. It fairly screamed, "I eat donuts, too!"

"Ooohh, me, too!" Jessie was in a revealing mood as well.

"Then, we'd better get a few extra of those," Mitch picked up the phone and dialed the bakery on Wolff Street. By the time she hung up, the order had increased to four dozen donuts, two huge pans of date bars, and an assortment of Danish that would've fed a small army.

"How is Jessie going to get all of that in her car?" Reb the Practical quizzed.

"They're going to deliver!" Mitch made it sound like it was the first time in recorded history that such an event would occur.

"Hope they have a really big truck," Reb yawned.

"Me, too!" Mitch smiled. This was just getting to be too much fun for her.

"You're really enjoying yourself, aren't you?"

"Haven't you heard? I'm the party animal of Utopia."

127

Chapter 24

I didn't think we'd be moving in quite this fast," Robbie was
sitting on one end of the couch that they had brought from
"Trish's condo." Robbie had, from habit, called it "Trish's
condo" for a long time after they got together. Which was why
Trish was so very ready to get a new house, or at least, a house
new to them. If there was one word that described the Livermore
house, "new" wasn't it. It had been an act of extreme courage to
even contemplate moving in, let alone actually carting in a
couch. Of course, Robbie wasn't carrying anything. Trish
wouldn't allow it. She had hired a full-blown gay moving
service to come in and handle everything. They were
consummate experts and had done everything from wrapping
personal clothing in tissue paper to custom crating what
remaining artwork Trish owned.

Still, it was an adjustment. Robbie continued sitting on the
couch as she meditated on the monumental amount of work that
was going to be necessary just to be able to fix a nice breakfast in
the morning, let alone setting up a brand new household. She
must've looked pensive, for Trish came over and sat next to her.
"Are you hungry?" Trish was psychic where thoughts of food
were concerned.
"I was thinking about breakfast…"
Trish checked her watch. "Gee, I was thinking more along the
lines of lunch, but if you're having a craving for waffles, I'm
sure we can find you some somewhere."
"I'm not craving waffles," Robbie tried to stem the tide of
fussing that Trish had been doing lately.
"Omelets?" Trish looked like she was going to start ticking
things off a list.
"Nothing breakfast. That's not what I meant."
Trish nodded her best expectant-father nod. "So, you want
lunch?"

"Lunch is fine."

"Whatever you want," Trish patted Robbie's knee, "But we can always go to Captain Flapjacks any time you want?"

"Take me to that little Italian place we passed on the way here." It was going to be an interesting next few months. That didn't seem to stop Trish from beaming ear to ear.

"We'd better stock up on antacids," Robbie added. "You know about me and meatball sandwiches."

"I could write a book about you and meatball sandwiches."

"If you ever write a book about me and anything other than meatball sandwiches, I'll break your pencil."

"Just you and meatball sandwiches, I swear to God!" Trish held her hands like one was on a Bible and the other was taking an oath of office. Robbie was convinced, for now.

They left the movers to their work and took off for a lunch break. The restaurant had a Formica and vinyl atmosphere, but it was clean enough to earn a 99 on the state's restaurant inspection. Or maybe it was an upside down 66? Either way, the meatball sandwiches were sumptuous. They ordered extra cheese because Robbie was craving all things milk lately, and two cups of dipping sauce for the garlic breadsticks.

"I should be eating a salad instead," Robbie said about halfway through the meal.

"Nonsense," Trish said, "you're making a baby, not a rabbit."

"If I'm not careful, I'm going to get as big as a house."

"You need to gain weight during a pregnancy," Trish practically sounded like a doctor.

"And so, now, you're an expert on pregnancy?" Robbie challenged. Just a little.

"I've read a book or two," Trish defended her new-found expertise.

"You have?"

"While you were napping."

Robbie's eyes welled up in sparkling tears.

"What?" Trish asked, trying hard to keep confusion out of her voice.

"I'm so lucky and so happy that I love you and that we're having this baby."

129

"Me, too," Trish felt tongue tied and suddenly inadequate where a command of English was concerned. Not that anything she ever said rose to Pulitzer Prize winning status to begin with.

"We have everything we ever wanted, except a way to cook breakfast tomorrow morning," Robbie explained kindly.

"I'll take you out for breakfast."

"Captain Flapjacks, I presume?"

"Anywhere."

"And what about the next meal?"

"Here?"

"And dinner?"

"Wherever your heart desires? Taco Bell?"

"We can't eat out for every meal!"

"Why not?"

"Because our arteries will clog up like the highway at rush hour."

"You want a new stove, right?"

"Either that, or some coal for the one that's there now."

"It does belong in the Smithsonian, doesn't it?" Trish laughed.

"Along with about everything else in the kitchen."

"So, let's make that our first priority. We can bring in a crew to strip and clean the entire kitchen and then install some appliances temporarily until you hit on a design that suits you."

"That sounds wonderful."

"Good. By that time, we'll be sick of flapjacks."

"I'll cook oatmeal for a month."

Trish only smiled.

Chapter 25

Mary had skipped breakfast altogether. She was too apprehensive to eat. Today was the day that she had prayed for and dreaded. Flashes of each emotion were going through her body so quickly that it felt like collisions were jarring every point in her nervous system. Lisa was coming home. She kept saying it over and over in her head, without even trying. It just kept drumming through her brain. Lisa was coming home. Lisa had been pretty upbeat lately. Until about two days ago, when the plans were finalized for the actual trip home. Right now, "home" wasn't so very far away. Mitch had kept paying the rent on the apartment, and Mary had the place all ready for Lisa. Including clean sheets on the bed where Lisa would still need to spend a lot of time resting. Most of Lisa's mood downturn was due to the plastic mask. The final fitting was complete and Lisa had been encased in it for twenty-two hours a day for two days and counting. There were weeks and weeks to go. She was already slipping back into depression, with Mary, for the most part, becoming a helpless spectator. Putting on a brave face had become far more important than makeup. Shielded with her best effort, Mary walked into the rehab center. Lisa was in a wheelchair, ready to go. She didn't look happy. She didn't look sad. She just looked ready to go. Much to Mary's chagrin, a small contingent of press people were waiting at the front door when they emerged. Had they all just arrived? She didn't care. She could've led them on a merry chase, but she felt no pressing need to do so. If it was big news that the lesbian daughter of a lesbian ex-United States Senator was taking her lesbian lover home from a burn center, they could snap as many pictures and ask as many questions as they could think up. Mary ignored them. The staff loaded Lisa, her suitcases, and a bouquet of roses that Mary had thought to bring and they were free and clear in five minutes. "How the hell did they know that I was leaving today?" Lisa fumed through her mask.

Mary caught a word here and there, but could tell by the tone of her voice the gist of the question.

"I didn't tell them."

"Who did, then?"

Mary was busy counting to ten. If she was going to be the scapegoat for everything that happened from now on, there was going to be a whole lot of counting to ten.

"Maybe someone on staff? It might have been an inadvertent slip."

"Patient information is supposed to be confidential!"

"I know. Try not to talk too much. Let your face rest."

Lisa's new face had had hours and hours of rest already. Just thinking about the weeks ahead was too overwhelming. Tears came to her eyes that she blinked back. It would be just her luck to have her mask fog up. And then Mary would know more than she wanted her to know. So, from now on, fogging up was not an option.

"I'm so happy that you're coming home," Mary drove along like nothing would be wrong ever again. They were going home. That was good enough for her. Thank goodness the press wasn't at the apartment. Apparently, it wasn't *that* slow of a news day. Mary carried the luggage across the threshold. Lisa carried herself. She looked around for about three seconds.

"*This* is where you've been living?"

"Yes."

"Well, no *wonder* you spent so much time at the hospital."

"You're not impressed?" Mary wasn't going to let this get to her. The counting to ten had started again. She was at "two."

"Oh, I'm impressed alright. This place is even more bleak than the hospital, something I would *not* have thought possible an hour ago."

Whatever sweet, wonderful fantasy homecoming Mary had envisioned in her mind earlier was now crushed like a dry oak leaf. She was at "five."

"Do you want to lie down and rest?"

"I've spent weeks lying down. I don't want to lie down."

Mary nodded. So, it wasn't a great idea to talk, either. She smiled, said a silent "seven" to herself, and then took the suitcases to the bedroom. Lisa followed right behind.

"What are you doing?" she demanded to know.

"Unpacking your stuff?"

"I'm not staying *here*."

"Ok," was Mary's only comment. Out loud. Silently, she was hovering at "nine."

"Have you called your mom lately?"

"Not lately," Mary admitted like she was under oath.

"Give her a buzz. Tell her we're coming as soon as we can get a flight."

"To Utopia?"

"That's where they are, right?"

"Right…"

"So, call 'em. Tell Mitch to, for God's sake, put clean sheets on the bed."

"You're sure you want to go back there?"

"You're going to need help. Your mom and Mitch are the only two people who would put up with me."

"I'll put up with you, too." Mary said in her own defense.

"You have to. You love me."

"Yes, I do."

Mary put down the suitcases and picked up the phone. Rebecca was thrilled. If she could have, she would've jumped up and down. Lisa was one smart daughter-in-law, making her mother-in-law so happy. Damn lucky guess.

It must have been the right choice because fate didn't usually allow for last-minute first-class airline seat availability on the afternoon flight to Kansas. Mitch would indeed change the sheets. Something she took in stride. She was on a roll. Her luck was improving. More than triple the number of guests had attended week two of their open-house-a-thon. This was beginning to get on Lucinda Cornwall's nerves. What Mitch didn't know was that Ms. Cornwall didn't take things lying down. The fanatic right wing had quite the large organizational network, which gave Lucinda the opportunity of support. She went to the top and made a wish. It was granted. In two weeks, these lesbian troublemakers would be shown just how much out of their league they were playing, by gosh.

133

Chapter 26

Max, Rose, and Silver stood speechless. Trish and Robbie had managed to get them through the front door of the Livermore Estate, but not much further.

"You bought the whole place?" Max asked obtusely.

He had been looking better after his apparent heart attack, until now. Now, he was swaying a bit. Maybe it was the draft.

"They wouldn't let us buy just half of it," Trish answered.

"It's very nice," Rose complimented with her usual old-world politeness.

"It's big for two people," Max stated the obvious.

"There will be three of us soon," Robbie reminded.

Max was ready to say that it was big for three people, but Rose shot him a warning look. It counted double. Max and Rose had remained reserved about the news of the pregnancy. Intellectually, they understood the process, but were, to this point, devoid of emotional glee about the outcome. This just wasn't how they made families back where they came from. Trish and Robbie weren't too concerned. They knew that things would change when the baby was born. Maybe even sooner.

"Come on and walk around," Trish motioned for everyone to follow her.

"It's going to look pretty empty," Robbie cautioned, particularly her mother.

"Right," Trish added, "It's going to look a little like the Beverly Hillbillies. We've moved all of our furniture in and barely made a dent."

"It looks downright foreboding," Silver finally made a comment. Silver Smith, upon reflection, was a wonderful addition to the family. She was brought on the scene as a bodyguard when Rose was being threatened. Silver was a big, African-American woman, and made a nice contrast to the diminutive Mrs. Goldstein. They garnered their fair share of curious stares in the grocery store. At least no one mistook them for mother and daughter.

"It's all the dark colors and old paint that make it gloomy. We have our work cut for us," Trish admitted.

"But you're not going to have Roberta doing any of that!" Rose was suddenly an impending Grandma.

"Absolutely not! Robbie's not going to do anything but sit, put her feet up and eat bon bons."

"I am not!" Robbie announced.

"You'd rather have cookies?" Trish asked with a twinkle.

"I'm not going to be treated like an invalid just because I'm pregnant!"

"Okay, okay, we understand," Trish promised and then added, "Don't we!" in the general direction of everyone else.

"Just don't inhale any paint fumes," Max admonished. Soon, he would be Grandpa Max.

Trish smiled inwardly. This was good stuff. Now was as good a time as any to bring up the subject of having Rose, Max and Silver move in. How best to put this?

"We want the three of you to move in," Trish held on to Robbie's hand as she said this. It was a sign of their solidarity on the matter.

"Move in? Here?" Rose asked as she looked around the room.

"Actually, we want you to have the bedroom this way," Robbie indicated the location of the master bedroom. They walked toward it like they were approaching the Wizard of Oz. The master bedroom of the Livermore Estate alone would easily hold every stick of furniture that Rose and Max had in their bedroom at home. In fact, just about everything that Rose and Max owned by way of chairs and tables and chests of drawers would shoehorn into the room as well. But there was no need for that. Some of it could go in Silver's room, which was right next door. Silver, the ever-vigilant one, had paid close attention to the windows.

"This place is going to need a serious security upgrade, if we're moving in, that is."

Rose looked at Max. Max looked at Rose. It dawned on Trish at this moment that she should never, ever play poker with either one of them.

"What do you want to do, Mrs. Goldstein?" Max asked reverently.

"Do you think we'll be a bother?" she asked back.

"In a house this big, you'd have to work hard to find someone, let alone bother them!"

It was weird for Trish to be listening in on a conversation as if it was being held in private. Rose fixed that little problem.

"Are you sure we won't be a bother to you?" Rose asked Robbie and Trish point blank.

Robbie pretended that she hadn't heard anything prior.

"We can't wait for you to move in," Robbie reassured them.

Trish nodded and then turned to Silver. "You'd better start drawing up plans for the security."

"What will we do with the other house?" Rose asked Max, now that the final decision was made.

"Keep it!" Max said. "It isn't like it isn't paid for and we won't need rent money for here."

"Right," Robbie was glowing.

Trish hadn't seen her that happy since their wedding day.

"Now, you're not going to be very happy with the kitchen," Trish brought them all back down to earth.

"We'll be happy with whatever it looks like," Rose was always so diplomatic.

As they turned the corner, Max remarked, "It looks like we'll be eating out!"

He was right on the mark. The room was bare.

"Where is everything?" Rose asked, now beginning to see the problem.

"We scrapped what the Smithsonian didn't want. If it wasn't broken, it was covered in grime."

Everyone looked around. It was going to be a long time before any serious baking would be possible. Hell, it would be a long time before oatmeal was possible.

Chapter 27

That second trailer came in real handy in Utopia. Mary and Lisa's plane had been delayed, making their arrival late into the night. Mitch made the trek to the airport while Reb stayed behind. She had been working out lately and was too tired for an airport vigil. By the time Lisa and Mary disembarked from the plane, they only had enough energy for a quick hug. They both dozed on the drive back and fell sound asleep in the as-yet-not-slept-in bed in the spare trailer.

When the four of them finally sat down to a meal together, it was lunch the next day. Lisa was allowed to remove her plastic mask long enough to eat. It was the only time she didn't feel like a freak.

"So, what have you been doing here?" Lisa asked. After all, everyone knew what she had been doing. Any new news was good news.

"Mitch has been holding Sunday socials," Reb tattled.

"Sunday socials?" Mary was puzzled.

"It's her answer to the protestors," Reb took her best shot at explaining.

"I see. How's the trial coming?" Mary changed subjects quickly.

"Slowly."

"Have you testified yet?"

"I'm due up later this week."

"Are you nervous?" Lisa piped up.

"No," Reb answered quietly. Not too much in life made her nervous anymore, but that didn't mean it was obvious to the casual bystander. Not that there was ever anything casual about Lisa.

"I want to testify, too. Can you arrange that?"

Mary and Reb exchanged glances. "Why didn't this sound like such a good idea?" was the general look on their faces.

Reb took a stab. "I'm not sure the prosecutor thinks your testimony is needed."

"Why not? I *was* there."

"Well, we didn't know if you had clear memories?" Mary attempted to carry the cause.

"I have clear memories. They come in my sleep. Every night."

"We don't want to make you go through anything that painful in public," Reb was determined to take the brunt of this conversation.

"Painful? PAINFUL! Things couldn't get much more painful than what I've already been through!"

"Well, I'm not sure if we can put you on the witness list so late in the process?" Reb tried to sound lawerly without appearing arrogant. A bold ambition.

"Matlock could figure it out," Lisa contested.

"Do I look like Matlock?"

"No, but you look a little like that assistant he had."

"Wasn't that his daughter?" Mary added like it was a trivia contest.

"Not the first season, I don't think?" Mitch was straining to remember.

"THAT'S NOT THE POINT!" Reb herded them back to the topic at hand. Loudly. "I think the case is already pretty well locked up. There's video footage and receipt evidence. So, unless you can say definitely that Miranda lit the match, my advice is to-"

"I *can* say that," Lisa remarked, with emphasis.

"You what?" Mary hadn't heard about this.

"I said I *can* testify to that. Why do you think I've been in such a hurry to get out here?"

"Truthfully?"

"Yes, truthfully."

"Testify truthfully?" Reb split hairs.

"Yes."

"Because if you're making this up or having a false memory, the defense lawyers will tear you apart."

"And how would that look?" Lisa asked as she worked to put her plastic bubble mask over her face. "Those mean lawyers picking on a disfigured victim."

Reb looked at Mitch, who shrugged as if to say, "You try and tell her what to do! I gave up a whole long time ago!"

138

"I'll call the prosecuting attorney first thing in the morning."
"Why not now?" Lisa was primed.
"He's working."
"You can leave him a message."
"You could've told me *sooner* about your plans!"

It was a good thing they had separate trailers to go to as Reb pondered the message she was going to leave for the prosecutor.

As Reb's luck would have it, the prosecuting attorney took her call and saw eye to eye with Lisa. So much so that he decided to juggle the schedule and put her ahead of Rebecca. Reb felt, among other things, upstaged. Mitch caught on after a stretch of stony silence. Even ex-Senators had an ego to assuage.
"I'm sure he's just making sure that he finishes the case with his strongest witness," Mitch offered her silver lining as she held the woman of her dreams close. Very close. Intensely close.
"Yeah," Reb was either unconvinced or playing hard to get. This was Mitch's favorite game, just in case anybody was keeping score.
"And that is you," Mitch nuzzled her ear. Just to be heard, mind you.
"Right."
"If I were him, I'd want to save you 'til last."

Reb pulled away just a little. A little was all her heart would allow, but it gave her perspective to study Mitch's face.
"You always know the right thing to say."
Mitch just smiled and was about to be kissed when, of course, the phone rang.
"Hello?" Mitch answered.
"Did you hear the news?" Jessie jumped right in as usual.
"I don't know, have I?"
"She's bringing in the big guns!"
As Jessie caught her breath, Mitch pictured several things in her mind. Things like Civil War type cannons and Panzer Tanks. She pretty much had already guessed who the "she" was.
"How big?" Mitch asked, just mostly to prod Jessie on.

139

"Big! National B-I-G big."

"National?"

"Right!" Jessie agreed, forgetting that she still hadn't told much of anything to begin with.

"A National Gun?" Mitch summarized.

"No, silly! It's Polly Perkell!"

"Who?" Mitch had no earthly clue who Polly Perkell was.

"You know! Polly Perkell. THE Polly Perkell!"

Mitch still had no idea. "Can you tell me what she's famous for?"

"She just happens to be the most famous gospel singer of all time."

In all fairness, this wasn't an area that Mitch knew much about. The last person she had heard sing gospel was Elvis. He couldn't have possibly been reincarnated into someone named Polly Perkell. If he was dead at all.

"Does she know her initials are PP?"

"What?"

"Never mind. So, why is this big news again?"

"Because she's coming here!"

"Why?"

"Because Lucinda Cornwall is bringing her here."

"Why?"

"Well, if I had to make a guess, it would be to get more people to protest instead of going to your Sunday morning socials."

"You mean to tell me that because I've been having a few folks to the house on Sunday, Cornwall's bringing some singer to town?"

"Polly Perkell isn't just some singer! How many people do you know can make a gospel album go platinum?"

"Elvis?"

"That doesn't count."

"Why not?"

"Because he's not coming to Utopia is why not!"

"Okay, and so, the best known alive gospel singer is coming to Utopia to do what again?"

Reb had been listening in on all of this and, bright woman that she was, mouthed the word, "Sing?"

"Sing!" Jessie answered simultaneously.

It sounded like a prison.

"And that's going to keep people from stopping over here for bacon and eggs?"

"You just don't quite get this, do you?" Jessie sounded disappointed.

"I guess I don't," Mitch agreed reluctantly. Falling off the smart pedestal always did bruise the ego.

"Polly Perkell is like an icon to these religious folks. If she smiles on you, you're blessed for life. If she frowns, you're history."

"So, Lucinda is bringing Polly here to frown at me?"

"Honey, you're in for a full-blown scowl from her."

"Oh well, I guess I can live with a pouty gospel singer," Mitch reassured Jessie.

"I suggest you just hunker down and hold on hard."

"Thanks."

Mitch hung up the phone, feeling miles away from where she and Reb were when the phone rang. "Do you know about this Polly person?"

"I certainly do."

"Oh," Mitch blinked. "Should I be concerned?"

"Yup."

Reb, not normally a woman of brevity, caught Mitch's attention with this succinct reply.

"What advice would you give me?"

"Just be yourself."

"That, I can do."

Once word spread that Ms. PP was coming to town, Mitch could've sworn that she could hear the buzzing clear out to the homestead. It didn't exactly preoccupy her every waking moment. She was too busy with other things. Things like getting used to having to cook for two more people, which although wasn't a lot after hosting a party a week, was still steady work. Four for breakfast, four for lunch, four for dinner. It was a labor of love.

Speaking of labor, the building contractors began arriving on a daily basis and although they brought their own food, Mitch was always good for a snack.

Reb was staying active as well, working out like she hadn't since rehab days. She was getting downright buff, except for her legs, which were showing the inevitable signs of waste. Mitch had spent time massaging them, but nothing took the place of actual walking.

"I don't know how you do it," Reb remarked one day as Mitch was working away on her left calf.

"Do what?"

"Everything."

"I don't do everything?" Mitch was puzzled.

"I meant everything you do do."

"Do do?"

"Are you making fun of me?" Reb asked like she knew better.

"No, I just don't understand," Mitch worked the calf muscle absently, because after all this time, it no longer required the energy of concentration.

"Do you even realize how much you do for me?"

"I could ask you the same thing," Mitch smiled.

"Now, don't you go and turn this around. I'm talking about you."

This never did make Mitch feel very comfortable, but she put up with it.

"Okay."

"How do you do it?"

"Well, first, I rub this muscle this way," Mitch demonstrated.

"That's not what I mean!"

Still confused, but undaunted, Mitch gently put Reb's leg back on the bed and then moved up so that she was straddling her. As she moved her face closer to Reb's, she pulled her into a kiss. This simple act sparked passion. As always.

"*That's* what I'm talking about," Reb explained.

Mitch waited for more. Of anything.

"How are you able to see me one minute as a patient and the next minute as a lover?"

"Oh that! Well, why didn't you just ask that in the first place."

"So, you *know* the answer?"

"Oh, sure."

"Do tell."

"It's because I *always* think of you as my lover."

"Even when you're massaging my legs?"

"*Especially* when I'm massaging your legs!"

"I don't massage your legs."

"It isn't my legs that needs massaging," Mitch made it clear.

"Oh, really?" Reb wasn't out of questions yet.

"Yeah, really!" Mitch smiled and continued to slowly kiss Reb's face. No reason to rush. They weren't going anywhere…except to answer the damn phone again!

It was Jessie.

Again.

She sounded different. Distraught. This didn't sound like it was more news about Polly what's her name. That kind of news was in the category of "Guess what?" This newest tone was more ominous.

"It's my sister," Jessie said in a whisper.

"What about your sister?" Mitch made eye contact with Reb as she spoke to convey the seriousness of the call.

"She's sick. She just called me."

"I'm sorry. I didn't know you had a sister, Jessie."

"She's my baby sister. My *baby* sister."

"Is she here?"

"No, she lives in Riley."

"Oh," Mitch nodded. Riley was a big town east of Utopia. Big only in comparison to Utopia. Then again, just about everything was big compared to Utopia.

"And…she's so…sick," Jessie's voice broke with deep emotion.

"What's the matter with her?" Mitch asked gently.

Jessie couldn't answer. She was crying full now.

"You want us to come over?"

Jessie snuffled for a moment. "I don't want to bother you."

"We're here to be bothered. We want to come over. Reb is right here and she's nodding agreement, okay?" even though she hadn't been.

"Okay."

"We'll be there in a few minutes."

"Okay."

When Mitch hung up the phone, she looked at Reb. "I volunteered you as well. Do you mind terribly?"

"No. Just tell me the part I didn't hear."

"You pretty much heard it all. Jessie's sister, who lives in Riley, is really sick."

"What's wrong?"

"Jessie couldn't even answer that. She's really shook up."

"I gathered as much."

They both got out of bed and readied themselves quickly. Which, translated, meant that Reb didn't put on any makeup. Mitch marveled at her beauty anyway. No use muddling up perfection.

Jessie was holding open the door long before Reb wheeled up the walk. It must have made her feel useful. Once they were all inside the small duplex, Jessie more or less grabbed on to Mitch in the form of a hug and showed no sign of letting go anytime soon. Mitch soothed her until she felt safe to let go. Jessie sat down without first fussing about coffee. This was serious.

"Tell us what's wrong," Reb said sensitively.

"My sister, my baby sister, has cancer," she answered quickly, afraid to talk slowly for fear of impending sobs.

"What kind of cancer?" Mitch pressed. If it was one of the types of cancer where recovery was viable, it might be easier to reassure Jessie.

"Some sort of bone cancer, she said."

Mitch cast an eye in Reb's direction. They both knew this wasn't good.

"So, you haven't seen her yet?" Reb tried to get to the facts.

"No. I called you right after she called me."

"So, you want to see her as quickly as possible?" Mitch nodded, hoping that the urgent nature of the question went unnoticed.

144

"But, I don't know about work?" Jessie was clearly overwhelmed.

"Don't worry about work. I'm sure everyone will understand."

"Would you call them?" Jessie's lower lip began to tremble.

"Sure," Reb volunteered.

Between Mitch and Reb, they accomplished everything necessary to arrange a sojourn to Riley. Except that Rebecca was going to stay behind. It was just easier that way. Mitch kissed her goodbye and whispered, "Just remember where we were when the call came in."

Reb nodded. She had a good memory.

With that, Mitch and Jessie got in Jessie's car and began the trip. It was only a hundred or so miles, but it was a quiet hundred or so miles. Small talk seemed inappropriate. Mitch drove and Jessie alternated between crying and sighing. Thankfully, she also slept.

Jessie awoke right before Mitch would've had to wake her up to ask directions. Between them, they found the local hospital and wound their way to the oncology section. Mitch hesitated at the doorway of the hospital room, but Jessie tugged her in.

"I didn't drag you all the way out here to wait in the hall."

For a place where death had so often visited, the room was cheery. An optimistic shade of green paint had been used in conjunction with a more standard taupe. The floor was sparkling clean and the window coverings were set to allow deflected sunlight to add to the ambiance.

Jessie's sister was the sole occupant of the room. If she wasn't careful, the bed would swallow her up. Jessie gave her a hug and then proceeded with the introductions.

"Mitch, this is my baby sister, Abigail."

As they murmured usual hellos between strangers, Mitch shook Abigail's hand. She felt warm, like she might have a fever. Instinctively, Mitch felt her forehead to confirm the diagnosis. It was an intimate gesture for only being introduced, but neither

Abigail nor Mitch thought another thing about it. Then, Mitch smiled. "How many more are in your family?"

"It's just us," Jessie answered.

"Yes, and I'm the younger of the two, *not* the baby," Abigail clarified.

Gee, she didn't act like she was staring death in the face. Mitch perched on the edge of the bed and became bold, or nosy, depending on your point of view.

"When did they diagnose your cancer?" she sounded positively medical.

"Just a couple days ago."

"Where is it?"

"It's in my hip socket."

"Are you sure?" Mitch didn't know why she asked. Questions just flowed out of her.

"That's what they told me."

Jessie had questions as well. "What are they going to do?"

"I don't know. I wanted to wait until you got here. I'm not sure I can face this alone..."

"I'm here for you," Jessie patted her baby sister's hand. The one that wasn't hooked into an IV.

Mitch stood up suddenly and wandered out to the meager waiting area. She was inexplicably tired and warm. This wasn't the time to get sick, she chided herself. Maybe it was just the long drive and the setting of the thermostat, but she sat in a chair and fell into a deep sleep. It could've been minutes, hours, or truly days later when Jessie shook her awake.

"Mitch? Mitch! Wake up!"

Normally, when Mitch was roused out of a sound sleep, she was irritable. Not so now. Something in Jessie's voice propelled her past cranky.

"My baby sister is better!"

"Better?" Mitch asked through a yawn.

"The doctor came to see her while you were out here snoring away-"

"I was snoring?"

"Yes! And anyway, the doctor was checking her and she was better!"

"How do they know?"

"I don't know. But they're doing more tests. I guess she wasn't in as much pain? So, they're doing something to check on the cancer. They used a bunch of big words, stuff I've never heard of."

Jessie was reduced to babbling from nerves. Mitch made her sit down and put an arm around her shoulders. It helped to calm her down.

"How long was I asleep?"

"A good hour or more. You okay?"

"I think so. Am I warm to you?"

"No," Jessie checked just to make sure.

"Good. I thought I was getting sick."

They sat a whole five minutes until the doctors reappeared with Abigail in tow. One motioned toward Jessie and she stood to join them.

"You coming?" she asked Mitch.

"I think I'll wait here."

Jessie nodded, mostly her assurances that she could handle things now.

The conference didn't last long. Funny thing, nobody could find any sign that Abigail ever had cancer. Her hip felt fine, good enough to put walking weight on it. In fact, it felt so good that she felt a little foolish when they put her in a wheel chair to send her home. Probably not nearly as foolish as the doctors felt.

Jessie, Abigail and Mitch crammed themselves into Jessie's car and drove Abigail home. They didn't even need to do any grocery shopping along the way. Abigail hadn't been gone all that long from home.

"Are you sure they didn't mix up the x-rays or something?" Jessie asked.

"How would that explain the pain going away?" Abigail countered.

"Well, maybe…" Jessie started and then stopped. No explanation made sense. Other than a miracle.

147

"Cancer does go into remission," Mitch added her two cents, cautiously.

"I guess so, but so quickly?" Jessie wondered.

"I don't know if remission has a timetable," Mitch admitted her ignorance.

"I wish you two would stop talking about my cancer like it's going to come back!" Abigail stated firmly.

"Sorry," Mitch said, and then added, "Why don't I rent a car or something so you two can spend a couple of days together?"

Two sisters nodded in unison. Mitch was on her way home to Utopia within the hour. That had a nice ring to it: Home to Utopia. More importantly, home to Rebecca. She pulled up into the driveway late. Everyone was in bed. Even Reb.

"Hey there," she greeted sleepily.

"Hi. I guess I should've called?"

"No, it's fine. I just didn't expect you home so soon."

"Oh, good. So, I'm not in trouble," Mitch settled herself on the bed facing Reb.

"How is Jessie's sister?"

"She's fine."

"Fine?"

"Yeah. Everything is okay."

"How can that be?" Reb sat up a little straighter. "She has cancer."

"Not anymore," Mitch stated matter-of-factly.

"People just don't get over cancer like that."

"Sure they do. One in 100,000 cancer patients go into remission."

"How do you know that?"

"I was reading the pamphlets in the waiting room," Mitch yawned.

"Did you eat?"

"I'm too tired to do anything but this," Mitch reached out and held Reb's hand.

"Take off your shoes and cuddle up."

"Yes, Ma'am."

Mitch took off more than her shoes. She stripped naked and was ready for that cuddle. That, and about ten or twelve hours of sleep.

Lisa dressed for court while Mary fixed breakfast. She was still unconvinced that this was such a great idea.

"You don't have to go through with this," replaced "good morning" as the first thing out of her mouth.

"If it doesn't bother me, why should it bother you?"

"I just don't want you to be reminded of it all over again."

"Every time I look in a mirror, I'm reminded of it."

"I guess so."

Mary sat opposite Lisa at the table. As Lisa removed her mask to eat, Mary studied the effect. She was healing quickly, but there were weeks to go.

"I give up. What's on your mind?" Lisa asked without looking up. Her intuitiveness was incredibly fine tuned.

What was on Mary's mind was that they had yet to be intimate all this time after the fire.

"I'm just thinking how beautiful you are," Mary blurted out. She didn't care anymore how ridiculous it might have sounded to the rest of the world.

"Oh, so, that's what's on your mind!" Lisa smiled in spite of her scars.

"It is not," Mary lied.

"It is, too," Lisa squeezed her hand.

"Okay. It is. I admit it."

"You understand why it's taken me so long?" Lisa asked and stated at the same time.

"Well, yes, and, no," Mary was as equivocal in her answer.

"I don't feel lovable."

"Why?"

"Because, I don't look lovable, I guess."

"I don't love you because of your looks," Mary assured her.

"Well, then, why do you love me?" Lisa made it sound like a challenge.

"If I start telling you all the reasons I love you, we'll never get to court on time."

"You promise to tell me later?"

"Consider it a vow."

Even when Mary hurried, they were still cutting it close to be ready on time. Reb was having kittens. She was the driver and fairly flew down the road leading to the courthouse. It was just fortunate happenstance that the county courthouse was in close proximity, or else they would've needed to rent a jet. As Mitch held on tight, she fielded questions about her trip to Riley, beginning with the obvious.

"So, what kind of cancer did Jessie's sister have, before it went away?" Reb picked up where they left off last night.

"It was in one of her legs. She had pain when she walked."

"Mom said it was bone cancer?" Mary got into the act.

"I think it was in her hip?" Mitch thought back to the various conversations.

"That's bad stuff. Are you sure it's completely gone?" Reb was getting more skeptical by the minute.

"I'm only telling you what the doctor said."

"Sounds like a mix up to me," Lisa offered her opinion.

"Well, when Jessie gets back, we can find out more," Mitch wanted to drop the conversation. It was wearing her out. And besides, she wanted to discuss something closer to home, namely, Aunt BeBe.

"You still haven't talked to your sister," Mitch said to Reb.

"There's nothing to say!" Reb snapped back.

"Actually, I think there's a lot to say. It's just that it's all painful," Mitch tried to soothe.

"I'll vouch for that!" Lisa came to the defense of Rebecca. Now, there was a case of strange bedfellows if ever there was one.

"Still, when the court case is over, we'll all need to live in the same town."

"Miranda will be in jail out east and everybody else can move the hell away if they don't like it here."

"That might very well happen, but don't you see that BeBe's heart is broken?"

"I haven't looked," Reb was still brittle.

"I have," Mitch said quietly.

"And you feel sorry for her and her treacherous daughter, I suppose?" Lisa was heating up as well.

"I always feel sorry for people who don't have the ability to love," Mitch answered softly.

Everyone grew quiet, mostly because no one had an adequate response. Good thing Reb was driving. They arrived at the courthouse before the silence became too awkward.

Inside was as silent as a church. If anyone cared to ponder it, the fact might be that just as much, if not more, praying went on in here than a place of worship. Don't we all pray for salvation in one way or another? Does it matter where we do it?
Mitch was cogitating about all this as she sat next to Reb.
"I didn't mean to snap."
"I'd rather you snap at me than your sister."
"I just can't talk to her right now."
"You never could talk to her. It's no surprise you can't now."
"She's the one so full of hatred. Not me."
"All the more reason to reach out to her."
"Are you sure you feel alright? Do you have a fever or something?" Reb felt Mitch's forearm as she asked.
"I felt a little warm yesterday."
Rebecca just naturally assumed that Mitch was referring to their time together and patted her knee. Before Mitch could elaborate, they had to "all rise" for the judge. Except for Reb, of course.
Judge Talbot, the closest thing to a hanging judge in Kansas, took the bench. If anyone had labored under the false impression that Miranda was going to get an easy ride just because the house she torched had been occupied by lesbians, hadn't been in Judge Talbot's realm lately. He had ruled in favor of about ninety-five percent of the prosecutor's motions and objections. The defense was already staggering when Lisa approached the witness stand to ostensibly deliver the final blow. Objections were raised again, just for the court record, over the sudden appearance of this surprise witness. Judge Talbot did what he had promised to do in his chambers, namely ruling in favor of the prosecution. It should be no shock to anyone with a lick of sense that the testimony of the victim of the crime would be the most logical witness, surprise or not. And, if anything, Judge Talbot was a logical man.

Lisa's testimony was brief. She answered what few questions the prosecutor had. Most of them were more or less for

151

foundation to lessen the objections the defense might raise with just simple straightforward queries. Then, the defense had to decide if they wanted to undermine Lisa's testimony, which would among other things, keep her on the stand in full view of the jury. Although Mary could see only beauty, everyone else in the room saw a scarred, disfigured victim. The defense had no questions.

Reb was next. And last. The defense's cross examination, intended to be withering, was a dud. They forgot that they were up against a brilliant lawyer. Mitch marveled at her adroit mind. There never had been any doubt who had the brains of the family. After Reb left the stand, the prosecution rested its case. The defense followed suit. A murmur of surprise rustled through the courtroom, stopped short by a fierce rapping of the gavel by the judge. Closing arguments were set for the following morning.

As the crowd milled out, Mitch caught the eye of Aunt BeBe. As they looked at each other, their silent exchange made it clear to Mitch that she was in agony over the events. BeBe tried to raise her guard, but Mitch saw through it. It could've been an hour for all Mitch could tell, but Reb's face came into focus through the haze.
"Come on. Let's go eat lunch."
A mere two or three seconds had ticked away. Mitch blinked.
"Are you sure you're okay?" Reb asked earnestly.
"I'm fine. Let's go to the diner. I'm hungry for a meatloaf sandwich."
"Oh, God," Reb muttered. Mitch could never use self-control where the diner was concerned.
"What did you say?" Mitch was finally focused on Reb.
"I said, 'oh, good.'"
"Oh."

Lunch at the diner was subdued without Jessie. Reb didn't feel like talking about the court case, Mitch didn't want to talk about Jessie's sister, and Mary and Lisa didn't want to talk about anything. When Mitch caught the wavelength between Mary and

Lisa, she skipped dessert. She felt that some things just shouldn't be stalled any longer than absolutely necessary. Mitch paid the check while everyone else went out to the car. They were soon back in their separate matching trailers behind their line of protestors. Mitch started rummaging around in the fridge two minutes after they got home.

"You just had lunch," Reb the Calorie Police pointed out.

"Yeah, but I skipped dessert."

"I noticed. Why?"

"Lisa and Mary were in a hurry, obviously."

"Obviously?"

"Yeah. They wanted to get home so they could make love."

"Now, how the hell do you know that?"

"I thought it was crystal clear."

"Oh, really," Reb sounded thoroughly unconvinced.

Mitch picked up the phone and handed it to Reb. "Go ahead and call. Ask them for yourself."

Reb took the phone and immediately hung it back up. "I guess it's not that unbelievable," she said with just a slight huff in her voice.

"Except that it's the first time since the accident," Mitch explained it all.

"And you know that how?"

"I don't know how I know. I just know."

"Did you find anything good for dessert?"

"No."

"Well, may I suggest that you and I proceed to the bedroom to search there?"

Mitch cocked an eyebrow. "Sounds like a…delicious idea to me."

There was never any hurry to their lovemaking before and there certainly wasn't any now. Everything Lisa did was deliberate, including foreplay. Mary had practiced in the past trying to relax under Lisa's touch, but her impatient nature had made it hard both then and now. She breathed in and out steadily, wanting to hurry and wanting not to hurry. Wanting Lisa to touch her deeper and wanting to wait for every gossamer touch.

"You're in quite the mood," Lisa whispered in her ear.

"I am?" Mary breathed.

"You're needing to enjoy every single second of this."

"That's because you make every single second so very enjoyable," Mary managed to say before Lisa made everything so much more intense. Mary dissolved.

She held on to Lisa like she was afraid she would float away. Mary's climax had been so splendid that it literally shook her to her core. It took time for her to begin to breath normally again, and Lisa held her close until her pulse and blood pressure returned to acceptable parameters. And then, they just stayed close and quiet for a long time. So long that Lisa prodded her.

"I think you were ready for that."

"I was."

"I'm ready now."

"You'd better be."

Chapter 28

Trish had been correct. All of the Goldstein's furniture fit easily into the new place. In fact, they would soon need to go out and get more. Much more. But, first things first, the kitchen needed tending. And in order to modernize it, there had to be a reworking of the electrical wiring. The contractor jerry rigged something temporary so that they could at least run a microwave. It was heartening to discover how many flavors of instant oatmeal you could choose. There was apple and peach and maple and just plain old plain. And that was just breakfast. For lunch and dinner, the selections available for microwaveable cuisine were an industry all unto themselves. There were healthy victuals and, by contrast, chow of which arteries are clogged.

Rose watched over Max like the proverbial hawk, swooping down on anything that could warrant a trip back to the emergency room.
"I didn't die last time," was his sole defense. He needed more law school to get around Rose.
"You won't always have a miracle," was her usual cryptic reply.

Speaking of miracles, Robbie had finally gotten over the worst of the morning sickness. For Trish, it was wonderful to wake up to the sound of peeping birds instead of tossing cookies. What hadn't been terrific lately was having a bowl of oatmeal for breakfast day in and day out. Trish had tried all the varieties at least once and then, she took to mixing them to achieve a more exotic blend of flavors. Nothing like a bowl of peach, apple, cinnamon, French vanilla oatmeal to set you on firm footing for the rest of the day. Still, the irony was that here Trish was, one of the richest women around, eating oatmeal out of a microwave and drinking coffee that was terrible. This she could only blame on herself, the coffee, that is. Maybe they needed one of those cappuccino machines? Max wandered into the kitchen.
"What's the flavor of the day?"
"Taste it for yourself and see if you can guess," Trish offered him a serving. He nailed everything but the French in the French vanilla.

"Not bad," he nodded.

In fact, it was quite the treat for him. Usually, he stuck to just plain oatmeal, but Trish had been a decidedly bad influence on him.

"Did you sleep well?"

"Like a kid!"

Trish studied him. Everyone should look so good after a heart attack.

"And Rose?"

"You can ask her yourself. She'll be out in a few minutes."

"I think I'll go check on Robbie. Maybe I'll pass her in the hall."

The hallways were deserted, and so was Trish and Robbie's bedroom. Trish wandered around until she spotted Robbie in the future nursery. Perhaps she was doing some mental redecorating?

"Hi," Trish greeted from the doorway.

Robbie jumped. "Don't sneak up on a pregnant woman that way."

"I clunked all the way down the hall."

"I didn't hear you."

"You were deep in thought," Trish walked up to her and put her hands around her waist. It was apparent that she was in an affectionate mood. Must have been that French in the French vanilla.

"You taste good," Robbie reported.

"So do you," Trish returned the compliment and then kissed her again. More arduously this time. Ah, being married was such a wonderful thing. The only thing missing was a bed. Trish didn't seem to care at the moment and began to seek out places on Robbie's body that would welcome her touch. Robbie was hesitant.

"Maybe we shouldn't," she said as she took hold of Trish's hands.

"You want to go somewhere more comfortable?" Trish was willing to make a plan. And stick to it.

Robbie shivered in response.

"Are you cold?"

"Yes, actually."

156

Trish wasn't. In fact, she was smoldering. But if Robbie was cold, it was probably one of those pregnancy things.

"Come on. I'll build a fire in the fireplace and we can cuddle up."

"But what about my parents?" Robbie whispered.

"I'll give them some money and send them to the movies."

"It's nine in the morning."

"Oh, I know that," Trish nodded mysteriously.

"And?"

"I figured I'm good for about seven or maybe eight hours of foreplay. By then, there's bound to be a matinee somewhere."

"Are you trying to be a bad girl on purpose?"

"Uh huh."

Robbie shivered again.

"Come on, let's go get warm."

Trish made a fire like she had gotten a merit badge in her past. Then, she brought Robbie a bowl of her gourmet oatmeal. That, and a cup of tea, warmed her clear to her toes. By now, Rose was up and touring the house for something to do. Trish, while snuggling under a soft thermal blanket with Robbie, engaged Rose in a conversation about kitchen plans.

"Do you approve of the idea of having two ovens?"

Rose thought it over. "I could bake two pies at the same time."

"In that case, maybe we should get a couple more ovens?" Trish winked at Robbie.

"What are you going to do, host a bakeoff?" Robbie asked.

"That's a great idea! We could have a bakeoff and a chili cookoff and a-"

"I think we need a fully-functioning kitchen first."

"I agree. Aren't the contractors starting for real first thing in the morning?" Trish asked even though she knew the answer.

"Yes. I'm going to need a dust mask," Robbie stated firmly.

"I can go get a bunch for all of us today," Trish offered.

"Let's send Max," Rose volunteered his services.

"I have a good idea," Trish had been waiting for just such an opening, "Why don't you and Max go out to dinner tonight? My treat."

"You trying to get us out of the house?" Max asked from the doorway.

"Yes," Trish answered truthfully.

Everyone laughed and then Max, bless his heart, said, "How about we go now."

"It's a little early for dinner?" Rose checked her watch.

"Come on Rose. Let's go to the hardware store."

"The hardware store? Doesn't sound like an evening of entertainment to me."

"I'll buy a broom and sweep you off your feet."

"Isn't he romantic," Rose pretended to be thrilled.

As they headed out of the room, Trish reminded them, "Don't forget the dust masks and take Silver with you."

"Who will guard the two of you?"

"We'll manage."

Indeed they managed. They managed *quite* well. At first, Robbie was a bit hesitant to make love right out in the open, but she soon warmed to the idea. Part of the warming came directly from the cherrywood fire glowing in the fireplace. Most of the warming, however, was due to the tender attentions of Trish. Robbie was cozy and tingly all over.

"I didn't realize there was an echo in this old place," Trish remarked after the fact.

"Is there an echo?"

"Well, it's either that or a ghost," she teased.

Robbie didn't say anything. She just shivered again. Trish covered her with the comforter and then they chatted about nothing in particular until Robbie brought up the subject of decorating the nursery.

"I won't know whether to paint it pink or blue?"

"We'll know soon enough. We can have them do an ultrasound."

"I'm not sure I want one of those."

"I thought they were standard procedure."

"Do you think it's a good idea?"

"I'm not a doctor. I don't know anything about birthing babies."

"You best start learning!" Robbie gave her a look like they were going to deliver in a cab.

"I'll pay a doctor to follow you around the last trimester."

"You will not!' Robbie giggled and then winced.

"Are you okay?" Trish asked immediately.

"Sure, I just need to get up and move around a little. I'm cramping up."

"Okay," Trish gave her a hand up and then fetched her a glass of milk and a banana.

"You don't need to wait on me."

"Of course I do! You're the mother of my child. You just snap your fingers and I'm at your beck and call."

"I'm going to need some maternity clothes soon."

"I'll have someone bring a selection to the house."

"I'd rather go out shopping."

"Are you sure?"

"Yes, I'm sure. Are you ready?"

"You mean, *now*? Isn't it a bit early?"

"The stores opened at ten."

"I meant, isn't it early in your pregnancy? How will you know what size to get?"

"I'm sure the clerks in maternity will advise us."

"Okay. If that's what you want, we'll do it."

Robbie beamed at Trish. Her look said that she couldn't ask for a better mate.

They headed out about eleven- thirty. It took a while to put out the fire and straighten up the house, which Trish did while Robbie tried on a number of outfits to go shopping in. It had to be easy to take off and put on and still be dressy enough in case they ate lunch somewhere nice. Trish stuck with jeans and a flannel shirt. Robbie kept her own counsel.

Shopping for maternity clothes was an interesting adventure in and of itself. It went way past interesting when you were a lesbian couple. The first clerk in the first store looked from one to the other and asked, "Who's the pregnant one?" Robbie 'fessed up and Trish proceeded to explain that she was the father. Seeming just a tad haughty, the clerk indicated a rack of clothes far over in a corner and then scurried off to help someone else

who frankly had given no indication that they needed help. Trish
gave Robbie's arm a tug and they were out of there.
"Let's try somewhere else."
"Maybe you shouldn't tell people that you're the father?"
"I'm not going to allow people's petty prejudices to deter me
from enjoying every minute of your pregnancy."
"Our pregnancy."
"Our pregnancy."

The next clerk in the next store was much more helpful. She
didn't seem to mind who the father was, and proceeded to advise
Robbie on style, fit and price.
"Money's no object," Trish assured her.
"I know," the clerk answered honestly. "You're those famous
gay women who bought that creepy old house."
Trish didn't know if she agreed with the entire gist, but she
nodded anyway. Meanwhile, Robbie was in Maternity Clothes
Heaven. There were indeed some very flattering outfits to
choose from. Of course, the more flattering they were, the more
they cost.
"This is a lot of money to spend on something I'm only going to
wear for a couple of months."
"You'll need them longer than that."
"Are you saying that I'm going to be big after the pregnancy?"
"No. No. Not at all!" Trish hurried to explain. "I was just
thinking that, with luck, we might have several children."
"Let's get through these pregnancies one at a time, please,"
Robbie stated firmly.
"Pick out as many beautiful things as you want. Get something
different for every day of the last three months."
"I'm not getting ninety different outfits!" Robbie was adamant.
"Eighty?" Trish adjusted slightly downward.
Meanwhile, the clerk's eyes were lighting up with visions of
profits. She worked hard to bring over a wide selection of
clothing. After trying on three, Robbie was tired. Trish made
arrangements to have them, and seven more, delivered to the
house. They went to lunch and had simple fare, soup, salad and
snapper. Trish hoped that it would revive Robbie, but she just
didn't have her usual reserve of energy.

"Let's go home and take a nap," Trish suggested guilelessly.

"Good idea."

Which they did. As Trish rested alongside her bride, she wondered how life could get any better. Not one single way came to mind.

Chapter 29

Closing arguments weren't anything like they were on TV. On
TV, lawyers were stunningly eloquent with precise arguments
and cohesive persuasions. Here in Breadbasket, America, it
resembled more a book report read backwards. Not that the
lawyers didn't try to do their best, but without a raft of writers to
help, the speeches were more dithering than anything else.
They'd be lucky to convict a bologna sandwich. Mitch dozed off
twice already and was heading for a third nap when things
abruptly came to a halt. The jury filed out, their brains chock
full of instructions, evidence and testimony. It was too early for
lunch, so Reb suggested a walk, in a manner of speaking. She
and Mitch circled the grounds of the courthouse twice before the
jury was back. Everybody reconvened to hear the verdict,
especially the newspaper people who had followed the trial like
it was a wandering bucket of water in the Sahara. They were
admonished to keep still. No applause. No show of emotion of
any kind. No wailing or gnashing of teeth was to be tolerated.
No kidding. It was a whole lot of verbiage just so the jury
foreperson could read a simple sentence. Miranda was found
guilty. Just like that. Aunt BeBe didn't wail, but tears streamed
down her face. Uncle Henry looked like he'd been hit on the
back of the head with a cast-iron skillet. Mitch put her head in
her hands to hide the myriad of emotions she was feeling. Part
of what she felt was relief, but it was the anguish that she wished
to hide from Reb. Miranda was a product of her upbringing and
had never had a chance to escape. Maybe in this sad, sorry
fashion she was breaking free the only way she knew how.
"Why so glum. We won," Mary said.
Mitch looked up. "Nobody won."
Mary, Reb and Lisa exchanged looks. It was just like Mitch to
see things from all sides. The press took this opportunity to
descend on Rebecca, having been rebuffed by the next of kin of
the guilty party. As Rebecca held court with reporters, Mitch
went over to BeBe and Henry. They were huddled together like

Hansel and Gretel, looking every bit the part of two frightened children.

"Is there anything I can do to help?"

"Oh, you've done quite enough already!" BeBe snapped blindly. Mitch knew better than to take it personally.

"I think Miranda needs counseling, and you could probably use some as well."

"I'll thank you to stay out of our family business! Come, Henry!"

As they stood to leave, the spectators began to flow away from them in any opposite direction. The ostracism had begun. If anyone thought the burg of Utopia could be cruel to gay people, it was nothing compared to what it could do to its own. It didn't matter that BeBe and Henry were former pillars of the community. What a community can forge, a community can destroy.

Reb had extracted herself from the voracious media and rolled unimpeded up to Mitch.

"You ready to go?"

"I want to know where Miranda's going to end up."

"There will be a sentencing phase of the trial. You must have missed that part."

"I'll admit, I didn't hear much after the word 'guilty.'"

"My guess is that she'll be sent to the women's correctional facility in Weaver."

"How far away is that?"

"Three-hundred miles east of here."

"That's a long way away."

"Women's prisons are few and far between."

"Henry and BeBe will have a long drive to visit her."

"It will give them time to talk."

Mitch didn't have a glib reply. In fact, she was clear out of glibness. "Let's go."

An entire week went by without incident. Miranda was being help in the county lockup pending her sentencing hearing. Construction began in earnest on the new homestead. Polly

Perkell was due in town the following Sunday. Utopia was atwitter. You couldn't buy a bag of groceries without hearing the gush. About the only two venues that were big enough to hold a performance by the world-famous Ms. Perkell were the fairgrounds and the high school gym. So, it wasn't the Met. Or the Grand Ole Opry. Viewpoints weren't the only thing narrow in a small town. Choices were right up there.

"Loretta Lynn probably got her start playing fairgrounds," Mitch remarked to Reb over breakfast mid week.

"Polly Perkell isn't just getting her start. She's already past famous."

"So, that rules out the fairgrounds, I take it."

"You haven't been paying attention, have you?"

"Nope, not really."

"The performance will be Sunday afternoon at the high school."

"I guess that's meant to put a damper on our little Sunday afternoon socials."

"Nothing gets past you after two cups of coffee, huh?"

Mitch smiled. She did depend on her coffee.

"Maybe we should forget about our party and go to theirs instead."

"You want to go to the party that's been designed solely to make our lives miserable?"

"Nobody but us can truly make our lives miserable."

"Try telling that to Lisa," Reb shot back.

"Lisa's life isn't miserable. She has your daughter for a partner and a luxurious trailer. She's about three-thousand and thirty-six miles away from miserable."

"And how many miles away from miserable are you?"

"A million billion."

"Just a million billion? Only a million billion?"

"A million billion three-thousand and thirty-six miles."

"That's more like it."

"Whew!" Mitch exhaled an exaggerated breath of relief.

"Are you going to try and see Miranda? Again?"

The emphasis on "again" was not lost of Mitch. She had tried and failed to visit Miranda twice before and was rebuffed by rules, regulations and relatives.

"No."

The brevity of the answer put a sudden end to that particular topic.

"So, what do you have planned for the day?"

"Maybe I'll go out and see if the construction crew needs my help."

"Just don't hit your thumb with a hammer. You don't look good in black and blue."

In truth, Mitch wasn't much help and didn't pretend otherwise. About the only thing accomplished by Mitch being outside was that it kept her out of Reb's way. Trailer living was great, to a point. And they were getting past that point. This new house needed to rise out of the dust. And soon. Which it was. Mitch was truly impressed by how quickly the project was going. One of the more complex issues was the electricity. Houses today could be wired for computers. If Mitch ever decided to start a dot com, at least the *house* would be ready. Mitch was back in the trailer at 10:45, wondering about lunch. Reb gave her a look. "It's times like this I wish the trial was still going on," Reb did her best to grumble in the general direction of the sight of Mitch rummaging around in the fridge.

"You know you love it when I forage for food."

"It's the highlight of my day."

"I could go try to see Miranda again?"

"By all means rummage."

By 11:15, Mitch had rummaged up some linguini drenched in butter and garnished with shrimp. Reb gave it one of her, "Just exactly which part of this is healthy" looks but ate her fair share of it.

"Not bad for a week's worth of calories and cholesterol all in one meal," Reb admitted.

"I promise to eat nothing but greens for the rest of the week."

"Does that include guacamole?"

"Hell yes!"

It had to have been Mitch's imagination, but she could've sworn that she heard more and louder excited buzzing as the end of the week approached. Good thing people as important as Polly

165

Perkell didn't come to town every week. This burg just wouldn't be able to handle it. Thankfully, Sunday rolled around and everyone who was inclined to do so went to early church. Then, folks made a beeline over to the high school so they could maybe get a glimpse of Polly before the show. This just wasn't some piddling deal here. Polly had some big bucks. The sound system toted around for her show was bigger than anything this old gymnasium had seen.

Mitch, Rebecca, Mary and Lisa caused somewhat of a stir when they took their place in the audience, but due to the size of the crowd, folks still had to sit close to them. That must've been torture. Jessie was in the aisle seat in the same row and waved nonchalantly to them. A tingle told Mitch that it was like the Five Musketeers. Being on the same side as Jessie was a good feeling. She'd take one Jessie over five Pollys any day of the week.

With a flourish, Polly swept onstage at exactly one o'clock. Her first number was rousing, her second was slower and by the third, Mitch was fending off sleep. Then, the sermon began. Overall, it was pretty ugly stuff in its intent. All sorts of jabber about those nasty gays and lesbians wanting to destroy everything and God, too. It dawned on Mitch that Ms. Perkell maybe hadn't a clue that she and Reb were in the audience. How could that possibly have happened? If Polly was in clueless land, Jessie was now on her feet, ready to change any misconceptions.

What happened next unfolded like a dream in slow motion. At first, Jessie hollered to be heard and then, as her words carried, the crowd grew quieter.
"What y'all don't know," Jessie was proclaiming at the top of her voice, "Is that we have a genuine miracle worker in our midst."
For a split second, everyone was thoroughly confused. Polly Perkell was billed as a singer, not necessarily a saint. Jessie soon cleared things up.
"Mitch Tanner is a faith healer!"

Right then and there, Mitch started to hear that buzzing in her ears, and figured she was a serious contender for tinnitus. Everyone craned to look as Jessie went on.

"She healed my sister of cancer! And a couple of other people as well! So, before you listen to any more of the mean things being said here today, you should know that Mitch has the healing touch of Jesus!!!"

Dear God in heaven.

Polly Perkell was not used to being interrupted, let alone upstaged. She put her microphone down with a thud and swept off the stage in a queen-size huff. Lucinda Cornwall was torn for a moment between two competing actions. In her efficient way, she chose the easier task to take care of first. She went right up to Mitch, shook a finger in her face like they were back in first grade and spat, "I'm not through with you yet."

Then, she turned and scurried off in the general direction of her bought and paid for star. Mitch only knew one thing. She liked her chances out here with the mob a lot better than Lucinda's with Hurricane Perkell.

Meanwhile, the buzzing had died down and was replaced by rapt stares of curiosity. There was honestly no other way to describe it. Mitch had made her way over to Jessie by now and asked her the first thing that popped into her head, "You want to go and get some fresh air?"

Jessie, who had finally realized how deep an impact her announcement had made, nodded. Mitch gave Reb and the rest of her group the plan via nonverbal means and then walked slowly to the back door of the gym with Jessie in tow. As they were doing so, Mitch checked out the stares. On balance, they were more curious than angry, and it surprised her. She figured that they'd be furious with them for putting the Polly Perkell show on the skids.

Once outside, Mitch steered Jessie to a shady spot and they sat together on a bench. They were quiet for a moment. It was restful. At least, that's how it felt to Mitch.

"I don't blame you if you're mad at me," Jessie said.
She had interpreted the silence between them as anger. Mitch
was quick to assure.
"I'm not mad at you at all," Mitch smiled. "I'm just a little in
shock, I guess. What made you do that in there?"
"Because I just couldn't sit there one more second and listen to
that horrible woman make up all those terrible lies about you and
your family. She's got some nerve!"
"So, you decided to make up a story?"
"What story?"
"The story about me being some kind of faith healer."

They had been talking so intensely that it was only now that
Mitch caught a glimpse of the approaching Lucinda. Maybe it
was just the light of day, but Mrs. Cornwall was white as milk.
She blurted out, "Mrs. Perkell wants to see the both of you *now*!"
It sounded like a command. Mitch did the unthinkable. She
questioned the realm.
"Why?"
"Well, to *explain* yourselves, of course!"
"That could take some time," was all Mitch could think of to say
in reply.
"Mrs. Perkell is waiting!"

Everything that came out of Lucinda's mouth sounded like a
command, and Mitch fought the urge to behave like a loyal
servant.
"We'll be there in a few minutes," Mitch said.
"You'll be there *now*!"
"Where's the meeting?" Jessie asked, all too happy to have
another shot at Polly.
"In the principal's office."
"Come on, let's go!" Jessie jumped up. This, too, was
disconcerting to Lucinda. Apparently, she was supposed to be
fetching sniveling apologists and neither Jessie nor Mitch fit the
profile. Since no one had left the gym, it was safe to assume that
everyone had been told to stay in their seats and that the concert
would continue as planned after a short intermission. Everyone
had apparently obeyed, except, of course, Reb, Mary and Lisa.

They crossed paths with Mitch and Jessie about midway to the office.

"Everything okay?" Reb sought and held Mitch's eye.

"It will be."

Lucinda reverently opened the door like she expected strobes of light to shoot out and strike her dead. Mitch caught the nuance. She and Jessie weren't the only ones in deep trouble.

Polly Perkell was one of those performers who, frankly, was two people. Her on-stage persona was the grander of the two. Offstage, she wasn't nearly so impressive. At least, not to Mitch. But she did have a steely glare that, no doubt, she had been directing Lucinda's way for moments unending. No wonder Lucinda was more than happy to provide newer, fresher targets. They weren't asked to sit down, but Mitch took the initiative, holding a chair for Jessie and then corralling another for herself. Polly had commandeered the principal's chair. He was nowhere to be seen. Lucky guy.

"I'm not in the habit of having my performances interrupted by trash like you!" was the opening salvo.

Gee, Mitch thought to herself. Whatever happened to a simple "Hello?"

"And I don't let people like you stand around and say nasty lies about my friends. I don't care who you are!" Jessie was good at fighting back.

"It's obvious you don't care who your friends are," Lucinda tossed in snidely.

This drew a look from Polly. It was one of those, "Shut the hell up. I'm handling this," kind of looks.

Lucinda shut her mouth. Mitch wondered if she could learn this trick. To Mitch, and company, Polly stated, "I must speak the word of Jesus as God as I see fit."

"You wouldn't know the word of Jesus if it served you a piece of pie," Jessie came right back at her in diner lingo.

"Dear child, I recite the word of Jesus as God in my sleep. Don't tell me I don't know what I'm talking about."

"Well, if you know so much, then you know that Jesus never had an unkind word to say about gay folks."

Undaunted, Polly changed the subject. She was one of those people who probably got straight A's in debate.

"You have blasphemed the glory of God by claiming that this vermin has healing powers. You must confess your sin and hope for the mercy of Jesus as Savior."

When Mitch heard the word "vermin," it finally dawned on her that this woman actually believed everything she said. Until now, it had seemed like an act. Now, it was real. As Mitch mused about this, Jessie carried on the fight.

"I have only told the truth! Go ahead, Mitch. Tell her about all the people you've healed. Go on."

This was the exact point that they were at a few minutes ago in the shade of the old oak tree. Mitch was still confused and thoroughly unconvinced that she had any kind of power, let alone a healing touch. But to argue with Jessie now would undermine the brave stand she had taken.

"Well, uh-" was all Mitch got out before Jessie took over again. Thankfully.

"She healed my sister of cancer and it wasn't no little bit of cancer either! It was a big, big cancer. The kind you just don't bounce back from like a teenager!!"

"Cancer goes into remission," Lucinda replied coldly, like she was somehow really unhappy that Jessie's sister hadn't gone ahead and died and saved her all this trouble.

"And it isn't just my sister, either!" Jessie was getting a full head of steam now. "She cured a Jewish guy of a heart attack!"

Mitch had to think fast. She was talking about Max. She didn't remember mentioning anything about Max to Jessie.

Meanwhile, Polly had a look on her face that suggested that it didn't count if Jews were involved.

"People get over heart attacks on a daily basis," she huffed. "All you need is oatmeal!"

Easy for her to say, Mitch thought as she recalled her time with Max. He had appeared so ill for a time that it had shaken her to her core. And now, he was going to be a granddad. In spite of the present circumstances, she smiled. Max and Rose as grandpa and grandma was a pleasant thought.

"You think this is funny!" Lucinda bellowed straight into Mitch's reverie.

"No, I think it's interesting."

"And then, there was Mrs. Johnson!"

"Who?" Mitch had to ask.

"You remember? The lady who was hurt when the tornado rolled her car."

"Oh yeah," Mitch nodded. Vaguely.

"She was in real bad shape with brain damage and everything. You told me you went to see her."

"Late one night…"

"And the next morning she was up and around like nothing had ever happened."

Mitch had three simultaneous thoughts, a record for her. First, Jessie had been paying attention. Second, there was a discernable pattern of healing. The third thought was the one she had to give voice to before things got truly out of hand.

"Jess, there's something that we need to consider here."

"What?"

"If I have healing powers, why haven't I been able to heal Rebecca?"

The question had a different effect on all parties present. Polly was gloating. She didn't know who Rebecca was right off the top of her head, but that didn't matter. Any chink in the armor was welcome at this point. Lucinda was beaming. As far as she was concerned, Rebecca could stay in her wheelchair forever. It would serve her right. Jessie was in denial.

"I've been reading about this," she argued, "not that the library has a lot of books on this subject, mind you. There are cases where faith healers are able to cure some people and not others." Mitch had always chalked that up to the quality of pretenders that charlatans were able to bribe, but kept her mouth shut.

"And then, there's Lisa."

"But, she's been able to get better by herself," Mitch said gently.

It was painfully obvious that Jessie absolutely believed in what she was saying and wouldn't be talked out of it. Polly took advantage of the lull. She jumped back into the conversation, directing her venom at Mitch.

"So, you admit that you're a fraud!" she went for the kill.

"No," Mitch countered, "I don't admit anything. I think we need to take some time and examine the events that Jessie has been kind enough to bring to our attention."

Polly wasn't in the mood for brokering a deal. She got up from her borrowed chair and crossed over to them.

"You're going to go out on that stage and retract everything you said," she was practically towering over them.

"No," was Jessie's one-word reply.

"No?" Polly couldn't believe what she had heard. Maybe nobody had tested the word out on her. There was a first time for everything.

"You heard her," Mitch backed up Jessie's decision. "The woman said 'no.'"

"You're making a grave mistake," Polly sounded ominous.

"I don't think so," Jessie raised up her entire five-foot-two frame and met Polly's stare with one of her own. Lucinda shifted from one foot to the other. Maybe she was expecting a lighting strike and needed to be ready to jump. More likely, she was aware that the crowd in the gym would be growing impatient and there was still the appeal that she wanted Polly to make to bolster the strength and number of the protestors. It was the original reason for bringing her all this way and time was wasting.

With a huff, Polly swept out the door, followed closely by Lucinda. To avoid being in their wake, Mitch and Jessie hung back. So much so that Reb poked her head into the room.

"Everything okay in here?"

"Oh, yeah. We're okay."

"Polly doesn't look so good," Reb reported, "and Lucinda is running a close second."

"I can imagine. Maybe this would be a good time to head home."

"You don't want to stay for the rest of the show?" Mary asked.

172

"I figure we've heard enough, haven't we?" Mitch looked from person to person. Everyone nodded. Halfway to the car, Jessie blurted, "I forgot my sweater vest."

"In the office?"

"No, in the gym," she grimaced.

"I'll get it," Mitch offered.

"I can wait and pick it up tomorrow."

"It's okay. It might get lost by then."

"You sure you want to go back in there?"

"Sure. Why not?" Mitch seemed disconnected to recent events. Jessie didn't reply, but she had a look on her face to suggest that Mitch was the Christians and the lions were waiting in the gym.

"I'll be right back.

Mitch walked with leisurely pace toward the gym. At the door was the ticket taker, but she didn't even need to show her stub. He even opened the door for her. Perhaps the order had gone out to facilitate any sign of apology on her part. After all, she couldn't apologize from outside the door. When Mitch had sprung for four tickets to this alleged concert, she had paid a pretty good price for them. It was clear that Jessie had done the same. That they were in the same row near the front was quite the coincidence. Now, that meant that she had to walk almost all the way to the front of the seating to retrieve the vest. It took only a moment to realize that everyone, and I mean everyone, was watching her instead of Polly. It was downright eerie, because they weren't looking at her in a mean way, but rather with wonderment. Mitch slowed to a stop about halfway to the stage and looked around. Every eye was on her. Every head turned her way. The room became deathly quiet and it dawned on Mitch that Polly was deathly quiet as well. Oh, yeah, and one other thing. Polly was turning a lovely shade of mad-as-hell red. Not being the center of attention was a real big issue with her. She'd need therapy after this little sojourn to Utopia.

Mitch resumed walking, willing her feet to move at a normal pace. She retrieved the sweater vest with as little a flourish as possible. As she turned to leave, a voice boomed out. It was only Polly and her best friend, the microphone, asking a question.

"Do you have something to say to everyone?"

"I forgot the vest," was all that came out of Mitch.

She continued her exit, walking only a pace or two before the strangest thing happened. A woman on the aisle reached out to touch the vest. Mitch didn't pull away, for she knew instinctively the gesture was benign. Then, another person wanted to touch the vest as well. And then another. Someone else reached out to touch Mitch's hand and another took hold of it like they were going to kiss it. It was, without a doubt, one of the strangest moments in Mitch's life. Obviously, all this talk about faith healing had gone to everyone's head. She reached the door and turned to take one last look. Everyone was paying rapt attention. Mitch waved and said, "Y'all go back to what you were doing."

She fought the urge to run once she cleared the building, mostly because she wasn't eighteen anymore. Still, she hurried to the car and nearly ordered Reb to gun it like they were in the getaway car.

"I told Jessie to follow us home and we'd have dinner."

"Good idea."

Mitch checked for Jessie and saw that she was right behind them. What she also saw was some people coming out of the gym and heading post haste to their cars. By the time they were on the road home, there was a convoy behind them. Polly's directive must've worked, the crowds were going to be even bigger. Sheesh.

They all obeyed the speed limit over the bumpy roads and arrived in good shape. All one-hundred of them. And counting.

The party of five disembarked and stretched like they had been traveling for hours. It had to be the tension creeping into their muscles. Mitch always had enough dinner for one more and she attempted to begin cooking, but her concentration kept hovering toward the new group who had assembled by the fence. Reb noticed the distracted Mitch.

"It's quite a group, isn't it?" Reb made small talk.

"It's different."

174

"What do you mean?"

"Come on, I'll show you."

Mitch helped Reb to approach the gate in her wheelchair. They were quite the pair. A purported faith healer and a paraplegic. Everyone was quiet, respectful, in awe. These weren't protestors. They were a brand new fan club.

"Hi, hello," was Mitch's brilliant opening statement.

Nobody said anything back. It was like the Stepford Townspeople.

"Thanks for…uh…following us home. We got here safe and sound. You all can go on back home now."

"Is it true you heal people?" a voice from the back traveled over the crowd.

Mitch was circumspect. "I don't know anything about healing and maybe even less about faith. I'm happy that some people are better. I wish everyone would get better. But I don't think I have anything to do with it. And if I do, I don't understand how or why."

If it was possible for an entire crowd to shift from one foot to the other, this was as close as you could get to the phenomenon. Folks were weighing Mitch's words carefully. They so achingly wanted to believe and hadn't heard anything to quash their hope. Mitch felt a tug at her sleeve. It was Reb. "As long as they're all here, ask them to next Sunday's brunch."

"Good idea!" Mitch nodded and then raised her voice again so all could hear. "Come over next Sunday for brunch after church."

"Late church?" someone asked.

"Any church!" Mitch answered with a smile.

Then, she helped Reb go back to the trailer. Even as they finished eating dinner, the crowd lingered outside. They didn't disperse until nightfall and then only reluctantly. Jessie had picked her way through the crowd not long after dinner and Mary and Lisa quietly headed to their trailer after helping with the dishes. For once, it was nice to just sit and relax.

"You were awfully quiet during dinner. Are you going to be okay with all of this?" Reb asked with a touch and a smile. It was that smile that made the world spin for Mitch. Every time.

"I don't know," Mitch replied honestly.

"Jessie is convinced."

"I know. I can't believe the coincidence myself."

"It may not be."

"What? A coincidence?"

"It might be for real."

"Honey, if I was some sort of faith healer, you would have been walking months ago."

"Maybe it doesn't work like that."

"What do you mean?"

"Have you stopped to consider that maybe you've healed me in other ways?"

"Other ways?"

"You healed my heart of prejudice. That's no small thing."

"Oh, I'm sure you would have come around sooner or later."

"I'm not sure. It was like you lifted a veil from my eyes."

"Well, don't tell Jessie. She'll start telling people I can cure the blind."

"I promise not to breathe a word."

"Thank you."

The morning sun was pesky. It stirred Mitch awake, albeit late. She wandered out to the kitchen where Reb was having a cup of coffee.

"Morning," Reb greeted succinctly.

"I slept in."

"That's good. You're going to need your sleep."

"I am?" Mitch smiled. It was one of those silly things that perpetual newlyweds said to each other to portend certain activities. Certain fun activities. But, gee, wasn't it kind of early in the day? Mitch hadn't even had her coffee yet.

"Look out the window," Reb instructed.

Mitch puzzled over the statement. Like we said, she hadn't had her coffee yet. She wandered over to the kitchen window and peered out.

"Oh, my God. What is going on now?"

"My guess is, *you*," Reb summed up.

Mitch looked again. There had to be five-hundred people out there. Plus a TV crew. With a satellite dish. This was nuts.

"At least they aren't protesting," Mitch pointed out as she poured herself a cup of coffee. "You need a warm-up?"

"Sure," Reb nodded.

Mitch brought the pot over to the table and drained it into Reb's cup.

"When did they show up?"

"They were out there when I got up."

"And you didn't wake me?"

"Like I said, you needed your sleep."

It dawned on Mitch that something was bothering Reb.

"You're upset."

"I'm worried."

"About what?"

"About five-hundred people standing vigil fifty yards away."

"They came in peace."

"On a Monday? It's Monday morning, for goodness sake. People go to work on Monday mornings. They don't go out and stand by someone's front gate to gawk!"

"If it bothers you that much, I'll go out and get rid of them."

"You think you can?" Reb was thoroughly unconvinced.

"I can try."

With barely half a cup of coffee under her belt, Mitch went out the door. There was sudden and rapt silence. She walked over to the gate, scanning the crowd for any familiar faces. There were none. As Mitch pondered her speech, someone yelled from a few rows back, "You healed me!"

"I'm sorry," Mitch strained to hear, "What was that?"

The crowd parted to let a woman to the front. It was the same lady who had touched Jessie's sweater vest yesterday.

"I'm cured. You cured me."

"I don't think so," Mitch was trying to let her down gently.

"Oh, but you did. I had an infection and the doctors had given me every medicine they could think of and now because I was able to touch your clothing, I was cured!"

How was Mitch going to ever explain to this dear sweet woman that first of all, her infection was probably viral in nature and probably went away on its own and besides it wasn't even her clothing. It was Jessie's sweater.

"I'm glad that you're feeling better," Mitch started out before a reporter descended on the interaction. There was a camera and a microphone and everything.

"Is it true that you can heal people?" was question number one.

"Who are you?" Mitch countered with a question of her own, mostly to stall for time.

"Pam Tracy, Channel Eleven News."

"Don't I know your brother, Dick?" Mitch asked with a straight face. In an audience of 500, nobody laughed. Apparently, faith healers weren't supposed to have a sense of humor.

"Are you a faith healer, Ms. Tanner?"

"Not that I know of."

"All these people seem to think so. Are they wrong?"

Gee, Mitch thought to herself. Pam Tracy really knew how to put a girl on the spot. Maybe it was the Dick joke?

"Everyone is entitled to their beliefs, Ms. Tracy, and I believe this interview is over."

Mitch walked back and forth along the fence for a few minutes, making it impossible for Pam to track her. She smiled and shook people's hands, listened to their stories and patted small children on the head. Then, she waved and went back to the trailer.

"What's for breakfast?" she asked matter-of-factly.

"Are they going away anytime soon?" Reb snapped.

"I assume so."

"You didn't ask them to leave?"

"That wouldn't be very polite, now would it."

"I get it now. You're actually enjoying this, aren't you?"

"Well, the reporter part wasn't exactly a barrel of laughs. Otherwise, it's okay."

"That's no ordinary reporter," Reb looked out the window. "That's Pam Tracy!"

"So?"

"*The* Pam Tracy. She's big around these parts. You didn't say anything stupid, did you?"

"Does a Dick joke count?" Mitch thought it sounded worse put that way.

"Pam Tracy comes all the way out here and you make Dick jokes? What else did you do?"

"I terminated the interview before it got started."

"Some people wait all their lives for an interview with Pam Tracy!"

"They should know that the experience is terribly overrated."

The contractors had arrived late for work, which was alright with Mitch. She could only imagine the traffic jam. When they came on the scene, Mitch went out in her jeans and flannel shirt to offer help. As the days had gone by these past months, Mitch had thinned down. It was all that farm work. She was perilously close to being photogenic. As she milled around, trying her best to look helpful, it began to dawn on her that there needed to be provisions made for the crowd. They would need food. And water. And a place to sit down once in a while. And every other necessity that human beings needed. She asked the contractors where they could find a more adequate number of portable restrooms. They only had one. It wasn't enough. Arrangements were made. It wasn't cheap, but it would be doable. And since no one who came to the Fairbanks farm went away hungry or thirsty, Mitch began to make plans for that as well. She went into the trailer and began to fill up all their two pitchers with water and scrounged as many glasses as she could find. By now, Mary and Lisa had gathered around the kitchen table.

"I suppose you have a plan for all that water?" Reb asked like she knew the answer already.

"People look thirsty."

"I see."

"You want some help with that?" Lisa was positively cheerful. Mitch looked at her carefully. She was healing nicely. Very nicely.

"All I can get," Mitch smiled back. "You don't mind?"

"Got nuthin better to do," Lisa assured her.

In a way, it was nice to have a crowd to tend to, now that the trial was over. Otherwise, they'd just be getting on each other's nerves. They carried their pitiful offering out to the crowd and apologized for the lack of glasses. Pam Tracy was probably memorializing this for posterity. It took several trips back and forth and a lot of glass washing to even make a dent in the thirst of the crowd. During one of the first trips, Mitch opened the gate to permit use of the construction worker's facilities.

"We're going to need a case of toilet tissue at this rate," Mitch said out loud to Lisa, hoping she would act as a human shopping list.

"Write it down," Lisa advised.

Mitch nodded. She was going to need a big piece of paper. Tissue, paper cups, and food. Lots and lots of food.

After doing a sufficient number of trips with water, Mitch went inside and settled at the kitchen table with the phone and phone book. It never ceased to amaze her how quickly things could be arranged when you had money. Within the hour, there would be pizza, chicken, burgers, pop and tea delivered to the farm. To her relief, the portable restrooms were also on the way. Reb had observed the goings on in silence. Pretty soon, even Mitch caught on. About five questions came to mind, but none seemed adequate.

"You want to just tell me what you're thinking?" was Mitch's final choice.

"Pizza for five-hundred?"

"Actually, pizza for two-hundred, burgers for two-hundred and chicken for the rest. Which reminds me, I'd better order five-hundred donuts for tomorrow."

As Mitch reached for the phone, Reb caught her hand. She had an unusual look on her face.

"You think they'll be back tomorrow?"

"I don't know. But I'd rather have food just in case."

"Five-hundred donuts?"

"Not enough? You're probably right. Maybe I'd better get a thousand?"

"And what if nobody shows up?"

"We'll make a full pot of coffee to wash down all that sugar."

Reb still had hold of Mitch's hand. It was suddenly very distracting. Eye contact was inevitable.

"Better make it a thousand, just to be on the safe side," Reb gave her seal of approval.

Mitch nodded. "This won't last long. Pretty soon, we'll be able to get back to life as usual."

"Life with you is never usual," Reb patted her arm. "That's why I'm still here."

"I'll do my best to always stay unusual just for you."

"I'll hold you to it."

Mitch gave the town baker a jolt and then went out to the crowd. "We're making arrangements for food and facilities for everyone. I hope you all don't get too tired out here." People sort of rustled around at the news. Mitch felt sorry for them. They were waiting on a vigil that frankly wasn't worth it. As people reached out to touch her, she obliged. She shook as many hands as she could reach and talked to folks she had never met before. The conversations were finally interrupted by the incoming feast on wheels. The crowd was orderly for a bunch of hungry people. Even Pam Tracy indulged. It was fun to watch a supposed icon of the television media industry munching down on a double deep fried drumstick. By four o'clock, many who had arrived early in the morning had drifted away. Those who had been in the back had filtered to the front and Mitch had taken time to say hello to most of them. At four-thirty, she sent the contractors on their way home and went inside to rest. Reb was ready with her robe, slippers and a cup of Earl Grey tea. It was a soothing treat. They snuggled together on the couch to watch the TV news. Mitch was the lead story. She nearly spilled her tea. Pam Tracy had stayed very busy all day conducting interviews of the "healed." The list was growing, and along with it, Mitch's miraculous reputation. The phone rang. It was Trish. A pleasant surprise.

"You're on the news!" was the "hello" for today.

"Even where you are?" Mitch asked lamely.

"It's national, Sweetie. What is going on out there? It looks like the cast of thousands from the Ten Commandments."

"That's how it feels. In winter vernacular, things have snowballed."

"More like an avalanche," Reb put in her comments too quietly for Trish to hear. Mitch got the drift.

"They are saying that you have some kind of healing power?"

"I don't"

"Are they talking about Max?"

Mitch sort of got that familiar "Uh-Oh" feeling in the pit of her stomach. Jessie had mentioned him as an example.

"I haven't been," Mitch split hairs.

"Well, maybe they should! He did have a miraculous recovery after your visit. You should see him! He chops wood and fixes things around here. You wouldn't believe he was on his death bed a few weeks ago."

Mitch didn't pray often, but she now prayed that no one, absolutely no one, was listening in on this phone conversation.

"You still there, Mitch?"

"Yes, I'm here. You don't actually believe all this stuff about healing powers, do you?"

"Honey, it doesn't matter what I think. All I know is that Max was dying and now he's better. If it was one isolated case, it would be different. But, according to Pam Tracy, there are all kinds of current examples."

"It's all coincidental, trust me."

"How's Reb holding out?"

"She's more than ready to have our new house built so she can buff up in the exercise room."

"And Lisa?"

"She's healing, and not at a miraculous pace, I can tell you!"

"I know. We saw snatches of her on the news. She's still in the plastic bubble."

"And will be for quite some time. I told her that she could be a Martian for Halloween."

"And what did she say?"

"My mommy told me to never repeat language like that."

They both got to giggling at this purely fictional story. Each knew that it was total fabrication. Mitch would've never told Lisa to go as a Martian. However, had she done so, Lisa would've no doubt said something salty in response.

"How's Robbie?" Mitch wedged in a question of her own.

"She's going along," Trish replied.

"Is it hard to be pregnant?" Mitch followed up, clueless to the entire experience.

"She's doing fine. We are going in for an ultrasound as soon as the doctor thinks it's going to be useful."

"An ultrasound? Is everything okay?"

"Oh, sure. Ultrasounds are pretty standard anymore. They do some looking around, you know, to make sure there aren't twins or triplets."

"And if there are?"

"We'll be ready."

Mitch nodded. No one would be more ready for triplets than Trish and Robbie. Mitch felt a slight twinge of envy, which she quickly buried in a hollow spot in her mind. Five- hundred people had come to stand in awe of her and she could hardly wait to buy baby clothes for her best friend's pending baby.

"Are you going to find out the sex of the baby so I can know whether to buy pink or blue?"

"Buy yellow. And orange. And deep purple if you can find it. We want a lot of variety."

"Consider it done."

"But don't go overboard."

"What? ME? Go overboard!"

"Yes, YOU. Don't go overboard!"

"That's my job."

Again with the giggling. They said their good-byes reluctantly and hung up. Thankfully, they had chatted clear through the portion of the newscast devoted to Miracle Mitch. The phone rang again. It was Dick's sister, Pam.

"How would you like to give me an exclusive on your day?" was her cheery question.

"An exclusive what?" Mitch asked.

"Interview, of course."

Mitch looked over at Reb. "Pam Tracy wants to come do a story."

Reb didn't say anything, but she had one of those, "You've already made up your mind, what are you asking me for," expressions on her face.

"Well, what do you say?" Pam was the impatient type.

183

Mitch exhaled, and if somehow this was a capitulation. "Sure. Why not."

"I'll be there in a few minutes with a crew."

"A what?"

"A crew. A camera crew."

"A camera crew?"

"Well, you didn't think I was going to bring crayons and paper, did you?"

Maybe it was just the smart alec quality of the answer, but Mitch made a snap decision. "No cameras." She could already hear the accusation – "Refused to be interviewed on camera." Tough.

"No cameras?" Pam asked in a pouty way, like that would make Mitch change her mind.

"Do you want your interview or not? I'm going to bed soon."

The phone clicked in Mitch's ear. Apparently, that was "yes" in reporter talk. Mitch checked in with Reb again.

"Thanks for not allowing cameras," she patted Mitch's arm. It would never be seen through Mitch's eyes the terrible toll Reb's paralysis was taking on her body. She was blind to all but Reb's stubborn beauty. Her selective vision was rewarded with a kiss. A really, really nice kiss.

"Well, now I'm damn angry that I agreed to this interview."

"Don't worry," Reb reassured. "I won't forget how to kiss in the meantime."

Further sensuous chit chat was interrupted by a knock at the door. Pam must've jogged. Mitch answered the door. It was Pam and her trusty tape recorder.

"No tape recorders either!" Mitch demanded, just because she could.

"But-"

"No tape recorders!" Mitch repeated.

Pam was one of those women who just got sexier looking the angrier she became. She was close to smoldering. This might get interesting, in a platonic sort of way.

"I can't take notes very fast."

"I talk slow."

Pam frowned, but left the tape recorder just outside on the step. Mitch motioned her into the trailer and toward a chair before picking up the tape recorder and tossing it a few yards down the path.

"That's a very expensive piece of equipment," she said in exaggerated importance.

"I'll buy you a new one. Would you like something to drink?"

"No."

"Have you met Rebecca?"

"Not formally."

"Pam, Reb, Reb, Pam," Mitch covered the niceties quickly.

"Senator Fairbanks," Pam extended her hand in that interesting hybrid way. Not quite vertical, like a man, and not quite horizontal, like the Queen. She took hold of Reb's hand and acted like she wasn't going to let go anytime soon. Gosh, where was a cattle prod when you really needed one? Mitch wondered.

"Have a seat," Mitch guided Pam more forcefully toward the pre-assigned chair. It was comfy enough.

"Thanks, now about these miracles-"

"You sure you don't want some coffee? Or tea? Or scotch straight up?"

Pam appeared disinterested until she heard about the scotch.

"Two fingers."

"Sure."

Mitch ambled over to the kitchen, all twenty feet of expanse, and took as much time as humanly possible pouring an inch of scotch into a glass. Suddenly, Pam didn't seem to be in any rush. She was content to be in the confines of the House of Fairbanks, and amused herself by memorizing Reb's face. Every square inch of it. Mitch noticed and blocked Pam's view as she delivered the drink and then sat close enough to Reb to deliver the silent but crystal clear message of "She's my woman, keep your eyeballs in their sockets." It wasn't like Mitch to be jealous and envious all in the same day. Maybe the strain was getting to her after all.

"Are you sure you're up to an interview?" Pam surprised her with a humanitarian question.

"I'm tired, but I'm always up to talking about myself."

Reb stifled a giggle, and Pam smiled wide. Gee, her teeth were pretty. Her folks were probably still paying off the orthodontist.

"So, tell me how all this stuff about miracles got started."

"I don't know."

"You don't know?"

"No."

"You weren't there?"

Maybe Mitch was too tired for this interview. They seemed to
be going around in circles.

"Where?"

"When you performed your first miracle healing."

"I've never done that."

"What?"

"I've never healed anyone."

"People beg to differ. There are at least three documented
cases."

"There are no documented cases."

"So, you deny your powers?"

This was all beginning to sound like the lovely conversation she
had with Polly and Lucinda.

"I don't know what to do," Mitch was brutally honest.

"Do you think you have healing powers?"

"I don't know. I would have never given it a second thought had
it not been for a friend of ours."

"The Polly Perkell incident. I heard about that."

"You and a few dozen other people."

"Try a few hundred dozen other people."

"No way!"

"Oh yes! You breaking up the Polly Perkell show was a big
deal. A very big deal."

"It wasn't planned that way."

"You didn't put Jessie up to it?"

"No, Ma'am," Mitch knew one thing. Pam had done her
homework.

"Are you willing to undergo a test of your powers?"

"No."

"That was quick. Are you afraid?"

"What would I be afraid of?"

"Disappointing the masses gathering at your doorstep, perhaps?"

Mitch had to stop and think about that possibility. Was any
fraction of her self-image tied up in their spontaneous awe?

"I feel that the only way I could disappoint them would be to not
be a good host to them."

186

"What does that mean?"

"I want to make sure that they have enough to eat, enough to drink. That sort of thing."

"The miracle of the loaves and fishes?"

"More like the miracle of the coffee and donuts."

"Tell me about that."

"You like donuts, Ms. Tracy?" Mitch replied in question form.

"I've had my share."

"You sure couldn't tell it."

That much was fact. Pam had the perfect figure. Perfect weight, perfect body type, perfect teeth. Which she now flashed again.

"Can you clear up one other thing for me?"

"If I can."

"The woman whom you cured first."

"I haven't cured anyone," Mitch reminded again. This was getting old, but necessary.

"Right, but the one I want to ask about was the woman with the head injury."

"Mrs. Johnson."

"Why did you go to the hospital?"

"I don't understand your question?" Mitch stalled for time.

"You went to the hospital to visit a total stranger. Why?"

Mitch looked at Reb and then back at Pam. She shrugged her shoulders. This was the same conversation she had had earlier with Reb and Jessie. "That's what it tells us to do in the Bible."

"It does?"

You might have thought Pam had never even picked up the book. Mitch became almost didactic. "It tells us to feed the hungry, clothe the naked, visit the sick and those in prison."

"It also says that people of your sexual persuasion are going to burn in hell."

So, she had perused the book after all. Mitch nodded. "I decided a long time ago to plight my troth with the New Testament."

Pam, who had been taking copious notes to this point, now hesitated. It was like she was stuck on the spelling rather than the concept.

"Do you need me to spell it?"

"No, I think I have it. It's an old-fashioned term."

"I'm an old-fashioned girl."

"You still haven't told me why you decided to visit this one patient?"

"I guess because we weren't welcome at the funeral."

Pam was really confused now. "What funeral?"

"The funeral of the other woman killed in the accident."

"The same car accident?" Pam was good at putting two and two together.

Mitch looked at her. It was the first time she noticed that her eyebrows were plucked in some sort of fancy pattern. They were angular, but not harsh. Right now, one was raised while the other kept closer to her eye. It was a surreal effect.

"I guess this is turning into a long story," Mitch mused.

"I hope I don't get writer's cramp."

If that was a complaint, she couched it in a charming way. It might have been a dare of sorts, challenging Mitch to become long winded purely for torture's sake.

"You won't. You see, there was this tornado. You can read up on the details in the local newspaper archives. It overturned a car. One woman was killed. Another injured. Hence the funeral."

"And why didn't you go to the funeral?"

Mitch was tired, but she wasn't so tired that she didn't recognize the reporter's tried and true ploy of incorrectly rephrasing previous statements to elicit further response.

"I said we weren't welcome at the funeral. We tried to go."

"Why?"

"Why?"

"Why did you try to go to the funeral?"

"Because the accident happened real close to here."

"The tornado was here?"

Mitch pointed to a spot over Pam's left shoulder. ""It came across our land. The people scattered."

"What people?"

"The protestors."

"What protestors?"

"Let me refresh your drink."

"No, thanks. I want to hear this sober. You're telling me that you had protestors and a tornado out here. All at the same time?"

It was a funny thing about some news reporters. The closer they got to a really good story, the more they resembled a person approaching a climax. At least, that had always been Mitch's observation of the reporters she had known. Maybe she just always had the luck to be interviewed by horny reporters? Mitch, staying true to character, began to stall.

"Well, tornadoes aren't all that uncommon around these parts," Mitch practically drawled.

"Can you remember exactly what happened?"

"I think so?"

"Just start from the beginning."

"Okay. Rebecca and I moved out here after the fire."

"That's quite a while ago?" Pam looked almost pained. She was moving away from that news orgasm that had been so close just moments ago. She even shifted in her chair. Gee whiz.

"Well, you did want me to start from the beginning, didn't you?"

"Of course," Pam almost grimaced, but not quite. "Go on."

"Actually, Sweetie, the story starts even before that," Reb suddenly jumped in.

"It does?" Pam seemed simultaneously downcast and interested. An interesting combination. She was longing for her tape recorder. That much was obvious.

"Why don't I go and see if your tape recorder in still in functioning condition?" Mitch said as she stood up.

"That would be helpful."

Mitch retrieved the machine for Pam and after doing a couple of sound tests, it was in good condition. It wasn't as if Mitch had drop kicked it over the barn. They were good to go.

"I think the problem started when my Aunt Bunny died," Reb started her part of the story.

"And when did that happen?"

"While I was still serving in the Senate."

If she had been Strom Thurmond, that answer would have done nothing to narrow down the time frame.

"I see," Pam said offhandedly. She could look it up later.

"And we came out for the funeral," Mitch told that part.

"And these protestors showed up," Reb added.

"At the funeral?" Pam asked to be sure.

189

"Yes, and at the house afterwards as well. They threw food at Mitch."

"Well, not exactly at me," Mitch lovingly patted Reb's arm.

"It got all over your clothes."

"On my slacks. It was just sort of a bounce and a splash."

Pam, who was now able to relax from her writing chores, sat in rapt attention. "A bounce and a splash?"

"Right."

"It wouldn't have been able to splash on you had it not been aimed in your direction!"

"I think we've covered that part," Pam said quickly, like she had only scant minutes of tape left. And then, it would be back to penmanship time.

"Oh, okay," Mitch said, "So then we talked Mary and Lisa into living here."

"And the protests started up all over again, only this time, things turned violent."

"The house was burned down," Pam was keeping, if not setting the pace.

"Right, so I talked Rebecca into moving out here long enough to rebuild."

"And the protests started up again?" Pam pushed.

"It must be like a cottage industry around here," Mitch mused.

"Then, Mitch decided to counter attitudes by having Sunday brunches after church."

"You go to church?" Pam asked like a jolt had gone through her body.

"We've been once or twice," Reb answered with a slight edge in her voice. "Does that surprise you?"

"It's just that with all the hostility directed toward you, it seems a little-"

Reporters weren't often lost for words, particularly the descriptive kind.

"Brave?" was Mitch's guess.

"No."

"Foolhardy?" Reb offered.

"I was thinking 'illogical.'"

Gee, Mitch thought to herself, she didn't look Vulcan. Out loud, she said, "Don't you think that, in a way, church itself is illogical?"

"In what way?" Pam asked warily, feeling that the conversation had drifted into something terribly esoteric and too far from the bounds of hard hitting journalism for comfort.

"A bunch of people gather together every Sunday to worship and obey something that they can neither see nor prove. Does that seem logical?"

"Perhaps not."

"So, if two lesbians go to a place of illogic, and it's illogical for them to do so, then it seems to me that the two illogics cancel each other out."

It all sounded so logical when Mitch explained it.

"We're not here to discuss logic," Pam hurried to escape the topic.

"You're the one who brought it up."

"What prompted the incident at the Polly Perkell concert?"

The word "incident" made it sound like something out of a police blotter.

"You mean, Jessie's speech?"

"Did you put her up to it?"

If this type of questioning was meant to catch them off guard, it didn't and wouldn't work.

"Nobody, I repeat nobody, can put Jessie up to anything. It was a big surprise to me."

"It was an even bigger surprise to Mrs. Perkell. She's considering a lawsuit."

Mitch just shrugged. "That's unfortunate." She didn't even want to know the details. What could possibly be the grounds for such foolishness? Concertus interruptus?

"You don't care if she sues you?"

"No."

Another avenue of interrogation shut down. Pam was running out of topics. Sensing this, Mitch came to the rescue with a question of her own. "Why don't you ask me what I really hope for."

"Okay," Pam nodded. "What do you really hope for?"

Mitch stated matter-of-factly, "I hope for what everyone else would hope for in a situation like this. I want my life to go back to normal. I'm married to the most loving, special woman in the world and everything that happens right outside my fence distracts my attention from her. I don't want that. I don't mean to sound selfish," Mitch paused for effect, "but if I truly have these mysterious healing powers, and if by touching some people, I can cure them, then I would give it my best effort. But I seriously doubt that what has happened to date has been anything other than a stunning coincidence."

"The people at the fence insist otherwise."

"They hunger for something to believe in and they would do well to lean on other people, like Mrs. Perkell, for validation."

"Saying nice things about the enemy?"

"Mrs. Perkell isn't my enemy. I have no enemies. I just have people who don't have a clear understanding of who I am and what's in my heart."

"They don't know that because you haven't done a very good job of telling them."

"Well, they haven't done a particularly good job of asking. Having your house burned to the ground isn't the most neighborly of gestures. Having family members threatened and critically injured shouldn't place the burden of communication on the injured party."

Pam studied Mitch. Her jaw was set. "Is your friend going to be okay?"

Mitch assumed rightly the question was about Lisa. "Lisa is more than a friend. She was my former lover and now she's an important member of our family. Is she going to be okay? That's hard to guess. Do you know what it's like to have part of your face burn away?"

A woman of obvious beauty, Pam now truly grimaced. "No, do you?"

"No, I don't. But we watched Lisa from the beginning as she fought to survive. Reb saved her life. Now, we work to save her spirit. What part of our loving, nurturing efforts demands or warrants protestors at our front gate?"

"They're not protesting now."

"Well, maybe they should because I don't have any magical powers. I can't even heal myself," Mitch lifted her bad arm. She was used to it by now, but every once in a while, she tried to see it with unvarnished vision.

"So, you hope they go away?"

"I hope they find what they are seeking. I don't think they'll find it here. Now, I don't mean to be rude, but it's past my bedtime."

"You go to bed this early?"

Mitch flashed a smile. "I go to bed with this lovely ex-Senator. Can you think of a better reason to turn in early?"

Pam had the good grace to smile back. That would probably make the ten o'clock news.

"Your mom and Mitch are on the news again," Lisa announced. She had removed her mask for a few minutes before bedtime, a habit that she had taken up lately. She had been a good patient for a very long time, but the depression that daunted her recovery was now tied directly to this damnable plastic contraption. Taking a break helped her keep her good mood, such as it was.

Mary peeked around the door. She had been brushing her teeth and took time to rinse. "What did you say?"

Lisa pointed to the image of Pam Tracy on the TV set. She was doing an adequate job of reporting all the family secrets, particularly the part about Lisa being Mitch's former lover.

"I don't know why they have to harp about that," Lisa groused. Mary listened to the rest of the report before remarking on Lisa's comment. "It's just a matter of fact. You know how it is, people never forget who a famous person's ex is."

"Like Liz and Dick."

"Meg and Russell."

"Ellen and Anne."

"Let's not even go there."

"Okay."

Mary crawled into bed and held Lisa's hand to her lips. It was her way of testing the waters. Things were tepid. Lisa was still troubled by events.

"If it doesn't bother me that you're Mitch's ex, why does it bother you?"

"That's not what bothers me. I just don't see why everyone else has to make a big deal out of it."

"Well, I wouldn't worry. This will all blow over soon anyway."

"What makes you think that?"

"Why wouldn't it?"

"Why would it?"

Mary intensely disliked these "would it or wouldn't it" types of conversations.

"You think that people will continue to gather at the fence?" Mary wanted a yes or no.

"I think that no one can say for certain whether or not Mitch truly has healing powers."

"You put stock in the story?"

"I'm just saying that what we don't know about this is more than we do know."

"I can guarantee that's true for me. I know zilch about faith healing. My only opinion is that it's quackcry."

"And yet, people are being healed."

"People may be getting better."

"And you think Mitch has nothing to do with it?"

"I haven't really given it that much thought."

"Honey, look at my face."

Mary noticed a tone in Lisa's voice that was strangely unfamiliar. She thought she had heard every nuance, every tremor before. She was wrong. She looked at Lisa's face.

"What?"

"I'm healing," Lisa said.

"Of course you're healing. You're supposed to be healing."

"What I mean is that I'm healing *completely*."

"Okay," Mary tried to be agreeable. About what, she wasn't quite sure.

"You don't even know what I'm talking about, do you?"

"Keep talking. I'm listening."

"I was never given the hope that I would heal completely."

"What do you mean, 'completely'?"

"I was always aware that no matter how many medical marvels there were in burn treatments, there would still be some scarring. Something that I would need to conceal with special makeup or even more plastic surgery. But, look at me! Look closely. You won't hardly be able to find a scar when this is all over."

"That's because you're young and a good healer."

"It's because of Mitch. What they're saying about her is true."

"If it were true, you'd be all healed up by now."

"Not necessarily."

"Why not?"

"Some miracles take time."

Mary, who had thought up a snappy comeback not at all related to the subject at hand, held her tongue.

"Why don't you want to believe in Mitch?" Lisa asked bluntly in the void.

"It isn't that I wouldn't want to believe. It's just that I honestly don't think there's anything to believe in."

"Fine."

Lisa put her plastic bubble back on and turned out the light.

Mary had the vague feeling that they had just had an argument, and that she was in the disbeliever's doghouse. At least she was in good company, Mitch was there as well.

Mitch was awakened by a drone of noise. It could've been many things. A distant airplane, a blender, a crowd of people... Oh yeah, that was it. That had to be it. She pulled herself out of bed and hid out in the bathroom long enough to take a shower and primp. Primping, for Mitch, consisted of running a hurried comb through her hair. Now, she was ready for the world. She strolled into the kitchen to find her favorite people present for breakfast. Reb was sipping coffee and got a big kiss just for being there. Lisa looked radiant. Mary looked like she needed another eight or ten hours of sleep.

"You feeling okay, Mary?"

"I've been better."

"Are you coming down with a cold or something?" Mitch went over and rubbed her shoulders. "You're as tight as a tick."

"I'm tired. Your adoring public showed up pretty early this morning."

"I wouldn't know. I slept in," she chatted as she continued to work over the muscles in Mary's shoulders and neck. Mary relaxed into the process and began to feel instantly better. This was the kind of touch she believed did some good.

"Lucky you."

"So, what's everybody up to today?" Mitch asked cheerfully.

"You obviously haven't looked out the front door yet."

"No. Why?"

"It might have some bearing on plans."

"Really?" Mitch padded over to the coffee pot, poured herself a cup and then proceeded to walk out the front door. What she saw absolutely flabbergasted her. If anything, the crowd had doubled from yesterday. This just didn't make sense. After the interview with Pam Tracy, she figured the troops would have dwindled in number. Not so.

As Mitch stood agape at the crowd, they more or less did the same. At least for a couple of seconds. Then, murmuring began as they talked among themselves. What could they possibly be saying? Mitch thought. On the perimeter were satellite trucks. The media had once again descended in a major way into Mitch's life. She scanned the crowd, trying to find the familiar face of Pam. Her comrades had gathered and the crowd was muddled. And through it all, Mitch had one thought stick in her mind. They didn't have half enough donuts being delivered. She took a couple of steps toward the crowd. They instantly turned silent, as if not to scare her away. They weren't too far off the mark on that one. If they chose to stampede, Mitch was dead meat. She took a couple of nerve-steeling deep breaths and walked closer to the fence. People wanted to be greeted and touched. Out of sheer sympathy, Mitch obliged. People said things to her that made no sense, mostly because they started in the middle of the story that was their lives. They talked of pain, ache, and heartbreak to Mitch and she listened and nodded and patted their hands and shoulders. After an hour, she hadn't even made a dent in the crowd. All at once, Pam Tracy popped into view.

"Did the donuts get here?" Mitch got in the first question. Quite a feat, she thought to herself.

"Those in the back got some. Those in the front got to see you."

"The front got shortchanged. Come inside while I try and solve that problem."

Mitch escorted Pam to the gate and then gave a general wave to the crowd. "I'll be out again soon."

Pam seemed to be just as relieved to be out of the crowd as Mitch. Then again, she had been out there longer. Mitch led the way to the trailer and then held the door open for her.

"How about some coffee?"

"Sure, thanks."

"Meet the whole family," Mitch pointed as she said names.

"Mary, Lisa."

"Nice to meet you all."

"I watch you on the news all the time," Lisa was just plain glowing.

"Thank you. You've been on the news yourself."

"More than I care to be. Particularly with my injuries. But that's quickly changing!"

"Why is that?" Pam was just a natural at this nosiness stuff. Mitch put a cup of coffee in her hand and practically sat her down in a kitchen chair.

"I'm healing beautifully!"

"Yes, you are," Pam looked at her the same way that she had gazed at Rebecca the night before.

Mary was getting tensed up all over again. Mitch understood this all too well and would try to calm her down later. Right now, she was on a mission involving donuts and other food. She picked up the phone.

"Who are you calling?" Reb asked.

"Anyone who can cook."

"That leaves me out," she smiled back.

"Oh, you can reheat tomato soup with the best of them," Mitch winked as she dialed the supermarket in Utopia. If anyone had a thousand of something, it would be them. Mitch had a nice long talk with the baker, the produce manager and the really nice deli lady. Food would be on delivery vans within the hour and would

197

continue throughout the day. And yes, they would run a tab.
Their credit was good.

"How can you afford to do this?" Pam asked. Like she didn't
know.

"Well, we can afford it for a short period of time. But after that,
we're going to need a backup plan." A nice non-answer, Mitch
thought.

"Why don't you just put out a request to have everyone bring
their own food?" Lisa offered her suggestion.

"I could do that," Pam made a note.

"And a blanket so they can sit down and have a picnic," Mitch
added.

"Why?" Pam asked. Gee, two seconds couldn't go by without a
question from her.

"Because it would be a lot less unnerving if they were all sitting
down. It would be easier to walk among them."

"You plan on doing that?"

"I don't mind talking to people if they're not pressed up against
the fence. I just don't want to get anyone hurt. Particularly me!"
Mitch finished with a grin.

"Okay, I'll put the word out. Anything else?"

"Stick around for lunch. Reb's re-heating tomato soup."

"I am not!" Reb pulled her up short.

"Chicken noodle?"

"Split pea."

"My favorite," Pam twinkled.

Mary had settled down by now, after realizing that Pam twinkled
at everybody. Mitch looked at her. "You want to go back out
with me? Help with the food?"

"Sure," Mary brightened suddenly.

"Let's go."

They went together back out to the fence and this time, Mitch led
the way through the gate. Her plan to make her way through the
crowd to where the food would eventually arrive went smoothly
but slowly. She stopped often to talk to people who hadn't held
much hope of getting this chance, but she kept her comments to a
minimum. There was food on the horizon. The first van had
fruit. Mitch and Mary stationed themselves on each side of the

back of the van and started handing out apples, bananas, pears and grapes. The produce disappeared in minutes, but there was no unruly crush of people to get more. When the next van showed up, other people followed Mitch's example and started an orderly distribution of cookies, muffins, and, yes, more donuts. By the time the deli food arrived, everyone who wanted something to eat had received at least one tidbit. Someone at the grocery store had a head on their shoulders, since a fourth and fifth van appeared chock full of pop, chips, crackers, paper plates, napkins, and plastic utensils. And, of course, boxes of trash bags.

As people ate their fill, Mitch and Mary wandered quietly back to the trailer. Split pea soup was ready and waiting in steaming hot bowls. Pam was still there, which surprised Mitch pleasantly. She had until now an image in her head of TV reporters being chronically nervous individuals who chased unsuspecting folks down with microphones. But here she was, calmly helping herself to soup and crackers. As was Mitch's custom, she washed her hands and then sat down at her place at the table. She always spent a contemplative moment before eating, and Pam just naturally assumed there would be prayers. She folded her hands. Mitch noticed this and asked, "Did you want to say a blessing?"
"I don't know any."
"Neither do I. Let's eat."
The simple meal was accompanied by simple conversation.
"Are the builders coming today?" Reb wanted to know. For a woman who hadn't even glanced at the blueprints until the third edition, she was now anxious.
"I don't think they can get through the throngs."
"We have to do something about that."
"I'd like to know where the sheriff is. We could use some crowd control," Mary stated.
"Are things getting out of hand?" Pam asked.
"Not really," Mary softened up. "There's just a lot of people in a limited amount of space."
"You wouldn't think that would ever be the case in Kansas," Mitch smiled at her observation.

"What else can we do besides call the sheriff?"

"We could let them on the property," Mitch suggested.

"ABSOLUTELY NOT!" Reb snapped back vehemently.

So much for simple conversation.

"You don't like my idea?" Mitch wanted to know.

"I won't stand for it! I'm not going to allow hundreds of people to wander the property and gawk!"

"I wouldn't worry much about the gawking part. Besides, they haven't come to see you."

Things suddenly went from simple conversation right through turbulence and clean into quietude. Real quietude. Real, real quietude. Reb excused herself and rolled to the bedroom. She had gotten over her penchant for slamming doors, but the click of the lock was still audible.

"Seems like you hit a nerve," Lisa gave her expert opinion without being asked for it. It was her forte.

Mary looked tense, again. Pam looked like she'd stumbled upon a veritable treasure trove of story ideas.

"You want some more soup?" was Mitch's offering.

"No, thanks," Pam held up her hand. "Are you going to open up the property?"

"I'm sure I need to consult on that a bit more. In the meantime, could you explain something to me?"

"If I can?" Pam had an expression on her face that suggested she was about to take the oral exam part of a Ph.D.

"I don't understand why it is that after I gave that interview last night, People flocked here in even greater numbers."

"Oh, that's easy."

"It is?"

"If there one thing that people love more than a miracle worker, it's a humble miracle worker."

"Why?"

"Because the more humble you appear, the more genuine you seem. Folks like that."

"Thanks for the heads up. Will you put out the word for folks to bring their own food and clear the road."

"Where will they go?"

"I'll get back to you on that," Mitch promised and then politely but firmly escorted Pam to the door.

"You can call me on my cell phone-"

"I'll come out later. You'll be there?"

"We're doing remotes."

"Fine."

Mitch closed the door and then faced Mary. "I'm going to go and talk to your mother."

"Good luck."

Mary and Lisa picked up and left. Just like that.

Mitch walked down the all-too-short hallway to the bedroom. She tried the knob, but as she knew, it was locked. She knocked. No response.

"Let me in."

"I'm resting."

"The door's locked."

"Well, why don't you try and *heal* it open."

"Oh, gee, I'm in stitches out here."

"Go away. I'm trying to sleep."

"It's not safe to have this door locked," Mitch said as she took inventory of all the keys on her chain. She found the right one and unlocked the door.

"I won't come in unless you want me to, but at least now I can get in in case of emergency," Mitch said and then waited patiently. Heck, if people could stand for hours at her fence, she could give Reb a few minutes.

"Are you going to stand out there until I say 'yes'?"

"Yes."

Mitch could hear her sigh. God, she could be maddening when she wanted to be.

"You might as well come in then. I won't get any rest otherwise."

Mitch pushed the door open slowly. Reb didn't look all that upset. There had been, for instance, no tears.

"It isn't like you to need a nap mid afternoon."

"And it isn't like you to have your head swell so big that it fills the whole room."

201

Mitch nodded for effect but she was confused. One person was telling her she was too puffed up for her own good and another was extolling her humility. She went over and stretched out beside Reb on the bed. There were literally dozens and dozens of responses that Mitch could utter. Choosing among them brought about only more silence.

"You're stumped for a response?" Reb looked over.

"Why does this bother you?"

"It doesn't bother me."

"You've taken to your bed! That isn't like you."

"Okay, I'll admit, having hundreds of people at our doorstep is a bit unnerving."

"Why?"

"Why! You need me to tell you why?"

"I need you to tell me why it's unnerving to *you*!"

Reb lapsed into silence. Maybe that's why she was here after all. Sorting out her feelings.

"They make noise."

"Yes, they do. We could play music."

"And they're making a mess. I can smell the banana peels from here."

"I'll talk to them about it."

"You make it sound like they are a couple of obnoxious house guests. It's a thousand people."

"Maybe that's what's bugging you?"

"What?"

"The sheer number. It is a lot."

"It's a whole lot."

"And you don't want them on the property."

"They'll kill off the vegetation."

Rebecca talked as if they lived in some botanical gardens. About all that stood threatened to be trampled was noxious weeds. Most farmers paid good money to eradicate these. They could get them stomped to death for free. Of course, they would always grow back from the root...

"What are you thinking about?"

"Nothing," Mitch snapped to.

"I'm telling you my concerns and you're thinking about nothing?"

"I was actually thinking about weeds."

"Weeds?"

"We could have the crowd go over to the part of the property where all those weeds grow."

"And you seriously believe that they would stay there?"

"You don't think so?"

"Before you know it, they'll be on the front steps and peeking in the windows."

"I can't imagine why?"

"You honestly can't, can you? Everyone came here to see you. Everyone wants to touch you and be in your presence. They all want something from you. They all need you."

"And none of that matters to me."

"It doesn't? That's not how it sounded a few minutes ago."

Mitch thought about this. Somehow, this all sounded like it was rooted in jealousy. Deep down, Mitch felt almost giddy. She knew that jealousy wasn't always the most positive of emotions, but the fact that Reb was jealous made sense. After all, Reb had always been the star of the family. Governor. Senator. She had always filled the spotlight beautifully.

"I'm with you. That's all that matters and all that will ever matter to me."

Reb was now quiet for a moment. Then, she said, "How do you always know the exact right thing to say?"

"I don't. You wouldn't be in here otherwise."

"I don't know why I reacted the way I did. You didn't say anything outrageous."

"You want my analysis?"

"Nope. Not right now."

"What do you want?"

"As long as you're here, I want you to hold me."

"I thought you'd never ask."

Mitch arranged her body to fulfill Reb's request. It was worlds nicer than walking along a fence in front of an adoring public.

"Maybe Polly Perkell would agree to entertain them?"

"After all the nasty things she said about you, they'd tar and feather her."

"I guess so. I really don't know what to do. I've tried being humble. That didn't work. And I don't want to order them to leave, like that would work anyway…"

"Maybe if they get bored enough, they'll go away."

"Maybe so."

"I know I would."

"Are you bored with me?" Mitch asked as she ran her fingers along Reb's least boring body areas.

"You are many things. Boring doesn't make the list."

"Not even close?" Mitch wanted facts.

"Not even close," was all that Reb cared to quantify.

"Good," Mitch stopped talking and concentrated fully on finger play. As did Reb.

They hid out until the dinner hour, at which time Mary called to see what the blue plate special was.

"We made lasagna," Mitch intoned.

"Sounds great. Got enough for four?"

"Got enough for fourteen. Come on over."

"What can we bring?"

"A big appetite."

This was, more or less, their average nightly routine. Mitch and Reb hosted dinner at their trailer. Once in a while, they ate separately, but not often. Mitch opened the door for them when she saw them approach and then quickly closed the door before the crowd could get excited about another appearance. They all sat down and had just passed the food around once when there was a knock at the door. A really assertive knock. Mitch went without hesitation to the door and opened it. Of course, it was Pam. No one else knocks quite like the press.

"There's been another miracle!" was her greeting. She was breathless. It gave her a sensual quality that offset the nature of the news. Sex and religion never did mix well.

"Suppose you come in and tell me what happened," Mitch tried to not sound too peeved at the interruption. Just enough to let her know that it was just that: an interruption.

"Thanks."

Pam stepped in and acted all surprised that they were just starting dinner. By now, Reb and company had found another chair and dished another plate.

"Oh, I'm sorry. You're eating. I can come back."

"We wouldn't hear of it," Mitch indicated her place at the table. They all settled in elbow to elbow. Pam tasted the creation. "This is marvelous!"

Everyone nodded agreement and continued to eat without comment. Mitch finally broke the silence when she realized that Pam was too polite to make further conversation until invited.

"I hope you asked everyone to bring a sack lunch tomorrow, if they show up."

"I didn't actually have time, with the latest miracle happening. I was busy tracking that story."

"I'll take the bait. What new miracle?" Mitch asked like she knew she was going to be sorry.

"A man has been cured of his ulcers! Apparently, he had these nasty bleeding ulcers, or maybe it was the kind that pus? Anyway, I talked to him and he was hard to understand so I'm waiting for the doctor's report."

Pam stopped long enough to poke some more lasagna in her mouth. She was now the only one still eating. At the mention of pustular, bloody ulcers, everyone else had choked down their current mouthful and then stopped eating altogether. Pam finally noticed. The press just doesn't miss a beat.

"Oh, gee, I guess this isn't exactly dinner-table conversation."

"It didn't seem to slow you down," Mary noted.

"When you're a member of the press, you develop a cast-iron stomach. If I let things like this bother me, I'd be even slimmer than I already am."

That would take some doing, Mitch thought to herself. Out loud, she said, "Why don't you and I go somewhere a little more private and talk about this?"

The idea bordered on the absurd. It wasn't as if the trailer had an upstairs library where they could retire with a snifter of brandy. Besides, the suggestion was destined to be overruled.

"I want to hear about this as well," Reb stated firmly. "Just not over a plate of lasagna."

They all milled over to the couch area of the room. It took fifteen, maybe twenty seconds.

"Well, I've really told you most of the news already," Pam said.

"Tell me why you said that the man was hard to understand?"

"He was in tears. These big, joyous tears and he talked fast in a sort of broken English."

"He had an accent?"

"It could've been Swedish or German. I'm still doing research on that."

"And he had some kind of ulcers?"

"He talked about stomach and skin ulcers during my interview."

"And when was this?"

"Just this afternoon."

"So, no one had heard about it yet?"

"You mean, have I put the story out yet?"

"Right."

"I'm going to run it on tonight's newscast."

"I don't want you to do that," Mitch said quietly and yet forcefully.

"The public has the right to know," Pam came back with the usual argument.

"Okay, so tell me what you can report so far without equivocation. Without guesswork of any kind."

When Pam didn't have a ready answer for this, Mitch pointed out the obvious. "You don't even know if the guy is German or Swedish let alone what kind of ulcers he did or didn't have pending a doctor's report."

"I may not have the minor details yet," Pam was getting miffed, "But I do have the gentleman's interview on tape. Check it out tonight on the news."

With that pronouncement, Pam stood up and let herself out of the trailer. Things got quiet.

"Who's up for more lasagna?" Mitch broke the snit spell. "As long as we have to stay up to watch the news, we might just as well get a good case of heartburn."

"My case of heartburn just left," Reb put on record.

"How bad can this be? Even she had a hard time with his English. Nobody's going to pay attention to a fifteen-second interview with a guy who's hard to understand."

"I sincerely hope you're right."

Mitch didn't make it to the late news. All the fresh country air did her in more days than not. Her sleep was sound. She didn't even hear Reb come to bed, and she didn't hear her get up either. By the time she stirred awake, it was just past six. A craving for a strong cup of coffee spurred her to roll out of bed. She wandered out to find Reb at the kitchen table.
"Morning."
"Sleep well?" Reb inquired.
"Yes, and you?"
"Your fan club woke me up early."
"I'm sorry. They are a bit louder this morning, aren't they?"
"It isn't that they're louder, it's just that there's more of them."
"More?" Mitch must not have heard right.
"Take a look," Reb gestured to the window. She had an interesting look in her eyes.
Mitch peeked out the window. Now, she understood the look from Reb. There was a veritable ocean of people where yesterday, there had been just a lake. In the figurative sense, of course.
"Tell me I'm seeing things."
"I'm afraid not."
"Where did they come from?" Mitch asked, knowing the answer was unknowable.
"I think you are now stop number one on the national pilgrimage tour."
"Is this at all related to the Pam Tracy interview?"
"You mean the one you slept through? You could say that." Reb's tone had an attitude. It was "ask if you dare" time.
"It must have been some interview."
"By the time it was over, we figured we'd be required to call you, "Saint Mitch."
"Why?"
"Well, according to this German guy, Otto Somebody, you healed his festering ulcers with just a touch of your hand on his head."
"I don't even remember anything like that."
"Well, it's your word against his and folks believe him."

Mitch checked the view from the window again. What was new today was a pronounced police presence. They had placed themselves between the crowd and the property line. Frankly, although they looked sharp and very professional, they were greatly outnumbered. The good news was that the crowd was well behaved. But then again, Mitch hadn't stepped foot out the door.

"You want some breakfast?" Reb asked.

"Maybe a piece of toast."

"How about a really big piece of toast?"

Mitch laughed. "You think I can stall my way out of this?"

"It's worth a try."

Despite the circumstances, they had a nice, leisurely breakfast. When left to their own devices, they still managed to enjoy each other's company.

"I'm not going to hide out," Mitch made her position clear after they finished the dishes.

"I don't want you to. Just keep track upon whose head you place your hands."

Mitch took Reb's face in both hands. "You first," she smiled. "And don't you forget it!"

They shared a kiss and then Mitch opened the front door. When she stepped outside, the gasp was audible. Thanks to the police, the house builders were once again on site. Mitch walked over to them and chatted for a few minutes. Things were going along quite well. She thanked them for their diligence in the face of adversity and then turned her attention to the crowd. There were so many. Hundreds and hundreds. And hundreds. She worried about the sheer crush of people at the fence. The closer she got, the more she realized that the crowd had created a sort of triage area. People closest to the fence appeared to be the very most needful of a cure. This stopped Mitch in her tracks. For the first time since this absurd drama had begun, Mitch felt at a loss. To fill so many people with false hope drained and angered her, all at the same instant. She scanned the crowd for the person she felt was the perpetrator, and it took a full minute to locate Ms. Tracy. She finally showed her face and Mitch indicted through gesture alone that she wanted to have a private discussion with her. The police let her through, reluctantly. She didn't get any farther than face-to-face with Mitch.

"Did you see the interview?" she seemed awfully proud of the chaos she had created.

"No."

"No?"

"I want to meet this guy."

"Again?"

"For the first time by my account."

"I don't understand.

"I don't remember this guy. I want you, him and his doctor in my living room by noon today."

"That might be tough to do," Pam tried to stare Mitch down.

"You're the famous Pam Tracy. I'm sure you can arrange it."

"If I do, I'm bringing a camera crew."

Mitch gave the bargain serious consideration. She was beginning to begrudgingly respect this woman. What she proposed didn't seem all that unreasonable. Besides, nothing Mitch had tried so far had worked to diminish the crowd. The straws she had been grasping at were becoming fewer. As all this went through her mind, Pam waited almost breathlessly. Maybe Mitch should've warned her that she was a slow thinker.

"I'll agree to a camera if you can get one other person to attend."

"Who?" Pam was in more of a mood to take down a name than be wary of the request.

"Lucinda Cornwall."

Pam nodded like Santa Claus had answered her letter. "I'll be back at noon."

She was on her cell phone making necessary arrangements before she even crossed the property line.

Mitch had put it off long enough. The crowd had become individual faces to her by now and she saw the spectrum of human emotion in their facial expressions. They were hopeless and yet hopeful. Joy and pain struggled for predominance. Mitch saw a hundred reasons to go to the fence and not one to not go. She went to them and listened to stories that were heart rendering. Imagine not walking. Imagine not seeing. Imagine a life with no respite from pain. There was all this and more at this most desolate of places on Earth. Mitch bent her head close to hear, held hands, touched heads and gave words of encouragement to all she could reach. When she remembered to check her watch, she was stunned to find that noon had rolled around. Her feet didn't ache. Her hands didn't hurt. Her voice held steady.

Pam ran late. Not much. By twelve-fifteen, she was at the gate with her lovely self, Otto, Lucinda and a cameraman.
"Where's the doctor?"
"In surgery," Pam answered and then waited in a dare-me mood for a reaction.
"His own or somebody else's?" Mitch quizzed like it mattered, which it didn't. She was going to grant the interview anyway. To do otherwise would be boorish.
"Somebody else's."
"Okay. I hope it turns out well. Come on in."
"I need to bring my sound guy as well. And hair and makeup."
"Sound, yes, hair and makeup, no."
It was Mitch that now had the dare-me look. A sound guy was okay. In fact, maybe he could take a look at the stereo if he had a spare minute? But makeup was out of the question.
Pam didn't challenge. The knot of people formed a rag tag parade as they made their way to the trailer. Although Mitch had neglected to inform Reb of this interview, she was ready and waiting. Must've been all those years as a public servant. Not even the dour presence of Lucinda could rattle her as she turned on that familiar charm. In fact, the only person rattled was Mitch. It made her swallow hard and strain to remember why they were here in the first place.

There was a lot more to being on camera than just turning on a button. The audience needed to be able to hear you as well, along with the nuance of your voice. The sound technician outfitted everyone with a little clip-on microphone. Now was not the time to divulge anything that you wouldn't want your sainted grandmother to hear.

And then, there was the matter of lighting. Too little was bad, too much was worse. It was like Goldilocks. Things had to be just right. For all the complexities, they were ready to roll in ten minutes. Throughout this lull, Mitch had been keeping an eye on Otto. He did look vaguely familiar, now that she had the chance to think about it. In all fairness, there had been so many faces. "So, tell us, Ms. Tanner, do you take credit for healing Mr. Walker's ulcers?" Pam's voice took on an ethereal quality when she was on camera. It took Mitch so by surprise that she hesitated. What came out next didn't sound at all brilliant. "Who's Mr. Walker?"

"That's me!" Otto raised his hand like they were in school.

"Oh," Mitch reached over and shook his hand like they had just met. "Nice to meet you."

He just nodded and remained speechless.

"So, do you?" Angel Pam asked again.

"Do I what?" Mitch asked back. She was sitting on the couch, holding hands with Rebecca. Even with this reinforcement, the experience of being on camera was a little more nerve-wracking than she had expected. As she felt Mitch tense up, Reb slowly moved her other hand over and began to massage Mitch's inner wrist. It was all-at-once calming. "Do you take credit for healing Mr. Walker?" Pam asked for the third time. She was getting a bit wan under the gills herself. This wasn't turning out at all like she had hoped.

"Ms. Tanner is a charlatan!" Lucinda couldn't hold back one more second. She had been building up to an eruption for days. Color rushed back to Pam's face. This wasn't going at all like she had planned. They had only one camera, for Christ's sake! Pam made some sort of head bob to the cameraman that must be TV journalism talk for "focus the camera on this one." Then, Pam transitioned her body so that she could carry on a conversation with Lucinda. The way she re-crossed her legs raised body transitioning to high art.

"Tell us who you are," Pam tried to wrestle back control of the interview-gone-bad.

"I'm Lucinda Cornwall, President of the Kansasans for Decency!"

"Oh, so that's who you are!" Mitch piped up, just skirting the mischievous side of her nature.

"You know perfectly well who I was!" Lucinda shot back, so incensed that she even mixed her tenses. Just try to get away with that on the SAT.

"Well, I knew you were important," Mitch admitted.

"You just didn't know how much!"

Because everything Lucinda said came out in exclamation mode, she was far better suited to sound bites than Mitch. Now, all she needed to figure out was whether or not Pam was more interested in sound bites or substance.

"Why have you accused Ms. Tanner of being a fake?"

"I called her a charlatan! Do I need to spell it for you!"

And this from a woman who mixed past and present tense like she was in a time machine! There are times when it's a really good idea to remember that you're on camera. Lucinda couldn't seem, or didn't care to remember. Mitch couldn't seem to forget. Otto joined the fun. "I can spell charlatan!" he assured everyone. He was probably, as a child, one of those kids who went to the state finals of the spelling bee.

"C-H-A--"

"Thank you, Mr. Walker. Thanks, but I do know how to spell charlatan," Pam was mentally gritting her pearly whites. "What I want to know is why you, Ms. Cornwall, consider Ms. Tanner to be a charlatan?"

"Well, she's obviously a fake!" Lucinda got all puffed up. If she was wheat, she'd be in somebody's cereal bowl by now.

"She is not!" Otto shot back. He was obviously put out at not being allowed to demonstrate his spelling ability and was just itching to take it out on someone.

"No one is given the power to heal who leads such a sinful, disgusting, aberrant lifestyle!" Lucinda finally made her point. It was like a festering abscess breaking loose. Which seemed to shift focus back to Otto and his ulcers.

"But Mr. Walker claims to have been healed."

"There's no proof that *she* did it, is there!" Lucinda continued to ooze, not at all in a positive way. When she used the pronoun "she," to refer to Mitch, Lucinda made it sound as if Mitch were the lowest form of pond scum in a really big pond. Mitch was beginning to get a headache.

"I think Ms. Cornwall has a point," Mitch all of a sudden wanted the interview to be over so she could lay her weary head down. For about a week or two.

"Excuse me?" Pam the Stunned asked.

"There are two words that we've been tossing around here today that need to be emphasized."

"Disgusting and aberrant?" Lucinda hoped to land on the correct answer like they were on a game show.

"No. Charlatan and proof," Mitch clarified. "Ms. Cornwall is correct in her statement that there's no *proof* of my ability to heal. We have Mr. Walker claiming that I've healed his ulcers, but let's not forget all the latest research on ulcers. There's a body of evidence that indicates that ulcers may be caused by bacteria or maybe even viruses. It could just be that the doctors either just found the correct medicine or that Mr. Walker's body healed itself."

"That may be true-" Pam tried to wedge in a statement, but Mitch interrupted her.

"And concerning the word charlatan, it's my understanding that the word refers to someone who claims to be able to do something but can't. If anything, we have the opposite occurring. I don't claim to be a faith healer, and yet, people are healing."

"But, you won't deny your alleged powers, either!" Lucinda sniped snottily. Geez, it would sure be a chore to sit next to her every Sunday in church, let alone spend an eternity with her in heaven. If salvation were a gift, could Mitch skip the party altogether?

Reb squeezed Mitch's hand. It was an unspoken signal to pay attention and answer the question. "I can't deny something I'm not sure I have."

There. See! Pam Tracy wasn't the only Vulcan in Utopia, Kansas.

"But, you do have the power," Otto found his voice, and his message. "No doctor or medicine could've healed me this quickly. It was an overnight miracle! I'll tell anyone who wants to listen, I'll swear on a stack of Bibles. Two stacks of Bibles." He held up two fingers on a hand that had seen many a year of hard work. No wonder the crowd had swelled overnight. Otto was as honest as the work day was long.

"Don't blaspheme!" Lucinda pointed at him with a finger of her own. Her index digit resembled a deadly weapon. Mitch wondered if she had to have it registered as such.

"Don't talk to me that way!" Otto was used to being called a blasphemer and didn't take kindly to it. This must've all centered around the two stacks of Bibles comment, but Mitch was getting lost. She asked Reb, "Didn't we hear that Otto's English was broken?"

"Sounds like you fixed that as well," Reb answered quietly. This seemed to make Mitch's headache worse instead of better. Pam looked like she was getting one of her own as well.

"I'm going to ask everyone to calm down," she asked nicely. Things did get quiet, but stares and glares abounded.

"I think we need to test the supposed powers of Ms. Tanner," Lucinda took advantage of the calm to spring this little gem.

"You're suggesting some sort of monitored experiment?" Pam asked.

"It seems to me that we need to know one way or the other, if only to be fair to the crowd gathered outside."

"At the risk of sounding hesitant," Mitch piped up, "I can't really tell if and when these powers come and go. How can we test that?"

"Sounds to me like you're already trying to weasel your way out of a fair test," Lucinda smiled like a gruesome cadaver. About the only thing Mitch would like to do about now would be to heal Lucinda's mouth. Shut.

"I'll do it," Mitch decided quickly. "Go find somebody in the crowd. I'll even let Lucinda make the choice. Pick somebody really tough. This is one test that I can hardly wait to flunk so that my life can just get back to normal."

Lucinda appeared momentarily stunned that her challenge had been accepted. She was back on her heels, but thinking quickly. "I haven't lined up a doctor to monitor the test."

Otto came to the rescue, gentleman that he was. "Use my doctor."

Who said chivalry was dead?

"I'll find my own doctor, thank you very much!"

"Well, you'd better hurry," Mitch said, "because I'm in a healing mood."

With those words, Mitch stood up.

"Where are you going?" Lucinda was practically stammering.

"Let's go heal somebody."

All attention was now on Lucinda. It was hard to have sympathy for her, since she had truly brought this on herself.

"Now?"

"I'm ready for your challenge. Are you?"

"Fine," she sounded put out.

God, this was going to be fun. After getting Reb ready to go out in her wheelchair, Mitch followed everyone out the door. Someone had alerted Mary and Lisa, since they were out there as well. Several cameras were now trained on Mitch as she waited patiently for Lucinda to find the least curable person on the front line. It as a circus-like atmosphere, and Mitch's headache showed no signs of retreat. Finally, after what seemed to be an eternity of pause, a young woman was brought before Mitch. She was maybe twenty-five and yet had the eyes of a forty-year old. Pain did that to people. Mitch felt a sudden, intense warmth in her neck and prickly spikes down her back. She chalked it up to the chill in the night air. She looked at Reb, worried that it was affecting her as well. She looked okay. Meanwhile, Lucinda handled the introductions with all the adroitness of a Kindergartner.

"Here, heal this one."

Mitch shook hands with the woman and asked her name.

"I'm Sheila."

"Hello, Sheila. Have you been waiting long?"

"Nearly all my life."

"Really?" Mitch didn't understand the answer but smiled politely.

"And then, I heard about you and I knew you were the one!'

"The one?"

"The healer who would cure me."

"Well, Sheila, I-"

"And I was so grateful."

Sheila's eyes were now brimming with tears. She was a
beautiful woman now that hope resided within her.

"I don't know if I have these healing powers everyone talks
about," Mitch broke the news as gently as she could.

"Everyone says you do!"

"There are times when everyone can be wrong."

As Mitch and Sheila held this understanding silently between
them, Lucinda broke in, "Will you just try to heal her and get this
over with!" The snappishness did nothing for Mitch's throbbing
head.

Doing nothing more than putting one hand on the young
woman's forehead, Mitch created a media circus anew. Between
the crush of people, the lights of the camera and the timpani of
drums in her head, Mitch fainted dead away. It couldn't have
been more dramatic if it had been on a stage in New York City.

Mitch came to about the time that a makeshift group of people
were hovering over her trying to figure out what to do next.

"We could call for the ambulance?" a voice of concern floated
by.

"They'd never get through the crowd."

"Maybe they're already here?"

"All we need is to get her to the trailer!" Reb's voice was taking
charge. "Is there a big, strong guy who could carry her in?"

"I'll help," a booming, masculine timbre rattled the still air.

Mitch was carefully scooped up like she was little more than a
feather pillow and carried to bed. She was woozy and warm, not
a fun combination. After a few minutes, she bravely opened her
eyes and saw the concerned face of Reb watching her cautiously.

"A doctor is on the way."

"Why?"

"You fainted, honey."

"People faint every day."

"And doctor's get called every day. Besides, you feel warm."

216

"I do?"

"You're running a fever."

"I don't feel so good."

"I know that! That's why I called the doctor!" Reb was firm but still smiling.

"Should I rest in the meantime?" Mitch asked.

"No, I think you should train for a marathon."

Now, even Mitch smiled. A bit. And then her head started to set fire to her brain.

"Do you have about twelve aspirin that I could take?"

"Just twelve?"

"Maybe thirteen. My head's about ready to crack open."

"I'd prefer to wait for the doctor."

"He'd better hurry. At this rate, there won't be a head left to examine."

Thankfully, the doctor was close by and did get police escort through the crowd. Imagine, a doctor that still made house calls. Who said miracles didn't happen anymore! His cool, dry hand was on Mitch's forehead before she could ruminate further.

"You've got yourself one good fever there," he told her the obvious with such gracious authority that all Mitch could do was nod in agreement.

"And you've also got yourself something else."

Mitch looked at him and then at Reb and then back again to hear the diagnosis. The doctor motioned to Rebecca to look where his finger was pointing. It was a place on Mitch's forehead, right up against her scalp.

"See that?"

"Uh huh," Reb nodded like she had a medical degree herself.

"What is it?" Mitch wanted to be in the know.

"You've got the Chickenpox."

"The Chickenpox? Aren't I a little long in the tooth to have the Chickenpox?"

"Young lady, you're never too old to have the Chickenpox!"

Oh, this man of medicine did ooze charm when he had a bona fide patient on his hands. He, fickle man that he was, now turned his attention to Rebecca. Like that hadn't happened a hundred times before. They were talking.

"Have you ever taken care of someone with Chickenpox before?"

"My daughter had them, but that's been years."

"Well, things haven't changed much. I'll prescribe something for the pain and something for the itch. If you can, get her into a warm bath tonight so she'll get all good and broken out. Then, later she can bathe in oatmeal. "I'll check her for Strep and then stop back by in the morning."

"Doctor?" Mitch took hold of his arm to capture his attention. "Yes?"

"Do I look like a healer to you?"

He crinkled up in a smile. For a guy in his sixties, he was kind of cute.

"I could ask you the same thing. Now, say AH."

He jabbed at the back of her throat like it was target practice time and her tonsils had circles on them. So much for being cute.

Reb escorted him to the door and by the time she got back, Mitch had managed to get all the way up to the sitting position. The prospect of taking a bath was suddenly overwhelming.

"You sit still while I get Mary and Lisa in here."

"Why?"

"To help you get into the bathtub."

"I don't want Mary and Lisa to help me into any bathtub!"

"I certainly can't help you."

"I'll get there all by myself."

"Okay."

Rebecca knew when to argue and when to remain silent. She waited and watched as Mitch sat…and sat…and sat. The pesky bed was calling softly to Mitch to lie back down. She was too busy resisting the urge to do much thinking about actually standing up.

"Who do you want—Mary or Lisa?" Reb gave her the choice. The real question was, "Who do you want to see you naked?"

"I think that's a question best answered by them," Mitch acquiesced.

"Fine. I'll be back."

She was back in ten seconds with Mary.

"You don't mind seeing me naked?" Mitch was slipping surely into delirium by now.

"I already have?"

"You have?" Mitch was aware enough to be puzzled.

"Come on. I'll tell you while you take that bath."

Mary drew a bath steamy enough to make a Swede blush. Then, she double checked to make sure that Mitch was indeed naked before she held her steady into the tub. Now, all she had to do was to make sure she didn't drown.

"Do you have any idea why I need to take this bath?" Mitch asked, mostly just to chit chat.

"I heard it will make you break out faster."

"And that's a good thing?"

"I guess so. My mom made me take a bath when I came down with Chickenpox."

"And when was that?"

"I was eight-years old."

"Just yesterday."

"Something like that."

"I finally figured it out."

"What?"

"When you saw me naked."

"So, you're not as sick as you appear."

"But, I was that time, as well. Sick, I mean."

"Right," Mary nodded.

When Mitch and Mary and Rebecca had first become acquainted, and things were still more strained than baby food, Mitch had come down with a sudden migraine headache at the Governor's Mansion. One minute she had blinding pain and, seemingly, the next moment she was lying in between cool, clean sheets without a stitch of clothing. Someone had to have undressed her, and surely it wasn't Governor Rebecca Fairbanks. At least, not at that early stage in their relationship.

"Why did you undress me that day?" Mitch was awfully nosy for a delirious person.

"I guess I thought that migraines had something to do with blood circulation."

"It certainly did, for your Mom. I got her blood circulating pretty good that day."

"I think you did most days…" Mary smiled.

"How long do I have to stay in the bathtub?"

"Do you feel like you're breaking out?"

"Honey, I'm already ten miles from the jailhouse!"

"Give it about five more minutes, okay?"

"Okay."

Mitch tried to relax in the water, but between all the toxins in her blood and the thought of crawling right back into bed made her restless. There was a polite knock at the door. It was Reb. She wheeled right in to observe the procedure.

"I should've charged admission."

"I suppose you're ready for bed?"

"Never readier. Don't take it personally."

"I won't."

Mitch took that as permission and began the attempt to get out of the tub. It was then that she realized that her muscles had turned to mush. This was even more embarrassing than being seen au natural by a majority of the people in the immediate family.

Mary, bless her soul, was strong as an ox. She single-handedly pulled Mitch from the vortex of draining water and sat her firmly on the closed toilet seat while she patted her dry. Then, they wrapped her in a cloud masquerading as a light robe and tucked her into bed. Mitch gazed out-of-focus into Reb's eyes.

"Have you had the Chickenpox?"

"When I was nine."

"Late bloomer?"

"Story of my life. Take this medication and go to sleep."

Mitch did so, almost immediately.

Mitch and the following morning had something in common. They both bloomed gloriously. Mitch stirred awake and moaned audibly. Reb was right there.

"Hi, Sweetie. How are you feeling?"

Mitch tried to think of an adequate word. It took an entire second. "How about miserable?" she answered.

"I believe it. I'll get you something to eat and your medicine."

"I'm not hungry."

"I have things cooked already. You need to eat to keep up your strength."

"I'm getting over the Chickenpox, not training for the Olympics."

"Don't argue with me. I'll be right back."

Mitch was just about to rub her eyes with her hand when she noticed the pocking. It wasn't something she wanted anywhere near her eyes. She knew one other thing-the bathroom was still as far away as it had been last night. And yet, she had to make the journey. She pulled back the covers and slowly swung her legs out of bed. They were a tad steadier than last night, but not much. The trip was uneventful, except for when Mitch caught a glimpse of her face. It was going to be a mess. It already was. She gathered up her strength and toddled out to the kitchen. Reb was putting the finishing touches on a breakfast tray.

"I want you back in bed!"

"You say the sweetest things."

"Go to bed. I'll be right behind you – with breakfast," was the sternest warning Reb could muster.

"Okay. Just as soon as I look out the window."

"Are you sure you really want to do that?"

"Is there a reason I shouldn't?"

"I just want you to rest and get well."

"Okay."

Mitch went back to bed. For only being away for a scant few minutes, the bed felt marvelous. She would've slipped off to sleep except that Reb was there with breakfast. It was oatmeal, bacon and eggs. A feast that overwhelmed her.

"I didn't know you could cook bacon."

"I'm just full of surprises," Reb talked as she placed a cup of coffee on Mitch's bedside table. After she had done so, Mitch caught up with her hand and tried to hold it. She was now too weak to give it a proper squeeze.

"Do you need help eating?"

"I don't know."

Reb understood all too well how humbling it was to need help with the most basic of life's tasks.

"Well, give it your best shot. There's no clock running."

Mitch did. She slowly fed herself a polite amount of oatmeal
and then ate the bacon as a reward. Before Reb had even left the
room with the dirty dishes. Mitch was back asleep. That
medicine was good stuff. It worked great for a whole hour.
Then, Mitch was back in the kitchen with her empty coffee cup.
"What do you need? Some more coffee? I'll get that for you!"
Reb wheeled over.
"You can't be waiting on me hand and foot," Mitch held on to
the kitchen counter while she talked. If she didn't hold on tight,
she might be holding on to the floor next.
"Oh, yes I can wait on you and I'm going to! And If I can't, I'll
hire someone to help. Now, the doctor told me to keep you in
bed for at least three days and maybe longer. So, you get
yourself back into that bed right now and I mean it!"
It was the most words strung together out of Reb since her
political days. What other choice did Mitch have but to
acquiesce.
"Yes, Ma'am."
The parade was slow with Mitch leading the pace. Normally,
they made much better time getting to the bedroom, but this was
the exception. Mitch was back under the covers before
conversation continued.
"Maybe that's a good idea," Mitch was being agreeable. About
what, Reb had to ask.
"Hiring someone to help," Mitch reminded.
"Mary will be over soon."
"Mary has her own patient to attend to. She doesn't need the
extra bother."
"I see your point. You're certainly not a bother, but I will need
someone to help you take two or three baths a day."
"Why so many?"
"You take a bath in this oatmeal stuff. It soothes the itching."
"I was going to suggest Jessie, but now that I think about it…"
"She's too busy anyway, what with the crowd at the diner."
"How is the crowd, anyway?" Mitch was suddenly curious.
"I'm sorry I said anything," Reb was blunt.
"Why?"
"The crowd is still there."
"Do they know I have the Chickenpox?"

"They know you fainted. Which reminds me, Pam Tracy sent you a bouquet of flowers."

"Does it have a listening device attached?"

"I checked," Reb was one step ahead of her. "It doesn't. I had to tip the delivery guy a bunch to make up for all the lost time trying to get through the crowd."

"So, it is getting bigger?" Mitch knew that if she just listened long enough, she'd hear the answer. Unfortunately, as she closed her eyes, she fell asleep and missed the answer.

Yes, it was.

By one in the afternoon, Mitch was cranky. Uncharacteristically so. Since food was beginning to be the central reward of the day, lunch was a letdown. Mitch was in the mood for something sinful, and tomato soup didn't even rate on the venial chart. But she ate quietly. Too quietly.

"What do you want for dinner?" Reb asked as if she were reading Mitch's mind and mood simultaneously.

"Chicken-fried steak, boiled new potatoes with lemon-butter sauce, onion rings, gravy, applesauce, a braunschweiger sandwich with mustard and mayonnaise both and warm blueberry pie. With ice cream. Butter pecan if you have it."

"Gee, but have you given it much thought?" Reb hid her delight with the renewed appetite in a cloak of droll.

"Maybe vanilla ice cream? I wouldn't want to overpower the blueberries? And maybe a latte?"

"I guess I'd better go shopping."

"Just call someplace and have stuff delivered. And if you want, hire someone to haul it in here. Okay?"

"Okay."

"The soup was great."

"Honey, your ability to lie hasn't improved with illness."

"The crackers were a nice touch."

"Are you ready for your bath?"

"I don't know? Am I?"

"Let me go get your new health care helper."

"My what?"

"It's a who, and her name is Hilda."

Well, at least it wasn't Horton. In a previous life, Hilda might've been a WWF wrestler. She was solid and muscled and had that look that made it clear that she didn't take guff from anybody. If it was time to take a bath, it was time to take a bath.

It was time to take a bath. Hilda was very businesslike, for a building. But, then again, weren't buildings usually pretty businesslike, Mitch pondered feverishly to herself. Except for the Fun House at the amusement park. Now, there was one fun building. And, then, of course, there was—
"I want to make one thing clear!" Hilda boomed as she sprinkled the magic oatmeal dust into the bath water.
"Glad it's only one thing," Mitch muttered as she popped her ears.
"I don't believe all that folderol about you being some kind of hocus pocus healer."
"Me, neither," Mitch told the solemn truth from her perch on the side of the tub.
"I mean, what kind of healer comes down with a first class case of the Chickenpox themselves?"
"Well said," Mitch nodded. She was itching, quite literally, to ask if Hilda had believed before the Chickenpox had struck, but wasn't up to properly conducting her side of the debate. Hilda was silent for a moment, apparently surprised that Mitch had agreed so readily. Then, she added, "Just try and tell that to the thousands gathered out there." She jerked her thumb in the general direction of the front yard.
"Did you say thousands?" Mitch thought she heard wrong.
"Yes."
Mitch put her robe back on and headed out the bathroom door.
"Where do you think you're going?" Hilda demanded to know.
"I'll be right back," Mitch promised. Right back would be a relative term, the Chickenpox breaking out on the bottoms of her feet made the going slow. But she escaped further questioning through sheer determination. Not even Reb could keep her away from the front door. Against all caution and good sense, she opened the door and stepped outside. Hilda wasn't kidding, not that she had seemed the kidding type in the first place. There were thousands. There were thousands of them and only one pocked-up Mitch in nothing but a robe. They stared at each

224

other in disbelief until Reb and Hilda managed to pull her back into the house.

"There's so many of them," Mitch mouthed as they guided her back to the bathroom.

"Come along, Ms. Tanner. It's alright," Hilda had transformed into someone almost motherly.

"I'm delirious, aren't I?"

"What do you mean?"

"I mean, I'm seeing things, right?"

"Depends on what things you're seeing?" Hilda reasoned as she managed successfully to get Mitch in the oatmeal bath. They were right about one thing. This oatmeal stuff was soothing.

"Why are they still out there? Can't they see that I'm sick?"

"If they didn't before, they sure got a good look just now," Hilda assured Mitch.

Everyone lapsed into silence. Mitch stayed in the tub until the water became tepid, and then Hilda poured her back into bed. Reb came in to check on things while Hilda cleaned the bathtub. She looked so innocent.

"Is there anything else you need?"

"How about you stick around for a few minutes and tell me what the hell is going on."

"I could do that, but it might take more than a few minutes."

"I'll try to stay awake this time."

"Everyone saw you faint on TV."

"Really?"

"They showed it about ten times on the news."

"Please tell me it wasn't in slow motion," Mitch would've been on her knees begging to make it not so were she able.

"Slow motion, super-slow motion, frame-by-frame in the newspaper."

"Oh, Dear Lord, I don't believe this. And that's why there's more people?"

Reb hesitated. That's all Mitch needed.

"What aren't you telling me?"

"You do remember Sheila?"

"Sheila? Sheila? Oh yeah. It's all a bit fuzzy, but she was that woman Lucinda picked out. Right?" Mitch was struggling to put it all together.

"Right."

"What about Sheila?"

"She's cured."

Mitch closed her eyes. "It can't be."

"It apparently is."

"I don't even know what she has. Or had."

"Something called fibromyalgia."

"Never heard of it."

"Apparently, that doesn't matter, whether or not you've heard of something."

"Although you have used the word "apparently" twice in the past minute, I'm still getting this funny feeling that you are beginning to believe all this hooey yourself."

"I'm not sure what I believe right this minute, but the TV has caught everything on tape. If it's any consolation, Lucinda Cornwall is having kittens."

"I imagine so. Wouldn't you give a crisp, clean, new hundred-dollar bill to get a candid view of Polly Perkell's face as well."

"A hundred dollars is a lot of money."

"How many boxes of oatmeal powder could we buy for a hundred dollars?" Mitch smiled wanly.

"Let's hope we don't have to find out," Reb patted her hand. "Take a nap."

Chapter 30

"Did you have a nice nap, Sweetie?" Trish had managed to tiptoe into the bedroom about the time Robbie was waking up. She had also managed to not quite hide two dozen roses behind her back.

"What have you got?" Robbie quizzed sleepily.

"Oh, just a small token of my love for the most amazing expectant mother in the state."

"Thank you," Robbie raised up in bed and grimaced.

"You okay, Sweetie?" Trish put the flowers down on the empty side of the bed and proceeded to fuss over Robbie.

"I'm just moving a little slow."

"You're supposed to. You're pregnant."

"I'm not so far into this pregnancy that I should be slowing up at all."

"Well, maybe it's something else?"

"Like what?"

"Maybe you have a cold? That would slow you down."

"I don't have a runny nose."

"You could have a mild flu bug. That might cause some muscle soreness."

"I don't have a fever."

Trish, who wasn't acquainted with the querulous side of Robbie, wasn't comfortable arguing about medical issues.

"I'm calling the doctor."

"Why?"

"Because it will make me feel better to have you checked."

"If we go to the doctor's office every time I have a pain, we're going to run up quite a bill."

"I don't care. If we want to pay to have a doctor sit with you for the second half of your pregnancy, it would be the best use of money I can think of."

Trish dialed the doctor's office and secured an appointment for one in the afternoon. That gave her time to cook up a nice lunch for the both of them. At best, Robbie nibbled. She definitely wasn't feeling her usual perky self.

"Did you see the news?" Trish chatted to keep Robbie's mind occupied. She never did enjoy visits to the doctor.

"No, not lately."

"Mitch is still in the top stories."

"What's going on now?"

"She fainted outside. Fell down right on the ground as she was touching some stranger. Now, she has the Chickenpox."

"Who has the Chickenpox?"

"Mitch."

"Not the stranger?"

"No, I don't think so. But she did have some illness that seems to have miraculously gone away."

"So, the stranger is well and now Mitch is sick?"

"Yeah."

"That hardly seems fair."

"And now, there's literally hundreds and hundreds of people standing vigil outside of the trailer."

"How terrible for them. They can't even live their lives in peace."

Trish cleared the lunch dishes and then did everything she could think of to help get Robbie out the door. One of the things that Trish had immediately liked about the OBGYN physician was her savvy and intuition. After performing a cursory exam, she had a talk with both women in her office.

"I think it's time to schedule an ultrasound."

"Why?" Robbie asked with a voice laced with concern.

"It's just a precaution. We probably won't find anything but a healthy pregnancy, but I want to err on the side of caution."

"So, everything's okay, you think?"

"Let's make the arrangements."

"You mean, we're going right now?"

"Not right now, but soon."

"Soon" turned out to be the next day. The amount of water that Robbie had to drink in order to have the test made her feel like she was going in and out with the tide. She all but ebbed on the car ride to the hospital. Trish had talked Max and Rose into staying home, only after promising to call them with any news. She was pleasantly surprised that she would be allowed into the room as they conducted the test. The technology was amazing. As Trish peered over the shoulder of the technician at the screen with the visible outline of the fetus, she realized how very, very amazing the technology was. A coldness seeped into her

228

stomach and made her shiver, a response she hid from Robbie, who couldn't see the screen from her position on the table. She had to keep reminding herself that she wasn't a doctor.

"Hey," Robbie squeezed Trish's hand, "You look like you're watching a football game."

Trish flashed a smile for show. "It's third down and goal to go."

"Rah rah for our team."

The technician looked backward at Trish. It was going to be a lot more complicated than football.

"There, we're done," the technician finished things up with a poker face unparalleled in the western hemisphere. After Robbie excused herself to use the restroom, Trish quizzed the technician.

"Tell me what you think."

"I can't discuss the test results with anyone."

"If you were me, what would you do?"

"I'd wait and talk to the doctor."

"How soon will we be able to do that?"

"I'm sure the doctor's office will be in touch with you."

"From the look of things, I think we'd better hurry home."

"That might be best."

No sooner had the technician disappeared than Robbie came back.

"You ready to go?" Robbie seemed drained in every sense of the word.

"Absolutely."

Trish drove home, carefully avoiding potholes and sharp turns. Max and Rose were waiting at the door, wondering about the generalities of the procedure. It helped to take Trish's mind off specifics. After all, she was no expert and was beginning to doubt her senses. Robbie was ready for a nap and accepted a quick kiss from Trish before closing her eyes.

Rose was waiting at the kitchen table for Trish.

"Do you want to talk?" Rose probed.

"Talk?" Trish stalled. She knew it was useless to do so.

"I can tell by looking at you that something isn't right."

"I really don't know anything," Trish hedged.

She should've known better than to try and hedge her way around Rose.

"Your eyes tell a different story."

Trish cast her eyes downward. Another tell-tell giveaway.

"What did you find out from the test?"

"Robbie didn't find out anything."

"I'm not asking what Robbie found out. I'm asking what you found out."

"I'm not quite sure," Trish told the version of the truth that best fit reality.

Further questioning was interrupted by the ringing of the phone. It was the doctor's office calling to schedule another appointment. That cold feeling that never really left Trish's stomach just went down a few more degrees.

"Is the doctor there now?" Trish asked.

"Yes, she's in with another patient, though."

"I'll hold."

It took about thirty seconds of classical music before the doctor took the call. In doctor standards, that was lightening quick.

"Hello, Trish."

"I was wondering why we need another appointment so quickly."

"I want to go over the results with you and Robbie."

"You've seen them already?"

"I was at the hospital and stopped in to check things out."

"And?"

"When do you want to come in tomorrow?"

"How about nine?" Trish threw out the first time that came to her mind.

"That's fine. See you then."

Trish hung up the phone and looked straight at Rose. Any time a doctor rearranged a schedule for a patient, it wasn't good. Those cold feeling previously held only by Robbie were now seeping into Rose as well. Winter had arrived early in the Goldstein house.

Chapter 31

By now, Mitch was truly delirious. She couldn't put a finger on herself that didn't hit a pock, and every last one of them was itching like mortal sin. Her temperature was making things more uncomfortable. Even with medication, it was still running above normal like it was trying to win a marathon. It was day three and counting.

"What day is it?" she asked Reb like Scrooge had done with the boy passing by the window on Christmas morning.

"It's Wednesday."

"That's not what I mean!"

"What did you mean?" Reb was so calm. She had probably been canonized already.

"I meant, how many days have I had the Chickenpox?"

It was as if time itself would now be measured by the event. Everything in history that had happened prior to the first day of Mitch's Chickenpox would be labeled BCP and everything after would therefore be ACP. They were in day three, ACP.

"You've *only* had them for three days."

"*Only?*" Mitch was grumpier that Scrooge. A fact not lost on Reb.

"Come now. Kids all over the world get Chickenpox every day and you don't hear them complaining about it."

"It's easier to be sick when you're little."

"You think so?"

"Did Mary have the Chickenpox?" Mitch asked. Again. For about the fortieth time.

"Yes, Mary has had the Chickenpox and I've had them as well." It sounded like a mantra.

"Why didn't I get the Chickenpox before?"

"I don't know."

"I was an only child."

"Mary was an only child. I'm sure she got them from her friends at school."

"I didn't have friends," Mitch admitted.

"You must have had friends in school."

"Nope," Mitch said and then closed her eyes. A sure sign that further discussion was off limits. Reb filed the confession away in a safe spot in her heart.

"Did I tell you about the oatmeal powder?" Reb asked.

"No. What about the oatmeal powder?"

"It seems that when everyone got a look at your Chickenpox ravaged body, they all ran out and bought you a box."

"They did?"

"Yes. There was quite the run on it at the local drug store. The shelves were empty in an hour. Then, according to reliable sources-"

"Pam Tracy?"

"Yeah. Anyway, all the stores in the surrounding counties were hit as well. You have boxes of oatmeal powder from as far away as British Columbia."

"Really?"

"And that's not all. When people couldn't buy the oatmeal stuff, they bought all kinds of creams and ointments and flowers."

"Flowers?"

"You know, bouquets of flowers and teddy bears."

"You're teasing me, aren't you?" Mitch trained her eyes on Reb. She wasn't teasing.

"Stuff is piling up out in the front yard like you wouldn't believe."

"So, it is Christmas. I haven't missed it after all."

"What?"

"Nothing."

Reb felt Mitch's forehead. The fever was running amok again. Time for more medicine. And another call to the doctor.

232

Trish did everything she could think of to hide her nervousness from Robbie while they waited for the doctor. Her attempts gave her away.

"What's wrong with you this morning?" Robbie asked point blank as they sat side by side.

"Nothing's wrong!" Trish patted Robbie's hand. For the third time that minute.

"I know you expectant father types are supposed to be nervous, but doesn't that happen closer to the actual delivery?"

"I'm not nervous."

"Are you sure?"

"I'm sure," Trish inhaled deeply to calm herself down.

"That's about the fifth time you've done that. If you keep it up, you're going to hyperventilate and need a bag to breathe into."

"I'm not going to need a bag."

"Okay. I'm just trying to be helpful. It just isn't like you to be this edgy."

"So, maybe I am a little nervous about this parenthood thing."

"And that's perfectly understandable."

"Uh huh," was all Trish got out before the doctor came in. She didn't look a bit nervous.

"I'd like you to repeat the ultrasound test," she came directly to the point with Robbie.

"Why?" Robbie asked.

"Some of the images were unclear. I'd like to be present at the procedure to monitor the technician. Are you up to it?"

Robbie had to think about it for a moment. For anyone who has never undergone an ultrasound during a pregnancy, which ruled out all men, it isn't like a walk through the park. One of the requirements is to drink a lot of liquid and then hold said fluid during most of the ultrasound, which includes running a hand-held sensor across the belly. This part puts added pressure on the bladder. There are worse tests, of course, but one time through the process is bad enough. Robbie would be a trooper to go along without complaint.

"When do you want to do it?" she asked calmly.

"This afternoon."

Trish bit her tongue. Not hard. Just enough to keep it from wagging out her concerns.

"Can I drink enough fluids in time?" Robbie was asking herself this question more than the doctor.

"I'm sure you can. If I were you, I'd stick to water as much as possible. Coffee and tea are diuretics."

Robbie nodded. She was already feeling the urge and the deluge hadn't even begun. So, as Trish measured out the fluid, Robbie drank. The trip to the hospital was eerily quiet, as if even dialogue would irritate the bladder. During the first ultrasound, the room had seemed a bit crowded. Now that the doctor was present, things were downright cramped. Which also adequately described the muscles in both Robbie's back and Trish's neck. Neither had slept very well the previous night, for different reasons. As the technician created more fuzzy images of the fetus, Trish watched over the doctor's shoulder like she was attempting to catch a headline. There was no pointing, no "ah hahing", no nothing. After a brief few moments, she had seen enough.

"I think we can finish up here. You've had enough for one day, right, Robbie?" the doctor was neutral and calm.

"This wasn't so bad."

"Go ahead and use the restroom. Take all the time you need." Something about all of this decorous talk was scaring the hell out of Trish. That wintry feeling was creeping clear into her bones. When Robbie was out of sight, the doctor turned to Trish.

"Would you be able to come back to the office this afternoon?"

Trish knew that the doctor knew that she knew.

"To consult."

"Right."

"I can take Robbie out to lunch. What time would you like us there?"

The doctor seemed to give the question an inordinate amount of consideration.

"How about three?"

"I guess I'll take Robbie out to a long lunch. Maybe we could squeeze in a shopping spree as well. Buy some more maternity clothes?"

Trish was fishing for a clue and came up empty.

"I thought you did that already?"

"Well, you know the old saying, an expectant mother can never have too many maternity outfits."

The doctor, if she had a comment, kept it to herself.

Trish took up a vigil outside the ladies room where Robbie had disappeared. She was taking her time, which was fine by Trish. It gave her a moment to come up with enough plans to fill up the hours until three o'clock. They could shop, do lunch, shop, have coffee, shop...

"Hellooo..." Robbie was right by her side.

"Oh, Hi!"

"You were just about to take a nap?"

"I'm sorry."

"Don't be sorry. I know you didn't sleep well last night."

"You do?"

"Yes, I do. Do you want to go home and catch up on your sleep?"

God, that sounded tempting.

"I wanted to take you to lunch."

"We can have lunch at home. In bed?"

Now, it really was tempting, except that Trish still had to work in the news about the doctor's appointment. Might as well get it over with.

"We're due back at the doctor's office at three."

"We are?"

Trish nodded. There wasn't much else to say.

"Then, let's do that lunch after all. I've had about all the liquid diet I can take this week."

Trish looked up at Robbie. She couldn't have fallen in love with a braver, more beautiful woman if she had tried for a thousand and one years.

"Lunch it is!"

And it wasn't just any old lunch either. They went to a nice, quiet, romantic spot where the tablecloths were actually linen and the glassware was musical when it clinked together. Robbie was trying hard to behave herself, nutrition-wise. Trish, however, was being a bad influence. Mostly on purpose.

"You must have some of this drawn butter with your lobster," Trish cajoled.

"I shouldn't even be having lobster!"

"Oh, sure you should. Fish is good for you."

"I think lobster is high in cholesterol?"

"One lobster won't hurt you."

"I suppose not. Unless it pinches me."

Trish laughed. Maybe a bit too loudly.

Robbie only rolled her eyes. "And this asparagus is good for me."

"That's something else you could dip into butter as well."

"Enough with the butter already. If I keep eating all this fat, our baby is going to slide right out on delivery day."

Robbie checked to see is Trish was smiling. It was a distracted expression she saw.

"Are you going to tell me what's wrong, or do I have to wait until three and hear it from the doctor?"

"What?" was the only word that Trish could utter. It was lame, just like how she felt.

"Something is going on with this ultrasound business and I want to know what it is that you know already."

"I don't know anything."

"You know something. Or you suspect something."

"I suspect that the doctor is looking for something specific. That's what we're paying her to do."

"What specific thing is she looking for?"

"She didn't say. I didn't ask."

"What did you see?"

"I saw a fuzzy image of a baby."

"And what else?"

"I'm not sure," Trish said, quite honestly.

"What bothered you?"

"I'm just not sure what proportions are expected at this stage."

"The head is big?" Robbie started to guess.

"Yes."

"Is it too big?"

"I don't think so. But I really don't know. I honestly don't."

Trish hadn't worried at all about the baby's head. It was other things that concerned her. She paid the check and then she and Robbie took a slow walk around a nearby shopping mall. They didn't feel much like shopping but that didn't stop Trish from buying a few things for Robbie that caught her eye. They didn't even go through the bother of trying anything on. Time dragged until they arrived back at the doctor's office. They were there early, but were shown right into the office.

"The doctor is on the phone. She'll be with you shortly," the perennially perky receptionist informed them. And, indeed, that did happen, almost immediately. The doctor took her place behind the desk and the only thing different from the last visit was the all-too-obvious presence of Kleenex within easy reach.

"I have made arrangements for you to go to Chicago."

One of the things Trish liked about this doctor was her directness.

"Why?" Robbie asked calmly, as if the doctor had simply requested that they go to the corner drugstore.

"There's another kind of ultrasound technology at the University of Chicago. It's called 4-D."

"Forty?" Trish asked.

"Four – D. It's a more accurate type of ultrasound."

"Why do we need a more accurate ultrasound?" Robbie was more curious than panicked.

"Because I'm a very cautious doctor and I want as much information as possible about your pregnancy."

"Do you send all your patients to Chicago?" Robbie sounded benign, but Trish could tell she was going to hone in very soon. The doctor weighed the question like the fate of the world depended on it. The fate of Robbie and Trish's world depended on it.

"I send about five to ten percent of my expectant mothers to other facilities for tests."

"Not all?"

"No."

"Then, what makes the difference for the other ten percent?"

"For you, this test will show more detail."

"What kind of detail?"

"The overall body structure of the fetus."

Robbie stopped asking questions. She knew that no amount of general questioning would make the doctor answer with any more detail and she didn't know enough to ask more educated questions. Frankly, she didn't want to hear anymore anyway. If the doctor wanted her to go to Chicago, she'd go to Chicago.

"Should we fly or drive?" Robbie asked the doctor.

"We should fly. I'll have my office make the airline reservations."

"You're going as well?" Trish had been paying attention to pronouns.

"I plan to accompany you, yes. I don't want to have anything go undone."

"In that case, let me take care of the flight details," Trish wanted to help take care of something and this was something she could handle. "What day do you want to go?"

"Let's have my appointment secretary talk to you."

It took them fifteen minutes to clear time on everyone's schedule between Denver and Chicago. The test would occur the day after tomorrow. Trish kept her mouth shut, but this did nothing but spell out the urgency of the situation for her. Hell, it wasn't this easy getting a tee time decided upon by two or more doctors. There was no time to waste. Trish needed to charter a jet, get Robbie and her parents organized and packed and make arrangements with the limousine company to provide ground transportation. In among all this activity, she managed to squeeze in a call to Mitch.

"You sound horrible!" she said in response to Mitch's croaked-out "Hello."

"I feel horrible. Just ask Reb. She's been putting up with me for days and days."

"I saw you on the news in your robe. You didn't look so bad then?"

"I've since bloomed. You know, I must have over a hundred of these pox all over me. I have one between my toes!"

"That must hurt."

"Not as much as itch. They make me take a bath twice a day. I used to get by on twice a week."

"Are you getting better, though?"

238

"Yeah. Slowly."

"Oh, good."

Even in her debilitated state, Mitch could sense a problem.

"What's new?" she fished.

"Robbie and I are going to take a trip to Chicago."

"Why?"

There was a significant pause. "Robbie needs a new-fangled sort of ultrasound."

"What's wrong?" Mitch went right to the heart of the matter.

"We're not sure anything's wrong."

"What are they looking for?"

"They won't say."

"And, you've asked, of course?"

"Every way we could think of."

"You want me to come out there? I'll have Reb prop me up in the car."

"No. Don't do that. I have enough to deal with right now."

"Including one very worried mother-to-be, I'm sure."

"Max and Rose are quietly frantic. You wouldn't believe how stoic they have been, but they are sick with fear."

"Okay, but, now, it's just another test, right?"

"Robbie had two ultrasounds before they arranged for this one."

"So, you've seen the baby?"

"It was pretty small."

"That's how they all start out," Mitch teased, just a little. Trish laughed, just a little.

"I can come out there, or meet you in Chicago," Mitch repeated her offer just before Reb's voice came on the line. "Hi, Trish."

"Hi, Reb."

"What's this about Chicago?"

"Please talk Mitch out of coming."

"Don't worry. She can't even get to the bathroom without help."

In the distance, Trish could hear Mitch objecting with a muffled, "I can so get to the bathroom all by myself."

"Just keep her there," Trish implored.

"I will. Is there anything we can do from here?"

"Let's keep in touch. I'll call you when we get there."

"Okay. And then, when you get back home and things calm down, we'll come to see you."

"That would be nice."

"You want to talk to the Chickenpox girl again?"

"Oh, sure."

Not a whole lot more talking went on. Mitch was tired and Trish was busy. After Mitch hung up, she looked at Reb. "This isn't going to be good, is it?"

"We can't know that for sure."

"I need to get well."

"You need to stay in bed until you get well."

"I will. I promise."

Flying on a charter jet to Chicago for a medical test wasn't nearly as much fun as the flight to New York had been what now seemed like eons ago. Back in the good old days when the only worry was drinking too much champagne. Making the arrangements for this flight had helped Trish to keep busy and now that she was consigned to sit and wait, she was once again faced with the onus of hiding her worry from Robbie. Meanwhile, Robbie was the epitome of calm. Max and Rose were putting on a brave face as well. The doctor was busy reading medical journals. Surrounded by all the serenity was a sudden comfort to Trish. She relaxed and dropped off to sleep. The next thing she knew, Robbie was waking her up in preparation for the landing.

"I was asleep?" she asked in disbelief.

"You were exhausted."

"I guess so."

Events blurred together after they touched down. The ride to the hospital, the test, the ride back, the flight home. They were back at the house, sitting in front of the fireplace like they had done nothing more than take a ride around town. Trish was holding Robbie close. Any other evening, it would be a prelude to romance. Tonight, it was just so she could marvel at this wonderful woman in her life.

"What if things aren't right?" Robbie asked the obvious quietly.

Trish gave the question due consideration. "You mean, with the pregnancy?"

"I mean with the baby."

"Life isn't meant to be perfect."

"It has been so far with you."

Trish looked at her. "You're the reason for that."

"I want to say something before we go back to talk to the doctor."

"Okay."

"I want to do whatever it takes to keep this baby. If it means I need to stay in bed, I'll stay in bed. If I need to go in for weekly checkups, I'll go in for weekly checkups."

"We don't even know for sure if something is wrong."

"Something is wrong. I can feel it."

Trish didn't argue. She just held Robbie closer and made her comfortable in her arms. They would know soon enough, one way or the other.

There was only one noticeable change in the doctor's office. An extra box of Kleenex had appeared on the desk. One for everybody. Trish didn't know if Robbie had noticed this, and made sure not to point it out. Lord knows, they were edgy enough after waiting for still more test results. The doctor came in and sat down. She was pale.

"I've been consulting with other physicians about the test results. Sorry to keep you waiting so long."

"And what have you come up with?" Robbie was calm.

"One of the things I do as a doctor is to try and balance what I can predict about a pregnancy against what I actually know about the pregnancy."

"Okay," Robbie remarked, hoping to prod the doctor along with agreeableness.

"What we know exactly right now is, obviously, not as much as we would know later in the pregnancy, but I will try to answer your questions fully."

"Okay," Robbie repeated.

"Our best guess right now is that the fetus might have T-A-R."

"Tar?" Robbie was totally in the dark.

"T-A-R is an acronym. It stands for Thrombosis Absent Radius."

"I've never heard of it," Robbie remarked, not knowing whether to be worried or downright scared out of her wits.

"That's not at all surprising. It's a very rare condition."

241

"Is it a birth defect, then?" Trish figured it was best to start at the beginning.

"Yes."

"And, what is it exactly. All those words? Throm…what?"

"Thrombosis absent radius. Thrombosis is a term that refers to bleeding."

"Bleeding? Is the baby bleeding?" Robbie asked. That line between worried and scared was disappearing.

"Not that I'm aware of."

"How would you know?"

The doctor paused. The answer pretty much dawned on Trish.

"The fetus is still viable."

"You mean, the baby is still alive," Robbie reworded the concept.

"Right."

"And what about the other words?" Trish forged ahead.

"Absent Radius. The radius is one of the bones in the arm between wrist and elbow."

"So, absent radius means…?" Trish didn't like where this was going. Not at all.

"The radius is affected, often absent. Not developed."

"The baby is missing its arms?" Robbie asked point blank.

"Not totally. The arm should be there from shoulder to elbow. And then, there's the other bone in the lower arm. Still, it could be a serious deformity."

"And that's what you saw in the ultrasound, isn't it? The arms?"

"Right. We're still hoping that we're wrong."

"But, you're not, are you?" Trish put a fine point on it.

"I don't think so."

As Trish had asked questions, Robbie had grown silent. It was a ponderous kind of silence, as if something were nagging at her. She found her question and voice.

"Are you surprised that I'm still pregnant?"

"Not especially."

"Could I still lose the baby?"

"Yes. Research indicates that if the fetus is male, it has a lesser chance of survival. But let me be clear about this, there are so very few instances of TAR, that I really can't quote research or statistics as reliable."

"So, it's rare? I just figured I'd never heard of it because I've just never read a lot about the subject."

"TAR is extremely rare. That's why we're still keeping our fingers crossed that we're wrong."

"I'm sure it's because I don't understand," Robbie said, "But as terrible as it is to be missing the bones, what else is the concern? What haven't you told us?"

"The thrombosis is actually the major concern here."

"The bleeding?"

"Right. Thrombosis is a bleeding condition that can have many profound effects."

"Profound, like, in what way?"

"Well, for instance," the doctor paused, "if there is bleeding in the brain, it can cause mental retardation."

Robbie had been the picture of bravery until now, but at the mention of retardation, her grasp tightened like a vice grip around Trish's fingers.

"The baby will be retarded?"

"There's a slight chance, yes."

"But there is a chance?"

"According to what little research we know of, the chance is roughly seven percent."

"So, my baby will be deformed, we know for certain, and might be retarded as well?"

"There's that chance, yes."

"And, what else, doctor?" Trish wanted to hear every unspoken fear.

"Would you like to take a break for a few minutes? Have some coffee?"

Trish looked at Robbie. They both knew what they wanted.

"We'd rather just hear the rest now."

"Okay. Well, if you do carry to term, and the birth goes well, there's still a ninety-percent chance that the baby will have a serious bout of bleeding in the first year."

"How serious?"

"Thirty percent of babies with TAR don't survive the first twelve months of life."

Trish looked over at Robbie. It was now time to take that break. Even with her strong resolve, Robbie was ashen. In fact, so

243

ashen that the doctor took immediate action. Between the doctor and Trish, they guided Robbie to a couch. Her blood pressure was elevated, but not out of bounds. Everything was within acceptable range as well. As Robbie's color slowly returned, Trish sat by her in a chair, soothing her with tranquil words that neither one would remember.

"I'll be okay in a minute," Robbie said in a voice stronger than Trish could muster.

"Of course you will," Trish struggled to sound as brave.

"And I have to get better because we'll have to break the news to my parents the minute we get home."

"I know. I'll do whatever I can to help."

"Just stay by my side."

"Always."

Robbie now patted Trish's hand and smiled. "I'm ready to go home."

"Okay."

When Robbie said she was ready to go home, she was ready to go home. There was no stalling, no putting off the inevitable. Max and Rose were practically camped out on the doorstep and knew without being told the gravity of the situation. Robbie began the story and then, when it got to be too much, Trish picked up the thread. As they finished the report, it was crystal clear where Robbie got her incredible strength. Rather than crumble, they were ready to do whatever was necessary to make things easier. So, other than dealing with a couple of bouts of paleness, Trish was ready to cook lunch and then get to work on the nursery. It wasn't until Trish had been sitting a good half hour on the French-style window sill in the nursery that Robbie came in to check on her. She took Trish's hand and wrist like she was counting her pulse.

"You okay?"

"I have to call Mitch. I promised. To call. When we knew more."

"And you're putting it off because...?"

"Why is it so hard to give good friends bad news?"

"It's because they know how deeply we feel, when strangers wouldn't. And it breaks us down. We know it's safe. Like it is with us."

And then, surrounded by light streaming in through the window, Robbie held Trish as she cried.

Robbie wouldn't let Trish make the call to Mitch until they were both stretched out on the bed, mainly so that they could hold each other for support. It took all of five minutes to convey the information to Mitch and hear that she would be there as soon as humanly possible. As Mitch hung up, Reb checked her expression. "I don't suppose I can talk you into staying in bed one more day?"

"I'm afraid not. Trish needs us."

"It's serious, isn't it?"

"Yes."

"I'll get the suitcases."

By the time word passed about the plan, Mary was over to visit and wondering if they needed a couple of spare drivers, namely herself and Lisa.

"It's a pretty short drive," Reb said.

"Don't leave us here. Alone. With *them*."

Reb nodded. She understood. Maybe if they all left for a couple of days, the crowd would thin out.

"Somebody should call Trish back and warn her that they'll be more guests," Mitch thought ahead.

"Do you think she'll mind?"

"No. She probably just needs to buy a couple more beds. And sheets. And pillows…"

"We could take our own, pillows."

"I'll just give her a quick call."

Robbie had answered the phone and gave Mitch the impression that they had planned all along to have Mary and Lisa as well.

"Order another bed," she informed Trish after hanging up.

"Another bed?"

"Mary and Lisa."

"Oh, okay. One more bed for Mary and Lisa coming right up."

Trish had already been on the phone to Furniture Plus once this morning and hoped to catch them before the truck was gone.

She did and was so thankful that she ordered four dressers to go along with the extra bed.

"Four dressers?" Robbie asked afterwards.

"We're having four women show up. Trust me, we'll need four dressers."

"Let's go sheet shopping."

"Good idea."

Under any other circumstances, shopping for sheets was cause for silly and suggestive dialogue between them. However, as they were picking out something for houseguests coming to give comfort and support, the shopping was more somber. Trish was surprised that Robbie had decided to go out at all, but it must have helped to stay busy and occupied.

"Do you think silk or percale for Rebecca and Mitch?" Robbie asked like Trish would know.

"I have no idea."

"No idea whatsoever?"

"Why would I?"

"I thought that this was something friends just knew about each other."

"You suppose they know that we sleep on flannel with a reindeer motif?"

"Well, now that you mention it, I guess it hasn't come up in conversation…"

"Why don't we just buy two of everything?"

"We *are* shopping for two beds worth."

"Okay, so, let's get four of everything. It's only money," Trish said.

"Four silk and four percale?"

"And four flannel as well. I don't want to spend time doing the laundry while we have guests."

"I can get the laundry done, no problem," Robbie explained.

"You're not going to do anymore laundry anyway," Trish explained back.

"We still need pillows and blankets and bedspreads and comforters. We need a lot, in fact."

Trish noted the fatigue in Robbie's voice. "You just pick things out, honey, and I'll do the rest."

About that time, a salesperson came to their rescue. Robbie pointed, Trish nodded, and the clerk gathered. It didn't take long for the stack to grow and take up two counters around the cash register. It obviously wasn't all going to fit in the car without blocking vision. They packed the essentials in the car and arranged for the rest to be delivered post haste. By the time they got home, the beds were set up in the only rooms left on the first floor that could be used as guest rooms. The dressers were still on the truck. Trish took hold of Robbie's hand and walked her to their bedroom.

"I want you to rest."

"I'm not going to *take to my bed* for the duration of this pregnancy!"

"I sincerely hope it doesn't come to that either, but I know when you're tired."

"How do you know?"

"I can tell by your voice. Now, go to bed. Please."

"Okay. I'll rest for a while. Wake me up when something exciting happens."

"I promise."

There was nothing very exciting about working against time to get bedrooms ready for guests. Rose helped with the first and then Trish had the bright idea to ask her and Max to do some grocery shopping, mainly to avoid treating Rose like a maid. They chatted about dinner ideas that would be easy. It really wasn't cheating if you used cream of chicken soup as a gravy base, particularly when the number of people to feed was about to double.

"In fact, although they won't hold a candle to yours, why don't you pick up a couple of pies from the bakery?"

"If I had time, I would bake."

Trish went to Rose and gave her a hug. "I'd rather you spend as much time as you can with Robbie, and leave the baking to someone else for a while."

"It's going to be a long next few months."

"Yes, it will. Would it be easier for you and Max if I hired some help? A cook? A maid?"

"I've never needed help yet around the house."

"You've never faced circumstances quite like this before, either."

"Sometimes, in circumstances like these, it's good to keep a little busy."

"You promise to let me know when busy gets to be too busy?"

"Yes."

With Max and Rose off to the store and Robbie resting, the house was still. Furniture movers had gone and the only thing to do now was to put sheets on beds and wait for the rest of the bedding. Trish resisted lying down. She knew she'd be a goner to lullaby land if she as much as closed he eyes. She went to the fireplace room and sat on the couch to await the arrival of whomever would appear next.

Robbie appeared next.
"You maybe want to wake up, Honey?" Robbie was rubbing her forearm like she had passed out.
"Hum?" Trish opened her eyes. She had fallen asleep on the couch and slept like a stone. Someone had even taken care to cover her up.
"Did you have a good nap?"
"I didn't even know I was asleep."
"Company is here."
"They are? I don't have all the beds made yet!" Trish was trying to will her sleepy body to get up.
"I took care of that."
"You did?"
"Yes, about an hour ago. The store delivered everything."
"An hour ago? How long have I been asleep?"
"You had a good, long nap. It's dinnertime."
"Already? And Mitch is here?"
"Mitch and everybody else."
Trish stood up slowly and stretched her muscles. It had been a long nap. She followed Robbie to where everyone had gathered. Mitch was a sight. Even with the worst of the Chickenpox over, the patient still looked a mess. It didn't matter to Trish. She pulled her close and held on like they hadn't seen each other in decades. It felt that was, with all that had happened recently. Usually, Mitch held on to people until she felt their tension ebb, but not this time. Trish was a bundle of unspent nerve, and Mitch couldn't take quite that much physical contact yet.
"You made it safe and sound?"
"Everything went well."
"Once we got out of our own driveway," Reb was waiting for her hug.

248

Trish obliged and then extended a welcome to Mary and Lisa.
"You certainly look better!" Trish was studying Lisa's face.
"I'm healing like a dream."
At the mention of the word "healing," everyone shifted from one foot to the other. It was a touchy subject.
"Yes, you are. Must be all the care and attention you're getting from Mary."
"And the good diet," Lisa said.
"And the nagging," Mary added like that was the secret ingredient.
Speaking of which, Rose had been cooking and was now ready to serve dinner. She had plenty of help, with five women in the house, and they all pitched in afterwards to clean up the kitchen. When it was once again safe to be lazy, Mitch and Trish went onto the fireplace room for a chat. They sat close together, like lovers.
"How is Robbie doing?"
"She's a pillar of strength. So are Max and Rose."
"And how about you?"
"Me? I'm a mess."
"You seem calm on the outside."
"I'm all jumbled up on the inside."
"Tell me about all the jumbles."
"I'm at the disbelief stage, I think."
"It's still sinking in, no doubt."
"Pretty soon, I expect I'll be throwing things."
"Big things or little things?" Mitch asked as she scanned the room for any heavy objects and Ming vases. Stuff like that.
"Probably whatever I get hold of first."
"I understand that mood completely."
Trish looked into Mitch's eyes. "You've been having an interesting time of it lately as well, haven't you?"
"Oh, gee, let's not go into all that."
"Touchy subject?"
"It's just so weird to wake up every morning to a crowd outside your door. And there's no reason for it."
"They say on the news that you can heal people."
"If I could heal people, don't you think Rebecca would be up and walking around by now?"

"Maybe it just doesn't work that way?"

"It doesn't work at all!" Mitch grew uncharacteristically testy and then immediately felt remorse. "I'm sorry. You're the last person I need to be snapping at about this."

"It's okay. That's what friends are for."

They sat quietly for a moment. So quietly that they heard noises in the night outside.

"Are you so far out in the country that you get visited by nocturnal critters?"

"Not that I'm aware of. But I do hear something."

They went to the front door together like they were trying to sneak up on a ninja. Indeed, there was something out there. As Robbie opened the door, flashbulbs went off in her eyes, creating those pesky, dancing-ball images. Behind the cameras were people. Some had come for photos, others had come to gawk. Either they had followed Mitch from Kansas or this was the local lookers. As Mitch stood up to them on the porch, Silver bounded onto the scene. She was at Mitch's side, gun drawn, ready to drop the first interloper in his or her tracks. Mitch remained calm, reaching over to slowly lower the gun.

"It's okay. No one's going to hurt anyone. Okay?"

Silver put the gun in her holster, but wouldn't budge from her spot. A voice from the crowd asked, "Are you the lady who heals people?"

It was a female voice. Mitch squinted her eyes to try and locate the interlocutor.

"I don't heal people," Mitch answered with her denial.

"I've seen you. You healed somebody on TV."

"I may have been on TV, but I don't have healing powers."

"Would you touch my baby anyway? Just in case?"

The voice sounded so sad and yet at the same time so hopeful that Mitch walked closer to the crowd. Neither Silver nor Trish were particularly happy about this, but couldn't stop her. Mitch went to the woman and saw a sweet baby in her arms.

"What about your baby?"

"He keeps getting ear infections. I'm worried that it will damage his hearing one day."

"Can I hold him?" Mitch surprised herself with the request. She hadn't held a baby in forever and the idea suddenly appealed to her. The mother didn't seem to mind handing her infant over to a world-famous healer and Mitch cuddled the child as she talked. "I wouldn't worry about the baby losing his hearing."

"I guess I'm just a worrier."

"That's okay. It's okay to be a bit of a worrier where your children are concerned. I think that kids outgrow ear infections, don't they?"

"But that will take a long time."

"No, it won't. I promise. In the blink of an eye, you won't be concerned about ear infections."

"I won't?"

"In the blink of an eye."

With that bit of homespun wisdom, she handed the baby back to the mother. Only after all this did the mother think to ask, "Are you still contagious?"

"I don't think so, why?"

"Because they said on the news tonight that there's such an outbreak of Chickenpox in Utopia that they had to call out the Red Cross."

Mitch only grimaced. So much pox, so few boxes of oatmeal powder. Maybe the sheriff would give away all those boxes to needy families. Since there were only a dozen or so people outside the house, Mitch took time to say hello and pose for pictures. No other person had a request for healing, so once Mitch came back inside, Trish closed the door for the night. Immediately, Silver launched into an apology, "They caught me off guard."

"Do you always pull a gun on strangers?" Mitch asked quietly.

"When I'm outnumbered twenty to one I do!"

"You wouldn't like it one little bit in Utopia right now. We're up to a thousand to one. And a Chickenpox epidemic to boot."

By now, Reb had joined the conference. "What's going on?"

"Some of my fans have shown up."

"It was only a matter of time. We didn't exactly travel in a secret convoy."

"You think they'll be back?" Silver looked at the trio for an answer.

"Hard telling if they'll even leave," Mitch sighed. "They stick around for days back home."

251

"What should we do?" Trish asked.

"I don't know about the rest of you, but I'm going to bed. It's been a long day," Mitch was showing wear around the edges.

"I'll guard the door," Silver announced.

"You don't need to," Mitch promised.

"Why not?"

"They won't try to break in. They never do. They are people of faith, not a band of outlaws."

Trish and Silver exchanged a look. No use wearing themselves out, at least not this early in the game.

Of course, Mitch and Reb had a downstairs bedroom. For such short notice, things were lovely. The sheets were crisp and new, as percale is. After having taken more than her fair share of baths over the past few days, Mitch was now more than happy to simply help Reb take her shower. Although it was nice to be close again in this way, Mitch tired quickly and chalked her fatigue up to her ongoing recuperation.

"Does it still hurt to hug?" Reb asked after they were settled side-by-side in bed.

"Not as much anymore," Mitch replied.

Reb wasted no time snuggling up. She, too, had missed their closeness.

"I sure have put you through a lot lately," Mitch snuggled back.

"No, you haven't!"

"I know I'm not an easy patient."

"I wasn't looking for easy when I took up with you. But you have made my life so complete, I would put up with anything to be with you."

Mitch studied Reb. For all intents and purposes, it was usually Mitch who waxed romantic. Reb was the leader, the strength, the pillar. Mitch was the dawdler, the wandered, the dilettante. Now, tonight, Reb was being downright mushy, at least, for her. Mitch could get used to this. Very, very used to this.

"Could you say that again?"

"What?"

"What you just said."

"I said I put up with a lot to be around you."

"That's not what you said the first time."

"Well, maybe we can have the court reporter read it back!"

So much for mushy.

"I gave the court reporter the night off."

"Huh?"

"Yeah, well, she wanted double-time and a half for evenings and weekends. And I thought that was just not in the budget."

Now, it was Reb's turn to study Mitch.

"Well, at least you've got your whacked-out sense of humor back."

"It comes in handy."

"So, you're saying that you need wacky sense of humor to put up with me?"

Mitch was oblivious to a lot of what went on in the world around her, but she did have a fine tuning where arguments were concerned. She could sense one bearing down from Reb's side of the bed.

"It has been a long day, hasn't it?" Mitch said, hoping to divert the storm.

"Yes."

"How do you think Robbie and Trish are holding up?"

"Very well, considering the circumstances."

"I can't even imagine what they are going through. Even after talking to Trish, I still don't have a sense of the depth of her feelings."

"Why don't we plan to stay on a few days? Take some of the load off Trish and anybody else who needs a break?"

"I'm sure we're welcome to stay as long as we want, but how can we help?" Mitch asked, not because she didn't have a clue how to help, but because the farther away they got from arguing, the better Mitch felt.

"You can cook."

"I'm touched that you've noticed."

"Not as good as Rose, of course."

"Of course," Mitch agreed. Agreeableness always went over well with Rebecca.

"Maybe not even as good as Max..."

"I could organize a bakeoff."

"It's going to feel that way, cooking for eight."

"I imagine so."

"You're awfully agreeable tonight."

"I don't want to fight."

"Me neither. Why would we be doing that?"

"Because it's been a long day."

"Hell, it's been a long week. We haven't fought even once."

"That's because we're so much in love."

Reb looked at Mitch. She was still very broken out, but crusting over nicely.

"You'd better get some sleep."

"Yes, Ma'am."

Mitch would've probably slept well past noon, but there was breakfast to cook. She vaguely remembered seeing a milk box off to the side of the front door on their arrival and wondered offhand if it would be full of edibles. As she walked toward the front door, she heard voices. She peeked out the door and saw another crowd of people. There were more than yesterday, and if the song was to be believed, less than tomorrow. Mitch sort of waved, forgot all about the milk box and closed the door. About then, Rose came down the hall.

"Is the milk here yet?"

"Uh...Should there be?"

"Yes! There should!"

"I'll check for it!" Mitch volunteered quickly.

"Are they still out there?"

"Uh...Yes."

"You want me to get the milk?"

"No. I'll get it."

"Okay. I'll see you in the kitchen."

Mitch opened the door again and checked the milk box under the scrutiny of dozens of pairs of eyes. There were lots of goodies in here: milk, eggs, bread. Now here was something she knew how to cook. Toast was a specialty of hers. She gathered everything up and kept her appointment with Rose in the kitchen. Mitch was midway through a yawn when Rose put a cup of coffee in her hand and told her to sit down at the table.

"I thought I could help you cook breakfast."

"You'll help by sitting down and staying out of the way."

That was probably true. Nothing was worse than trying to cook with an amateur underfoot.

"What are you making?"

"Breakfast, of course!"

Mitch nodded. Rose was clearly affected by recent events and was trying hard not to be distracted. One of the first casualties at a time like this was the power of concentration.

"When did folks gather again at the door?"

"Some have been there all night."

"Did they keep you awake?"

"Yes."

"I'm sorry."

"If you're sorry about it, go out and make them go away."

"It doesn't work."

"You haven't tried."

"Not here. No." Mitch had to remember that Rose didn't have perfect knowledge about all the goings on in Kansas.

"Then, you must want them to be here."

Mitch actually took time to think about this as she added cream and sugar to her coffee. Farm chores, such as they were, had tightened her up to the point where she could add a few frivolous calories here and there. Was Rose correct? Did Mitch secretly enjoy the adulation even as she openly protested the attention? She stood up and went to the front door. There were only about fifty people gathered by now. Good. She wouldn't need a bullhorn.

"Can I ask all of you to please leave?"

They all sort of shifted from one foot to the other. It was eerie, like watching an unrehearsed dance. Somebody in front said, "We didn't mean no harm. It's just that, well, you're famous."

"I guess I am. But I'm at the home of a friend, and the crowd makes them uneasy."

"Is there somewhere else we can wait?"

It dawned on Mitch that, yes, there was. There was her old house in the poor part of town, way far away from Mansionville. Could she persuade folks to hang out at that house only to see her for an hour or two? This was the stupidest idea Mitch had ever come up with, but she had to do something.

"Everybody got a car?"

They were all nodding. Nobody walked here.

"Good. Follow me."

Mitch got into the van and began to drive slowly across town. It was worse than any funeral procession she had ever seen. They were fine on the major roads, but once they entered residential areas, mayhem ensued. They attracted the attention of the police about two-thirds of the way there. Mitch, the obvious ringleader, got pulled over, sirens and all.

"Good morning, Officer."

"License, registration and proof of insurance, please."

It took a bit of fumbling through her wallet and the glove box, but she produced all the documents forthwith. The officer took all of the paperwork back to his vehicle and ran whatever it was they ran through the computer. He was back at her window in three minutes.

"You're that faith healer, aren't you?"

Mitch felt a little like banging her head on the steering wheel, but refrained.

"Alleged faith healer."

"The one on TV, right?"

There were several faith healers on TV, what with all those channels to choose from.

"I've been on the news."

"Can you tell me why all those cars are following you?"

"Because I told them to?"

"I see."

"I suppose I'm breaking a law?"

"Well, it's not like you were having a parade and needed a permit?" the officer was thinking this through orally.

In the meantime, one of the parade participants decided to come to Mitch's rescue, a thoroughly unnecessary endeavor. To say a scuffle eventuated would have been a bit of an exaggeration, but Mitch wasn't the most reliable witness. She was cold cocked by the first errant fist. They must've taught "ducking a punch" early and often at the police academy. When she came to, she was loaded in an ambulance. Well, at least she'd gotten the crowd away from Trish's house. After answering a bunch of questions to satisfy the EMTs that she wasn't going to die on the way to the hospital, she racked her brain to recall Trish's phone number. It was elusive, scattered among other brain cells, playing hide and seek.

Before she could remember it, she was at the hospital, being trundled on a gurney between the emergency room and x-ray. Finally, they let her rest for a few minutes in a curtained-off cubicle while doctors she had never met deliberated her fate in faraway hallways. Surprise, the next person who pulled back the curtain was Reb.

"What are you doing here?" Mitch smiled through the pain.

"I could ask you the same thing!"

"I forgot to duck. How did you find me?"

"You're on the news. Again."

"So soon?"

"It's that twenty-four hour news thing. Never a moment of peace. The story went something like, "Famous Faith Healer gets socked in the jaw by follower" or some such other nonsense."

"I'm lucky he didn't break my jaw."

"A glancing blow?"

"I was caught off guard and lost my balance."

"They said if you behave yourself that I can take you home."

"Do they know how hard it is for me to behave myself around you?"

"Let's just have that be our little secret, unless you want to spend the night here?"

"My lips are sealed."

In no certain attempt to break the land speed record, someone came in with a written set of prescriptions likened both in length and decipherability to the Dead Sea Scrolls. The main concern was a concussion. Mitch had had one of these before, she thought? Anyway, Reb knew what to do. Reb always knew what to do. She had had a child, after all.

"Did Mary ever have a concussion?"

"No."

"Oh, well."

Another pleasant surprise was awaiting Mitch in the patient pickup area. Trish was there with a car. A really big nice car. One that could hold Reb's wheelchair and everything.

"The van is in police impound."

"It is?"

"We'll bail it out tomorrow."

The trip back to Trish's estate was long enough to tire Mitch out. She asked for and received permission from Intern Reb to go to bed when they got home.

"You know I'll need to keep checking up on you through the day and night, don't you?"

"Santa Claus answered my letter," was Mitch's final thought on the matter.

Shift number one was manned by Robbie. She came in just to see what an almost broken jaw looked like and then lingered.

"Have a seat," Mitch patted the side of the bed.

Robbie did so.

"I'm sorry to be such a bother as a house guest," Mitch talked just to be talking and her jaw let her know about it. Ouch.

"Don't let that worry you. You and the Senator are wonderful house guests."

"You already have enough on your mind without all the fuss I've caused."

When Robbie remained silent, Mitch carried on with her usual directness. "How are you holding up? Under the circumstances and all."

"Some days are better than others," Robbie answered. Seeing as how there hadn't been all that many days, the evasive answer prompted Mitch to go on.

"I have a theory about this. Do you want to hear it?"

"Sure."

It was enough of an affirmation to prod Mitch along.

"Imagine for a moment that you are God."

"I wouldn't even do that."

"I know. Most people don't. But give it a try."

"Okay."

"Now think about all those babies up in heaven waiting to be born. And you know that some of those babies are going to face many challenges. Like, your baby."

"Okay."

"And so, if you were God, wouldn't you want to try and choose a really strong couple of parents for that baby?"

"Sure."

"You and Trish have been chosen to help this little baby through some pretty rough times. If God knows you're up to the challenge, then so should you."

It took a moment or two, but then Robbie brightened, as if she understood fully and was now ready to fulfill the role of parenthood under duress. She gave Mitch a quick hug as Reb rolled into the room.

"How's our patient?"

"She's brilliant," Robbie answered as she stood to leave.

"Really?" Reb didn't sound too puzzled.

"I have to go and see to dinner plans. You'll probably need something soft?" Robbie directed the remark to Mitch.

"I could probably get a bowl of lumpy oatmeal down."

"I'll see what else we have, too."

Robbie more or less floated out of the room like a great weight had been lifted from her shoulders.

"The two of you must've been having quite the conversation."

"I asked her to put herself in God's shoes for a moment."

"I see. And?"

"God doesn't look half bad barefoot."

"Uh huh," Reb nodded like this was all making sense, like maybe from someone who had recently been hit in the head.

"Why don't you come to bed with me...just to make sure I don't fall asleep."

"You're incorrigible."

"And that's on a good day.

Reb followed Mitch's suggestion, even though she remained fully clothed. That was okay with Mitch. Right now, Reb felt every bit as wonderful clothed as naked. It took a moment or two before Mitch was fully tuned in to Reb's mood.

"You want to talk about it?" Mitch asked.

"What?"

"You've been breathing these deep sighs, like you're upset with me."

"I'm not upset with you."

"Then, what?"

"It's just very unnerving when I have to go and bail you out of the hospital."

"I'm sorry I worried you."

"You don't need to apologize for someone hitting you in the jaw."

"Okay."

"But you do need to tell me what was going through your mind when you left the house this morning."

"I was thinking that I would lead everyone away from here over to the old place in the woods."

"Well, I'm glad then that someone hit you in the jaw."

"You are?"

"Well, I'm not *glad* exactly, but I don't want your new fan club to know that we have a house in Colorado and the exact location of it."

"Why not?"

"We may want to move back here someday."

"We might?"

"And wouldn't it be nice if we could for once sneak into town and stay somewhere far away from the maddening crowd."

Mitch raised up on one elbow, even though it hurt from stem to stern to do so. Why a simple punch in the face made everything hurt was a deep mystery crafted for the likes of Scotland Yard.

"You want to move back to Colorado?"

"I just don't want everyone tramping around the old house."

Mitch smiled. There were some pretty special memories tied up in the old place. Oh yeah, like…recovering from a gunshot wound to the elbow.

"You want to move back, don't you," Mitch got to the point. Since it really wasn't a question, Reb didn't treat it as such. It would've been like asking Julia Roberts if she knew just how sexy her pouty lips were. It really wasn't a question if you knew the answer.

"I've given it serious consideration."

"Spoken like a true politician."

"I think we need to consider the circumstances."

At the word "circumstances," Mitch's ears perked up. When Reb used big words like "circumstances," it meant adult talk was impending. And not the kind in X-rated movies.

"What about our circumstances?"

260

"Have you ever stopped to think about what would happen to me if I didn't have you in my life?"

Mitch now understood what was at the root of Reb's sighs. If anything more serious than a simple sore jaw were to happen to Mitch, Reb was out a caregiver.

"There's a dozen or so women lined up to take my place."

"There are not."

"Of course there are. I'm the envy of at least ten women in every state in the union. Maybe more in California?"

"And I wouldn't have any of them."

"I imagine not. You can be so picky sometimes," Mitch smiled. Reb didn't. Mitch noticed.

"What's really going on in your mind?"

"I'm worried about ending up in a care facility."

"A care facility?"

"A nursing home."

"Why would you ever end up in a nursing home? Even if you didn't have me, you'd still have Mary."

"I'd never impose on Mary!"

"You think it would be an imposition?"

"I know it would be. I'm not about to ruin Mary and Lisa's lives by asking them to be my nursemaids!"

"Sweetie, with the kind of money you have, you could hire five or six people to take my place."

"It would take more than five or six people to take your place."

"Don't try and flatter me when you already have me in bed."

"Would you please get sex off your brain for five minutes so we can continue our discussion."

"Well, I was being serious. I mean, we do check for bed sores in bed. And some other therapy things."

"And that's exactly what I'm talking about. You do so much for me. Maybe it's too much?"

"What do you mean?"

"Maybe it's time that we get serious about hiring someone to help out."

"And get serious about moving back to Colorado?"

"That too."

"Would doing all that make you less afraid of the future?"

"I think so."

"Then that's what we'll do. The less you worry about the future, the more you can enjoy today. We'll move back to the ranch house and hire some help."

"Do we even need to go back to Kansas?"

Mitch pursed her lips and crinkled her brow just like a supreme court judge. "No. I'm sure we can handle everything by phone. The builders can finish the house and then we can put it on the market. And I'm sure we can get somebody to pack up the trailers. There isn't much stuff. We seem to travel light."

"I'll help all I can. I can make phone calls. Just don't ask me to go back. Okay?"

"Sure," Mitch nodded. "There's no need to go back."

They were quiet for a moment. Mitch was stunned at how much better she felt. A calmness enveloped them. How did Reb always know the best path to choose? She had the most perfectly-honed feminine intuition of any female Mitch had ever known. Which really wasn't *that* many.

"Are you okay with all of this?" Reb checked one more time.

"Never better. We can finish remodeling the ranch house at our leisure. Get you into some serious rehab habits. Do some swimming, some weight training, some serious necking..."

"Now, that sounds like a plan!"

"The swimming?"

"The necking!"

"Sounds like our serious discussion is over for the moment," Mitch grinned, and then grimaced. Damn jaw!

"You just take it easy and let me handle things," Reb intoned. And if there was one thing that Reb excelled at, it was handling things. For twenty whole minutes, Mitch forgot all about her jaw and the rest of the world as well.

She didn't know how long she had slept, but when Mitch woke up, Reb was gone and it was dark. Her watch indicated that it was after eight. If someone had rung the dinner bell, they must've done so quietly. Mitch willed herself out of bed and wandered through the house toward the noise. Someone was talking in the kitchen. Maybe it wasn't too late after all. Mitch walked right into the middle of a conversation between Reb,

Mary and Lisa. It was clear that they were discussion the impending move. They all looked so…happy.

"Oh, hi there! We saved you some dinner," Reb indicated a chair for Mitch.

"I hope it's something soft."

"If you can't chew it, we'll just run everything through the blender."

"Liquid meatloaf?"

"Yum huh?" Lisa knew what this was like.

"My favorite."

"We were just chatting about moving back here," Mary recapped.

"Yeah," Lisa added, "And Trish has offered us room and board until we get settled."

"After all the hopping around the two of you have been doing lately, I'd think you'd have 'settling in' down to a science," Mitch poked a small bit of meatloaf into her mouth and began to chew gingerly. Easy…easy…

"At least you have a house to move back into," Mary said matter-of-factly.

"We can all live in the ranch house until you find something," Mitch answered equally matter-of-factly.

Reb looked like she was going to have a stroke. "Are you sure there's enough elbow room for everyone?" she asked, trying to not sound too panicked at the thought of sharing a tiny living space with Lisa. Being in separate trailers in Kansas was about as close as she cared to be to the girl.

"Well, we did do that remodeling?" Mitch thought out loud. That was true enough, Reb had to nod. Her affirmation was mistaken for total and unconditional agreement to Plan A.

"Oh, good," Mary was as happy as was legally allowed. "It'll be just like old times!"

There were better things to wish for than "old times." It's just that none of those things immediately popped into Reb's mind.

The logistics of moving from Point A to Point B were pretty complicated if nobody wanted to return to Point A to button up the details. After much consideration, it was decided that Mitch and Mary needed to go back to Kansas long enough to do the

263

necessary paperwork. There were homes and farms to sell and trailers to clear out. If Reb had any qualms about selling the family homestead to complete strangers, they didn't manifest themselves. Papers with notarized signatures crossed through the mail and before you could say, "We're not in Kansas anymore," they weren't.

Through this particular phase, Trish had been, in spite of the burden she herself carried, a Godsend. In a way, she was very much relieved that everyone was moving closer. She and Robbie would need the moral support. What was to be done about the crush of miracle seekers hadn't yet been divined. Still, before the heaviest of snows were due to nurture the earth, Reb, Mitch, Mary and Lisa were all settled in at the ranch house. It was…cozy. Real cozy. Sort of like, "Let's knock out a few walls and quadruple the floor space" kind of cozy. Which was unthinkable with the approach of winter. Buying another house for Mary and Lisa seemed the more logical thing to do, but before that could happen, they all needed to put their brainpower to good use to come up with a scheme to rid the property once and for all of the crowds that were once again starting to gather like storm clouds. A simple call to the police solved most of the problem. That's not to imply that where enforcing the law is concerned, city police outshine their country counterparts. It's more a matter of realizing a potential for revenue. One day, the city workers came out and posted over a dozen No Parking signs along the stretch of road beside Mitch's property. The next thing you knew, nobody could legally park close enough to create a traffic jam. Now, that's not to say that this solved the whole problem. But between the parking fines and the onset of cooler weather, the crowds thinned. No more miracles by Mitch. At least, none that made headlines. The real miracle now was managing a house full of women. This was going to take some divine intervention.

"Who wants pizza?" Lisa had the phone in her hand, poised to dial.
"You're ordering pizza again?" Reb was sitting in the other room, but it was still close.

"Sure. Why not?"

"It has a lot of calories and cholesterol is why not."

"So, I'll get you a veggie pizza. What does everyone else want?" Mitch had been reading a book in bed. Until she heard the plan. Why she felt compelled to calm every little ripple of waters was beyond her, but she entered the impending fray with her usual tact and good judgment.

"They have salads, don't they?"

"I guess so," Lisa shrugged. The motion added character to her scars, what few there were.

"Order a bunch of those, could you please?"

"What kind of dressing?"

"Something lo-cal."

"I should've figured as much," Lisa mused.

Reb held her tongue. Mitch appreciated the restraint. Later, in bed, after eating perhaps just a teeny tiny more pizza than at first planned, Mitch was nursing a case of heartburn. Reb couldn't help but notice.

"Do you need some antacid?"

"I think I have some," Mitch rummaged through her bedside stand.

"Was it the meal, or is it something else?"

Mitch recognized an opening when she saw one. "It is sort of close quarters around here."

"Makes a submarine seem roomy."

"You've been in a submarine?"

"That's for me to know and you to find out."

"So, I'm married to a woman with a salty past?"

"We're not married."

"Would you like to be?" Mitch followed up quickly. It had been a while since they had discussed the matter and it never hurt to keep tabs. Reb checked to see if Mitch really wanted to talk about the subject. Seemed she did.

"Is that a proposal?"

"If it is, it was a rather lame attempt."

"It certainly was."

"Tell you what," Mitch took hold of Reb's hand. "Give me a couple of days, maybe a week. A lady like you deserves a much better attempt."

"Well, okay," Reb sounded bemused at best.

The following day, Mitch went out house hunting. She had thought about calling Trish for advice, or maybe just to see if she wanted to tag along, but then decided against it at the last minute. Besides, she didn't want everyone within listening distance to know that she was looking in the first place. It saved her from answering a bunch of nosy questions, which could include the dreaded, "You want us to move out?" that she expected to her from Mary and Lisa. Well, maybe just Lisa…

Anyway, Mitch was just really looking right now. She just sort of got in the car and roamed around the neighborhood. It could've only been providence that led her to turn right instead of left on Hilltop Drive. Halfway down the block, she spotted a "For Sale" sign in front of a quaint little house. Actually, it wasn't so little, but how often do you hear the phrase, "quaint big?" It was as if nothing large could ever be considered quaint. Mitch made note of the realtor's number and punched it into her cell phone. A really cheery someone picked up and within fifteen minutes, the realtor was on the premises and ready to conduct a tour. For once, Mitch followed along with no comment, other than to say at the conclusion that she would meet whatever price the seller asked and to draw up the paperwork.
"We can even start the loan-qualification paperwork," the realtor said casually.
"There's no need for that. It will be a cash transaction."
The realtor didn't seem so casual anymore. But she still said, "Okay."
"So, you'll call me when the papers need to be signed?"
"Of course. Let me take you to lunch."
"Oh, gee, thanks but I have more shopping to do. Maybe on the day I sign the papers?"
"Of course. I'll call you soon."
"Thanks."
Mitch got in the car and drove straight to the mall. She really didn't have much shopping to do and was probably using the time to delay going home and having to confess to buying a house unilaterally. So, she sipped down a scalding cup of coffee

and then milled through the clothing sections of the department stores for bargains. Two sweaters and a pair of slacks jumped off the rack and Mitch was soon heading home with tell-tale sacks from the store.

"What did you buy today?" was Reb's hello.

She was in the kitchen, tending a pot of vegetable soup previously canned and now bubbling.

"You mean, what's in the sacks?" Mitch said innocently enough. Not innocently enough for Reb.

"Did you buy something besides what's in the sacks?" Reb turned her lawyer stare to focus on Mitch. It worked.

"I bought a house, too. It was too big for the sack."

Reb sized up Mitch's facial expression. "You're serious, aren't you?"

"Yup."

"You bought a house?"

"Right."

"Without telling anyone?"

"I'm telling you."

"Now!"

"Right. I didn't think you'd mind."

"I guess that depends on who you bought it for."

"I bought it for Mary and Lisa. If they don't like it, they can sell it and buy something else."

"And who's going to tell them they're moving?"

"When they see the place, they'll jump at the upgrade."

"I see."

Things were real quiet for a minute or two.

"So, what's in the bag?"

"Oh, that. I bought you a couple of sweaters. Cold weather's coming."

"That's nice."

"And a pair of pants."

"I see."

Things were quiet again.

"Did you want a new house instead?" Mitch ventured a guess.

"No, I don't want a new house instead," Reb assured her as she divided the soup equally into two bowls. Mitch carried them over to the tiny kitchen table and sat down. Reb wheeled into place and they started eating.

"We really should do some more remodeling around here, though," Reb finished her thought.

"Absolutely," Mitch nodded. "Where do you want to start?"

"We need room for more exercise equipment. And a kitchen that's easier to use."

"Then how about twice more room? We can knock out the back wall and really get serious about space."

Reb only smiled.

"What?" Mitch asked.

"You're never happier than when you're in 'build mode.'"

"I like making plans for the future with the woman I love."

"That has a nice ring to it."

At the mention of the word "ring" Mitch remembered that she was supposed to be coming up with a good proposal. Why she hadn't browsed through the jewelry store at the mall was anyone's guess. Maybe she had an aversion to making more than one major purchase in any given day? Or maybe she knew instinctively that whatever she wanted to shop for in the way of jewelry wasn't going to be in the mall?

"You're not hungry?"

The question poked through Mitch's thoughts. "Huh?"

"You're not eating your soup."

"I'm waiting for it to cool."

"Ah."

As soon as was humanly possible, Mitch consumed her lunch and then cleaned up the kitchen while Reb took a shower. Usually that meant that there was a chance for a snuggle on the couch in the near future. She was not to be disappointed. At least, not right away. There they were, Mitch and Reb, dreamily gazing into each other's eyes when Mary and Lisa arrived home. Damn the timing.

"Hello, we're home!" Mary called out breezily, not at all aware of the intrusion.

"I'm already appreciating your purchase of today," Reb whispered.

"Yeah," Mitch breathed back. "You look great in that sweater."

"That's not what I meant."

"I know."

"Anybody home?" Mary came in and found the cuddlers.

"Hello, Honey. You're home already?"

"We got tired. What's for dinner?"

"We just had lunch."

"Well," Lisa wandered in, "We can always order a pizza."
Mitch could feel the tension in Reb's body.

"Let's talk first. Mitch has something she wants to tell you,"
Reb adroitly shifted the burden to Mitch.

"You do?" Mary said. "Let's hear it."

"Okay," Mitch inhaled and then announced, "Your mother and I
are getting married."

"Yeah. And?" Lisa was unimpressed with the announcement.
But not Reb.

"What?" she said.

"Well, we are just as soon as I figure out a really romantic way
to propose. Aren't we?"
The silence was deafening.

"That's not the announcement I was talking about," Reb finally
clarified.

"It wasn't?"

"You mean you have an announcement that's bigger than getting
hitched?" Even Lisa was now intrigued.

"Perhaps not, but one that's for *public* consumption," Reb stated
firmly and then gave Mitch a knowing look. Oh, yeah, the
house…

"Well, uh…" Mitch started out slow. Too slow.

"Mitch bought a house for you," Reb broke the news.

"A house? For us?" Mary was curious.

"We had planned to for a while," Reb told it like it was her story,
which it appeared to be now.

"I guess that makes sense, but why don't the two of you live in
the new house?" Mary asked.

"It has stairs," Mitch explained.

"Besides, this place has memories," Reb mellowed.

"So, you want us to move out," Lisa put it bluntly.

"Not yet. There's still some paperwork to complete," Mitch
said.

"Can we go and see it?" Mary was practical as usual.

"Sure. We can drive by, but we'd need an appointment for a walk through."

"Can you set that up?"

"I can make a call."

Mitch was more than happy to make her escape. Obviously, bringing up the subject of the impending but not yet perfected proposal was not the brightest of moves. The realtor, ever chirpy, could hardly wait to show the house again. Apparently, the owners were out of town. Everyone was in the van and travelling within fifteen minutes. When they pulled up in front of the house, Mitch could've sworn she heard a low whistle. She just didn't know from whom.

"When you buy a house, you *buy a house*," Mary commented.

"You like it so far?" Mitch asked as they viewed the façade.

"Is it this nice on the inside?"

"You can judge for yourselves. Here's the realtor now."

Mary and Lisa spent a good deal longer that Mitch had checking out the premises. It could've been a crime scene the way Lisa appeared to be looking for trace evidence on the carpets, in the corners, and every closet and drawer. Cops with a search warrant weren't this thorough. At least, not in the movies. Mitch shifted her weight from foot to foot, loathe to sit on someone else's furniture.

"Lucky me, I bring my chair everywhere I go," Reb noticed Mitch's two-step. At least she didn't sound peeved.

"Let's go out to dinner when we're finished."

"I hope the restaurants stay open that late," Reb remarked with just a touch of sarcasm.

"Oh, I'm sure Detective Lisa will have her investigation wrapped up by happy hour."

About that time, the trio of Lisa, Mary and the realtor appeared around the corner.

"We're finished," Mary stated.

"You like it?"

"When can we move in?"

"Only the realtor knows for sure."

"Things will take a couple of weeks."

"We'll be packed and ready by then," Lisa verified.

Mitch was relieved. Nobody sounded disappointed by the new living arrangements. Besides, they were only moving ten minutes away. They could practically jog to each other's house. Well, maybe one or two of them could. Mitch wasn't even going to attempt the feat.

Two weeks plus five more days went by in a snap. Time has a way of skimming right by when there are things to do. And buy. With all the ups and downs and moves that Mary and Lisa had been through lately, they had whittled their personal belongings down to the barest of the bare essentials. All of a sudden, they needed to fill up a twenty-room house. Like Mary said, when Mitch bought a house, she bought a house. If you took all of Mary and Lisa's stuff and piled it up, it might, just might, fill up two rooms. Lisa commented, in Mitch's general direction, "two down, eighteen to go."

The price Mitch paid willingly for having Reb all to herself was to foot the bill for eighteen rooms of furniture. Every credit card swipe got her one step closer to the golden moment.

"I don't know if I like this shade of gold or not?" Lisa was picking out drapes.

"Imagine that! A shade of gold that you don't like," Mitch said drolly.

"What's that supposed to mean?" Lisa came back, not at all amused.

It certainly was wonderful to be split up all these years and still be able to bicker like an old married couple.

"I thought gold was your favorite color."

"Next to platinum, sure."

Now, Mitch had to chuckle. The platinum card had practically lost its spots from all the use.

"Too bad drapes don't come in platinum."

"It's a crying shame. Let's go look at the more expensive ones."

Ah, yes, the price Mitch paid for being funny. Literally. You wouldn't believe the cost of drapes, particularly when they needed to be custom made. Lisa had measured the windows and, wouldn't you know it, every one was a non-standard size. Mitch watched as Lisa and the Drapery Specialist discussed every teeny tiny bit of minutia about window coverings. This kind of torture was even out of the league of Marquis de Sade. You could send a kid through college on the kind of money they were talking about. Well, maybe a community college. Finally, they almost gleefully totaled the bill. Mitch handed over the much-used card with just a trace of reluctance.

"I don't know why you're acting this way," Lisa remarked. "After all, you're the one who picked out the house with all the weird windows."

Mitch remained silent. Some mistakes were easier to pay for than others. This was in that category, so she just counted her blessings, deducted the balance and held her tongue. After all the papers were filled out and the documents signed and the delivery date set, Lisa was glowing. There was nothing quite like spending someone else's money to put a genuine radiance in her cheeks.

"Are you taking me somewhere nice for lunch?"

"Would today be any different?" was Mitch's standard reply. Anything to get out of the store with the shirt still on her back. Lisa had acquired a taste lately for French cuisine in expensive restaurants, at least when Mitch was footing the bill. You could buy one pretty good snow tire for the price of one of the luncheon entrees.

"What are you thinking about?" Lisa peered over the menu.

"Snow tires."

"Snow tires? Why, they aren't even on the menu!" Lisa teased. God, even after all these years and burn scars to boot, she could still crimp Mitch's stomach like it was ravioli edges.

"I'm going to need snow tires soon. Winter is coming."

"It only comes once a year, poor thing." Lisa smiled and then realized what she had said. "Sorry. I wasn't thinking."

"It's okay. Reb and I are used to our situation by now."

"You must be. You're talking about having some sort of ceremony?"

"It's taken Reb a while to get over her first marriage."

"I know how that is!" Lisa nodded.

"Oh really?"

"I've been left before. I know how it feels."

"Hmmm," Mitch replied and went back to studying the menu. Everything had a sauce. Good thing Reb wasn't here to fuss about the extra calories. After they ordered, Lisa got nosy. Nothing new there.

"So, when are you buying the ring?"

"I don't know."

"We have time after lunch. I'll help."

Mitch wondered about the wisdom of having the old girlfriend help select the diamond ring for the current girlfriend.

"Oh, I think I've had enough shopping for one day."

"You're out of practice."

"You're right."

Lisa was quiet for a moment and then remarked, "You really do take good care of her. She's lucky to have you. I hope she knows that."

"If she forgets, I remind her."

"You do not! I know better."

They savored all those extra calories in relative silence and headed back to the cramped ranch house. Mary and Reb were watching a movie, so Mitch puttered around the kitchen while Lisa took a nap. She was still healing, after all. So was Mitch's pocketbook. Due mostly to caloric guilt, Mitch prepared a healthy dinner for everyone and then Mitch and Reb relaxed together in bed. It was still the best part of the day. Mitch said so. Out loud.

Reb replied, "You mean that picking out curtains with Lisa wasn't the highlight of the day?"

"It was downright scary."

"Where did you have lunch?"

"At L'EXPENSIVE, I swear."

"I figured something like that."

"You did, huh?"

"Lisa always does take advantage of your generosity."

"You should do that more often," Mitch admonished.

"I'm trying, I'm trying!"

"You've been lagging behind."

"Oh, I don't think so. You up and moved from Kansas just for me."

"Well, that's not exactly true."

"It isn't?" Reb asked.

"I had had enough of Kansas by the time you suggested the move."

"I wasn't sure about you, but I know I had had enough. But I felt guilty. Until now?"

"Why?"

"I felt guilty depriving you of your followers."

"You needn't have."

"And perhaps your gift entirely?"

"You think the 'gift' only works when I'm a resident of Kansas?" Mitch mused out loud.

"I haven't seen proof otherwise."

"Hopefully, you never will."

"You're a strange one."

"Why?"

"Some people would give their eyeteeth to have powers and be famous. You run the other way."

"And the faster, the better."

"Why?"

"Because if everything were true, it would've eventually come between us. There are too many sick and hurting people in the world for one person to heal them all."

"You put me ahead of everyone else in the world. Even yourself."

"That's just how love is."

"You know how we've been bantering back and forth about proposals?"

Mitch wouldn't have necessarily classified it as "bantering," but she said, "Uh huh" anyway.

"Well for the record, you probably won't improve over the previous sentiment."

"Perhaps not, but I will still give it my best shot. Soon."

Mitch closed her eyes and the next thing she knew, it was morning and she had slept in. It wasn't like she was on a time clock, other than the internal tick tock she heard from the impending proposal attempt. Where should she go ring shopping? Maybe Reb didn't even want a ring? Who would know for sure? Mitch wrestled her way out of bed and wandered out to take roll. Mary was drinking coffee at the kitchen table.

"Where's everybody?" Mitch asked.

"*I'm* here," Mary replied rather pointedly.

"Good. You're just the person I want to talk to."

"In that case, pull up a cup."

Mitch did so and asked point blank, "Should I buy your mom a ring?"

"Curtain or diamond?"

"Definitely diamond."

"You two already wear matching rings. I wouldn't necessarily buy another."

"What should I do to propose to her then?"

"Do something romantic."

"You mean like take her out to dinner or something like that?"

"Right."

"Your mom doesn't like to go out to fancy dinners much…"

"Unlike Lisa."

"Right."

"Then, take her somewhere else romantic."

Mitch didn't reply. She was thinking. Mary talked on.

"Why did you let Lisa spend so much money on drapes?"

"Uh, I guess because I figured that I didn't have a say in the matter?"

"She understands the word 'no.'"

"She sure didn't when we were together…as a couple I meant."

"I know what you meant."

"Okay. Well, don't you like the drapes?" Mitch was still puzzled.

"It's a lot to spend. By you. Don't you understand that it makes it hard to compete with you?"

"I didn't, until you pointed it out. I never even consider that we're competing with each other."

"I guess we're not. Really. I know we're not. I've just heard all I want to hear about drapes and houses and lunches in French restaurants."

"Next shopping spree, I'll take you instead. Lisa can keep your mom company."

"Let's not have too many more shopping sprees, okay?"

"You need furniture."

"We'll make do. We can shop at garage sales."

"Not in the dead of winter."

"We'll wait until spring."

"You're willing to eat dinner off a card table until spring?"

"I've done it before."

"When?"

"Well, the last time Lisa and I found ourselves without a thing to our names. We got through then."

"And you think I could *ever* compete?"

Mary didn't say anything but just smiled faintly.

Where is everybody anyway?" Mitch asked again.

"Lisa's at the grocery store and mom is shopping for exercise equipment."

"All by herself? Boy, are we in trouble."

"Yeah, in both cases!"

Lisa crossed the finish line first, but it was damn close. When she went grocery shopping, nothing, it appeared, escaped her perusal.

"What's this?" Mitch held up a package.

"Gruyere cheese," Lisa replied.

"What the hell do you use that for?"

"Cooking!" Lisa defended her cheeses well.

"Like, macaroni and cheese?"

"You put that Gruyere anywhere close to macaroni and you'll have KP duty for a month."

"I already do," Mitch squawked.

Further inquisitions about food were put on hold with the arrival of Reb. She didn't have anything to bring in.

"It's all being delivered."

"How soon?" Mitch wondered if she had time to find suitable room. And maybe even a hiding place to avoid exercise.

"In three days. In the afternoon."

"Oh, boy," Mitch answered with as much enthusiasm as she could muster. Somehow, this was a lot less fun than picking on Lisa and her cheese.

"I even got something for you!" Reb poked Mitch's arm.

"You did?"

"A really nice new multi-station exercise machine. You could work out for two hours easy and never need another piece of equipment."

"Two hours *easy*?"

"It won't be long before you're ready for the Olympics."

"Do they still have curling?" Mitch asked tentatively.

"Have you got ice skates?"

"I think I have a broom."

"Good," Lisa butted in, "You can practice on the kitchen floor."

"Gee, thanks, I think?"

After finishing up all her chores, Mitch made plans to arrange a romantic getaway. The logical choice had dawned on her during her talk with Mary. Santa Fe. Nothing like a few days of dusty quiet in a small town to have romance blossom. A couple of phone calls out of earshot of Reb was all it took to ensure that their vacation home in Santa Fe would be clean and ready for them by tomorrow. For this, they relied on the trusty Bella. Bella was the housekeeper who cooked for Mitch and Reb when they visited the house. Otherwise, it sat empty. All too often, Mitch was reminded after the phone call.

"What are you up to?" Reb asked the minute she wheeled into the room.

"Nothing."

"Right..."

"You don't believe me?"

"You're as transparent as cling wrap."

"But not nearly as difficult to handle."

"I'm sure you'll tell me in your own sweet time what you're up to."

"I'm sure I will."

"Should I plan for anything?"

"Just be sure you've got clean underwear."

"On, or in the drawer?"

Even Mitch had to think about this. "Both."

"Gee, you're demanding."

"That's my middle name."

"Anything else?"

"Get a good night's sleep."

"I always do when I'm next to you."

It was probably the packing of the suitcases the following morning that gave Reb the clue she needed. "Are we going somewhere?"

"Yes."

"Both of us?"

"Of course."

"Where?"

"I figured if you watch me pack long enough, you'd know."

"You're packing practically everything we own. Are we going on a round-the-world trip?"

"Would you like to?" Mitch was mildly curious. That, too, could be arranged. After a few days in Santa Fe.

"Not really. Around the world is so very…far away."

"So, you'd like to go someplace closer?"

Depends on what you have in mind."

"If we go the opposite direction from Kansas, would that suit you?"

"One-hundred percent. Does that mean that we're going to Disneyland?"

Mitch chuckled again and asked, again, "Is that where you'd like to go?"

Reb gave this serious thought. "Nah. Too many mice."

"But they have Snow White."

"Why would I want Snow White? I have you instead."

"I'll consider that a compliment until notified otherwise."

"Please do."

Mitch finished up the packing and loaded up the van while Reb gave last-minute instructions to Mary.

"Don't forget that the exercise equipment is being delivered Tuesday."

"Right."

"You can sign for it."

"Okay."

"Just have them put it anywhere."

"Sure."

"I hope the floor is strong enough?"

278

"Would you go already! Mitch looks like she's about to have kittens."

"Okay. We'll be back…when we get back."

"It usually works out that way."

Reb wheeled out the door and was whisked up by Mitch. They were gone in two minutes.

"Are they gone yet?" Lisa peered from around the corner.

"Yes."

"Oh, good!"

"You seem happy."

"Hey, we have the place all to ourselves. You…me…" Lisa had a beaming smile on her face. The scars barely showed, or maybe Mary was just so used to them.

"I guess we do, don't we?" Mary pretended to be somewhat reserved. Lisa knew otherwise. It was Mary's way of saying, "Come and get me."

And Lisa knew very well how to play this game. She went over and took hold of Mary's hand. "How about I make you breakfast in bed?"

"I'm not very hungry."

"Who said anything about cooking?"

Now, it was Mary's turn to beam. This was indeed going to be a lovely couple of days.

After about two miles on the road, Reb had divined where Mitch was taking her. In her subconscious mind, she had known all along.

"It should be pretty this time of year in Santa Fe."

"More so with your arrival," Mitch added.

"You're such a romantic."

"I hope so."

"I know so."

With the mystery now out of the way, the drive was soothing and comfortable. Of course, they stopped several times to stretch and once to have lunch. The green chili at the small restaurant was extra zingy. Reb was smart, she took it easy. Mitch couldn't help herself and burned her mouth to hell and back. Oh, but it was worth it.

"I think I see smoke curling out of your ears." Reb teased.

279

"Almost!"

"Well, do me a favor and take it easy. I want your tongue in good working order later."

"Yes, Ma'am," Mitch smiled.

"Are you blushing?"

"It's the peppers!"

"Uh huh," Reb smiled back. She was right. It was blushing.

"Are you ready to hit the road?"

"Ready when you are."

By early afternoon, they were at the house in Santa Fe. Bella nearly bowled them over.

"Jou made it! Jou make it!"

She made it sound like they were the only two survivors on the Titanic.

"Hello, Bella," Mitch winced through a mama-bear-type hug.

"I have everything ready. 'Cept dinner. Dinner's usual time. Jou know the rules."

Yeah, Mitch and Reb knew the rules. Dinner was ready when Bella decided and not sooner or later. The way Mitch had it figured, whoever cooked dinner should get to set the rules. Especially when they cooked the way Bella did.

"Are we going to have your specialty?" Mitch was just being nosy.

"Jou 'spect something different?"

It was like talking to Ricky Ricardo. In drag.

"I expect the usual sumptuous meals that we always have when you cook."

"I spoil jou rotten!"

"We love it," Reb assured her.

Enough fussing. Bella had to get back to the kitchen so Mitch took over valet duties. It didn't take long to unpack in spite of Reb's earlier consternation that they were bringing everything they owned. There was no formal wear. Jeans and shorts and t-shirts didn't need much space but a spot to occupy. Mitch looked over at Reb. She looked tired.

"Why don't you lie down for a while. You look road weary."

"Why don't you think of something more flattering to say to me?"

"You look gorgeous when you're road weary?"

"I suppose I do," she sighed.

"What's wrong?"

"I just sometimes wish that I had the energy I used to."

"Gee, Honey, we've been awfully busy lately with all the crowds in Kansas and the moving around. Even I'm a bit on the tired side."

"You don't look it."

"Is that why we're buying all that exercise equipment?"

"I really need to start building up my muscles again," Reb said as she arranged herself in bed.

"You look pretty good from here," Mitch smiled.

"Maybe you need a closer look."

Mitch took her up on the offer, stretching out next to her.

"This alone was worth the trip," Mitch whispered.

They were content to relax together, no hot and heavy passion flowed between them at this moment. Just a contentment that could last for eternity.

"Will you marry me?" Mitch heard herself ask from the depths of her soul. A decade or two of time seemed to slip by and evaporate.

"Yes."

"Okay."

From the outer reaches of the universe, a voice called out, "Dinner it's served!"

Mitch knew she was eating. She was chewing and everything, but her mind was a million miles away from paella.

"Are you okay?" Reb checked in.

"Oh, yeah," Mitch answered and then chewed some more.

"Are you sure?"

"Yeah, why?"

"You just seem awfully quiet."

"Aren't all grooms-to-be quiet?"

"Are you going to be this way for a while?"

"I don't know. I've never been a groom-to-be before."

"I suppose not," Reb chuckled. "Since you've decided, unilaterally I might add, that you're the groom, does that mean that you're going to have a bachelor party with a big cake and one of those scantily-clad girls popping out of it?"

"Honey, the only thing I ever want popping out of the middle of my cake is jam filling."

"What flavor?"

"Huh?"

"What flavor of jam?"

"Boysenberry," Mitch dashed off a glib answer.

"I'll alert the pastry chef."

"The pastry chef?"

"Well, you do want a real wedding cake, don't you?"

"I suppose so."

"That means we'll need to find a pastry chef."

"For one cake?"

"No. There will be other things."

"Like what?"

"Well, like mints, for instance."

"Mints?" Mitch was puzzled.

"Right."

"You mean those things that you can buy by the bag-full at the grocery store?"

"Heaven's no! I mean real mints."

"I don't understand?"

"You can have mints made to order in these really pretty shapes. I think pastel colors are best, don't you?"

"I guess so?" Mitch realized two things simultaneously. The first was that she was *way* out of her league. The second was that Reb wanted a *real* wedding.

"And, of course, we'll do a dinner."

"A dinner."

"And a rehearsal dinner."

"Two dinners?"

"Right."

"Ah," Mitch was retreating back into the world of one-syllable answers.

Even Reb was now aware of Mitch's non-responsive answer.

"Are you sure you're okay?"

"Me?"

"You seem a little on edge."

"I've just never planned a wedding before. Not a lot of my friends had weddings. Except for Trish. But she didn't have mints."

"Of course she did."

"She did?"

"They were on the cake table."

"I guess I didn't notice."

"I guess you didn't."

"What else was on the cake table besides mints…and cake?"

"There were mixed nuts."

"Of course."

"And that's just the cake table. If we want a dinner, then that's one consideration. But if we want a reception and dance, then we'll need to plan differently."

"What did you and Jeff do?"

"For our wedding?"

"Yes."

"Well," Reb thought back like it was the Mesozoic period. "We got married in the afternoon and had a formal dinner party."

"Then, let's *not* do that."

"I take it that you don't want this wedding to be anything like my first."

"I don't mind *some* similarities. It sounds like you want a traditional wedding cake and that's fine with me."

"Okay. It can be a different color."

"You can do that?"

"Oh sure. In fact, before we get too far into planning, we need to pick colors."

"Pick colors?"

"You know, like dress colors."

"I thought brides wore white."

"Well, most do. But, I'm talking about bridesmaid's dresses."

"Oh."

"First, you select colors and then get everything else to match."

"Okay…so what color did you pick the first time around?"

"Promise you won't laugh?"

"I would never laugh at your choice of colors."

"Blue."

"Blue?"

"That's right. What's wrong with blue?"

"Nothing's wrong with blue. So, now, we've ruled out blue?"
Mitch was doing her best to keep track. Without laughing.

"That's correct. Do you have any suggestions?"
Mitch thought about this. According to all the wedding lore that she knew, the groom was supposed to shut up, do everything asked by the bride, and then show up sober to the ceremony.

"I'm not very good with colors. I think we should go with your selection."

"Really?" Reb sounded a bit skeptical. It wasn't like Mitch to defer so readily.

"Uh huh."

"You know, before we make too many more decisions, I think we should hire a consultant."

"A consultant?"

"A wedding consultant."

"People actually do that…for a living?"

"You have a hard time believing that? You must think a wedding is an easy thing to plan!"

"I imagine a big wedding is hard to plan. I figured a small wedding would be…" Mitch's voice just sort of trailed off. Perhaps, Reb wanted that big wedding after all.

"Any wedding is hard to plan, but at least we already know some of the important things."

"Like mints?"

"Like, who's going to pay for the wedding, for one."

"Oh, that's easy. I'm paying," Mitch announced.

"No. The bride's side of the family pays for the wedding, which means I'm paying."

"I can be the bride if you want." Mitch offered. "Then, I can pay."

"Oh, I think I'll keep you as groom."

"You don't think I could be a bride, do you?"

"Well, you haven't been yet," Reb was so maddeningly logical.

"And I have."
Mitch knew when she was licked.

"But there are some things the groom pays for."

"Like what?"

"Well, the rehearsal dinner, for one."

284

"The rehearsal dinner. Check. What else?"

"The honeymoon."

"Honeymoon. Check. How about here?"

"Here? For the wedding or the honeymoon?"

"Either, I guess."

"I think we need to plan where to have the wedding before we get too carried away."

Mitch thought they already had, gotten carried away, but she didn't mention it.

"Sure. Where do you suggest?"

"Probably back in Colorado." Reb was thinking every minute. "That's where most of our friends are."

"That makes sense. No use making people travel all over."

"So, where in Colorado do you want to get married?"

"Neither one of us belongs to a church. I guess that rules out that idea."

"Not necessarily. There are lots of people who don't go to church as a rule and yet get married in one."

"I bet that's lots of straight people."

"Either way, I'm sure it can be arranged."

"It can be, but do you think it's appropriate for us?"

"You don't like the idea?" Reb took note.

"It isn't that I don't like the idea. It's just..." Mitch voice trailed off. She didn't know quite what she was trying to say.

"It's just what?" Reb asked gently.

"Churches just don't feel right to me anymore. I've seen what comes out of them."

"We can always get married at home."

"It's too small."

"So, give me an idea."

"How about Trish's house?"

"I'd never thought of that. With everything going on in their lives, I wonder if that would be too much?"

"Let's call and find out."

Mitch was on the phone before Reb could think of any more reasons why they shouldn't get hitched at Trish's. Meanwhile, Mitch and Trish had entered into an animated conversation.

"So, your Casanova days are over," Trish teased upon hearing the news of the impending nuptials.

"Heck, yeah! I've been out of circulation a long time."

"I guess. So, when's the big day?"

"Oh, gee, I guess we haven't decided that yet."

"Well, what have you got figured out so far?"

"Reb wants wedding mints."

"Of course. It just wouldn't *be* a wedding without wedding mints."

"Yeah."

Apparently, everyone but Mitch knew all about wedding mints.

"Where are you having the ceremony?"

"We don't know."

"Have it here, at our house," Trish offered as if she had read Mitch's mind.

"That would be okay?" Mitch asked.

"It would be way past okay, right, Honey?"

Mitch realized that Trish was now talking to Robbie and didn't want to interrupt.

"She wants to know when the big day is?" Trish reiterated now for the both of them.

"When's the big day?" Mitch asked Reb in turn and Trish knew not to interrupt.

"It takes a while to plan a wedding," Reb answered seriously.

"How about Valentine's Day?" Mitch asked.

"Sounds good," Trish answered, figuring it was her turn at conversation.

"That might be pushing it a little?" Reb was looking panicked. Mitch was too busy setting things in stone with Trish to worry about the hundred and one details coursing through Reb's mind. And, too, did Trish agree before consulting Robbie, forgetting for the moment that they were talking about the birth window. So, when the phone call was over, two very similar conversations took place. Reb was giving Mitch a few choice reasons why a wedding would be tough to pull together on such short notice. The more Reb talked, the clearer it dawned on Mitch's consciousness just how elaborate an event Reb had in mind.

"I'm sure you can do it," Mitch answered feebly.

"I sincerely hope so. And with *your* help!"

Meanwhile, Robbie was gently but firmly reminding Trish of their due date, which was March 1.

"Well, it's not February 14," was Trish's equally feeble reply.

"Do you know what I'll look like then?" Robbie made her point distinctly.

"Do you want me to call her back and tell her we can't do it? I will. I'm going to," Trish was reaching for the phone.

Robbie caught her hand. "No, you're not going to call her back. It will be okay."

"No, really, I will. Honest. And she won't mind one bit."

"It's okay. Don't worry. I'll just need to wear something big enough."

"You'll be gorgeous. As usual. If they're planning a Valentine's Day wedding, I'm wondering if it's going to be all reds and pinks. You look wonderful in pink, just like those yummy mellocreme candies."

If Trish knew nothing else, she sure was an expert at talking her way out of trouble.

"Now, you stop it!" Robbie was by now blushing as pink as any Valentine should.

Back in Santa Fe, things were a bit more somber.

"We need to get our colors done," Reb announced after they had settled in for the night.

"Get our what's done?"

"Our colors."

Mitch looked at her arms. She didn't know if Reb was talking about tan lines or hair dye.

"I think I'm pale?" Mitch ventured a guess.

"That's not what I mean!" Reb could sound so haute couture when she wanted to.

"Well, what do you mean?"

"You're supposed to find out if you're a winter, summer, spring or autumn bride."

"February's in winter, isn't it?"

"That hasn't got anything to do with it! It's all about your skin tone, eye color, shade of hair."

"It all matters?"

"You take all those into consideration. Then, you know what season you are and then certain colors look better on you than others."

"So, we could plug in my answers and find out that green is my color."

"Nobody wears green to a wedding. It's the color of jealousy!"

"Really?"

"It's one of those rules that one shouldn't break. No green!"

"Even if it's your color?"

"Even if."

"This all sounds too complex. I have an idea."

"You do?"

"Don't sound so surprised."

"Sorry."

"Since it's a Valentine's Day event, why don't we pick red and white and pink."

It was really quiet for a moment. Mitch began to think that Reb had dozed off.

"That would work," she finally said.

Every psychic wedding consultant on the planet cringed in unison. It didn't matter. The idea was an original Mitch Tanner. It would have to do.

"How hard would it be to rent a white tux in my size?" Mitch mused.

"We'll have one made for you. There will be no renting."

"Doesn't that take time?"

"You're the one with your foot on the gas pedal."

"I'll start looking the minute we get back to Denver."

"That's not the only issue. We will need to select attendants and have them outfitted as well."

"Oh yeah. Attendants. Like maid of honor and stuff."

"I keep forgetting that this is your first wedding."

"And my last. Who's going to be your maid of honor?"

"That's easy. Mary. What about your best man?"

Reb held her breath. She knew who she didn't want."

"Trish, of course."

Reb exhaled, "Good choice!"

"But," Mitch intoned, "We still need to find a role for Lisa. She is part of the family."

"Of course," Reb answered like it was her intention all along.

"She could be one of your groomsmen."

"She could be one of your bridesmaids."

"Does she look better in a tux or a dress?"

Somehow, it didn't seem like a wise question to answer. Mitch stalled by pretending to think.

"Well?" Reb the wedding planner wanted an answer. Now!

"Why don't we ask her which she prefers?"

Well, it wasn't a definite answer, but it satisfied Reb. For now.

"How long are we staying in Santa Fe?"

Mitch checked her watch. Hadn't they just gotten here?

"How long do you want to stay?"

"Look, I know you think I'm diving headfirst into this entire wedding business, but somebody has to."

"Sweetie, I'll be here for you every step of the way. You just tell me what you want and I'll make it happen for you."

"Okay. Let's head home tomorrow."

"Bella will be disappointed."

Reb nodded. A couple of days wouldn't hurt. "I guess we can stay through the weekend."

Mitch smiled big. "Good."

They made wise use of their vacation by getting a spiral notebook and writing down ideas as they discussed them. This had a calming effect on Reb, but Mitch was getting writer's cramp. So far, the list included: wedding dress, tux, matching wardrobe for attendants, flowers, decorations for Trish's house, food, rehearsal dinner, invitations, type of ceremony, reception, wedding cake, mints (duh) gifts for attendants, groom's cake, photography, guest book, cake knife, silverware, plates, glasses, caterer, music, liquor, and champagne. So far.

A wedding the size and scope of Reb's dreams wasn't something you threw together in a week. There were a couple of things they didn't need to worry about, namely blood tests and a marriage license.

"Should we get another set of matching rings?" Reb asked during the drive home.

They had ended up staying an entire week in Santa Fe. There was just something about the area and Bella's cooking that made it conducive to rest and relaxation. Mitch felt like a new person.

"Absolutely! And let's have them inscribed. Something poetic."

"Speaking of poetic, we need to think about vows."

"Vows?"

"Wedding vows. The things we're going to say to each other. In front of all our friends and family."

"I thought we just repeated what the preacher told us to say?"

"We could do that. Or we can include something original."

"I guess so…" Mitch's sense of calm was sifting away. She never thought of herself as a poet and was easily overwhelmed at the prospect of penning something even halfway decent.

"Or, you can just repeat what the preacher says," Reb mouthed. Mitch nodded. She was happier talking about rings.

"You want gold, silver, or white gold?"

"What about diamonds?"

"We can do diamonds and/or any other precious gems your heart desires."

"I'm wondering about rubies."

"Red is a passionate color. Sounds a lot like you."

"But I'm also thinking about emeralds."

"Those are my favorite."

"Really? I never knew that."

"I guess that's one of those things you find out when you're getting married."

"You don't mind that we use the word 'marriage' I take it?"

"Well, I know that we're really not getting married, but I'm still going to use the word because it's just too much trouble to say something else."

"Like 'commitment ceremony' for instance?"

"Right. You start inviting people to a 'commitment ceremony' and they might shy away."

"I see your point."

Having had enough of wedding talk for now, they lapsed into companionable silence. When they chatted, it was about finally having the entire house all to themselves. Mary and Lisa would be moving out soon. And then, they'd get to do everything they wanted. Like, exercise?

"Mary said that the exercise equipment arrived in good order."

"That's nice."

"It's all set up and everything."

"Good."

"You sound thrilled," Reb used her best sarcastic tone of voice.

"It shows, huh?"

"I know that working out isn't your idea of fun, but I really need to try and maintain the parts of me that still work."

"And I'd better try and keep up with you!"

Reb smiled. For the most part, it was true. But she still needed to fight osteoporosis. In order to do that, she would need to engage in serious physical therapy, something she had avoided until now. For this she would need the help of professionals and pray that no bones would be broken.

"You know what I have to do, don't you?" Reb asked.

"I know."

"And, you're okay?"

"I'm okay."

"Okay."

After a week, Mitch realized that life was now divided into two different time zones: Before Wedding (BW) and After Wedding (AW). Logically, all wedding plans were in the BW category. One thing in the AW category included redecorating the house. Of course, some things like physical therapy, fell into the Everyday Things to Do category. Other things in this grouping were eating, sleeping, bathing, Thanksgiving and Christmas. Lest anyone think that the last two items on the list were any less festive just because they fell into the ETTD category didn't know how much of a kid Mitch could be during the holidays. For the more subdued holiday of Thanksgiving, Mitch cooked turkey for four after wrist-wrestling Mary for the honor. The argument went something like:

Mary, "I'll cook the turkey!"

Mitch, "You don't want to mess up your new kitchen! I'll cook the turkey!"

Mary, "The kitchen will need to get messed up sooner or later."

Mitch, "Let's opt for later."

Mary remembered this conversation when Christmas rolled around and insisted that Christmas Dinner be at their new house. Mitch and Reb could do little but agree, since it still left them the sanctity of Christmas Eve all to themselves. Which they celebrated together in bed with eggnog.

Across town, the celebration at Trish and Robbie's house had been centered around Hanukkah. Perhaps because there would soon be an infant child born to the household, Rose and Max had become more religious. They went to temple more often and when Robbie felt like it, she went along. Trish stayed home. She had gotten this far without organized religion being a part of her life and starting now felt akin to engaging in superstition. No amount of praying to God was going to change the fact that their baby was going to be born with a devastating birth defect. With each new ultrasound, the fact was absolutely undeniable. No amount of faith would make arms appear on a fetus where stumps were now formed. If that was the only concern, it might be bearable. But it wasn't. The crushing possibility that the baby might not even make it to birth weighed on Trish's mind constantly. Conversely, Robbie was a picture of courage every day. Trish had offered at least a half dozen times to call Mitch and change the wedding plans. But Robbie had put her foot down and in the common sense way that guided her through life finally explained to Trish that being at home for the event was a benefit.

In this way, Trish fretted all the time Robbie was gone to temple, so as to get it all out of her system. Otherwise, Robbie would know and be troubled. And it wasn't good for pregnant ladies to be troubled. During the days of Hanukkah, Trish had gone a tiny bit overboard on gifts for Robbie. She gave her three gifts every day. In the morning, it was jewelry. And not just any jewelry either. It was diamonds and sapphires and emeralds and rubies as big as the fingernail on your pinkie finger. After a couple of days, Robbie sparkled like champagne. The afternoon was clothing. Robbie had a stylish outfit for every day. In the evening, there was sleepwear, and we're not talking flannel. There was enough lace to throw together a small tablecloth with matching napkins. The colors were exquisite and Robbie's favorite was a midnight blue number.

"You make me feel beautiful," Robbie would say.

"You are beautiful," Trish would reply in turn.

Usually, that was all that Robbie needed to hear to fall sound asleep after each long day. Make no mistake about it, every day that you were six-plus months pregnant was a long day. Robbie was glad that they had spent time early on to decorate the nursery. Their preparation had been every bit as meticulous as a space shuttle launch and now, all they had to do was wait.

"You're not asleep yet?" Trish asked quietly.

"I guess not."

"What are you thinking about?"

"Oh, nothing in particular."

That always meant that she was thinking about something in particular and it was Trish's duty to get to the bottom of it. Gently.

"You're thinking about the baby?"

"Yes."

Trish pulled her into an embrace. At least, as much of an embrace as they could manage at this point.

"And what else?"

"I'm thinking that I don't know if I can go through this again."

Trish thought about this for a moment. They had talked about having lots and lots of children.

"I'm not sure we should go through this again," she said.

"We wanted more children," Robbie reminded.

Now, Trish didn't know what to say. On one hand, she could always be the birth mother, but frankly, while Robbie was making it look easy, the very concept frightened Trish. She had never had the urge to be a mother in that way.

"Gee, it sure got quiet all of a sudden," Robbie half teased Trish.

"It did, didn't it."

"What are you thinking?"

"I'm thinking that you're about eighty-five times braver than I am."

"You never did want to be a birth mother, did you?"

"It shows?"

"It shows."

Now, it was Robbie's turn to be silent for a moment. Then, she said, "I think it will take about all we have in us to care for this baby. At least, for the time being."

The remark must have settled the issue comfortably for Robbie, for she fell sound asleep.

Chapter 33

"Are you ever coming to bed?" Lisa called out. The sound must've carried far enough. An answer floated back, "In a minute."

It was a long minute. When Mary finally showed up, Lisa had to know, "What took you so long?"

"I was cleaning the kitchen."

"Within an inch of its life?"

"Pretty much," Mary said as she walked over to Lisa's side of the bed and perched there. It had taken a long, long time but things were finally returning to normal for them. Having a house all to themselves had helped immensely. So had the speed of Lisa's healing process. Sure there were scars, but Mary hardly noticed anymore. In fact, she busied herself nuzzling them as Lisa put up with the rapt attention.

"You know I don't quite feel that the way I used to," she reminded Mary.

"I know. But I still do."

It had taken Lisa extra time before she had even allowed any kind of contact with this area. Now that it seemed to be one of Mary's favorite starting points, Lisa went along. Besides, Mary never stayed in one spot too long, with one exception. And they weren't there yet.

"Are you in a hurry?" Mary asked out of the blue. Lisa never knew quite how to answer this. So, she vacillated, "I don't know."

"Let's find out."

Which Mary did and Lisa was. The passion that had eluded them during rehab was now back and in fine fettle. Really, really fine. Speeding tickets didn't have this much fine.

"I think you just broke the land-speed record," Mary teased.

"You helped," Lisa breathed.

"I did, didn't I. I'll just have to go slower next time."

How could Lisa argue with that? Mary had been the paradigm of patience. Making up for lost time would be fun.

"What are you thinking about?" Mary asked.

"I'm thinking about the upcoming nuptials," Lisa fibbed. She had been thinking of them earlier, so it wasn't that big of a lie.

"Really?"

"How is your mother going to manage a wedding dress in her wheel chair?"

"Last I heard, the dress was going to be uncomplicated attire."

"The bridesmaid's dresses are gorgeous," Lisa commented. It had been decided that every attendant on Reb's side would be in dresses. That short list included Reb, Mary and Robbie. Mitch, Trish and Lisa were opting for tuxedos. It was going to be a stylish affair. The bigger question was, with all those attendants, who was left to be in the audience? It wasn't like the Pitt-Aniston wedding where the list was so long that parking was a problem. Over time, it seemed that Mitch and Rebecca had made few friends. Family was practically nonexistent. Mitch had broached the idea of inviting Reb's family and suffered a withering stare.

"The general rule is," Reb explained it like it was gospel, "that the bride invites people who she likes! It's a special day and I'm not going to have it be ruined by my sister."

"Maybe she'll behave herself?" Mitch offered.

"Do you want to take the risk of her ruining the entire day for us?"

Mitch thought about this for a mere second, just to sort out the concept in her mind.

"I don't believe that your sister could ruin the day."

Reb got that "you've got to be kidding" look on her face.

"What makes you so sure?"

"Maybe it's just me, but about the only thing I can think of that could ruin our wedding day is if you didn't show up. Any other problem would be just a minor inconvenience. So what if your sister shows up and creates a scene? The only person she'll be hurting is herself."

"It wouldn't bother you if she started proselytizing against our relationship?"

"What else could she say that I haven't already heard?"

"You haven't heard her on the subject of gay weddings. Hell, she wasn't all that thrilled about my first marriage!"

"I remember Jeff saying something about it. He is on the guest
list, isn't he?"

"You want to invite Jeff to our wedding?"

"The worst he could do is not show up."

"I'll pop an invitation in the mail tomorrow."

"I mean, it isn't like we're inviting thousands. Are we even up
to a dozen invitations yet?"

"I've sent out ninety-seven so far."

"You have?" Mitch sounded shocked.

"And if you keep adding people, I'll need to order a second
printing."

"And just think of the postage!" Mitch said in mock horror.

Reb finally smiled. Mitch was reminded of why they were going
through all this. Ordering the invitations had been an experience
all unto itself. Of course, there were gay printers. There were
gay everything. Gay printers understood the differences between
gay and straight weddings. You couldn't always say that about
straight printers. Anyway, the differences started right on the
very first line of the invitation. Normally, the parents of the
bride were the people who did the inviting. Since neither the
bride nor the groom had living parents, Reb's and Mitch's names
were listed as those honored to request the presence of those
hundred or so people Reb was inviting.

"Is there anyone else on your last-minute list?"

"Last minute?"

"Invitations need to be hitting mailboxes soon. It isn't like
people aren't already making big plans for Valentine's Day."

"Did we send one to Jane?"

"Jane who?"

"Jane, the woman who named her restaurant after you..."

"Oh, that Jane. What's her address?"

"I bet if we send it to the restaurant, she'll get it."

"Okay, now, are there any other people who have named things
after me whom I've forgotten to invite?"

"Not that I'm aware of."

"Good. So, we have the date and time and place. How's the
music coming?" Reb was just full of questions.

"Music? What music?"

"You're supposed to be arranging for the music!"

"Every time you kiss me, I hear violins," Mitch explained.

"Well, that's peachy for you, but what's everybody else going to do?"

"You put me in charge of the music. Don't worry about it."

"If you bring in some sort of kazoo band from Cleveland, you don't even want to know what's going to happen to you."

Mitch pretended to be crossing a certain kazoo band off an imaginary list, and only for Reb's edification. She had a decent combo band lined up. And they weren't cheap.

"What else is on your mind?"

"You won't even talk to me about flowers."

That was true enough. Mitch didn't know a nasturtium from a geranium. She was florally challenged in the worst way.

"I thought you were choosing roses?" Mitch scoured her memory for this small factoid.

"They're very expensive."

"They grow on bushes. How expensive could they possibly be?"

Reb sighed audibly. Mitch had been hearing this sound a lot lately. Planning a wedding was not for the faint of heart.

"You can spend hundreds if not thousands of dollars on flowers."

"If you don't pick roses, what's your next flower of choice?"

"A lot of people choose carnations."

"Do you like carnations?"

"Carnations are okay."

"But you like roses better," Mitch summed it up.

"To me, roses are romantic and carnations are happy."

"That's a tough choice, since both apply."

"Yes, they do. I'll talk to the floral consultant tomorrow."

"Good," Mitch was happy to be off the hook on this decision.

"Just get as many of each as you want," she added quickly.

"You're feeling rich?"

"The feeling is going away slowly," Mitch grinned playfully.

Reb smiled back. At least it wasn't a sigh.

The notebook that they had started a scant few weeks ago was now filling up with checkmarks. Those were good things. They meant that someone had made a call, a decision, or a deposit. Mitch was due in for a tux fitting, as were Trish and Lisa. They decided to make a day of it, which meant, of course, another really fancy lunch for Lisa. The biggest decision was whether to eat first or be fitted first.

"Do you want your tux to fit tight or loose?" Lisa asked bluntly. To her, it didn't matter. Lisa would have the same beautiful figure until the day she died and beyond. Mitch could hear it now, people bending over her open casket commenting, "And would you look at that perfect figure!"

"Well!?" Lisa was waiting for her answer.

"What?" Mitch came out of her funereal stupor.

"Where is your mind?"

"Hey, I'm allowed to be distracted. I'm getting married!"

"Yes! I know! That's why we've all been standing at attention lately awaiting our orders."

"What was the original question?"

"Are we eating before or after?"

"The fitting is at two. We can either have an early lunch or an early dinner."

This sent the tough decision back to Lisa. She could have a nice lunch or a more expensive dinner.

"Why not both?" she asked like it was just a matter of logic and not the more obvious attempt to spend as much of Mitch's money as possible.

"Why don't the hell we just go out for breakfast as well and make it a trifecta?" Mitch tried to sound sarcastic, but it all came out sounding like an idea worthy of a Nobel Peace Prize.

"Trifecta? Is that one of those new skillet meals at Village Inn?" Mitch only shook her head. Lisa never had played the ponies.

"Do you think Trish will be up for this?"

If you looked up the word "doting father-to-be" in the dictionary, Trish's picture would've been the accompanying illustration. As she and Robbie sailed unwaveringly toward the due date, they had practically gone into seclusion. Howard Hughes had seen more daylight in his waning years than Trish had this past month.

"I personally think she needs a break. You can only pack and repack the hospital suitcase so many times!"

It was true. Trish had been in hover mode for a while now. Maybe it was Robbie who needed a break. After much debate, Trish agreed to at least the lunch part of the day. And the fitting. Which left Mitch and Lisa all by themselves at the local pancake house. How Reb put up with this was anyone's guess. Maybe, like Robbie, she needed a break as well.

Lisa pored over the menu like it was the Dead Sea Scrolls. The word "trifecta" wasn't anywhere to be found, but omelet was everywhere as were pancakes, bacon, steak, and biscuits and gravy. Mitch was starving, but knew better than to go overboard so early in the day.
"What are you having?" Lisa asked like it might help her decide.
"Toast."
"Toast! You've got to be kidding!"
"Why?"
"I know you're hungry."
"You do? How?"
"We did spend some time together once upon a time."
"And that makes you psychic?"
"About some things, yes."
"Hmmm," Mitch said noncommittally. That didn't deter Lisa.
"I kept track of all your appetites pretty closely."
"I see," Mitch resorted to Reb's standard reply. It came in handy when there was nothing else to say.
"So, don't think I don't notice," Lisa sounded mysterious. Why it was that Mitch always took the bait was beyond her comprehension.
"Notice what?"
"Things," Lisa intoned.
Before Mitch could reply, probably with another stab at clarification, the waitress was there to take their order.
"What can I bring you?"
Lisa popped up first with her answer. "I'll have toast."
Mitch looked up, puzzled. For a moment. Then, without further hesitation, she ordered "a western omelet, strawberry pancakes, corned beef hash, two eggs and hash browns."
"I thought you weren't hungry?" Lisa asked immediately.
"I changed my mind."
"You don't just change your mind about being hungry. Either you are or you aren't."
"A little like being in love, huh?"
"Exactly."

Things were quiet for a moment, which meant that Lisa was finally getting to the point that she had been working toward. Mitch was braced for the real question.

"Why didn't you choose to memorialize our relationship with a wedding?"

When Lisa got to the point of the matter, she got to the point of the matter. Mitch fought every urge to dash off a glib reply. In fact, she sat dumbfounded for so long that Lisa said, "Gee, don't everybody answer all at once."

"I'm sorry. Did you want to get married?"

"It's a little late to be asking now, isn't it?" Lisa said in that certain way of hers that inferred that she really knew it wasn't a serious inquiry on Mitch's part but couldn't pass up the opportunity to make her swing in the wind. Meanwhile, Mitch went way past swinging in the wind.

"You walked out on me. Remember?"

"After a long time."

"You took my savings."

"Consider it palimony."

"If you wanted to get married so badly, why didn't you propose to me?"

"Don't be ridiculous. You're the man! You were supposed to do the proposing!"

"I was?" Mitch was muddled.

"Who did the proposing between you and Rebecca?" Lisa asked but she really knew the answer.

"I did. But that's different," Mitch was now truly mired in verbal quicksand.

"Why was it different?" Lisa asked.

Mitch could feel the sensation of logic pulling her under. Lisa, God bless her, had a point. Why hadn't Mitch jumped on the matrimonial bandwagon with her? Her earlier answer came back around for a repeat performance.

"You just didn't stick around."

"I'm here now."

"The first time."

"You really do love her, don't you?" Lisa smiled suddenly.

"I wouldn't settle for less."

"Good."

With that out of the way, Lisa's appetite took on a life of its own. She went clean through her toast and then proceeded to scavenge Mitch's breakfast as well. The pancakes were history and the omelet was teetering on the brink of destruction. Mitch nibbled around the edges of the hash brown. After all, there was another meal before the fitting.

"You going to eat your corned beef hash?" Lisa the Conqueror asked.

"Help yourself."

After Lisa had finished laying waste to everything on the table, she talked Mitch into going to the mall to ostensibly buy a wedding present.

"The invitation said 'no gifts,'" Mitch reminded sternly.

Lisa was having none of it.

"I'm sure you need something for the wedding night. Remember, I have seen what you wear to bed!"

Way back when, Mitch's standard pajama outfit was a t-shirt.

"I've changed since then."

"What? Are you wearing a better brand of t-shirt?"

"Ouch!" Mitch tried to sound mortally wounded.

"Well, I am right, aren't I?"

"Yes."

"Come on."

Lisa led the way to the sexy lingerie department like she could get there blindfolded. She skimmed the racks and, before Mitch could check to price tags for sticker shock, Lisa had three little nothings for Mitch to try on.

"Okay, but I'm not doing any modeling."

"Oh, thank you, thank you, thank you!" Lisa sounded like she was getting an Academy Award. Mitch retreated before she could hear more of the speech. Damn that Lisa! She did have good, no make that superior taste in lingerie. Everything Mitch tried on was tasteful yet flattering. It was going to be a tough choice.

"Hey, are you reading War and Peace in there or what?" Lisa's voice carried through the fitting rooms. Thank goodness they were alone.

"I'm trying to choose one."

"Get all three if you want. Or, I can find more…"

"I'm not getting all three."

"Get all three. You've got an entire honeymoon to think about."

Oh geez, the honeymoon. In order to make life fair, society dictates that while the bride's family foot the bill for the wedding, the groom is responsible for everything after that. The first joy and expense being the honeymoon. When Mitch suggested that they just hang around the house for a week, Reb declared that she might just go out and buy a ladder. Well, at least everyone knew where they stood on those issues! So, Mitch had pondered travel brochure upon travel brochure, trying to come up with a workable plan. She wasn't big on traveling abroad. Too many tropical or exotic diseases to be concerned about. And as lovely as Niagara Falls sounded, it was going to be mid-February. That could be a good thing. It would give them a good excuse to stay indoors. And in bed…But they could do that any old time. For a while, she contemplated Hawaii. It would be nice and warm. They could lounge on the beach. Drink those luscious liquor-loaded cocktails. And not remember a damn thing afterwards. Which didn't seem like such a good idea. So, Mitch did the logical thing. She had asked Reb's opinion a few days ago.

"Where do you want to go on our honeymoon?" Mitch remembered the conversation. It had started out so well…

"You haven't taken care of that *yet*?"

"I can't decide."

"Why not?" Reb sounded on the edge of irritation. The Before-Wedding jitters were beginning to show.

"I guess it's because no matter where we are, I'm happy just because you're there."

"That's really romantic. Let's go to the place where we fell in love."

Mitch had opened her mouth to say something and then immediately closed it. She had no idea where Rebecca was referring to. Mitch knew where she was when she first fell in love with Reb, and that was at The Lucky U. Reb obviously had somewhere different in mind. Mitch was thoroughly stumped. If she had to ask, she knew she would be in the biggest doghouse of all time. So instead of doing the sensible thing, namely opting for the doghouse, she had blurted out, "I'll make reservations first thing in the morning."

"Good. There, now. That's settled!" Reb was happy.

Mitch was panicked.

The panic now returned, thanks to Lisa. Mitch hadn't made reservations yet because she still had no earthly clue where it was they were going.

"What did I say?" Lisa asked.

"What?" Mitch came back to the moment.

"You're getting all white-knuckled on me. What's wrong?"

"I'm supposed to be making reservation for the honeymoon at the place where Reb and I fell in love..."

"So?"

"And I don't know where that is!"

"Oh, sure you do. You're just not thinking about it logically."

Mitch looked skeptical.

"You've got to think back to the beginning of the relationship, probably prior to the time when you were *sleeping together*, and figure out where the two of you were that takes reservations. It's as simple as that!"

Mitch turned this homespun advice over in her mind once or twice before the answer tumbled out clear as day.

"Thank you!" Mitch would've kissed Lisa had it not been for their history.

They gathered up Trish and went to lunch at La Wallet. An apt name for such an expensive restaurant. Every time Lisa dragged Mitch to one of these French bistros, the check escalated. Holy Mother of God, twelve dollars for just an appetizer. Now, she wished she had ordered the large stack of pancakes for Lisa at Le Cheapo Breakfast Place. It probably wouldn't have made one whit of difference. Lisa was in a gourmand mood. And, happily, so was Trish. Once Trish had decided to leave the house, only after telling Robbie about twelve times to call her if anything happened, she managed to relax about things after the first fifteen minutes or so. In fact, it was doing her a world of good to conspire with Lisa over the menu. They figured out that if they all ordered something different, then they could all have a taste of three entrees. But then Lisa got the wild idea to get one each of the appetizers. Mitch couldn't complain. She had done that kind of thing before herself. Mitch knew it was only a matter of time before they had one each dessert on the table as well. If it brought a smile to their faces, it was worth it. They had both been through so much, and the balance for Trish was yet to come. Taking on the responsibilities of a baby was one thing. Bearing the burden of a child whom you knew wasn't going to come out of the womb with twenty digits was quite another.

"So, how is Robbie doing?" Mitch asked, probably for the millionth time since the news of the conception.

"She feels big," Trish said the first salient thing that was in her mind.

"But, she's okay?"

"Yes. She's beginning to worry about her bridesmaid's dress." Mitch's side of the aisle had not the market cornered on fittings. Reb, Mary and Robbie had been catered to as well by the dressmakers. But even they could only do so much with measurements, prognostications and elastic.

"Tell her not to worry. She'll be as lovely as ever."

Lunch and the subsequent fitting went well. In honor of Valentine's Day motif, they had decided upon white tuxedos with red cummerbunds. The bride's attendants were sticking with pink. It was all going to be yummy.

Trish was delivered back home by 3:30. Lisa, for whatever reason, opted out of dinner plans. Maybe it was those appetizers and desserts finally catching up? Mitch was home by four thirty. Reb was shocked. Shocked!

"I thought you had dinner plans? What happened?"

"Breakfast and lunch happened."

"You mean, Lisa got filled up!"

"Who says miracles don't happen."

"So, what were you going to do for dinner?" Mitch asked.

"I was going to nibble on some saltines and maybe have a dill pickle."

"How about a steak?"

"What kind?"

"A really expensive kind."

"I'll get my shoes."

Although dress shoes were mostly just a formality for Reb nowadays, she still had some nice pairs. For a steak dinner, she wore her best. They had a favorite out-of-the-way spot where the menu was meaty, and they arrived early enough to get seated immediately. No use even looking at the menu. The order was always the same. Large filet mignon, baked potato, salad, coffee. They really didn't do this very often, so it didn't feel like a big sin. Until they caved in to the dessert menu. Actually, it was more like spelunking by the time all was said and done. Mitch sighed. "This is like pigging out after getting weighed at the doctor's."

"At least we'll have time to work all this off before the wedding."

"That sounds like fun," Mitch perked up.

"I was talking about all the errands and things left to do."

"Oh, yeah, that, too."

"I guess the fitting went okay?"

"Perfectly."

"That was a quick answer."

"What more do you want to know?"

"Well, how was Trish?"

"Once we got her out of the house, she was fine."

"She wasn't before?"

"She's on edge."

"Of course she is. And how was Lisa?"

"Full of questions," Mitch blurted out before thinking.

"Questions? What kind of questions?"

Now, Mitch was stuck. She forged ahead. "She had a lot of questions about relationships."

"Really?"

"Uh huh."

"What did she want to know about relationships?"

"Well, what she really wanted to know was why I never asked her to marry me."

"And what did you say?"

"I told her she could've asked me."

"What did she say to that?"

"She told me that I was the man."

Reb smiled. "Only Lisa would come up with something like that."

"Yeah," Mitch agreed, happy to be off the hook. Or so she thought.

"So, why didn't you propose to her way back when?"

"She didn't stick around long enough."

"And I did."

"Right."

"And that's all someone has to do to get a proposal out of you?" Oh brother, Mitch thought to herself! Whoever said that honesty pays must've been trading in a different currency.

"There is one other stipulation," Mitch hinted.

"And that would be?" Reb wanted to know, and pretty quickly at that.

"I would need to be so deeply in love that I couldn't have imagined ever living without her."

"That's really sweet. Pay the check."

Mitch knew she was getting off cheap, in every sense of the word.

If the impending wedding was to be visualized, it would most probably resemble a runaway train. So magnificent and yet at the same time, ominous. It couldn't be stopped or slowed and about all Mitch could do was blow the whistle occasionally and hope for the best. Her main concern was for Trish and Robbie hosting the gala event, but as Rose pointed out, it kept them busy. Which was an important thing apparently. If idle hands were the devil's workshop, or whatever that saying was, then the Goldstein household was approaching Godliness. Old carpet was unceremoniously ripped out and replaced with new. An extremely beautiful and expensive new flooring was installed in the kitchen just so the caterer Reb hired would have the very best to walk upon. The appliance upgrade was every bit as ambitious. Heck, they needed to do it anyway, Trish reasoned. Soon, they would be cooking for five. Not that you necessarily needed a convection oven to heat up baby formula, but with what was in store for them, Robbie should have every luxury available. And yet, she remained totally uninterested in the renovations. Almost on the verge of sullen whenever the topic came up. Trish wondered if this was just a natural part of expectant motherhood, and asked just to be sure.

"Are you feeling okay?"

"I'm fine."

"You want me to massage your feet?"

"No, thanks. They're fine. What little I can still see of them."

That much was true. As Robbie's tummy grew out, her toes were in eclipse mode most of the time.

"They are still as beautiful as ever, as are you," Trish complimented readily.

Robbie didn't say anything. Trish got even nosier, "Is something troubling you? I mean, something new?"

Robbie gave the question serious consideration. "I guess it's the word 'new' that gives me pause to think."

"Why is that?"

"We're doing a lot of changing things around here."

"You mean, all the redecorating?"

"Everything is changing."

"That's true. We didn't buy this old place to keep it the same old way, did we?"

"Yes, but don't you think it would be okay if some of it stayed the same?"

Trish hadn't honestly given this concept even ten seconds of consideration. Until now.

"I figured it was a good idea to renovate the areas we were going to use for the wedding."

"And then wait on everything else?"

"Sure."

"And it will all be so lovely, too," Robbie brightened right up. Maybe she had just felt a little left out of the whole process? Trish thought to herself as they snuggled off to sleep.

February 14 dawned gloriously. It was as if the Heavens knew that somewhere in Colorado two people were about to plight their troths to one another and created the perfect day for it. Of course, weddings happened all the time, just not a wedding like this one. The press had gotten wind of the event and if you thought you had a lot of satellite trucks at Trish and Robbie's ceremony, it was nothing like what was happening today.

Because today, unlike the "other" wedding where it was just two lesbians tying the knot, this was the celebration where a paraplegic ex-Senator ex-Governor was going down the aisle with a recently world-famous healer of dubious credibility, only in the healing department, that is. Mitch found Reb at the kitchen table early in the morning, frowning over *the* notebook.

"Good morning, my dear bride-to-be," Mitch greeted, hoping to make at least a modest dent in the frown.

"Ummmm," Reb answered, totally absorbed in her studies.

"Going over the last-minute details?"

"Ummmm," Reb nodded.

"Is breakfast on the list?"

Things were quiet for a solemn moment and then a "What?" rose out of the reverie.

"Breakfast. You know…first meal of the day…?"

"There's some cereal in the cupboard. Knock yourself out."

"Yum Yum," Mitch exaggerated her reaction. "Do we have milk?"

"Of course not. I never get milk before a trip."

Ah yes, the honeymoon. After Mitch had remembered where Reb wanted to go on the honeymoon, she had been stubborn enough to keep all the plans secret. This had so irritated Reb that she had placed a moratorium on buying perishables. No fresh fruit. No fresh vegetables. Mitch could've sworn she was coming down with scurvy. She deposited her frame in the chair opposite Reb. Sans cereal.

"What?" Reb looked up.

"I'll take you to breakfast."

"No, thanks."

"You'll have to eat sometime."

"I'm saving my appetite for cake."

"That's a long way off."

"We're getting married at noon."

"Yeah, but we won't even get near the cake until two. Come on. I'll buy you a bowl of oatmeal," Mitch wheedled.

"Oatmeal?"

"With cream and sugar and strawberries."

"Strawberries?"

"Big, fat, plump, red, juicy ones."

308

"It's the middle of February. Nobody has really good strawberries in the middle of February."

"Particularly here," Mitch muttered.

"I heard that."

"I'm going to breakfast. Who's going with?"

"Give me ten minutes."

"Ten minutes it is."

They were off to the Breakfast Palace in eight and one-half minutes exactly. After checking the menu, Reb lost all interest in oatmeal and ordered bacon and eggs instead. After hearing that she had a choice of toast, biscuits or pancakes with that, she simply said, "Yes."

The waitress didn't question the answer. Mitch went for fresh fruit and cereal. And milk. And juice. And coffee.

"My mouth is dry," she explained to Reb.

"Just wait until you try and say your vows."

"Don't remind me."

"You do have them written, don't you?"

"Oh, sure."

Mitch had them written, sort of. There was a sentence or two on a piece of notebook paper. And then there were a couple of post-it notes with ideas jotted down on them. And then, of course, there was the jumble of adlib thoughts racing through Mitch's mind.

"I typed mine," Reb made it sound like a term paper.

"Good for you."

Reb chuckled.

"What's so funny?" Mitch wanted to know.

"For two people who are going to exchange vows in a few hours, we sure act like an old married couple already."

"And that's not all bad, is it?"

"No, it's not. I'm looking forward to the honeymoon. Wherever that's going to be."

"Yeah, me, too."

Further "old couple" dialogue was postponed by the arrival of breakfast. It was splendid. Fresh food and plenty of it. It beat the socks off of cold corn flakes. By nine, Mitch was sated. Reb had only picked.

"Does getting married kill your appetite?" Mitch asked.

"It seems to have. This time, anyway."

"So, you weren't nervous the first time around?"

"No."

"Why?"

"Because the first time around, I thought I was doing the right thing."

"And now?"

"Now I know I'm doing the right thing."

"Doing the right thing makes you nervous?"

"Yes."

"Why?"

"Because now I know what I can lose. And that makes me nervous."

From a woman who had already lost a lot of things, this revelation helped put things in perspective.

"You're not going to lose me."

"You can't guarantee that."

"No. But I'll do my level best to make sure it doesn't happen."

"Well, then we'd better get back to the house and commence with the wedding."

Other than sounding like something Jed Clampett would've said, it made sense. People would be calling. People like Trish wondering where Mitch was and people like Mary wondering where her mother was and heaven knows who else. As expected, the phone was ringing when they got in the door. But it was neither Trish nor Mary. In fact, Reb almost fell out of her wheelchair. It was her sister, BeBe. Her sister BeBe who had received an invitation to the wedding and hadn't RSVP'd. Until now. Reb said "uh huh" a few times, nodding as she listened. It had "no, we're not coming written all over it until Reb started giving directions to the house. Trish's, not theirs. Whew. Enough people were already gathering here. Mitch referred to them as the second-string press corps. The first stringers were already assembled at Trish's mansion. They would be ankle deep in cables if they weren't careful. Reb hung up.

"So, Aunt BeBe will be there?"

"And Henry."

"I suppose he had to buy a new suit?"

"And complained every minute in the store, I'm sure."

"I know the feeling."

Before Mitch could elaborate further, the phone rang. Now, it was Trish, the worried best man. "Where have you been?" she asked in a kind and gentle way.

"At breakfast."

"Eating again?"

They both laughed. Last night, at the rehearsal dinner, it would be safe to say that both Mitch and Trish overdid it a wee bit in the calorie department. They had made a pact to not eat for at least another twelve hours.

"I made it a whole eleven hours and fifty-five minutes."

"Better than me. I was in the refrigerator at the crack of dawn."

"How are things over there?"

"Hectic. When are you going to be here?"

"When are we going to be there?" Mitch turned the question over to Reb.

"We'll head out in a few minutes."

"Maybe a half hour?" Mitch informed Trish.

"Good. That will give us time to sit over here and relax."

"I'm not nervous."

"Well, I am!" Trish laughed. "I've never been a best man before."

"It's a snap. Just keep me from tripping over my shoe laces and you've done your job."

"Okay. No tripping over shoe laces. Got it. You'll be here soon?"

"We'll be there soon."

After Mitch hung up, she noticed that Reb had left the room. She was probably checking the luggage one last time. There wasn't much to check. She had packed *everything*.

"Where did you go?" Mitch called out.

"In here."

Mitch followed the voice to their bedroom. Reb was fiddling with a box.

"Come over here," Reb directed.

Mitch obeyed. She could "come over here" with the best of them.

"I wanted to give you this before the day gets away from us," Reb handed her the box.

"What's this?" Mitch sat on the bed.

"It's your groom present."

Mitch got a squelchy feeling in the pit of her stomach. She hadn't gotten Reb a bride's present.

"Of course, your gift to me is the honeymoon," Reb explained.

"Oh," was Mitch's reply.

She opened the box to find perhaps the most exquisite diamond-encrusted watch that she had ever seen. And she had seen her share of jewelry over the years shopping for Reb. On the watch face where normally numerals appeared, there were, instead, twelve hearts.

"We'll never have enough time together," Reb said, "But at least now you can keep track of it."

"This is...overwhelming," Mitch whispered. A whisper was about all she could manage about now.

Reb was thoroughly enjoying the moment. It wasn't every day she could reduce Mitch to a whisper.

"Try it on."

"I might need to sit down first."

"You are sitting down."

"Oh...yeah," Mitch smiled. She was getting color back in her face now. It was sure warm in the house.

With help from Reb, Mitch hooked the clasp and admired the watch. It was practically blinding.

"I'm going to need sunglasses just to tell the time."

"I'll pick up a pair for you when we reach our mystery honeymoon destination."

Mitch leaned close and kissed Reb. "This is the most astounding present anyone has ever given to me. Ever."

"Ever?"

"Ever, ever."

"Is it time to leave?" Reb asked.

Mitch checked her new timekeeper. "It sure is."

Witnessed by the dozen or so TV and media cameras, Mitch put their suitcases in the van. It appeared that just about every minute of this day was to be documented. At least there would be some privacy at the ceremony. Silver staked her reputation on it. Nobody was getting past her without an authentic invitation and a photo ID. She had driven the catering staff up the wall already and the party hadn't even started. Maybe that was why Trish was edgy.

"You'd better sit down, Honey," Robbie urged Trish. Serious pacing had been going on since she had called Mitch. Back and forth. Back and forth. Robbie was queasy just from watching.

"Are you okay?" Trish cast a look at Robbie. She seemed paler than usual.

"I'm fine. You've made me sit with my feet up for so long that my backside is beginning to hurt."

"You want to take a walk with me before all the confusion begins?"

"How long a walk?"

Trish gazed lovingly at Robbie. She was so large with child and yet so breathtakingly beautiful.

"Oh, not more than thirty miles."

"Fifteen out, fifteen back?"

"Maybe once around the house."

"Inside or outside?"

"Whichever you want."

"How bad is the crowd outside?"

"It's pretty thick."

"Let's stick to the inside."

"Okay."

Trish helped Robbie to her feet and they took a lovely stroll around the house. Things were lovely. Fresh flowers adorned all the rooms. Even the kitchen, which was abuzz with perfectly-orchestrated activity.

"Are those mini cream puffs?" Robbie asked, almost reverently.

"Let's see," Trish reached over and plucked one off a silver tray. Without missing a beat, another was put in its place by someone who didn't even look up to see what had happened. Trish offered the tidbit to Robbie, who ate a small bite. It was soothing on her stomach, which had been very selective of late.

"It's wonderful."

"You want another?" Trish was ready to create another vacancy on the tray but Robbie stopped her.

"I need to save room for later."

"You've got your eye on the wedding cake?"

"Who wouldn't!"

Who wouldn't indeed. Those who had managed to steal a glance at the multi-tiered masterpiece were in awe of the artistry. If anyone noticed that the top decoration was nondescript, they kept the observation to themselves. It consisted of two larger-than-life silver wedding bands interlocked. It resembled something out of a magician's kit. It wasn't the only thing magical about the day. Just the most tangible at the moment. Robbie finished off the cream puff and then gave Trish's arm a squeeze.

"I think I'm ready to rest a little before the ceremony."

"Okay," Trish masked the concern in her voice. She had had ample practice lately. Robbie's lack of stamina had her worried sick for weeks now. Robbie reassured Trish that this was normal for pregnancy. How she knew this was anyone's guess. Trish walked with Robbie back to their bedroom and after making sure she was all comfy, went in search of Rose. Rose was double checking Max's wardrobe, from socks to bow tie.

"Everything okay?" Trish asked from the doorway.

"We're fine, Dear. How are you? How is Robbie?"

The questions were one after the other. Trish ignored the first and pondered the second for so long that Rose looked up to see why there was a delay.

"She's really tired lately."

"Wouldn't you be?" Rose had a reassuring smile on her face.

"Of course," Trish smiled back. Rose knew more about this than Trish did. A case of been there, done that, and having enough common sense to share.

"Why, when I carried Robbie, I couldn't get from one room to the other without sitting down to rest."

Trish nodded and then just to be on the safe side, she went back to check on Robbie. She was resting comfortably. Not sleeping. And now curious.

"What?" Robbie asked.

"I was just checking on you."

"You just left me five minutes ago."

"It was ten minutes."

"Seven at the most."

"What? Are you timing me?"

"Someone has to," Robbie smiled. It still had the same familiar effect on Trish.

"You look like an angel."

"Stop it."

"You do."

"I'm big and awkward and I have a case of heartburn that would strangle a yak."

"Why didn't you say something sooner? What can I bring you?"

"How about a ginger ale."

"I'll be right back."

Trish practically bounded down the hall and before she could turn the corner, she saw Mitch and Reb come through the front door amid a sparkling of flashbulbs. The crowd outside had grown in number. There was the press, the believers, the skeptics and the curious. Trish gave Mitch a quick hug and bussed Reb.

"You look like you're in a hurry," Mitch noticed the breathless nature of the greeting.

"I'm getting a drink for Robbie."

"Let me help," Reb offered. "Where's the kitchen, where's Robbie and what does she want to drink?"

Trish gave excellent directions and then Reb wheeled away to take care of the task.

"I shouldn't have her be doing chores. It's her wedding day."

"She won't mind. Besides, you've been all too busy doing things for us. Come over here and sit down," Mitch walked Trish to the sofa. "The house looks lovely."

"Yes, it does."

"The flowers are perfect."

"Uh huh."

"What's going on? You're more nervous than I am."

"I've just been trying to keep a close eye on Robbie."

"Ah, that explains a lot. How is she doing?"

"She's really tired."

"Wouldn't you be?"

"That's exactly what Rose said."

"How are Rose and Max doing?"

"Come and see for yourself."

Trish led the way past the maze of tables and chairs to the last place she saw Rose. No one was there now, but Max's clothes were still laid out on the bed. It was too early to get dressed, so

315

Max and Rose must've found another task to help with. The kitchen was the next logical place to look, but of all the faces, none was familiar. From there, they trekked over to Robbie's room, where they found Reb and Robbie exchanging stories about childbirth. Reb could be excellent company when circumstances called for it. Robbie seemed a whole lot more relaxed than Trish.

"Have you seen your folks lately?" Trish asked breezily.

"No, not lately. Why?"

"I was just wondering if Rose needed help with her dress."

"I know I will!"

"I'm leaving you until last."

"Okay."

Trish and Mitch regrouped in the hallway. "Where haven't we looked?" Mitch asked.

"That's just the problem. We've looked in all the logical places."

"Then, let's start looking in illogical places. How many of those are there?"

"This old place has a bunch of hidey holes. Even I haven't paid much attention to them. There's no reason for Max and Rose to be in any of them."

"I have an idea. Let's double check the places we've looked just in case we crossed paths and then if we haven't seen them, we'll visit those illogical places."

"Okay."

Step one went fast. Max and Rose were nowhere to be found on the ground level of the house. Two choices remained: upstairs and downstairs.

"There's nothing much in either area," Trish explained. "We haven't even started renovating the upstairs and I haven't been downstairs since we moved in."

"Is there anything stored downstairs? Something they might be looking for? Jewelry? Silverware? Hidden wedding presents?"

"Not that I know of, but we'd better check."

Treacherously narrow steps, those most common in the old days before safety standards dictated step rise and length measurements, led the way down from the back door by the kitchen. It was musty and dim, a whole lot like those old black-

316

and-white scenes from the Munsters. Mitch wasn't exactly spooked, but she wouldn't want to spend an enormous amount of unsupervised time down here. Trish, meanwhile, was being her usual methodical self. She walked to the farthest reaches of the basement and began to check rooms. Things were empty so far but one rooms' door was shut. Trish pulled it open.

"Thank goodness!!" Rose said.

"Did you find the key?" Max asked.

"What are you two doing down here and what key?" Trish asked as Mitch joined them.

"The door was locked!" Max explained. "We've been knocking and yelling for ten minutes!"

"We didn't hear a thing. I just pushed the door open. Here, let me close it again to show you-"

"No!" Rose was pushing her way out of the room. "I don't want to be locked in again!"

Max hurried out behind her. Apparently, he'd had had enough as well.

"Well, why don't you close me in," Mitch felt suddenly brave. "Maybe there's a trick to it?"

Mitch went in the room and closed the door behind her. And then opened it. And then closed it. And then opened it. And then banged it shut. And then opened it again with ease.

"Maybe it was just stuck and now it's loose?" Trish offered her explanation.

Rose didn't look like she was buying it.

"Why were you down here anyway?" Trish asked. She knew that nobody ever wandered down here under normal circumstances.

"One of the people working for the caterer asked us to come down here and get something," Max answered.

"They did?" Mitch was now very curious in a heads-will-roll kind of way.

"She was a pretty young thing dressed in a white silk blouse and black slacks," Max filled in the details like he had been paying very good attention. Which now caught Rose's attention. "That blouse didn't look like silk to me. More like rayon."

"What did she ask you to bring from down here?" Mitch steered the conversation to a more germane area. It didn't matter

317

whether or not it was silk or rayon at this point. What mattered was finding this person and firing them on the spot.

"She said that there was some wine stored down here and that she needed it upstairs," Rose remembered that much.

"And she also said that everyone else was too busy to help," Max filled in.

"And when you got down here, there was no wine?"

"Not a drop. Nothing."

"And then the door shut and we couldn't get out," Max wound up the story.

"Let's go upstairs," Trish said.

Mitch steadied Rose and Trish watched over Max as they navigated the creaky stairs. Once in the kitchen, they looked around briefly to see if Max or Rose could identify the wine girl. No luck. It would have to wait. The time of the wedding was nearly upon them. Mary and Lisa had arrived and it was time to get dressed. As Mitch, Lisa and Trish dressed in their tuxedos, they chatted about nothing in particular until Trish suddenly said, "the catering staff were only wearing cotton."

"That's right," Mitch agreed.

"What's that got to do with anything?" Lisa piped up.

Mitch looked over at her. It wasn't fair. Lisa looked so damn good in anything she wore.

"We were under the assumption that they were wearing silk."

"Well, *that* would be a silly thing for a kitchen staff to wear. Now, maybe the servers would be a little dressier…"

Mitch glanced over at Trish. "Maybe she was a server? Did we get a look at all the servers?"

"I'm not sure. I doubt it."

"Why would you want to do that?" Lisa just wasn't going to let up.

Mitch thought it through. Another pair of eyes wouldn't hurt. "Some young lady sent Max and Rose downstairs on an errand and then somehow locked them in a room."

"What do you mean, somehow?" Lisa drove straight to the core.

"Well, they couldn't get out of the room but we don't know why not."

"And now you can't find this young lady?"

"Right."

"But Rose and Max are okay?"

"They're fine."

"Hmmm," Lisa said as she adjusted her bow tie.

"Hmmm what?" Trish asked.

"Oh, just, hmmm," Lisa replied.

Mitch gave a look to Trish that conveyed the iron-clad belief that it wouldn't do one bit of good to press Lisa. When she was in one of her "just hmmm" moods, there was no moving her off the mark.

"Let's just keep our eyes open for her," Trish said and then, as an afterthought, added with a smile, "while we get this one married off!"

A wedding required a lot of planning and after weeks and weeks of detailed preparation, the walk down the aisle was just moments away. Trish gave Mitch one final look.

"Are you ready?"

"Yes."

"Are you nervous?"

"No."

"Good. Let's go."

The lineup was simple, if not quite logical. As Robbie walked down the makeshift runway, she was situated close to Lisa. Mary was across from Trish. Mitch and Reb came together and then faced the minister. He was a jovial elderly man who looked more like somebody's grandpa than a representative of a church. It hadn't been the easiest feat to find a minister amenable to gay weddings, but Reb had been persistent. Her efforts paid off. He was a gem. As words began to come out of his mouth, Mitch's mind drifted, a carryover from a childhood chock full of Sunday services. Soon, she felt the gentle jab of Reb's elbow. Oops! Mitch looked over.

"It's time for the vows!"

"Already?" Mitch focused on the moment.

"Well?" Reb prodded.

"Senators first."

"Oh. Okay. Well. It took me a while to think of the words that describe our relationship and the only word that kept coming back to my mind over and over again was 'unbelievable.'"

319

Mitch let this sink in. It made sense, when she said it. After all, most folks would've gladly put them in the category of "unbelievable."

"I cannot believe," Reb smiled, "how unbelievable lucky I was to have found you in the first place."

Mitch could only nod. She hadn't been hiding. But it had been so good to be found by Reb

"And we certainly have had some pretty unbelievable things happen to us along the way."

Which was true. The story of their relationship would've been rejected by writers of soap operas as being too fantastic. Or maybe just too gay?

"You are listening to me, right?"

Mitch focused back on Reb. "Unbelievable, right?"

"Are you okay?"

"Are you finished?"

"Finished?"

"With your vows?"

"No!"

"Well, maybe we'd better hurry it up."

"Why?"

"Because Robbie's going to go into labor."

Everyone at the wedding turned to look at Robbie, who seemed fine. And then, the strangest look crossed her face. Trish went to her side. Robbie held on to her arm and said quietly, "My water just broke."

As rides to the hospital go, this one was fairly calm. Once the reality sunk in, Mitch directed traffic. She sent Trish and Robbie to the hospital in their van with Reb as chauffeur and Mary as helper. Then, she told Max to exhort all the guests to stay and enjoy the food and drink.

"Don't let them touch the cake," was her only admonition.

Once that was settled, Mitch, Max, Rose and Lisa gathered up the suitcases that Trish had packed days ago and headed for the hospital. The fact that Robbie had gone into labor prematurely weighed heavily on Rose's mind.

"It's too early," she said two or three times on the way over.

Lisa comforted both expectant grandparents during the drive and then helped them out of the car in the emergency room parking area. Mary was on the lookout for them and guided everyone to the appropriate waiting area. Reb was there with the latest news. "Robbie is fine so far and the doctors are considering a cesarean section."

"Why are they doing that?" Rose asked.

"I'm not quite sure," Reb said. She didn't want to take any wild guesses at this point. Trish might know more by now, but she was nowhere to be found. Everyone took a seat and used small talk to ease the tension. They were undoubtedly the best-dressed group of people to ever grace the likes of this waiting room. A fact not wasted on a volunteer in charge of keeping order in the area. "I guess you're all together?" she asked as she peered over her bifocals.

They must have been a sight indeed. Those who weren't in tuxedos were in something about three steps above a prom formal. Reb, the formalist of them all, spoke up. "Yes, we are. Is there news about Robbie?"

"Are any of you immediate family?" woman-peering-over-her-glasses asked.

"We are," Max indicated himself and Rose.

"Perhaps we could go somewhere and talk."

It was pretty obvious that this particular volunteer believed in the "blood and adoption" strict definition of families.

"Whatever you have to say, you can say in front of everyone," Rose made it quite clear quite quickly.

"Ms. Goldstein is in surgery. I'll let you know when she's out." The news hardly seemed earth-shattering, certainly not warranting the privacy that the volunteer had hinted at. She then went over to a desk, sat down, and proceeded to ignore them altogether.

"Where do you suppose Trish is?" Mitch asked Reb.

"Good question. You don't suppose they allowed her in the operating room, do you?"

"Even if they had, I guarantee she won't be in there long. She's way too squeamish for that sort of thing."

"Where would you be if you were the squeamish type?"

"I'd be in the bathroom."

321

"Probably the one closest to the operating room," Reb added. She could be so logical in times of stress. It was decided that Mitch should be a scouting party of one, while the others keep vigil in the waiting room. Mitch found Trish readily enough. She was ghastly pale, and leaning up against the gleaming wall of the restroom for support.

"I'm not feeling so good," she explained like it wasn't obvious.

"That's understandable."

"Is Robbie out of surgery yet?"

"Not that I know of."

"They sure whisked her right in."

"They sure did," Mitch went closer to see if Trish was clammy.

"I'm pretty shook up, I guess you can tell?"

"Of course you are. Would you like to go lie down somewhere?"

"That would look pretty feeble, wouldn't it?" Trish tried to smile. "I mean, Robbie's the one in surgery and I'm falling apart."

"You're not falling apart. You're just having the natural 'going to be a new daddy' reaction. You're allowed by law to get a little wobbly in the knees."

Even as Mitch talked, color started to flow back into Trish's face. She washed her hands, splashed some water on her face and then turned to Mitch.

"I'm ready when you are."

That was good enough for Mitch. Arm in arm, they ventured out of the restroom and rejoined the group. Everyone had just gotten settled back in when news came that the baby was born, mother was being stitched up, and the newest member of the world was on his way to the incubator.

"Can I see any of them?" Trish asked.

"You can go to the nursery to view the baby. Your pediatrician is still working on him, however."

At the words, "working on him," Trish's grip on Mitch's hand got tighter. Even Reb noticed the wince.

"Let's all go down there," Reb suggested.

"You all cannot go in to see the baby," the volunteer was being officious. And snippy.

"We understand that," Reb was Senator-like in her response, "But we are allowed in the area, correct?"

"Well, yes," the volunteer backed down.

The evolution of hospital policy where birthing babies was concerned had allowed for more contact with newborns. Mommies and daddies had almost full access to their offspring. But, for now, Trish was separated by a wall of glass. The baby boy was in an incubator with tubes stuck here and there. He was precious, even if he didn't have much in the way of arms from the elbows down.

"He's beautiful," Trish pointed out the obvious.

"So, are you handing out cigars?" Mitch asked as they admired the newest wonder in the universe. Miraculously, all the color had returned to her face, along with a smile of relief.

"Robbie said I couldn't."

"But, I can!" Max stated triumphantly.

Grandpa Max and Grandma Rose had been watching every move their grandbaby had been making.

"He's a fighter," Rose stated knowingly.

"He has to be," Trish nodded.

And although there would be uphill battles yet to face, baby boy Goldstein couldn't have a better group of people on his team.